THAT STILL AND WH.

G000272616

Kathy Shuker was born in Wigan, England. After training and working as a physiotherapist, she studied design and went on to work as a freelance artist in oils and watercolours. Now writing full-time, she lives in Devon with her husband.
That Still and Whispering Place is her third novel.

To find out more about Kathy and her other novels, please visit:
www.kathyshuker.co.uk

Also by Kathy Shuker

Deep Water, Thin Ice

Silent Faces, Painted Ghosts

THAT STILL AND WHISPERING PLACE

Kathy Shuker

Published by Shuker Publishing

All enquiries to kathyshuker@kathyshuker.co.uk

ISBN: 978-0-9932257-3-4

Cover design by Design for Writers

For my parents

Chapter 1

Claire knew this tree. She remembered climbing it as a child, annoying the boys because, long-limbed, she could do it faster. Not that she hadn't skinned herself doing it - but that had never stopped her. She reached out an uncertain hand to touch its trunk. It was strange to be back. The alder flanked one of the footpaths weaving through the woods to the east of the village, a stone's throw from the banks of the sleepy river which cut the settlement in two. Claire knew all the woods round Bohenna - and the sly tapestry of footpaths that crossed them. It surprised her how little any of it had changed. Strange to be back, but good too.

And yet there was something wrong because she couldn't hear the river and there was no birdsong either; the woods had never been this quiet. Then the piercing scream of a girl split the air and Claire's unease quickly turned to panic. She turned, was certain she knew where the scream had come from and ducked away from the tree, starting to run.

She cut right, then left, weaving in and out of the trees, picking a footpath here, one there. She veered right again. This path wasn't one she'd used before but she ran on anyway, blindly, urgently, driven, unable to hear anything save the thump of blood in her ears and the cracking of broken twigs underfoot.

Her headlong search came to an abrupt end. She'd found her: a limp twisted bundle on the ground, her blonde hair filthy with mud, her skinny arms thrown out sideways as they always were when she slept. The little girl was barefoot, wearing just a tee shirt and shorts, and Claire fell to her knees, reaching out to gather the child into her arms and hug her close. She must take her indoors, wrap her in blankets, give her hot drinks, never let the girl out of her sight again.

But Gilly's white skin was covered in bruises, her clothes torn and blood-stained. To the touch her flesh felt frozen. Claire couldn't get a grip on her and now the child was melting into the ground, her features rapidly dissolving away. Claire felt her heart twist inside her chest, as if someone was wrenching it out of her body. She was screaming her daughter's name and turning in circles, anguished, searching for her...but there was nothing she could do because she was falling...falling...

A radio blared into life and music twittered into her head - a stupid, silly little jingle – but that didn't make any sense because there were no radios in the wood. And it was getting louder. Claire opened her eyes and struggled to focus, her heart still thumping, her skin damp with perspiration. She was sprawled along the sofa, her left arm stretched up behind her, the hand tucked beneath her head. For a moment she couldn't recognise the room though the furniture looked familiar. Her hand had gone to sleep and she unfolded her arm and stretched it, trying to make it feel again.

Slowly reality sank in and her heart rate subsided. She'd had that dream again. She remembered moving in - was it only yesterday? - remembered the old man next door watching suspiciously as the removal men carried each piece of furniture into the cottage. She remembered all the cleaning and unpacking and then she'd sat down and fallen asleep.

The stupid jingle was still playing and Claire sat up, shaking her left hand as it started to throb and simultaneously

2

reaching with her right for the mobile phone on the coffee table, wondering why she had chosen such an inane ringtone. Glancing at the name on the screen, she hesitated before accepting the call.

'Hello Neil.'

'Claire? At last. You've finally deigned to answer. What the hell are you doing? Have you gone mad?'

'Don't start, Neil.'

'But what possessed you to go dashing back to Bohenna? If you're trying to make me feel guilty, it won't work. I won't be manipulated.' He paused. 'Are you all right?'

She swallowed, taking her time. 'Of course I am.'

He was silent, long enough for her to wonder if he was still there.

'How did you know I was here?' she asked eventually.

'I called at the house and one of the neighbours told me. So I tried ringing you, and when I couldn't get a reply I rang Laura.'

'You shouldn't have gone bothering Laura.'

'I wouldn't have needed to bother her if you'd answered your damn phone. I just wanted to know what was going on. And she's not happy about what you're doing either. In fact she sounded quite upset. She's worried about you.' He hesitated. 'What were you thinking?'

Claire shook her head silently and tipped her head back, rolling her eyes up to look at the ceiling. She'd missed a cobweb and she watched it dance in the draught coming under the front door.

'Claire?' he insisted in her ear.

'My coming here is not about you,' she said slowly. She watched a tiny spider abseil down an invisible silken thread from the edge of the web. 'It has absolutely nothing to do with you. Why should it? Soon we'll be divorced. You wanted the divorce as much as I did.' More, she thought. Much more. 'You're in no position to dictate what I should do with the rest of my life. I told you I was planning to come back but you obviously weren't listening. I wasn't going to hang around waiting for our house to sell. And our daughter's all grown up now with plans of her own. Maybe you've been too busy to notice? So I've come home.'

Claire stopped short. It was the first time she'd put it that way. Home. She nodded. Yes, that was exactly right.

'Anyway,' she added, 'I explained what I was doing to Laura and she was fine about it. You're using her as emotional blackmail. It's typical of you. You say you want a new life so get on with it and leave me alone. How is Samantha by the way?'

'Damn it, Claire. You know very well our marriage had fallen apart way before Sam came on the scene. You were impossible to live with. You wouldn't move on. And look at you now: you're back chasing shadows.'

Claire said nothing. Neil constantly put the blame on her as if he'd done nothing, as if he had been easy to live with, and it made her angry. But she was tired of all the arguments and recriminations and didn't bother to retaliate. She was tempted to cut him off – he'd done it to her several times over recent months – but couldn't quite bring herself to do it. She was pleased to hear his voice and that made her cross too.

She got up stiffly and walked to the window, looking out to the front. The old man from next door was standing on the rough ground opposite the house, staring into the interior of her car as if it was an invention he hadn't seen before.

'Claire…darling…' Neil's voice in her ear now held something of the old familiar warmth. It was easy – tempting - to believe he still cared. 'Stop blaming yourself. Please. It wasn't your fault. You know these things happen. She's gone.

4

You've got to let her go.'

Claire hesitated, squeezing her lips together hard, feeling tears prick at her eyes but refusing to let herself cry.

'You think you understand me,' she said. 'But you have no idea why I'm here. None at all. And I'm not convinced you care, Neil. I think it's about your pride. You think Bohenna is your patch, the Pennymans' patch, but it's mine too, remember? Well, I've made the choice to come back. That's all there is to it.'

He grunted. 'I'm sure you didn't tell me and I wish I'd known before.' He now sounded sulky; she could imagine his expression perfectly, the pout of his lips, the frown making the top of his nose crease up.

'I did tell you. We discussed which furniture I could take.'

'I thought that was for the future. I didn't expect you to run away like this. It's insane.' He sighed. 'Does mum know you're there? I'd better tell her.'

'There's no need. I'm going to tell her myself.'

'It might be better coming from me… Claire, are you listening?'

'Neil, it's my life. Butt out.'

This time she closed the call without giving him a chance to respond and stood for a moment, painfully aware of the sudden silence and the pressing insistent heaviness of it. If there was birdsong now, she didn't hear it. She was back in the past, a succession of painful images running through her head. That dream had unnerved her but she had known it would be like this. It was never going to be easy to come back.

She saw the old man walk away from her car with his bent, lurching gait and the movement brought her back to the present. Old Eddie. She had known of him growing up, had seen him round the small Cornish village, but had never had a single conversation with the man. He'd been an agricultural

5

worker, she dimly remembered, lived alone and didn't bother much with anyone except maybe a walk to the pub now and then. And he kept chickens. She knew that because the cock kept crowing all hours.

And now the weak October sun was already setting; gloom was descending. The nearby bank of trees appeared to suck what little light remained. She moved away from the window, hesitated, then brought up Eve's number on her phone. But no, she couldn't face it now. Neil's mother could wait. It was hardly urgent and, despite what the Pennymans might think, the woman did not rule the world. She put the phone down.

She needed to go for a run to get that dream out of her system. Jogging was the only thing she had ever found which helped. She went upstairs to change.

*

Standing outside the pub, Adam Thomas shuffled his feet and glanced at his watch again: it was six fifteen and still there was no sign of Zoe. He sighed heavily. She had forgotten again - or maybe not. A small voice at the back of his head told him that she was doing it deliberately, trying to prove some kind of point. But it was rapidly going dark and it had been a long day; he could do without this.

He pulled the phone out of his pocket. There was only one bar. Reception was sometimes patchy along the valley, especially if the weather closed in. He punched in her number but there was no answer and it cut through to the answering service. A couple of men heading for The Swan looked his way curiously and Adam turned away, mumbled a brief message into the phone and closed it down. This was the second time in the last couple of weeks that he'd been stood up. It was becoming more and more difficult not to accept that there was something wrong. At home, Zoe had become increasingly moody, one minute full of some plan or other, the next crabby and confrontational. He felt like he was walking a tightrope all the time.

He glanced at his watch again. He needed a beer but Zoe always insisted that they meet outside because she didn't like walking into the pub alone. For an apparently self-assured Mancunian, she was ridiculously nervous of country pubs. They're too dark, she would complain, and everyone stops talking as soon as you walk in. What Zoe liked was the anonymity of a crowded, raucous city pub where an extra body was ignored and where you had to shout to make yourself heard. The Swan was old-fashioned and cosy: it still had its original lounge bar and a separate public bar and a snug - and a menu where virtually every meal came with chips and the word *jus* didn't appear once. Adam liked it, though it had occurred to him that, at thirty-eight, he was already turning into his father.

He saw a woman jogging up the road from the direction of the bridge, her long legs sheathed in leggings, a huge long-sleeved tee shirt draped over the top and cinched in with one of those funny little bum bags that cyclists wore. Her curly hair had been pulled into a short, stubby bunch at the back. He was pretty sure he'd never seen her before. Not that he had lived here very long - five months, in village terms, was the blink of an eye, or so one of the locals had told him.

Bored, he watched the jogger stop, panting, in front of the shop on the other side of the road and now she seemed to be reading the adverts in the window. That was a novelty; he didn't know anyone ever read the adverts. He thought they were put up more in hope than expectation, then went yellow and curled up at the corners in the sun.

In the harsh fluorescent light cast from the shop, he saw

7

her scrabbling in her bag, looking for something. Then a taxi drew up not far from him and his attention was distracted. The driver was Nick Lawer and he was alone in the car. He lived in the village and Adam had met him in the bar a few times where he was sometimes friendly and sometimes ignored everyone. He was a surly man with a lascivious tongue and a short fuse. Adam watched him get out of the car then stand, motionless, looking across at the woman who was now writing something down. A moment later she was jogging down the road again with Nick pointedly watching her.

Then he turned and took a few steps towards Adam, a cheap grin on his face.

'Not bad, eh - for her age anyway? Get those legs. I'd maybe give her eight.' Nick liked to rate women on a scale out of ten - Adam had heard him do it in the pub several times. Anyone would think he was God's gift to women. Adam disliked the man and was surprised he ever managed to get any fares. 'D'you know who she is?' Nick enquired, eyebrows raised knowingly.

'No idea,' said Adam.

'That's Claire Pennyman. Neil's wife.'

'You mean like the Pennymans from the vineyard? I don't know Neil.'

'Well you wouldn't. Neil is Tim and Julia's brother. Left here about five years ago. Had two daughters. Then... Don't tell me you haven't heard about the younger Pennyman girl? Thought every last bugger knew about that.'

Adam frowned, reluctant to get drawn into this conversation but curious to know all the same.

'What about her?'

'Disappeared,' said Nick. 'About a year before they left. Came home from school one day, went out to play and never came back. Police were here for ages, questioned everyone.

Spent a lot of time with the family, they say. It was all over the telly for days. Where were you, mate? Outer Mongolia or something?'

'Didn't they ever find her?'

Nick laughed. 'Nah. Police chasing their own tails. Didn't have a clue what they were doing. Anyway, this place is crawling with visitors in the summer. She was probably miles away by the time she was even reported missing. Waste of time searching the village. They admitted as much themselves in the end.'

'How old was the kid?'

'I dunno,' Nick said carelessly. 'Eight or nine maybe.' He leaned forward conspiratorially though there was no-one around to hear. 'Course there were some said Claire Pennyman was to blame herself. I mean, not just careless of the kid but the one who made her disappear - if you know what I mean.' He gave an exaggerated wink and straightened up. 'But, hey, there's some people in this village'd condemn you for farting. And if they don't know the whole story about something, they make it up themselves. Anyway, I need some fags.'

He crossed the road, glanced up the lane in the direction Claire Pennyman had gone, then walked into the shop.

Adam pulled out his phone and checked the screen. There was no word from Zoe. He toyed with going into the pub anyway but wasn't in the mood any more and began the walk home.

*

Claire stepped out of the shower, dried herself quickly in the draughty bathroom, dressed and put a quick brush to her hair. She threw a jacket on, slipped on some shoes and left the house. Running had focussed her mind as it often did. She had decided she had to see Eve that day and get it over with. In any case, there was good strategy in speaking to the woman so soon after her arrival: it showed that Claire was in charge of the situation; it suggested that she didn't feel guilty, that she wouldn't be intimidated. A phone call wouldn't do: it looked weak.

Neil's mother was a widow, the matriarch of the Pennyman dynasty and still the lynch pin of their wine business: domineering, hard-working, astute. It was more than three years since Claire had been back to Bohenna and seen her. Too many missed family gatherings and events had frayed her already tenuous link to the Pennymans. But Eve had never liked Claire much, had never thought her good enough for her eldest boy, and had liked her still less when she had failed to give Neil a son. Even so, she was Laura's grandmother and if Claire was going to live in the village again she would have to face her sooner or later.

There was no moon and it was dark outside, forcing Claire to immediately duck back into the house and grab a torch. She was surprised at herself, at how quickly she had forgotten what living in a small Cornish village was like: the lack of streetlights, the obscurity of the black winter nights. And walking the narrow lane back into the village, she was immediately reminded of the stillness of these evenings in a community of little more than five hundred people. There was the odd bark of a dog, the twitter of a late-settling bird, somebody banging a garden gate closed. She could smell wood smoke in the air. Mains gas didn't extend to places like this so people burnt wood, coal and oil.

Claire reached the bridge over the river, turned right to cross it and kept on walking up the hill. The White House and its accompanying vineyard stood on the northern side of the valley, the white-rendered old farmhouse half way up the hillside, looking down on the village below, virtually surrounded by field upon sloping field of vines. If Claire paused and flicked her torch beam that way she could see the vines now, tall and still bushy with growth.

She reached the turning to the vineyard on her right, but found herself looking to the left instead. The ground on that side of the lane was called Tom's Acre and had belonged to her father. All her life he had run a nursery there. When he'd retired, not long after she and Neil had moved away, he had sold the land to the Pennymans and she'd heard that the courtyard with its ramshackle old farm buildings had recently been turned into a craft centre. The Pennyman enterprise grew each year, it seemed, carrying all before it.

She turned away and walked through the car park to the vineyard buildings. The house was further on but a bright light shone in the winery, its open double doors shedding the glow in an arc across the yard. Voices sounded inside. Claire approached the edge of the doorway and looked in. She could see leaves and stems strewn on the floor, odd grapes too, broken and bleeding. Her nose filled with the sharp, fruity smell of grape juice. Of course, it was October and they had been harvesting. That meant long hours and weary backs and they would be working late. It wasn't the best time to visit.

A jet of water sprayed on the ground in front of her and she jumped aside with a yelp of surprise as it splashed her and ran pell-mell down the slope into the broken gravel of the yard.

'Sorry.' The hosepipe was switched off and a man appeared in the doorway, the nozzle still in his hand. He stared at her, frowning. 'Claire? It is you. I'm sorry I didn't know you were there. I was just washing down. Are you OK?'

'Hi Tim. I'm fine, thanks.' She glanced down at her jeans but they were barely damp. 'Just took me by surprise.'

She smiled warily. Tim was Neil's younger brother, a bit introspective sometimes but he was all right. Once upon a time they'd been friends. He threw the hosepipe down and, after a blink of hesitation, leaned in to give her a peck on the cheek.

'I got a text from Neil,' he said, 'saying you were here. I wasn't sure if he was joking.'

'No, no joke.' She looked him over. 'Short hair, Tim? I nearly didn't recognise you.'

'We decided it was about time he lost the hippy look.'

Julia had joined them. Her wiry frame was covered in juice-stained dungarees which looked too big for her, her short hair now more steely grey than brown. She produced a strained smile. 'Hello Claire. Long time, no see.'

'Hi Julia.'

Julia jerked her head in her brother's direction. 'The earrings and leather jewellery frightened the punters. They had to go. I hadn't heard you were over. Where are you staying?'

'I'm renting Woodbine Cottage, down on Dark Lane.'

Tim frowned. 'That's somewhere by old Eddie isn't it?'

'Right next door. The last house before the woods.'

'You're renting?' said Julia, frowning.

'Yes, just until…'

'Who is it?' The voice was authoritative and female. A small, slightly stooped woman came forward, her steps stiff, her eyes keen. She frowned heavily. 'Oh, it's you, Claire.' She managed to make her sound like an illness.

'Hello Eve. I see I've chosen a bad time but I wanted to see you.'

Eve had aged since Claire had seen her last: the skin of her face sagged more and she had shrunk. The gimlet eyes were as sharp as ever though.

'You wanted to see me?' Eve sniffed disdainfully. 'If you're going to tell me that you've come back, I already know. Neil rang me.'

'Come back?' Julia exchanged a look with Timothy. 'You

mean, like, permanently?'

Claire nodded. 'I'm sure you've heard about the divorce. We're waiting on the sale of the house. When I get my share of the money, I'm hoping to buy somewhere.'

'And yet you were so keen to go,' said Eve, her lip curling. 'Taking the family with you.'

'That's not true, Eve. I wasn't keen to go. I was confused and desperate. So was Neil. That's why *he* suggested it.'

Eve made a derisive noise and fixed her flinty gaze on her daughter-in-law. Claire stared back, unflinching.

No-one else spoke.

Julia shifted uncomfortably. 'I suppose Laura's at Oxford now?' she asked loudly.

Claire pulled her eyes from Eve and smiled. 'Yes. She started a couple of weeks ago.' Again there was silence. 'Anyway…I can see you're busy. The harvest is late isn't it?'

'I'm surprised you noticed.' Eve was already moving stiffly away towards the house. 'You never showed any interest in it before. Come and see me before you go, Tim.'

Julia waited pointedly until Eve was out of earshot.

'You're right: the harvest is late. We had a good, sunny autumn so we held back. We've only just finished.' She glanced towards the sky. 'Just as well since they've forecast rain for tonight.'

Claire nodded, fidgeted. 'Right… well, I'll be off then.'

'Claire?' Julia flicked Tim another look. 'Have you heard about the Craft Yard? Only the builders found a couple of things belonging to your dad when they were doing the conversions. If you'll just wait, I'll get them for you.'

She hurried to the office next door, leaving Claire alone with Tim. He rammed his hands in his pockets and shifted the gravel with the toe of his shoe. She cast about for something to say.

'Have you seen Neil recently?'

'In the summer. He came over and helped with the stall at the fête.'

There was another awkward silence.

'And you?' she said. 'Are you still with Monica?'

He laughed. 'You're out of date, Claire. Monica's ancient history. I've had another girlfriend since then. And that finished months ago too.'

'I'm sorry.'

'Hey, you know me,' he said dismissively. 'I'm not the settling kind.'

She saw him study her face speculatively, a smile teasing at his mouth, a mischievous glint in his eye.

'You know, you should take a look at the Craft Yard,' he said. 'Jane's got a unit there.'

Her mouth fell open. He'd caught her out and he knew it.

'Do you mean Jane Sawdy?' she said. 'I didn't know she was back in the village.'

'A few months ago. She's living in her mother's house out on the road to Lostwithiel. Her mother died a while back.' He produced that taunting smile again. 'I take it you two have never made up then?'

Julia's return saved her the need to reply. She handed Claire a plastic carrier bag. 'There's a watch in there and a few other odds and ends. I thought you'd want to have them.'

'Thanks. I do.'

Claire raised the bag in a half-hearted gesture and gratefully said her farewells. Julia managed a smile. Tim just nodded. She walked briskly away, suspected that she was being watched, was sure she was being talked about.

Reaching the bridge, she stopped to lean on the rough stone wall and look down into the river, though it was much too dark to see anything. The breeze rustled the trees along the river banks and sent a flurry of falling leaves drifting past her and down onto the water below.

She took a few slow breaths, then turned for home, relieved. She had negotiated her first hurdle.

*

Julia finished her last check in the winery, came outside and turned to lock the door. It was after nine now and pitch dark, not a single star in sight. Standing here she was out of range of the light sensor on the barn restaurant and she stayed there, happy to be enveloped by the night. She looked down the valley towards the village. Illuminated windows showed the extent of the straggling settlement either side of the river and made a faint halo of light. Pale smoke drifted up from a chimney here and there and a tawny owl hooted somewhere below her, sounding absurdly loud in the stillness. A car engine started and lights flashed on the road towards Penmarna. It looked peaceful, a village at rest.

But Julia didn't feel peaceful. Her mind was occupied with Claire, her thoughts automatically flicking back through the years: Claire the curious and overactive kid, then Claire, the gangly-limbed teenager, enthusiastic, funny, stubborn, independent, awkward. Brave even.

'You all right there?'

She recognised her husband's smoke-gravelled voice and turned as he came alongside.

'Just enjoying the quiet.' She hesitated. 'And I was thinking about Claire.'

Phil grunted in a non-committal way.

'Are you surprised she's back?' she asked.

'Not really. She was born and bred here. You don't get it out of your system as easy as that. Can you imagine leaving?'

She frowned and shook her head. 'You off to the pub?'

'Just for a pint. Won't be late.' He leaned across to kiss her then strode off, torch in hand, though she was sure he'd know the way blindfold.

Her thoughts returned to Claire. Julia's father had found her once in the lower part of the vineyard with a toad sitting, glassy-eyed, on her hand. 'She's like a Gerald Durrell with curls,' he'd joked, slightly disconcerted. If she saw something interesting, she always had to follow it, be it a moth, a beetle, a mouse, even ants. She was dogged about things, persistent.

Julia was ill at ease. In many ways, she liked her sister-in-law, always had. She even liked the way she stood up to Eve. But she didn't feel good about the woman being here. It might not be her fault, but trouble seemed to follow Claire around like a shadow. And now, with Jane back in Bohenna too, Julia couldn't shake off the fear that Claire's return was like putting a light to a tinderbox.

Chapter 2

The rain that had been forecast arrived later that night, heavy and persistent, and the late sunny days of summer seemed to be washed away with it in the space of a few short hours, along with the last tenacious petals of the asters and geraniums. By morning, the rain had stopped but the mild balmy air of a Cornish autumn held a thick veil of moisture and Claire looked out of her front cottage window onto a clinging white mist. She knew these mists of old; here in the river valley, trapped between the woods, it might last all day.

She turned away. Walking back to the kitchen past the sideboard, she automatically stroked a finger across the frame of a photograph of Gilly. The girl was grinning broadly, eyes shining. Claire's gaze shifted to the only other photograph: Laura, not quite looking at the camera, a shy smile tugging at her lips. She paused, wondering how her elder daughter was doing in Oxford, worrying about her as she habitually did. Further along the cupboard top was the crumpled receipt she had scribbled a phone number on the night before and she picked it up and looked at it as if she might see something new there, some wisdom that would indicate what she should do about it. The *Vintage and Collectible* unit in the Craft Yard was advertising for help. She really needed a job - her meagre savings weren't going to go very far - but the vineyard was the last place she wanted to work. She'd only written it down out of desperation.

She poured milk over a bowl of cereal and sat to eat it at the tiny table crammed into a corner of the kitchen. There was no dining room. The cottage was small and dark, two up, two down, with a tiny afterthought bathroom built on the back. Showing her round with a breezy, disinterested air, the estate agent had turned her nose up at the musty smell, had tried to talk persuasively of the larger, more modern - and more expensive - semi the agency had available higher up the valley side.

'Unless you particularly want to be near the river?' she'd added, doubtfully.

Did Claire want to be near the river? Not especially, given that a significant tract of woodland separated her from it. But she didn't want to rent the modern semi either, not when it was a stone's throw from the last house she'd shared with Neil. In any case, this tiny little cottage, with its lichen covered thatch and damp cob walls, was all she could afford. There was no way she was going to go asking Neil for money. And Woodbine Cottage had simply been left unoccupied and shut up for too long. She knew about cob walls because she had grown up in a cob house. They were like living things, they needed air to let them breathe. Otherwise the place was fine: it had a telephone line and a television aerial and it had been reasonably decorated in a neutral way. It could be made into a comfortable home for a while.

Her father's belongings lay on the table where she had abandoned them the night before: as well as the watch, there were a couple of ball point pens and an old pocket diary. She picked up the watch with her free hand as she ate, handling it for a moment, remembering. It was hardly surprising it had been left behind. Her father never wore the thing, said he hated the feel of it on his wrist and he kept his own hours anyway.

Not that he wore any kind of jewellery, not even his wedding ring which he complained irritated him and which he regularly removed and left lying around. Claire wondered where that had ended up and smiled. In a flower pot maybe.

'It shows what you think of our marriage if you won't wear my ring,' Sally, Claire's mother, used to say peevishly. Then he'd apologise, try to explain, but Sally, an incomer and restless, wanting excitement and change, had never been cut out for life in Bohenna. She had never been likely to be content - as her husband was - exclaiming each year at the wonder of the clematis rambling over the fence or the beauty of the wildflowers in the hedgerows. It wasn't the ring - or the lack of it - which had made her leave.

The cereal finished, Claire sat, staring into space, her thoughts now on her meeting at the vineyard and the news that Jane was living back in Bohenna. It had been on her mind off and on ever since.

She got up suddenly, walked back into the living room and pulled a photograph album out of a drawer of the sideboard. She flipped through the pages of snaps, then paused and took the album across to the window. Here was a photo of 'the gang' when they were teenagers: Neil, Tim, Julia, Phil and Jane. She hadn't looked at these pictures in years. The one below included Fiona too, Jane's scatter-brained cousin who sometimes came to stay with her. How young we were, she thought, how naïve. She shook her head, smiling ruefully. And yet we thought we knew everything.

Over the page was one of Claire by herself, sitting on the famous horizontal branch over the river where the rope swing hung - their favourite hang-out. Tim must have taken it because it was a good shot and no-one else took decent pictures. Photography had been a bit of a hobby of his. Claire was posing, balancing casually but precariously as if a fall onto the stony river bed below didn't concern her a jot. Long skinny limbs, curly blonde hair shaggy and untidy, jeans rolled up below her knees, nose in the air. Cocky. Was that really the same person? She barely recognised herself. She was forty-two now. Where had all that self-assurance gone?

She turned a page. And here was Jane, her class-mate and best friend, leaning against the trunk of the same tree. Jane could have been a model. She had the looks for it: the soft, swinging dark hair, the large limpid eyes and a grace none of her contemporaries could match. She and Claire had been chalk and cheese but it had worked…for a while anyway. Jane had been quiet, introspective, moody even. She had been smart and academic too and she'd gone away to university and had never returned to Bohenna.

Now she was back and running a unit at the Craft Yard which was odd: Jane had never been into crafts. *I take it you two have never made up then?* Tim knew very well that they'd never made up.

Claire closed the album and watched Eddie hoeing his front garden, cutting through the top soil, turning weeds over. He had barely exchanged five words with her since she'd moved in. He didn't want company, he had made that clear; he wanted to be left alone. She could hear his television sometimes - he was deaf and he had the sound turned up - and that only seemed to emphasise how alone she was. It was proving a challenge, living by herself after all these years.

A few minutes later she eased her trainers on, grabbed her jacket and went out.

*

Claire paused at the entrance to the old yard. The once dilapidated farm buildings the old nursery had inherited now had new windows, doors and security lights and the uneven yard had been relaid with fake stone slabs and was eerily smooth. Hand-painted wooden signs hung beside each door and tubs of plants were dotted here and there - the only nod to its previous life as a nursery. Claire wondered what her father would have made of this modern theme park. Nothing, probably, because he had been more pragmatic than she was. At least the place is being used, he'd probably have said.

There were eight units in all, arranged around three sides of the yard. One was empty but the rest were occupied: wood-turning, stained-glass, fabric crafts, paintings and pottery. Two of them had nothing to do with crafts: the *Vintage and Collectible* unit and one called *Natural Healing.*

V and C - the initials were intertwined on the sign - was the first unit on her left and she wandered across to look in the window. The display held a couple of old enamel advertising signs, a big Victorian kitchen chair draped with a patchwork quilt, an inlaid chest of drawers and a low shelf unit with a selection of glazed pottery. It had been nicely done - better than she had expected - but the interior beyond looked dark and cluttered. She noticed a thick-set woman looking at her from behind a desk near the entrance and she turned away.

She wandered round the corner to the artist's studio - the first in the next run of units. The sign read: *Adam Thomas.* There were a couple of big figurative, highly textured, canvases in the window. The door stood open and she could see him inside, shaven head bowed over a table, earphones rammed in his ears. Next door was the *Natural Healing* unit. The place was deserted but the lights were on and the door stood ajar so she walked in.

It was a bright space, the walls painted a chalky pastel yellow, and mobiles of crystals hung from the ceiling, catching the light and bouncing it round the room. A tall fibre-optic table lamp in the shape of a tree stood on the cupboard in one corner and silver jewellery hung on the back wall - earrings and pendants set with an assortment of stones, the properties of the stones listed nearby. On the wall to the left hung a large poster showing the chakras on a human body. There were shelves of books about healing and meditation and others stacked with ointments and powders produced by a herbal company. Near the open window at the front a wind-chime oscillated in the movement of air, its bamboo chimes piping softly. And there were mottos all over the place, random, occasionally sugary, inspirational quotes.

Claire was mildly interested in herbal medicine but some of the stock looked like superstitious nonsense. *What goes round comes round*, she read on a sign propped up on the table in front of her.

'Claire. How lovely to see you again.'

She turned quickly. The woman standing behind her smiled. The beautiful brown eyes were still there though now they were couched in heavy dark make-up. Her face was rounder but her hair hung long, shiny and sleek, partly masking it. She was still striking. Draped around her shoulders was a fringed shawl.

'Jane,' said Claire. 'I knew you were here but I didn't realise this was your place.'

'And I'd heard you were back in Bohenna, Claire, but didn't know whether to believe it or not.' Jane still smiled as if the expression was stuck on. 'You know what the rumour machine's like here: the sighting of a helicopter landing in a field can become news of a full scale invasion. Would you like a cup of tea? I was just about to make some.'

'Yes, Thanks.'

'Take a seat.' Jane indicated two small bamboo armchairs either side of a round bamboo and glass table, and disappeared into a room at the rear.

Claire sat down, leaned back, crossed her legs, uncrossed them, then restlessly bounced one heel on the ground the way she always did when she was nervous. Jane was different to the girl she remembered – more assured and yet strangely remote, her voice smooth and inexpressive. Claire was reminded uncomfortably of a plastic doll.

'I sometimes use the table for consultations,' Jane called through. 'It's a bit more relaxed.'

'Consultations?'

Jane reappeared in the doorway. 'You know, if someone wants to discuss their problems and what therapies might help.'

'Ah.' Claire nodded but Jane had gone again.

After several minutes she brought through a tray bearing two mugs, a teapot and a plate of aniseed biscuits. She offered Claire a biscuit then took one for herself and they sat, chewing, silent, as if both searching for something safe to say.

'So are you planning to stay here?' Jane asked.

'Yes. Yes, I am.'

Jane looked her over thoughtfully. Claire waited for a comment. None came.

'When did you come back?' Claire asked. 'I heard you'd gone to live in East Anglia.'

'Oh, that was a long time ago.' Jane shrugged. 'I was a fool. I met this guy at university and thought he was wonderful so I followed him to Norwich and abandoned the degree. We split up - of course - and I did a secretarial course. Then I got interested in this…' She waved an elegant hand towards the room. '…when someone gave me a herbal treatment for something and it worked. Transformed me actually.' She paused and looked up. The heavy make-up round her eyes made her gaze strangely compelling in her otherwise blank face and Claire found herself fixed in its beam. 'And that's when I realised I had a gift - though I think I'd always known it really.'

'A gift? What sort of gift?'

'For sensing people's pain; for understanding energies, both good and bad. I use it to help treat people and make them well again. When I heard about the Craft Yard I thought it was a good opportunity so I applied straight away and got in at the beginning.' She finished her biscuit and leaned forward, resting a hand on Claire's knee. 'I was sorry to hear about your daughter. Very sorry.'

'Thank you. You heard then? I suppose everyone did.'

'I saw it on the news. Terrible. I couldn't believe it.' Jane straightened up again. She hesitated. 'Is that why you moved away?'

'Yes. We wanted a new life. But it's not that easy, of course.'

'No. You take your life with you.'

Jane lifted the teapot, pouring tea through a strainer into each of the mugs. It was pale yellow as if it had been chosen to match the walls. She put a mug in front of Claire.

'Chamomile,' she said. 'Calming.' She glanced at Claire's bouncing leg and Claire immediately quelled it.

The tea was still steaming. Claire tried a sip but it was too hot and she sat back, gingerly holding the mug. She rested her gaze on Jane warily. 'I wanted to see you again but I wasn't sure how we'd be now.' She hesitated. 'I know we had our differences, Jane, but when I apologised to you, I did mean it you know. It wasn't intentional but I *was* sorry for what happened.'

Jane shrugged and offered a tight smile.

'I know you were. But I did some terrible things too and I don't think I ever apologised. Let's just forget about it. It's so long ago, it's ancient history.'

Claire managed a sip of tea. It wasn't good.

'Tell me about you,' said Jane. 'I heard your father moved to Lostwithiel when he retired. And where's your brother now?'

'I'm afraid Dad died of a stroke a couple of years ago. Jon's been living in Canada for years - married but no children. Says they don't want them.' She hesitated. 'Tell me: have you heard from Fiona at all? I was looking at some photos of us all before I came out. I can't remember when I last saw her.'

An expression of distaste fleetingly distorted Jane's impassive expression.

'No, I haven't heard,' she said, with finality. 'But then, we've never been that close. And I gather she's had some mental health issues too. Had a breakdown or something.' She paused. 'I heard you were getting a divorce. So what's Neil doing now?'

'Neil's still in Kent. He's got a job at a vineyard there…and a girlfriend.'

'Oh. Serious?'

'I have no idea.'

A leaden silence fell between them. Claire had been hoping to renew their friendship, had thought the passage of the years might have rubbed away that tarnish from the past. But it didn't feel like it. And Jane had definitely changed, had become more intense and probing and yet oddly evasive. Claire supposed she wasn't the same any more either but, whatever the reason, she didn't feel comfortable here. The room felt too small as if it was crowding in on her. She forced down another mouthful of tea and put the mug down.

'Thanks for the drink.' She stood up. 'I'd better go. It was good to see you again.'

'I'm glad you called.' Jane got up too and reached out a hand again to place on Claire's arm. Claire didn't remember her being so touchy-feely either. 'Don't be a stranger.' She raised enquiring eyebrows. 'By the way, are you still doing your beautiful illustrations?'

Something in the way it was said suggested Jane already knew the answer. In fact, Claire had the disconcerting feeling that Jane knew a great deal about her.

'No. In Kent I was working at a garden centre.'

'Ah yes, plants can be very soothing can't they? I grow several of my own herbs. Well, if you happen to be looking for a job, Penny Shalcross wants someone at V and C.'

'Yes. I saw. But it wouldn't be easy to work up here, what with the family and all the memories.'

'But you can't get away from the Pennymans, Claire,' Jane murmured, eyes stretched knowingly wide. 'Not if you live in Bohenna. You must have known that. And you'll have to learn to live with the memories. They're everywhere.'

*

Claire arrived back at Woodbine Cottage to find a man by her front door, bending over and moving the empty flower pots, swearing.

'Neil? What are you doing?' she demanded.

He straightened up and turned.

'Looking for a key. Waiting for you. I've been here half an hour already. Where've you been?'

She pushed the gate open and walked the short path to the front door.

'What's that got to do with you?'

He frowned, apparently surprised at the question. 'I wanted to see you.'

'Really? Why do I find that so hard to believe?' She turned the key in the lock. 'Then I suppose you'd better come in. And for future reference...' She pushed the door back and

26

stepped inside, turning to hang her jacket on a hook behind the door, '…I don't leave a key under those flower pots. In any case, I don't remember inviting you to poke around my home.'

'Don't be like that.'

He followed her in and looked around. The front door opened straight into the living room and, taller than average, he only just missed the bottom of the old beams and made the room look small. He looked back at her. She thought she saw pity in his eyes and she hated him for it.

'Oh Claire, what are you doing?' he said.

'We've been through this, Neil.' She pushed past him and walked briskly into the kitchen. 'Look, I'm making tea. Do you want one?' She had to get the taste of Jane's chamomile out of her mouth and the activity would occupy the space between them.

He moved to stand in the kitchen doorway, leaning against the frame. 'This isn't a good place to be, Claire.'

She ignored him. 'So tell me why you're here? There's no special occasion, is there? A birthday perhaps? Something I've forgotten?'

'I came to see the family…and you.'

'Check up on me, you mean.'

'No. I just wanted to…well, yes, check that you were all right.'

'I'm fine. Why wouldn't I be?'

He sighed. 'Can't we get ahead of this? Must you always fight?'

The kettle boiled but she ignored it and turned to face him, full square.

'Get ahead of this? You're the one who needs to do that. You criticise, you find another woman to share your life and then you turn up here, unannounced, and expect me to be here, available for you. Like what? A servant? And you keep patronising me. Now, if I don't want to keep playing the same games - by your rules - I'm the one who's accused of fighting.'

He managed to look astonished, as if they hadn't had similar arguments before, and didn't reply. She reboiled the kettle and poured the water into the teapot, glaring at it as if daring it to answer her back. They were both silent until she'd poured the tea into two mugs and they'd taken them through to the living room.

Claire hugged the mug of tea like a friend. She had drunk so many cups of tea these last years. Lost your daughter? Let me make you a nice cup of tea. No sign she'll ever be found? I'll make you a cup of tea, dear. Getting hate mail for neglecting her? Have a cup of tea - you'll feel better. All terribly British. She was surprised no-one had suggested she keep a stiff upper lip.

'You've let your hair grow again,' Neil said. He smiled. 'I always thought it suited you like that. Never understood why you wanted to cut it…get rid of all those lovely curls.'

She flicked him a look.

'Sorry. Criticising again. I know. What I'm saying is: you look good. And I'm glad, Claire. Really I am.'

She frowned at him, unsure where this was leading. She supposed he wanted something.

'Are you staying up at the house?' she asked.

'No. I stayed with Tim last night.'

'I went to see them, you know. I spoke to your mum.'

'Tim said.'

She took a sip of tea. 'I was amazed at him. He's looking very proper these days. I think I preferred him the way he was before.'

'You would. You've always liked 'free spirits'. But everyone else gave him grief for it and he finally succumbed to the pressure. It was about time he grew up.'

Claire let it drop. 'Did you know Jane's back in Bohenna too? She's got a unit up at the Craft Yard.'

'I know.'

'How?'

'I suppose Tim told me.'

'Have you seen her?'

'No. Have you?'

'Yes, I was just there. She's…' Claire searched for a way to describe her but abandoned it. 'It seems old John Matthews was right. Do you remember - when we left - he told us we'd be back? People always come back to Bohenna, he said.'

Neil didn't reply and they drank their tea. He emptied his mug first and put it on the table.

'Gilly won't come back, Claire,' he said, gently. 'I wish you'd accept that. I really do.'

She looked up. 'I have.'

'I don't think so. Isn't that what this is all about: waiting for her to come home? Being here ready?'

'No. No, it's not. It's about moving on, Neil.'

He scoffed. 'Coming back here is moving on?'

Her voice rose in frustration. 'It had to be here. Because this is where it all started and this is where it all went wrong. How else could I pick up the pieces?' She tried to find a better way to explain it but his pained expression stopped her. There was no point.

'OK…good,' he said placatingly. 'Moving on. I'm glad.' His expression softened. 'You know, I'd like us to be friends again. Do you think that's possible?'

Claire pressed her lips together and nodded, refusing to meet his eye. 'I don't want us to be enemies, Neil. That would make it hard for Laura.' She stood up. 'Anyway, I've got things to do.'

'Yes. Well, so have I.'

He got up, walked to the door and opened it, then paused.

'Are you all right for money?' he asked coolly.

'Fine, thanks.'

'Look Claire, I'll be down for Christmas and I should warn you: Mum's going to ask you to join us…and Laura of course. You will come, won't you?' When she didn't immediately reply, he added, 'It'll be awkward for Laura if you don't come.'

'Will Samantha be there?'

He looked wrong-footed. 'I don't know yet.'

He hesitated, opened his mouth then closed it again and walked away. Claire shut the door with the smell of his after-shave in her nostrils, a smell she knew only too well. She felt very weary all of a sudden.

*

When Adam got home from work that afternoon, Zoe was already there, lolling on the sofa watching a TV film. She worked as a receptionist at a dental practice in Lostwithiel and was still wearing what he thought of as her work clothes: a formal skirt and a crisp blouse. She'd thrown an oversized cardigan over the top and was hugging it fiercely to herself though the central heating was already on and, to him, the house felt warm.

They lived in a rented sixties bungalow, a two-bedroomed square building of cream-rendered breeze-block with old and inefficient UPVC double glazing. It stood in a large overgrown garden on a lane running south from Long Lane, the main street of the village, and had originally been built for an elderly relative of the neighbouring farmer. It stood alone, surrounded by fields of cows, and was in desperate need of modernisation though Adam barely noticed.

Now he walked across to the sofa, leaned over and gave

30

Zoe a kiss. She didn't respond and he straightened up.

'Are you OK?' He peeled off his fleece jacket.

She grunted, eyes still on the screen. 'I thought you said you couldn't work as late with the nights drawing in.'

'There was something I particularly wanted to finish and the light wasn't an issue.' He looked at her but she was ignoring him. 'I'm going to get a beer. Do you want anything?'

'No thanks.'

Adam got a bottle from the fridge, prised the cap off and tipped back a generous mouthful. He went back into the lounge and dropped into the only armchair. The film appeared to be an American detective mystery and he watched it idly.

'Who's he?' he said, gesturing with the bottle towards the screen.

'You don't really expect me to tell you the whole story now, do you? It's more than half way through. Anyway, I didn't see the beginning myself.'

Then why are you watching it, he felt like saying. But he often watched a football match which had already started, even when he didn't know where the teams came from.

He watched her sidelong. Eight years they had been together now and mostly it had been great. They had met in a queue for a cinema in Bristol, both waiting to see Casino Royale, and there had been an immediate attraction. Zoe was fun, light-hearted and incredibly pretty and she had a wonderful, infectious laugh. He thought she was the perfect antidote to him. He could be funny - in a dry sort of way - but he could be intense and preoccupied too. She helped him keep things in proportion. But lately she hadn't smiled much and she never laughed and he was scared to ask why.

The adverts came on and Zoe hit the mute button. The silence felt explosive.

'We've had a reminder that the rental contract is due for

31

renewal.' Zoe flicked a glance towards the table where Adam could see an envelope and an unfolded piece of A4 paper. She turned her head, looking at him accusingly. 'How long do we have to live here?'

He frowned. 'Well, we're saving up aren't we?' He was aware she didn't like the location of the bungalow much because she found it too quiet and the cattle spooked her, so they had talked several times about going somewhere else - sometime. 'Maybe when the next contract finishes we'll be able to find something better.'

'Where better?'

'I dunno. Nearer the centre of the village maybe. Where would you like to be?'

She shook her head crossly. 'You don't listen, do you, Adam? I've told you before: I don't want to live anywhere in Bohenna. There's nothing going on here.'

'But we talked about what coming here would be like. You were quite keen.'

'You said we'd be near the sea.'

'You're saying I lied to you? That's not fair. I showed you where it was on the map.'

'Yes, and on the map it does look close to the sea. But it's not really is it? It's in the middle of the country and the roads are so narrow and twisty that it takes forever to get anywhere. There's just mud and cows and…and cabbages everywhere. I had no idea it would be like this.'

'It's not that far to the sea. I know you can't walk there but it's only fifteen minutes in the car. And there's all sorts of great places not far away. Anyway, we haven't been here very long. It takes time to settle in and get to know the place.'

He got up and went across to kneel down by the side of her, putting his arm round her shoulders and resting his head against hers. She let him so that was a start.

'We're together aren't we?' he said softly. 'It's an adventure. We both said we wanted to try something new. And it's wonderful here for my work. I got that print deal after doing those pictures of the river. That's going to make a big difference to our income and it'll make all sorts of things easier.'

He felt her relax into him and he turned his head and kissed her lingeringly on the mouth. She responded and he felt the arousal immediately. It was almost embarrassingly quick. He let his hands wander down her body, kissing her back greedily. He'd begun to think she didn't want him any more. It had been a while.

But she was turning her head away again and he had to force himself to let her go.

'If our income's going to be better then it's time we talked about starting a family. Again.' Zoe fixed him with a penetrating look. 'I'm thirty-four, Adam. I can't put it off much longer. And it'll maybe take me a few months to catch. You said that this would be a good place to bring up children.'

Adam sat back on his heels, staring at her. He felt like he'd been tricked. She was manipulating him.

'We've talked about this,' he said coldly. 'We agreed to wait until we'd got ourselves established.'

'We didn't agree, Adam. You insisted. How established do we have to be?'

Adam got to his feet and looked down on her. 'We're not ready to do this yet. We'll talk about it again. Anyway, I need something to eat.' He headed for the kitchen.

'That's right. Walk away. Why do we always have to talk about it again?' he heard her shout after him.

He didn't reply.

Chapter 3

Walking into the village shop the next morning to buy the local newspaper, Claire became aware of the other shoppers stopping to glance at her, of voices dropping and people turning away. At the till, she could tell from the way the owner, Steve Carthy, looked at her, at the things he didn't say, that he had been talking about her. He was a little too polite. She had been back three days and already the word had got around. She wondered what the gossipmongers were saying about her now, after all this time, but didn't want to know. Had it changed from what had been said before? Had it become more benign with time or more extreme?

Back home, she trawled through the job adverts: a care home assistant - experience required - and a bar job at a pub in a neighbouring village. She checked the internet on her phone for anything else she could find. There were more bar jobs in Lostwithiel and Fowey and a chef and an early morning office cleaner required. Nothing that appealed. The job at V and C taunted her. It was close - she could walk there - which meant she'd use no money in travelling, and the hours were sociable. And she'd probably never see the Pennymans - certainly not Eve. And maybe her dad would be pleased to think that she was up there, back in the old place, even if it had changed out of all recognition. At the end of the day it was work, and she needed the money. It was becoming a major issue.

A couple of days later, swallowing her pride, she went to see Penny Shalcross. Penny, big and sardonic with a deceptively languid manner, had clearly heard the gossip too because she already knew who Claire was and she had only lived in the village a couple of years.

'You're the poor woman whose child disappeared,' she said, with refreshing directness. 'I'm so sorry. That must have been dreadful.'

'Yes. Thank you. It was.'

Penny studied her with a shrewd gaze and Claire felt like a schoolchild called up to see the headmistress, though Penny could have been her senior by barely eight or nine years.

'I had a school leaver here until a couple of weeks ago,' Penny said in the brisk, no-nonsense manner Claire would come to know well. 'She couldn't hack it. Too slow for her, she said. Boring. Well, of course it's got slower now the summer's over. If the girl was looking for excitement I don't know why she came here.' Her eyes narrowed. 'Can you cope with boring? It'll pick up again near Christmas but it's going to be slow till then. I need you to clean, iron, sort through things. And serve. You'll have to man the place while I go out sourcing stock. Can you do that?'

'Yes, I can do that.'

The job was hers.

Claire started the following Monday, working four days a week, nine-thirty to five, and alternate weekends. Penny stayed with her to start with, explaining the stock, the till and the record-keeping. Having always favoured old things with a bit of history, Claire hoped the job might actually prove interesting. Penny sourced most of her goods from house clearances and auctions and made occasional trips to France to buy from the street flea markets. The stock was varied: shelves of folded quilts and racks of antique linens; an assortment of pottery and china and bundles of silver cutlery; old wooden trays, rusting advertising boards and kitchen storage tins. A couple of pieces of fine furniture were prominently displayed but the rest were covered in items to sell. There were two bookcases of second-hand books and a rack of vintage clothes. At the back of the room stood a locked, glazed cabinet with a display of valuable, 'easily pocketed' items, mostly jewellery. Behind a partition wall at the rear was a small kitchen, just big enough for a sink unit, an electric kettle and an automatic washing machine and tumble drier.

On the Monday of the second week, Claire worked her first day alone. The unit felt empty without Penny's larger than life presence and she switched on the CD player behind the counter and flicked through the discs piled beside it. They were mostly compilations of French ballads or classical albums. She put on something by Ravel to fill the silence, pushed the vacuum cleaner over the floor, swiped a duster over the polished surfaces then got out the silver polish and began cleaning an old canteen of cutlery.

Her phone started its familiar stupid jingle and she smiled when she saw the name.

'Hi Laura. Are you all right? I tried to ring you last night.'

'I know mum. Sorry. I was out. No reception.'

Out where? thought Claire. And who with?

'Did you have a good time?' she asked, rubbing her thumb ineffectually at the black marks on her fingers.

'It was OK. Just a few of us freshers getting together.'

'You've made some friends then? Anyone in particular?'

'I've only been here a month, mum. Give me a chance. I have been doing some work too.'

Of course she had. Laura was conscientious and hard-working. She had managed to get a place at Oxford reading history and philosophy. How she had been able to study and concentrate when everything around her had been falling to pieces, her mother couldn't imagine. Though maybe the work and the reading were what had kept Laura sane.

'You're enjoying the course?'

'Yes. It's good.'

Claire waited but there was no further comment. Laura was never very forthcoming. Too quiet, Neil used to say, too serious, but that was probably their fault.

'Laura, I've been thinking about Christmas. Is there anything you particularly want?'

'I haven't thought.' There was a brief silence at the other end of the line. 'Are you going back to Kent for Christmas?'

Claire hesitated. 'No Laura. I've brought some furniture down here, remember. I wanted to make this place feel more like home.' She paused. 'I think your grandmother wants to have us over for Christmas Day. Did your dad mention it?'

'He might have.'

There was another silence.

'Well we can decide what we want to do nearer the time, can't we?' Claire said brightly. 'The cottage here'll be lovely with decorations up. And there's a wood-burner to roast chestnuts in too. Do you remember how we used to roast chestnuts when we lived down here before?'

'Yes.' The word came out flat and empty, like the sound of a torn drum.

'Is there a problem about coming here?' Claire asked gently. 'You can tell me if there is Laura.' She'd thought Laura was genuinely unperturbed by her move; she'd said all the right things when Claire explained.

'No, it's fine. It's just going to be…odd.'

'I know. But I think it's an oddness we need to get over, don't you?'

'Sure. Don't go on about it, mum.'

'No. OK.' Silence. 'Oh, by the way, I've got a job.'

'Really? Good. Well done. Look mum, I've got to go. I've got a tutorial.'

'OK. But, don't forget to think about what you'd like for Christmas, will you?'

Claire closed the call and stared at her phone thoughtfully. Laura had never talked much about her sister's disappearance despite much intrusive though well-intentioned prompting. Her feelings had been kept all bottled up, untouchable. In the end Claire had thought it best to let it lie.

The bell over the door tinkled and she looked up as Jane walked in.

'So you took the job. I'm so glad.' Jane stood by the sales desk and glanced around, shaping her lips into a little moue of disdain. 'It's pretty crammed in here, isn't it? A bit claustrophobic. Much healthier to allow room for the energy to flow, you know. Though you'd better not tell Penny I said that. Anyway, I can't stay. I've got a client coming to see me. Soon though, we must spend some quality time together.'

Claire forced a smile.

Jane reached out a sympathetic and unwelcome hand to touch Claire's arm, then walked out. Claire watched her walk away and saw her duck in at the door of the art studio before returning to her own unit next door.

Her thoughts quickly returned to Laura, doubts crowding in on her again. They had dragged their eldest daughter away when she was a confused and vulnerable adolescent. Was it fair now to make her return, as if the intervening five years had changed everything? Had they? She and Neil had run away, desperate not to keep seeing Gilly out of the corner of their eyes or lie awake at night wondering where she had gone. And they'd assumed it would be better for Laura too. They were doing it partly for her benefit, they'd said. Then they'd turned their frustration, guilt and anger on each other instead and eaten their marriage away from the inside out.

But Claire didn't want Laura's memories of Bohenna to be tainted in that way. She was young enough to wash it out of her mind and make fresh memories. And she had to come back to do that, had to see the family and experience the place again. Bohenna was in her blood, like it or not.

'She'll be fine, once she's here,' Claire murmured to herself, turning resolutely away from the window and going back to the cutlery. 'We'll have a good time. We will.'

*

Julia, Phil and their son Daniel lived in a self-contained extension to the back of The White House. It was convenient and cheap, but also meant that they were always on the job and, at this time of year, Julia started work early.

That morning, she had been in the winery for three hours already. She and Tim, with the help of Chris - a young man from the village - were working their way round the vats of red wine, pressing the cap of skins, stalks and seeds down into the liquid in each one, breaking it up, allowing the flavours and tannins to enrich the juice. It was demanding work, the more so because it had to be done three times a day.

Or maybe I'm just getting old, thought Julia, rubbing at her shoulder as she moved on to the next vat. There were machines you could get to do the job of course, but they cost money, and there wasn't that much spare to go round. They had recently bought a new bottling machine. In any case, Julia preferred working the more traditional way and, despite their expansion over the years, they were still small enough to be able to do that. It was one of the things that made them special.

She placed the steps by the new vat, climbed to the top and glanced round. There was no sign of Phil. He'd gone to have a smoke half an hour since and still hadn't returned. It was dry so maybe he'd gone down into the vineyard. There wasn't much to do there this time of year but Phil always found room for a bit of 'housekeeping'. He didn't like to spend much time indoors anyway, said he couldn't breathe.

She pushed the plunger down into the wine with a grunt, working her way systematically over the crust. She'd seen the signs: Phil was smoking cannabis again though there was no point confronting him about it. He'd only deny it. And he swore it was harmless but they both knew that wasn't true. Normally Phil was a quiet man, protective of his own routines, but good-natured and a patient and caring father. But grass made him irascible and forgetful and in the past it had fuelled his anxiety and even made him paranoid. He was fine while he was smoking it - he felt good and it calmed him down; it was afterwards the problems kicked in. He was a fool to be dabbling in it again. She was concerned - and cross too - and gave the last push into the wine an extra effort in her frustration, managing to splash juice up her arms. Damn.

She stepped down to the floor to find Tim waiting for her.

'We're done,' he said. 'I've sent Chris for his break. Where's Phil?'

'Not sure.'

Tim gave her a meaningful look but she refused to rise to it. It was none of his business.

'Coffee?' he said. 'Mum's out. She's at the dentist's this morning.'

Julia nodded, relieved. It was vineyard lore that they all went up to the house for a break each morning but it was a great deal more relaxing when Eve wasn't there.

They rinsed off the plunging discs, washed their hands and walked up together.

'Chris was having another go at me about a pay rise.' Tim

filled the coffee machine in the big breakfast kitchen and switched it on.

'If we put his pay up, we'll have to put all the wages up.' Julia put a pan of milk to heat on the Aga. She turned to face him. 'I don't think we can afford to do that.'

'No, I know, but it must be difficult for him. He's trying to save up to buy a car. Maybe we could increase the Christmas bonus? It'd be something.'

Julia grabbed a couple of mugs from one cupboard and the biscuit tin from another. She put them on the table and turned to look at him, smiling indulgently.

'You're a soft touch, aren't you? We'll talk about it at the next meeting.' She took a biscuit out of the tin, bit into it and went back to watch the milk. 'How's the new brochure coming on?'

'Fine. The new photos work well.'

There was the sound of boots being dumped by the back door and Phil walked in. He said nothing, pulled out a chair and sat down at the table. Where Tim was slight and wiry, Phil was solid and strongly built, his hair receding off his forehead and grizzled. Julia glanced at him as she poured hot milk into a jug and put it on the table.

'Problem?'

'Kids messing about in the vines again. I went down to see them off. Threatened them with a hiding. They've pushed down the wire on the fence.' He shook his head, lips compressed. 'As if I haven't got enough to do. Trouble is, there's too many places along that river path where they can push through. You mend one bit, they just come in somewhere else.'

'Who were they?'

'Dunno. Maybe from the new estate.'

Julia looked at him just a little too long and he caught her eye.

'They're only kids, Phil,' she murmured. 'Playing.'

He didn't respond and she looked away, grabbing another mug and the sugar bowl.

'They won't be back in a hurry,' Timothy was saying with a grin. 'If I know Phil, they won't have stopped shaking yet.'

He tipped coffee into the three mugs and sat down. The smile faded and he stared into his mug pensively.

'Claire's working in the yard,' he said. 'At V and C.' He looked up, flicking each of them a glance. 'Did you know?'

Julia shook her head, frowning.

'I knew,' said Phil. He reached into the biscuit tin and took a custard cream.

Julia watched him and looked away again. She wondered how he knew and what he thought about it. The Craft Yard was very close.

They lapsed into silence and no-one mentioned Claire again but Julia could still feel the resonance of her name lingering in the air around them.

*

The days of November grew shorter. Autumn settled on the village softly like the drifting fallen leaves at the sides of the road. There were morning mists along the river, showers of squally rain and brief spells of vapid sunshine. It was a quiet spell, uneventful, and just what Claire needed. If she wanted to jog - and these last years it had become a regular part of her routine - she was usually obliged to do it in the dark, morning or evening, and she took to wearing a head-strap torch. She knew it looked stupid but there were few out to see her and she developed a couple of familiar routes: running the roads through the village or cutting through the woods and along the riverside footpaths. Added to her new working routine, the

42

regularity and monotony of it were soothing.

There were memories round every corner: police and villagers walking the village, scouring it for the missing girl, poking in every ditch and compost heap and shed; posters printed with Gilly's photograph on every fence and every telegraph pole, begging for information; Gilly tumbling out of the gates of the little primary school at three o'clock, laughing and joking with the other children.

Gilly had been a live-wire, always doing something, inquisitive, only still when she had a butterfly on her hand or when she was watching damselflies mating on a stem. Claire was certain it was the reason she had been taken. Gilly had a wonderful giggle and bright, inquisitive eyes and, though she hadn't been exceptionally pretty, she had inherited her mother's blonde curls. She was a child who drew attention. Some tourist, some visitor from a big city somewhere perhaps, had found her too tempting to resist. And she had an open, chatty personality. She was the sort of kid who'd talk to anyone, whatever warnings she'd been given to the contrary and she'd had plenty of those.

Claire was surprised to find she could think about it now, certainly not without pain, but at least she could cope with it. Maybe she had learnt to manage the pain, had pushed it deeper down and cushioned it in some way. These last months it had become clear that she had to, for otherwise it would poison her life and, more importantly, it would poison Laura's too.

Somehow, she was settling. Around the village she bumped into people she had known in the past. Beattie Foster - who, with husband George, had been Claire and Neil's neighbours - was now in her sixties and as smiling and friendly as Claire remembered her. And Greg Bingham, who had been one of Gilly's teachers from the school, said how good it was to see her back. The atmosphere had lightened; the suspicion had dissipated. Or perhaps she didn't look for it quite so much and didn't see it in every innocent glance. Maybe her own feeling of guilt had made her assume everyone blamed her. Now she dared to feel a little triumphant: Neil didn't think she could do this and she was proving him wrong.

She even liked the job. Despite her intimidating manner, Penny was fair and she was straightforward. Yes, the work was boring some days but, glad to have found reliable help and knowing how quiet it was, Penny was relaxed about Claire closing the unit for a break now and then. So Claire tried learning more about the goods she was selling and about their history. And she visited the other units too, admiring the pots and the wood turner's beautifully shaped cherry wood bowls, wondering if there was something that Laura might like for Christmas, unsure how much money she dared spend.

She looked in on Adam Thomas, the artist, too. His pictures were bold multi-media works, images both of the river and the undulating countryside around the village and also further afield to the coast: shingly beaches, rugged cliffs and the harbours of Fowey, Polperro and Looe. Imaginative and emotive paintings with unexpected colours, some were bright and cheerful, others were sombre, heavy and doleful. She wasn't sure if she liked them or not. And Adam was as moody as the pictures. The first time she went in he was friendly, pulled the earphones out of his ears, apologising for ignoring her. The second time he looked at her, barely nodded and sullenly carried on working.

'It's his love-life,' Penny confided when she mentioned it. 'Stormy, I hear.'

A stormy love-life was something Claire understood.

As the month neared its end, Penny went on a trip to France, leaving Claire to look after the unit alone for five days. She left behind a large cardboard box for Claire to sort through, unsold items from the village fête's bric-à-brac stall which had only just been handed over.

'There won't be anything I can sell,' Penny complained bitterly. 'Most of the stuff they're given is no good to me. Megan even suggested I make a donation to the fête funds in return for taking them off her hands. Cheek of the woman. Do you know Megan Davies - chair of the village fête committee? There's no talking to her.' Penny sighed heavily. 'Still, you'd better take a look.'

So on the Monday morning, Claire made herself coffee, hefted the box onto a small oak table and started picking through its contents. She pulled out a couple of worn soft toys, a single, silver-plated candlestick, a jigsaw of a steam train with *3 pieces missing* scribbled on the box, a milk jug and sugar bowl in a garish printed design and a teapot with a chipped spout. Beneath she found an embroidered tray cloth with some broken stitches, a pair of plated sugar tongs and a pile of mismatched modern dinner plates. Nothing so far that Penny would be likely to sell. But then she pulled out a couple of Beatrix Potter books which, though not first editions, still had their dust jackets and were fully intact. And there was a hardback copy of The Old Curiosity Shop too and a couple of Agatha Christie paperbacks. She put them to one side.

Further down was a pretty lace table runner, another tray cloth and, at the bottom, a motley selection of jewellery and ornaments. Claire sat back, stretched her back and finished her coffee, then slowly sorted through them. The ornaments were mostly modern and much of the jewellery was too. There were a couple of earrings without their pairs and a brightly-coloured bead necklace with a broken clasp. An old brooch with a silver setting had lost two of its stones. But there were a few nice pieces which were worth salvaging.

Finally, in a paper bag in a corner of the box, someone

had thrown together yet more ropes of beads and pendants and they had become tangled together. As she emptied them out onto the table a couple of brooches fell out. And there was a hair slide too, a chunky little plastic child's clip in a rich aquamarine hue, set with shells and a few cheap sparkling stones.

Claire stared at it. Something clutched at her stomach and she felt sick. With a shaking hand she cautiously touched it as if it might burn her then gingerly picked it up, turning it over and back again, dimly aware that her heart was hammering in her chest.

This was the hair slide Gilly had been wearing the day she disappeared. She was sure it was; absolutely certain. Again she turned it over, brain almost numb with the implication. Her little girl was still here then, after all. In Bohenna. Someone must have known all along. Someone - maybe someone she knew in the village - had been lying.

She groped for a chair and sat down quickly as her knees gave way.

Chapter 4

The policewoman turned the slide over on her hand in exactly the same way Claire had done, pursing her lips together thoughtfully, flipping it over and over. Claire sat and watched her, her foot doing its usual jig. The police officer was Family Liaison Officer, Constable Lyn James. Claire was surprised she didn't look more excited – or perhaps excited wasn't the right word. But she should be pleased, surely? After all this time, wasn't this the breakthrough they needed?

They were sitting in Claire's living room. She had rung the police from the unit as soon as she had got over the shock of finding the slide. In the last few years she had lost touch with the Family Liaison Officer originally allocated to them when Gilly disappeared and, in any case, that policewoman had left to start a family of her own so it had been late afternoon before anyone else was available. Claire had been obliged to potter round the shop all day, desperately trying to find things to do to keep herself occupied, waiting for the clock to tick round and give her the chance to escape. Now she sat, picking at a loose piece of dry skin on her right thumb while she fixedly watched the policewoman's face in the light shed from the lamp on the sideboard. Lyn James was older than the officer with whom they had all spent all that time six years ago. She wondered if she had any children herself.

'And she was wearing this the day she disappeared?' Lyn

was saying. 'You're sure?'

'Yes…' Claire hesitated. Some parts of that day were etched in her memory, vivid and sharp; others were woolly and sometimes seemed to mutate the harder she tried to remember them. 'Yes, I think so.' She was aware of the lack of conviction in her voice and knew that the policewoman had heard it too. 'I don't remember seeing it in her things afterwards anyway.'

The policewoman nodded, ambiguously. 'Where did you buy it?'

'Buy it? In Truro. At Pzazzies.'

'The national chain?'

'Yes.'

'And what makes you so certain that this one belonged to your daughter?'

'Certain?' Claire frowned, surprised at the question but starting to see where this was leading. 'Well because it did. I recognise it. When we bought it I remember looking at them with her in the shop. There were a few different designs and this one came in two colours: that turquoise and a soft pink. I thought she'd choose the pink one but she preferred that.' Claire felt her throat thicken and she swallowed hard. 'She said it was the colour of the sea. She wore it a lot. She had other hair slides but that was her favourite. Of course you weren't here when she went missing so you wouldn't know but she had shoulder length hair – curly - and she used the slide to clip it back on one side.'

Claire demonstrated vaguely with her own hair. She stopped talking, looking at the policewoman with a knot of frustration forming in her stomach. Why didn't she understand how significant this was?

'But there's nothing about it that makes it especially hers?' Lyn prompted gently, turning the slide over again. 'I mean are there any particular distinguishing marks?' She

48

looked up at Claire with a kind smile. 'You see where I'm coming from here? You bought this from a national retail chain. There will have been thousands of these slides sold. It would be very difficult if not impossible to prove that this one belonged to your daughter. If I'm frank, Mrs Pennyman, it seems unlikely after all this time that your daughter's slide would turn up at the church fête.'

Claire stared at her. The policewoman was breaking it gently but it was clear she thought this was a wild goose chase. Claire could imagine Neil's reaction too. *Really Claire, get a grip. You're making a fool of yourself.* And yet she wasn't mad; she knew it was Gilly's slide.

'But surely,' she said desperately, 'the likelihood of the same slide appearing in a little village like this is incredibly small?'

Lyn raised her eyebrows and offered a weak smile. 'Not really. The village has a couple of new estates, doesn't it? There are more children here now. I know because I visited the school not long ago. And like I said: that chain would have sold thousands of these. Anyway, is it just village people who give to the fête? There are a lot of holiday cottages in the village too aren't there?'

'Ye-es.' Claire's frown deepened. She had been on the village fête committee for a couple of years way back and yes, she did vaguely remember that they had made a point of targeting the holiday cottages with leaflets too. 'OK then, so…couldn't you test the slide for…I don't know, DNA or something?'

'With the number of people who will have handled this, just in the last few weeks, Mrs Pennyman, I don't think it's going to offer us any valid information now. I mean, for example, if it still had one of Gilly's hairs caught in it…' She shrugged. 'But certainly I can take it with me if you like and see what I can do.'

Claire imagined the slide being put in one of their neat polythene bags, filed away somewhere, carefully forgotten, the offer merely a sop to keep the victim's family happy. She reached out her hand.

'No, of course, you're right. And when I think about it maybe Gilly was wearing something else that day. She had another slide she used a lot. I'll keep this, thanks. I'm sorry I've wasted your time.'

Lyn relinquished the slide into Claire's grip and smiled kindly. She stood up.

'Not at all. I can entirely understand why you contacted us. Since as you say I wasn't here when your daughter disappeared, I'll have another look at the case file and have a word with my senior officer, see if there are any leads which might be worth following up. I'll let you know if we come up with anything.'

Claire saw the woman to the door, closed it behind her and leaned heavily against it. The slide was still in her hand and she straightened up, opening her fingers, watching the light glint dully from the little stones. She walked across the room and put it down on the sideboard, then went into the kitchen and poured herself a glass of wine from a bottle she'd opened the previous Saturday night.

Back on the sofa, the glass in one hand and the slide in the other she let the alcohol gradually numb the edges of the pain inside her, felt her breathing slow and the tension in her muscles ease a little. She stared at the slide. Of course there would be no fingerprints or DNA on it now, nothing to check. Even if the abductor's prints had been there, they'd be smudged or more likely obliterated. And Claire couldn't prove it was Gilly's slide. She flipped it over in her fingers then gripped it hard, feeling the edges of the plastic dig into the flesh of her fingers, then quickly eased the grip. She didn't want to break it. It was a tangible link and whatever the police thought, she knew it was important.

The wine finished, she put the glass down and sat staring at the hair slide, her thoughts slipping back in time. The policewoman who had liaised with her when Gilly disappeared had been called Mariella. Mariella Jansen. She'd been a big, broad-shouldered girl with a hearty grip and a calm, firm manner; at the start she had felt like a mountain of security and reassurance. She had sat with the distraught Claire patiently coaxing her to explain repeatedly the order in which everything had happened.

'Tell me again, Mrs Pennyman, just so I can get this straight in my head, in case there's anything new which might occur to you. Anything at all might help.'

'She came home from school,' Claire had begun.

'Came home how?'

'She walked. The school isn't far away and she kept asking to come by herself because that's what her friends did. She wanted to feel grown up. When she turned eight we decided to let her.'

'Yes,' prompted Mariella. 'So she walked home from school. What happened then?'

'I was working. I do illustrations, usually for books. I had a commission which was getting really close to the deadline so I gave her a drink – orange – and a chocolate bar to keep her going. Then I told her I needed to work for another hour so I asked her to be good and play quietly till I'd finished. She asked if she could go and play with Danny - he's her cousin and the same age. They'd arranged it when they were coming out of school - to meet at the village playground. She was like that – very…independent. I said OK but that they mustn't wander off. But I've spoken to him and he didn't stay long and

51

he went home. He left her at the playground.'

'Does Gilly sometimes wander off?'

'Well yes. She's fascinated by nature, you know, insects and butterflies and birds, fish in the stream...anything like that. She's more of an outdoor girl and sometimes follows things or goes looking...' Claire's voice trailed away.

'She hasn't actually run away before then?'

'No, no, nothing like that. She just loses track of time.' Claire frowned, feeling increasingly cross. 'Are you trying to say she's run away now? She wouldn't do that.'

'You're sure? There hasn't been an argument or anything...or something she had been told off for? Sometimes a really trivial thing can make a child go off.'

'No. There hasn't been anything like that.'

'So what made you worry this time?'

'It's been too long.' Claire automatically glanced again at the clock. She had been doing it regularly every few minutes. 'She's never been so long before. Never.'

'OK. Look, now I know how difficult this is for you Mrs Pennyman but you mustn't panic. The majority of children turn up again. Like Gilly they wander off, get lost sometimes, lose track of time. It's possible she fell over and hurt her leg – something quite innocent but which is stopping her coming back. We'll go and search for her. Try not to worry. You just tell me where her favourite places are to explore. That'll be a good start.'

Sitting staring into space now, Claire reflected yet again that she had made a mistake in admitting that Gilly sometimes wandered. She had become increasingly certain of it over the years. Once the police knew that the girl had absented herself before, they felt less urgency; they were sure she would turn up again of her own volition. Claire had even accused them of it and of course they had denied it but she had no doubt: by the time they had taken the problem seriously all hope of finding Gilly's trail had gone. And then their very real concern about Gilly's welfare had turned subtly into suspicion and endless questioning. Where had all the family been when Gilly disappeared? What were their relationships like? Had there been any rows between the parents, jealousies, affairs? Had anyone seen her that afternoon…? Mariella had been charming and yet thorough, if not ruthless. Claire had slowly become convinced that she wasn't so much an ally as a spy in their midst, waiting for someone to make a mistake.

Claire picked up the slide thoughtfully. Gilly had been wearing a necklace too, a pretty little beaded affair that Sally had sent to her granddaughter for her birthday. Unfortunately there had been no sign of it with the other things in the box. If that had been there too, it would have proved the link.

She flipped the slide over and brought it closer to examine a couple of fine scratches on the back. Any particular distinguishing marks, the policewoman had asked. Did she recognise these scratches? Claire wasn't sure. She hadn't handled it that much. Gilly was past the age when she wanted her mother to do her hair for her. From the moment she mastered any skill she had always wanted to do it for herself. She was, in almost all things, her mother's daughter. The only time she tolerated having things done for her was when she was ill. Would she still be the same?

Claire felt a wrenching sigh escape her. She would be fifteen now. How pretty she would be. Of course Neil had been right, at least up to a point. At one time, Claire had been convinced that Gilly would simply walk in the door one day. Living in Kent, she had cursed herself that she had agreed to leave and effectively abandon her little girl, and she had blamed Neil for suggesting it as much as she had blamed herself for agreeing. But she'd comforted herself with the

53

thought that there was still family in Bohenna if Gilly did return and eventually the hope had slowly died.

But now the slide had turned up in Bohenna. Gilly hadn't been taken by a tourist; she had never left. Claire thought she should tell Neil. But no. He wouldn't believe her either. They would simply have another row and he would be obstructive. She had to keep this to herself.

She fixed on the slide again. If this was Gilly's, maybe her daughter was very close after all. Didn't you read about girls being abducted and held captive a stone's throw from their homes? Or maybe she was dead and the killer had thrown the slide away… But as always, she fought the thought, unable to grasp its exquisite pain, fending it off like she might fend off someone trying to sear her with a branding iron. In any case, it didn't make sense. Why would it turn up at the fête? In truth, it didn't make sense whichever way you looked at it though that didn't change her certainty that the slide had belonged to Gilly. Tears began to run down her cheeks unnoticed.

What was important was to track the slide back to the person who had put it to be sold at the fête. The police didn't take her seriously so she would do it herself. Gilly might be depending on her. She felt a twinge of fear, mindful that if Gilly was still alive and waiting to be rescued, Claire would have to be very careful. Nothing rash, she told herself. Nothing rash to risk Gilly. Softly, softly…

*

Adam hesitated at the door to V and C, opened it and walked in. Twice before he had been in the unit: once to see what Penny was selling and a second time to borrow her staple gun when his own had broken down. Penny had given him the impression that she thought painting pictures for a living was frivolous and could hardly be expected to keep a grown man fed. She hadn't articulated the opinion but he could see it in the line of her mouth and her disdainful gaze. Glancing round at racks of goods which his parents would probably have considered junk, he thought her attitude a bit precious.

But this week Claire Pennyman appeared to be working alone so this was a good time to call. He closed the door behind him and wandered in and Claire emerged from the back room, drying her hands on a towel.

'Hello,' she said, looking surprised. 'Can I help?'

'I believe you had some old perfume bottles for sale. Have you still got them?'

'Yes, they're in the case over there. I'll need to unlock it for you.'

Claire disappeared into the back room again and emerged with a key in her hand. Adam had already walked across to the glass cabinet and was standing staring in at its contents dolefully. He watched her put the key in the lock and wondered which of the things he'd heard about her since her return were true. There's no smoke without fire, his grandmother used to say - all too often - but Adam had already come to the conclusion that, in Bohenna at least, sometimes there was an awful lot of smoke created by a very tiny fire. Now Claire was removing each perfume bottle in turn and placing it on a table top next to where a china dinner service had been laid out. There were four bottles. She put the last one down and straightened up, looking at him expectantly.

Adam stared at them dumbly, reached out a hand to the nearest and lifted the price tag which hung from its neck.

'Ouch. I didn't realise they'd be that expensive,' he said. 'Sorry. I'm not sure…'

His voice trailed away but he continued to stare at them, uncertain. Zoe had made such a fuss about how lovely these bottles were a few weeks ago. He'd thought it would be the perfect thing to get, something to make her realise that he did listen to what she said, that he did care about her.

'It's my girlfriend's birthday soon,' he explained. 'She saw these here and loved them, so I thought I'd get one before they sold. But they're a bit steep.' He shrugged.

'They aren't all the same price.' Claire picked a different one up and read out the price tag. 'The one you looked at first is the most expensive. It's Victorian and probably the oldest.' She picked up the other two in turn and told him their prices.

'Those aren't so bad.' He flicked her a look. 'Hey, I'm not being mean here but, you know...'

'You don't need to explain to me,' said Claire with feeling. 'We all have to watch our pennies.'

He was surprised and it must have shown in his face.

'I'm not part of the empire,' she said crisply, waving a hand vaguely towards the vineyard.

'No, sorry. I didn't mean to suggest anything.' He grinned. 'I'm not doing very well here, am I?' He looked back down at the bottles. 'Honestly, I know nothing about them. Do you like them? If you had to choose one, which would you go for?'

She glanced questioningly into his face then looked down, studying the bottles, and pointed to the second most expensive one. It had a pyramidal base of palest blue cut glass and a silver ball top delicately designed with a bee feeding on a wild rose.

'I like this one,' she said. 'It's art deco, I think.' She produced a weak smile and a half shrug. 'And I like bees.'

Adam picked it up and looked it over. It was pretty.

'Of course, your girlfriend might have very different taste,' Claire added.

And just at the moment, thought Adam, she'll probably hate whatever I get on principle.

Claire turned away, fiddling with the position of a couple

of plates in the service, giving him some space.

'I'll take this,' he said heavily.

Claire smiled again, put the other bottles back in the case and locked the door, then took the art deco bottle to the counter.

'What's good about this one,' she said, wrapping it up in a couple of sheets of tissue paper, 'is that, being art deco, it looks modern as well as being vintage.'

'I see you've got the patter down already,' said Adam.

'What do you mean by that?'

'Nothing. It's just that you've only been here a couple of weeks. You must have been swotting up on the stock or something. Jane was telling me you worked in a garden centre before you came here.'

'Are you suggesting I don't know what I'm doing?' she replied indignantly. 'Of course I've made an effort to know the stock.' She finished wrapping the tissue paper round the bottle and ferociously ripped a piece of adhesive tape off the dispenser to fasten it. 'Do you want a bag?' she said curtly. 'I don't want to give you one because you don't need it and all these bags are ruining the planet.'

'I don't want a bag.'

She glanced at him warily. 'Jane say anything else about me?'

'No.' He offered his credit card and watched her put it in the machine, wondering why she was so touchy all of a sudden. She had been friendly enough when she had visited his studio. Now she was all bristles and sourness. 'Jane only told me about the garden centre because she said you used to be an illustrator.'

'You can put your number in now.'

He tapped at the machine.

'Jane was concerned you'd stopped painting.' Adam

waited for the machine to finish and took his card. 'She said you used to love it. I gather you know each other well.'

'We did - a long time ago. It seems you know her pretty well too. I didn't realise she confided in you.'

'Confided? Hardly.' He picked up the tissue-wrapped bundle from the counter but didn't move and fixed Claire with a withering look. 'Jane strikes me as being lonely. She comes into my studio and likes to talk. To be honest I don't always listen to what she's saying 'cause I'm involved in my work - I trust you won't tell her that - but if it makes her feel better…' He shrugged. 'Maybe if her old friends still bothered with her, she wouldn't need to talk to a relative stranger.' He gestured with the package, said, 'Thanks,' and walked out.

He noticed her frowning, pinching her lips thoughtfully as he closed the door.

*

Claire got the phone number of Megan Davies from the noticeboard in the church porch but when she called her, Megan stated briskly that she knew nothing about the contents of the box she had given to Penny. She was a busy woman with a lot on her mind, she said, and she simply got people from the various stalls to put whatever was unsold into boxes at the end of the fête then passed them on as appropriate. The bric-a-brac stall was run by Patsy Miller and Megan grudgingly gave Claire the woman's phone number. But Patsy, though pleasant and helpful, didn't live in Bohenna. She lived in a hamlet some three miles away and didn't know much either. Most of the donations were left anonymously. The people who owned the pub in the village kindly left the doors of their old garages open and people put their offerings into various plastic boxes, labelled according to stall: bric-a-brac, bottle, raffle prizes and so on. Patsy only knew the people who had turned up on the afternoon when the table was already set up.

'Which is always a bit of a nuisance really,' she remarked, 'though it's kind of them to give, of course. But it means a rush to price everything before the fête starts.'

'But can you remember who those people were and what they gave?' Claire asked.

'Oh, my dear - I don't know. Let me see. Well yes, I remember Philippa Johnson – you know, the new vicar's wife - gave us a baby doll with two spare sets of clothes. Lovely condition. That sold very quickly. There was a young woman who gave a few things, but I can't remember what exactly and I didn't know her. And there was Beattie Foster, of course…she'd left some donations at the garages but had forgotten to include…what was it she brought on the day? A teapot I think. There were a couple of others but I can't remember who they were. Sorry. Why do you want to know?'

'There were some interesting pieces in with the jewellery and we're always looking for stock at V and C. I wondered if they might have any other things to sell.' The spurious excuse seemed to placate and the call was ended.

So that was no help; there was no way sweet old Beattie could be a suspect. Claire would have to go and ask at The Swan. Already she felt that she was clutching at straws.

*

The new landlord at the pub had been there barely a year. Terry Donovan who ran the place when Claire and Neil were younger had gone but even before their hasty departure from Bohenna, they had rarely visited The Swan. Neil had been the marketing manager for the vineyard and had travelled a lot. The pressures of both work and a young family had curtailed their social life to a minimum.

Now the licensing plaque over the pub door read *Dave*

Spenser. Claire arrived there at five to six on the Wednesday evening, hoping he might open early so they could talk before the regulars arrived, but it was six o'clock exactly when she saw the lights being switched on and heard the clunk of the key turning in the big old lock. She waited a couple of minutes then went inside.

It was said that there had been a public house on the site of The Swan for more than four hundred years. The present building was a mere two hundred and twenty years old. It had low, beamed ceilings, a sloping wooden floor and a fireplace in every room. Claire walked into the lounge bar. Not much had changed though the dark old tables and chairs had been replaced by paler, more modern ones and the bench seat in one corner had been reupholstered. A shovel full of coal smouldered disinterestedly in the open fire; the logs stacked up to the side seemed optimistic. The bar at the centre of the public rooms was formed in a square. A partition with shelving and optics divided it and meant that you could only see into the opposing room from certain places along the bar, looking at an angle.

Claire stood at the bar now but there was no sign of the landlord. Away to her right, she could hear voices in the kitchen and she cleared her throat loudly. Dave quickly appeared.

'Sorry to keep you waiting. What can I get you?'

She ordered a small glass of white wine and watched him pour it. She could feel his curiosity and saw the way his eyes slid sideways to glance at her. Already she was convinced that he knew who she was.

'I don't think I've seen you in here before, have I?' He put the glass down in front of her.

'No. There was a different landlord when I used to live here.'

60

She gave him a five pound note and he put it through the till.

'You used to live here?' He handed her the change.

'Yes. I left a few years ago. But I'm back now and working up at V and C in the Craft Yard.'

'That's right,' he said, and nodded. 'You were married to Neil Pennyman. Claire, isn't it?' He smiled; it looked genuine enough.

'Yes.' She glanced along the bar. 'Quiet tonight.'

'Early yet. But November's always quiet. Much business up at the Yard?'

'Not a lot. I've been told it'll get busier in the run up to Christmas.'

'That's what we're all hoping anyway.' He grinned and looked about to move away.

She leaned forward. 'I understand you let people put things in your garages for the fête in the summer?'

'Yes, we did.' He frowned. 'Why?'

'We've had a box of leftover items given to us and I wondered if you happened to see anyone bringing things to leave there? Did anyone keep an eye on it?'

'You mean in case anything was stolen? That's not very likely. No, sorry. I spend most of the day in here.' He shook his head, pulling a face. 'I might have seen a couple of people but I didn't really notice. I assumed they were taking stuff in. Maybe they were taking bags in and filling them up to nick.' He laughed.

Claire smiled politely. She angled a glance towards the public bar but it still looked empty.

'Can you remember who you saw?' she persisted, trying to sound casual.

'Who? I told you, I didn't really register.' He pursed up his lips. 'Though, come to think of it, I did see Mandy Turner

61

when I was out sorting the bins one day. She's Nick Lawer's girlfriend. You probably know Nick? He's lived here forever, so he says. Runs his own taxi business.'

Claire nodded. The name rang a vague bell.

'No-one else?'

He shrugged, shaking his head.

Claire noticed a pile of business cards on the end of the bar nearest her and she picked one up and read it, brow furrowed.

JANE SAWDY
Natural healer and psychic.

She turned it over.

Stressed? Struggling to cope? Niggling ailments? I can help rebalance your life. Private, affordable consultations. Find your inner peace.

Dave nodded at the card. 'That's that woman who works up at the yard. It's quite a claim, isn't it? I gather she does séances sometimes. Sessions, she calls them. Says she can commune with people's nearest and dearest...' He put on a spooky, wobbly voice, eyes big. '...on the other side.' He looked at her with frank curiosity. 'Know her, do you?'

'Only a little.' She felt a pang of guilt. Adam's words had stayed with her. *Maybe if her old friends still bothered with her...* But Claire found Jane's behaviour disturbing. She quickly replaced the card.

Dave was grinning. 'P'rhaps she'll look into her crystal ball for you and see who gave what to the fête. Tell me again why you're so interested?'

Claire repeated the excuse she had given to Patsy Miller about looking for more jewellery stock.

'Oh. Right.' Dave turned and walked towards the kitchen.

The public bar door banged and Claire heard the voices of two men. They came to stand at the counter and one of them was at the right angle to look directly across at her.

'Annie,' Dave shouted. 'Did you see any of the people who put stuff in the garages? Someone who donated jewellery maybe?'

Claire couldn't hear the reply. She found herself trying not to look at the man at the bar who was staring at her with frank and intrusive interest.

Dave came back. 'Annie didn't see anyone. I could ask around, if you like.'

'No, don't worry, thanks. It's not important. I just thought I'd ask since I was here anyway.'

Dave served the men in the public bar and Claire took her glass across to a table and sat down, out of sight. She couldn't just go; she had to make her questions look like an afterthought. She swallowed a couple of mouthfuls of wine, trying to look at ease, and stayed another ten minutes before making for the door and slipping out into the cloak of darkness.

Claire did remember Nick Lawer now. He was a womaniser and there had been a rumour going round, years ago, that he beat his wife up - before she left him, that was. Sensible woman, everyone had said, though no-one knew for certain what had gone on. That was the thing in Bohenna: everyone knew and yet no-one knew. And Nick was the man in the bar who had been looking at her, undressing her with his eyes. She was certain he knew who she was too and, if he didn't before, he soon would because Dave Spenser would be sure tell him.

The question was: did his taste extend to little girls too? Nick Lawer was definitely worth investigating.

Chapter 5

By the first week of December, the wine had stopped fermenting. By the end of the second, Julia had started racking each tank off its sediment into another freshly cleaned one. If they left it too long on the dead yeast cells and grape residue, the flavour of the wine would be compromised.

Like most of their jobs, racking was the sort of work which didn't respect weekends off: it was done when it had to be done. On the Saturday, Julia, Tim, Chris and another lad called Mike were working in pairs, moving the pumps from tank to tank, dragging suction tubes and attaching them, taking care not to disturb the debris at the bottom of the wine. Phil was working outside, carrying the pressed sediment away, driving up and down the rows of vines in his tractor to deposit it around the base of the plants as a fertiliser.

Julia fitted the tube to the spout on the next stainless steel tank and turned the tap. Tim had already put the tube from the pump into a clean empty tank and he flicked the pump on. They had done it so often that they worked automatically, barely speaking, and, standing waiting for the tank to empty, Julia found herself thinking about Gilly. She had done that a lot since Claire's return.

The little girl used to come up to the winery, sometimes with her father, far more rarely with Claire. She wasn't supposed to go there alone but she often spent an hour or two with her grandfather at the nursery and sometimes she would wander across, occasionally with his permission, often without him knowing. She hadn't been a naughty child - Julia had always found her good-tempered and polite - but she'd been inquisitive and curious and fiercely independent. And stubborn. She liked to 'help'. When they were racking she would ask to put the tube on or switch the pump on, then she'd climb the steps and watch the wine frothing into the new clean tank. Everything seemed to fascinate her.

Julia had been fond of her; she would have liked to have had a daughter of her own. It was ironic that Neil had fathered two girls when he had been so keen to have a boy. Maybe that was why he had seemed to struggle to connect with his daughters. Or maybe it was because Neil was such an ambitious person. His children weren't necessarily the first thing on his mind. Indeed, he had sometimes given the impression that they held him back.

'Done.' Tim switched the pump off and turned to look at her then waved a hand slowly in front of her face. 'Julia? Finished.' He grinned. 'Jesus, where were you then?'

'Sorry Tim. Miles away.'

They moved on to the next tank.

Half an hour later, Eve turned up at the winery and stood, watching intently, saying nothing. Julia saw her out of the corner of her eye but carried on working. Eve appeared there virtually every day at some point. She couldn't physically work any more because her arthritis had weakened her and gave her too much pain, but she had to keep making suggestions or commenting, had to feel involved. Julia suspected she would feel the same way one day, a thought which generally managed to make her more tolerant.

'All right, mum?' she said, coming across to join her.

'How's it going?' Eve's beady eyes watched Chris attach

the pipe onto a tank.

'Fine. Nearly half way through now.'

Eve nodded. Her gaze shifted, searching the winery, frowning.

'No Daniel, I see.'

'No. He went out. Football this afternoon.'

'He should be helping you, Julia, learning the trade. You're too soft with him.' Her voice had risen.

Tim walked slowly across to join them.

'He's only fifteen, mum,' said Julia. 'He's got time. He's got to have some fun.'

'You were working in the vineyard at his age.'

'But I wanted to.' Julia looked at her brother. 'Tim didn't do much in the winery till he was older, did you?'

'Not really.' He glanced uneasily between them. 'Why?'

'I worry about the future of the vineyard,' Eve said curtly. 'It seems I'm the only one who does.' She glared at Julia. 'You're saying Daniel doesn't want to work in the winery. But since you only had one child and this one…' She gripped Timothy's arm with her bent fingers. '…has so far chosen not to have any, where's the next winemaker to come from? Hmm? I think about that. Your father would be desperate to think the vineyard would leave the family.'

No, *you're* the one who's desperate to think that, Julia thought. My father would have just wanted his grandson to be happy.

'Anyway,' Eve was saying, 'maybe Neil can have a word with him at Christmas. He's always been good with Danny.'

'Neil?' Julia frowned. 'He's coming, is he?'

'Yes, he'll be staying here a couple of days. He's got a new girlfriend, you know. Samantha. I told him to bring her too if he wants.'

Eve smiled sweetly and left. Julia knew that smile. Eve

was at her most dangerous when she was being charming.

She turned to Timothy. 'But hasn't she invited Claire?'

'Yes. She had to because she wanted Laura to be there. You know how she believes in getting the family together.' His mouth twisted wryly. 'Should be interesting.'

Back at the tanks, Julia forgot Gilly and thought about her mother instead, wondering what plans she was hatching now, schemes which she clearly wasn't planning to share.

*

Nick Lawer lived in a semi-detached house on Tap Lane, a road which ran south from Long Lane, climbing the valley side, and which eventually, after a few winding miles, reached the coast. His home was a small, rough-rendered cottage with a gravelled front garden and a glimpse of washing hanging on the line at the back. On the drive stood an ancient Ford Fiesta which looked as though it might fall apart at any moment.

Claire walked slowly past, glancing idly at the other houses stretching along the lane. They were a mixture of new build infill and the old cottages of agricultural workers. On the other side of the road, about twenty yards higher up, was the turning to the estate - The Paddocks - where she had lived with Neil. Gilly had walked this way every day to and from school. Beyond The Paddocks, on higher ground behind a hedge, was a gently banked field where sheep grazed and a stile gave access to a footpath. Claire crossed the road, climbed the stile and took a few steps along the path. Stopping and looking back, she could see the house through the bare branches of a tree growing out of the hedge.

She had been here before, several times already. Nick Lawer had quickly obsessed her. Having found out where he lived, her days off had been organised around visiting this place and checking out his movements. Increasingly she was convinced that he knew what had happened to Gilly. She suspected - was certain in fact - that he might be keeping her captive. His girlfriend had donated things to the fête and Nick's salacious and violent reputation spoke for itself. And, glancing down the drive of the house, she had seen sheds in his back garden.

But she needed him to be out so that she could investigate. He was out now, clearly, because his Toyota was nowhere in sight but the Fiesta on the drive suggested his girlfriend Mandy was still at home. Claire made a pretence of walking a few steps along the path then turned to come back. The sound of an old engine turning over made her look up quickly and hurry back to her vantage point. Mandy had got in the car. The ignition didn't fire and the engine turned again. Reluctantly it started and, rattling disconcertingly, the car reversed out of the drive.

Claire waited until the car was out of sight then crossed over the stile and walked briskly back down the road. Glancing each way in case anyone was watching, she hurried down the drive to the back of the house.

The back garden was scruffy. There had been an attempt to plant a border up but it was choked with weeds and the small square area of lawn was uneven and overgrown. On the left was a single brick garage with two rotting wooden doors. Behind it were two sheds built of corrugated iron which had both been painted jet black. The first was small, the second much larger and given the size of the house, surprisingly big. Claire was barely breathing. Neither shed had windows and both were padlocked. She stood by the side of the first one, listening, but could hear nothing. She tried the door and pulled at the padlock but it was locked and wouldn't move. She did the same thing on the larger shed, leaning her ear against the metal this time, hearing nothing but the beating of her own heart. She tapped gently.

'Gilly?' she murmured, then repeated it a little louder. 'Gilly? Are you there?'

Was it her imagination or did she hear something, a rustle maybe, a movement? She tapped again but now heard nothing.

She straightened up, unsure what to do next, and stood, staring at the shed then slowly glancing round the scruffy garden in case there might be any sign that Gilly had been there. What did she really expect: a child's toys? Gilly would be fifteen by now. She'd be grown up, wearing trendy clothes and make-up, listening to music Claire wouldn't understand and drooling over posters of boy bands Claire had never heard of. Except that she wouldn't. Not if she was shut up in a shed. She wondered if she could pick the padlock or maybe even break it. She glanced around for a large stone.

'What the hell are you doing in my garden?'

Claire spun round. Lost in her own thoughts, she hadn't registered the taxi pulling onto the drive and now Nick Lawer was standing just a few yards away. He was wearing his 'taxi' clothes: dark, neatly creased trousers and a thin navy sweater over an open-necked shirt, but his legs were spread aggressively wide as if spoiling for a fight, his expression black as thunder. Her mind went blank. He took a step closer.

'Oh, it's you,' he said. He looked her up and down, stuck a tongue in his cheek, then glanced towards the sheds and back at her as if he'd been checking that they were still locked up. 'What are you after here?' The aggression had dropped a little and his eyes challenged her suggestively. He surveyed her a second time, slowly, in that offensive way he had. 'Come to see me, have you?'

'No. I was walking down the lane, and I...I saw a cat come in your garden. It was limping badly and I was worried about it. But I can't see it now. Do you keep a cat?'

69

'No.'

Claire gestured a hand towards the sheds.

'Maybe it's gone in one of your sheds.'

'It couldn't have. They're locked.' His eyes narrowed. 'Did I hear you talking to someone just now?'

'I was singing to myself,' she said. 'I do that a lot.' She glanced round the garden again. 'Well. No sign of the cat.'

She moved to go but Nick stayed where he was, saying nothing, obliging her to walk round him. He grabbed her arm as she passed, holding her tight with steely fingers and leaned his head close to hers.

'Don't come on my property again...' He spoke low with just a grumble of menace. She could see the heavy stubble on his chin starting to show through and the broken veins on his cheeks. '...not without an invitation.' He raised his free hand and ran one lewd finger over her lips, then down her chin and neck. 'That could be arranged, mind. Fancy a bit of fun, do you?'

'Leave me alone,' she said, pulling her head away and trying to shake him off.

He let go of her and she walked away as calmly as she could, her arm burning where his fingers had dug into her flesh. She heard him laugh as he watched her go.

*

'It couldn't have been Nick Lawer,' the Family Liaison Officer told Claire firmly. 'I promised I'd look into the case when I saw you last, Mrs. Pennyman. And I did. We checked his whereabouts at the time of your daughter's disappearance and he wasn't in the village; he was taking a couple to Exeter airport. We checked the flight times and spoke to the couple as well. There was no doubt about it. He was telling the truth.'

Claire stared at the constable. She heard what she was

saying but struggled to accept it. She had rung Lyn James as soon as she'd got home because she had been so sure that Gilly was shut inside one of those sheds. She wanted someone to come and break them open, straight away, as soon as possible. But she had been obliged to leave a message and it had been a couple of hours later before Lyn had called her back. And now it was early evening and the officer had turned up at her door, her frustration clear at what she saw as more time-wasting.

'Mrs Pennyman,' she was saying now, 'I'm concerned that you're trying to take the law into your own hands here. It's quite clear from the records that we looked into everything. We spoke to everyone who was anywhere near Bohenna at the time, anyone who had a connection with the case in any way. If any new information comes forward we'll look at it again - of course we will. But you must let us do the asking and investigating. You aren't helping by digging around like this.'

'Then how will your 'new information' come to light if I don't do the digging?' said Claire, getting to her feet, pacing a couple of steps then turning to face the constable. She raised her arms in a gesture of despair. 'You're not doing it are you? And yet I know that Gilly never left this village.'

'How do you know? The hair slide?' Lyn's expression softened. 'It's not evidence, Claire.'

'But I know,' repeated Claire. She stabbed the air in front of her with an incisive finger. 'I know she's here somewhere.'

'You're going to make yourself upset. Please don't do this. I did read the report into the investigation, checking if there was anything to follow up on. There was nothing.'

'You checked everyone in the village? Everyone? Do you know where they all were when Gilly disappeared?' Claire could hear the hysterical note in her voice but she couldn't let it go now.

'Yes, we checked. Of course we checked. That's what we

71

do. We followed up family, friends, acquaintances. We did a door to door. You know that.' Lyn James frowned. 'You'll make yourself ill if you keeping worrying at it like this, Mrs. Pennyman.'

The officer stood up. Her manner had become impersonal again; the interview was at an end.

'You mustn't go causing trouble, nosing into other people's private lives or trespassing. You'll only make living here uncomfortable for yourself and maybe provoke complaints to us. And if someone complains, we have to follow it up. Let it go…please?' She offered a kind smile and walked to the door.

Claire watched her go but didn't move to show her out. She sat down and stared into space.

Half an hour went by. She picked up the phone and rang her mother. She had rung her once since arriving in Bohenna only to get a well-meaning lecture on how strange Sally Hitchen thought her daughter's behaviour was in going back to Cornwall at all. It had proved pointless trying to explain but just at the moment Claire needed to talk to someone.

'Claire darling,' her mother said with genuine enthusiasm. 'Are you all right? You sound tired. How's the new job?'

'It's fine.'

'Good. Antiques, didn't you say? I was a bit surprised; I didn't know you were interested in antiques.'

Sally Hitchen's voice sounded remarkably clear. Claire could imagine her mother in her bright, airy Greek house, her only garden a few pot plants in a courtyard, the sea five minutes away and the nearest taverna even closer.

'I suppose some of them could be classed as antiques, mum, but mostly they're collectibles. You know, kitchen things and old advertising boards and bits of designer pottery. Some of it's junk but there are some nice things too. Anyway,

I needed a job. It's fine. And it's convenient.'

'Yes, but you had a job, Claire - in Kent. I can't understand why you've gone back to Bohenna, especially after what happened. Of course, you know what I think of the place: it gives me claustrophobia. And it's so dismal this time of year. Is that why you rang? Are you unhappy there darling? Why don't you come and stay with me for a while? The spare room's free. Graham wouldn't mind.'

Claire thanked her but brushed the invitation aside. She'd heard it before. She loved her mother. Despite her endless maternal words of advice there was nothing judgmental about her and she did care about her children - from a distance. But even if she wanted to go, Claire couldn't leave Bohenna now. She listened to her mother chatter on and found it vaguely comforting but when she finished the call the house felt emptier and more silent than ever.

She flicked the television on but didn't watch it, then got up again and went upstairs to her bedroom. From the bottom of her wardrobe she pulled out a box, laid it on the bed and ripped back the brown tape holding the flaps down.

'We should get rid of some things,' Neil had said.

'We can't get rid of them,' Claire replied. 'Gilly might want them.'

'She'll have grown out of them…' If she ever comes back, she knew he wanted to add. 'It's already been three years. Her clothes wouldn't fit her.'

'No. No, you're right.'

Of course he was right. She knew that. You can't keep everything. And they didn't. It became an issue as soon as they decided to move. Did they create another bedroom for her, the girl who didn't live with them any more? Or did they package things up and 'rationalise', as Neil put it. They argued. Claire thought there should be a room that was Gilly's; Neil thought it inappropriate. He said they would be creating a museum piece, that it was unhealthy, especially for Laura. Laura, when asked, didn't express an opinion.

'But what will Gilly think if she comes back and finds we've removed her from our lives?' Claire argued. 'She'll think we don't care, that we don't want her.'

So they had compromised and had got rid of some things and kept others, and they kept one bedroom 'available' and put her remaining things in it. With the passage of time, more clothes and toys had gone. I'll buy her more, Claire had thought repeatedly, feeling treacherous. It's not as though it's final.

And this box now contained most of what was left: a few of Gilly's favourite games and books, some much loved trinkets and cuddly toys and her magnifying lenses and 'bug traps' for examining beetles and butterflies and anything else that strayed her way. Claire pulled out the soft toy that sat on the top. It was a hedgehog. Gilly loved hedgehogs.

Claire sat with it on her lap and stroked its unrealistically soft coat absent-mindedly. She hadn't told her mother about the hair slide but had she really thought she would? Sally Hitchen would have thought it foolish too.

She thought back over the conversation with the policewoman again. She had been so certain that Nick Lawer had Gilly in one of his sheds that her disappointment was like a punch in the stomach - she felt winded by it, knocked back, unsure where to go next.

Chapter 6

At the beginning of December, Claire and Penny decorated the unit for Christmas, stretching tiny fairy lights round the window, putting candles in gilded glass bowls and spreading tinsel and holly about. Penny brought in Christmas music - carols and schmaltzy selections from a variety of crooners - and, exactly as she had predicted, the number of visitors rose dramatically as the days passed. Claire was busy serving customers for the first time since she had started there.

She had been looking forward to Laura's return from university for the holidays but her daughter had rung up at the last minute to ask if she could delay her arrival in Bohenna. There were a couple of parties going on in Oxford after term ended and a college friend had invited her back to Surrey for a few days. They would go up to London, do some shopping, see the lights.

'Do you know her well?' Claire had asked.

'Of course. She's all right mum. Her father's a doctor. You don't need to worry about me.' Laura hesitated. 'Is that OK? Do you mind? I'd love to go.'

So Claire had said yes, had been glad that Laura - at eighteen - still thought to ask, but warned her not to stray from the busy thoroughfares and insisted that the girls always stayed together. She was fussing, she knew, but she couldn't help herself. And now the much anticipated reunion with her daughter had been put back until Christmas Eve.

On the last Saturday before Christmas, Claire was working at V and C alone, a recording of *Carols from King's* playing yet again. She had just sold a man a nine carat gold ring set with a garnet. His wife had seen it the day before so he had come in to buy it for her as a surprise Christmas gift. He had been excited, apparently thrilled with his own subterfuge.

'Happy Christmas,' he'd said as he was leaving.

Claire returned the greeting and smiled but she wasn't feeling very festive. The day before she had received the Decree Nisi in the post. It had never been in doubt, her lawyer had said, but still it shocked her to see it in black and white and it felt a little unreal, a sort of emptiness. In six weeks she could apply for the Absolute, or she could wait. But the marriage was over and the sooner the details were finalised, the better.

The music had stopped while she had been day-dreaming but it was already four twenty: she would be closing in ten minutes. She bent to take the CD out of the machine just as the bell tinkled over the door. She straightened up. Jane had come in, the habitual fringed shawl thrown tightly round her neck.

'Jane.' Claire smiled warily. 'How are you?'

'I'm fine.' She approached the counter. 'I'm having one of my sessions next week.' She handed Claire a card, identical to the ones in the pub. 'I thought you might like to come. You might find it helpful.'

'Helpful?' Claire avoided making eye contact and stared at the card. 'When is it?'

'Wednesday evening. In a private house at the top of the village. I've scribbled the address on the back. There's just a small admission fee.'

'I'm afraid I can't. Sorry. Laura's coming home for

Christmas.'

Claire offered the card back but Jane shook her head.

'Keep it. You might want to use my services another time. Think about it.' Jane smiled, fixing Claire with her magnetic gaze. 'Of course, Laura could come too. I'd love to meet her.'

'I'll tell her about it. See what she thinks. She's quite shy.'

'Is she? What a shame.' She looked disappointed.

'I hope it goes well.' Claire tried to sound like she meant it.

Jane paused, frowning. 'By the way, have you seen Adam today? He hasn't opened his studio at all.'

'No, I haven't seen him.'

'I just *knew* something was going to happen. I could feel it and I'm never wrong. I hope he's all right.'

Jane moved towards the door. On an impulse, Claire leaned forward. 'Perhaps you'd like to come to my place sometime over Christmas? Maybe have a drink with us?'

Jane turned back. 'Thank you. I'd like that.'

'Do you still drink alcohol?' Claire asked doubtfully.

Jane grinned suddenly – a refreshingly normal grin - and Claire was suddenly reminded of the friend she once knew. It was reassuring to know she was still there, buried somewhere inside.

'Yes, I do drink. Wine usually.'

'I'll give you a ring then and we'll fix something up.'

Jane nodded and left and Claire immediately wondered if she'd done the right thing.

*

It was pitch dark by the time Claire left work and a miserable intermittent drizzle hung in the air. Even so, with her mind too active to allow her to relax, she changed into her jogging kit and trainers and went straight out again. She headed into the

77

village, cutting through the back lanes, narrow tracks barely greater than the width of a car which twisted and looped round to yet another lane, then another. Going out further than usual, she reached a field gateway on the far side of the village and paused, gasping, enjoying the cleansing rush of blood thumping in her veins and the charge of electricity in her system. She had been passed by only two cars so far. By the light of her head torch, her watch read six forty-five so Nick Lawer would probably be safely in the pub by now too. She didn't want to risk bumping into him, especially in the dark.

Breath easing, she set off back through the middle of the village and, reaching the stone bridge, stopped as she so often did and walked to the wall, staring down into the water. The clouds had lifted a little and the water looked steely grey in the wispy moonlight.

A dark figure was sitting on the bank by the footpath from the green. A man. She'd assumed he was a fisherman but then she watched him put a bottle to his mouth, tip it right back, curse and then toss it away. Now he was groaning and throwing himself backwards, arms out to the sides till he was spread-eagled across the path, eyes staring vaguely to the night sky. She recognised that shaven head and looked harder. It was Adam.

'Oh, for Pete's sake,' she muttered.

To the side of the bridge was a low stile. She climbed over it and walked down the path till she stood looking down on him. His eyes were closed and she wondered if he was asleep - or maybe unconscious. He was breathing at least, slowly and heavily.

'You're blocking the path,' she said tartly.

There was a brief pause but he didn't move. 'You could step on me,' he said, a little indistinctly. 'Why not? Everyone else does.'

She almost smiled. 'Everyone?'

He grunted, grimaced, then opened his eyes as if with effort. After staring at her a minute with questionable focus, he closed them again.

'Yep.' He waved an indolent hand. 'Feel free.'

She hesitated a minute then sat down beside him. The ground was damp. The man was an idiot.

'Are you doing this for your image?' she enquired drily. '*Starving artist gets drunk because no-one understands his work*. I'm not sure it's a good tactic for selling paintings.'

Showing surprising vigour, Adam sat up suddenly and leaned his head towards her. She could smell the beer on his breath and maybe whisky too.

'No-one understands *me*,' he said. 'End of story.'

'Crikey, Adam, how much have you had to drink? You smell like a brewery. And, ugh, this ground is wet and freezing. I'm getting cold.' She scrambled to her feet and brushed her leggings off. 'Get up and go home. You're making a fool of yourself.'

He shook his head and attempted a shrug though only one shoulder seemed to move.

'No point. My girlfriend's left me.'

'I'm not surprised.'

Still, he worried her. His speech was slurred and his head had dropped limply forward. He did look as if he might pass out.

Claire glanced up and down the path. Of course there was no-one else stupid enough to be hanging around the river in the damp and the dark, though maybe that was just as well since this wasn't likely to improve Adam's reputation with the majority of Bohenna's residents. She bent over, grabbed him under the arm and pulled. Nothing happened except that his arm lifted.

'Come on, Adam. You're far too heavy for me to get you up unless you help. Let's go back to my house and I'll make you some coffee.'

He peered up at her. 'Coffee?' He snorted derisively. 'Haven't you got anything stronger? I'm out of money and I've got nothing left to drink.'

'I might have something but you'll never know if you don't shift yourself. Get up.'

He grunted again, then made an exaggerated effort to get to his feet and, with her help, finally made it and, supporting him as best she could, she guided him back to her cottage. The movement seemed to have brought him round. She pushed him in the direction of the sofa and went into the kitchen to make two mugs of coffee. Handing him one, he took it reluctantly and looked at it with distaste.

'I thought we were going to have a drink,' he said.

'I've only got one bottle of wine in the house and I was saving it up for a special occasion. This isn't it.'

'Oh? Don't you get freebie bottles from the vineyard - for old times' sake or something?'

'Nope. I don't have a cheap and continuous supply of alcohol and, frankly, even if I did, I wouldn't be giving you any now. You're already smashed.'

He grunted and sipped at the coffee, then sat back, still cradling it. His eyes, though glazed, were at least open.

'So this girlfriend,' said Claire, 'she's the one you were buying the perfume bottle for?'

'Yes. Zoe. But I never had a chance to give it to her. Her birthday isn't till Monday.'

'And what happened exactly to make her go?'

'We had a row. I accused her of seeing another man.'

'Ah. And that didn't go down well.'

He shook his head exaggeratedly. 'But it's true. I followed

her. And when I told her that, she completely lost it. Spying on me, she said. What kind of a man goes spying on his girlfriend, she said. The kind who knows that she's not telling him everything, I said. Then she denied it. Said she'd just been talking to a friend and I was using it as an excuse to give her grief.' He moaned, drank some more coffee and pulled a face. 'Can't we open the wine? I'll pay you for it.'

'No. So why were you following her?'

'Because she's been behaving oddly, going away, not turning up to things when she said she would. Just being…weird.'

Claire nodded. 'How long have you been together?'

He frowned. 'Eight years, more or less.'

'Eight years and this is your first bust-up?'

'Yes. No. It's the first time she's walked out.' He hesitated, rolled bleary eyes to look at Claire. 'She keeps banging on about having a family. Thinks I don't want one and I'm just making excuses.'

'And do you want one?'

'Yes. Of course. We just need to be more settled first. I keep telling her that.'

'How old is Zoe?'

'Thirty-five nearly.'

'So she's worried the clock's ticking. I had my first child at twenty-four. Everything about it gets harder as you get older. Are you *sure* you're not making excuses?'

'What do you know about me?' he said crossly. 'Nothing. I love Zoe.' He drank another mouthful of coffee then looked at her, eyes narrowed. 'How do you do it?'

'How do I do what?'

'Cope. You've had all this gut-wrenching stuff with your daughter and now your marriage and you seem pretty cool with it all. How d'you do it?'

81

'Pretty cool?' She stared at him then began to laugh and found she couldn't stop.

Adam was both smiling and frowning at her, bemused. She got a hold of herself.

'Believe me, Adam, I've never been cool about anything. Ever. I just...' She snorted and shrugged. '...muddle on somehow. When I was young I thought I had it all sorted. I was happy. I was married to a guy I adored and we had plans. I lived in a village I adored. But life turns round and kicks you, doesn't it? Nothing works out the way you expect. What's that joke: if you want God to laugh, tell him your plans?' She shrugged again and finished her coffee.

Adam stared at her dumbly, mouth open.

'Zoe said I was selfish,' he muttered. 'Said I dragged her down here where there's nothing going on and I didn't care that she hated it.'

'And did you?'

'What?'

'Do all that?'

'No.' He bristled indignantly, then sighed. 'When I first suggested moving down here she seemed keen. I think she saw Cornwall as all big surfing beaches and wall to wall sunshine. Bohenna wasn't what she had in mind.' He paused, rested his head back and allowed it to loll side to side. Claire got up and took the mug from his hands. It was still half full and she put it on the table. 'But in the summer she seemed happy for a while. We did stuff, travelled around a bit. Then when autumn started...' His speech was getting slower. 'Can you imagine? She's from Manchester. It's in the north. Doesn't it rain every other day up there? But she said it was never like this: moist and misty and gloomy. I said that's only because there was so much smoke in the air that you couldn't see anything anyway.'

'Maybe not a good move.'

'I was only joking…sort of.' His eyes closed. 'I went up there with her once…God, it was cold…' He fell silent; his breathing slowed.

'Don't sleep, Adam.' Claire stood up and put a hand to his knee, trying to shake him awake. 'Adam?'

He'd gone.

'So much for the coffee,' she muttered.

She didn't like the angle of his head. If he was sick he'd maybe choke on it and she didn't fancy him being ill on her sofa either. She found a plastic sheet and stretched it out on the sofa to his right, covered it with a bath towel, then tipped him over onto his side with a cushion under his head. She took off his shoes and heaved his legs up onto the sofa too. Finally she covered him with a travel rug, looked at him and resigned herself to leaving him there. He'd have to sleep it off.

*

When Adam came to his neck hurt. And his mouth felt like he'd swallowed the contents of his car battery. Whoa - and his head… He didn't want to think what that felt like. He tentatively opened his eyes but it took him a minute to focus. He was looking sideways at a small fireplace and a rusty old woodburning stove, burning dully. There was a chunky wooden mantelpiece over the top where a clock ticked much too loudly. Twenty past eleven. Was it? Had he read that right? He moved his eyes cautiously because that seemed to make his head hurt more and saw the bright glow of a lamp, then someone's legs. Following them up, he saw that someone holding an open book and then Claire's head.

'Hello,' she said. 'You OK?'

He pulled a face and pushed himself slowly into a sitting position, then put a hand to his head and rubbed it. He rubbed his neck too. And he felt queasy.

83

'Everything hurts,' he mumbled.

'I can imagine.'

Upright, he suddenly realised his bladder felt like it would burst.

'I need to pee,' he said, struggling to his feet.

'The bathroom's through the kitchen.' She pointed. 'There are paracetamol in the cupboard in there and I've put a fresh towel out for you if you want to freshen up.'

It sounded like an order but he felt too ill to care and stumbled through the kitchen to the bathroom. It was small but clean and smelt of bath lotion - something like vanilla - and he immediately thought of Zoe and groaned, flooded with self-pity. After relieving himself he washed his hands and threw some cold water over his face, then enjoyed the softness of the towel on his skin. It smelt of fabric conditioner. Every smell reminded him of Zoe and every scent seemed to be heightened. Shit. Two paracetamol later, he dragged himself back into the sitting room and eased himself gently back down onto the sofa. He shifted his gaze to Claire who appeared to be watching him with amusement.

'I'm glad you find this funny,' he said acerbically.

'Funny isn't the word I'd have used. Not when you passed out on my sofa.'

'Sorry.' He rubbed ineffectually at his forehead again.

'Can I get you something? Tea, coffee, water? Maybe you should try eating something. Neil always had dry toast when he was like this.'

He pulled a face.

'You should have something,' she insisted.

'Maybe some tea, thanks. Black.'

She put her book down and went out to the kitchen. When she came back she had a tray with two mugs on it and a plate with two slices of dry toast. He'd certainly give her full marks for persistence. She handed him one of the mugs and dumped the plate of toast on the table in front of him. He sipped the tea but it was too hot and he burnt his mouth. He put it down next to the toast.

'So this is why you didn't open the studio today,' said Claire.

He shook his head, then wished he hadn't.

'Wasn't any point. I wouldn't have done anything useful anyway.'

Claire drank some tea. Hers had milk in; presumably it was cooler.

'Jane was worried about you. Said she could feel that something was the matter. Had you told her about your issues with Zoe?'

'My issues?' He pulled a face. 'No. But Jane sees trouble everywhere she looks.'

They sat in silence. A couple of minutes passed.

'When Gilly disappeared,' said Claire slowly, 'everyone told me that work would help to keep me going. Those that didn't think I was the one to blame in the first place, that is.'

'And did you? Work it off, I mean.'

'No. I couldn't concentrate.' She took another sip of tea. 'In any case I beat myself up for working when I should have been watching her so…' She shrugged. '…I suppose I blamed the work and then punished myself by not doing it again. It was a pathetic little sacrifice but then the whole association of painting with Gilly was too painful anyway.' She shook her head and stopped talking.

He frowned but said nothing, picked up the plate and nibbled at the corner of one of the pieces of toast. It tasted surprisingly good and he tried a bit more.

'Anyway, I'd suggest you don't leave it too long to get back in the studio,' she said, 'because it gets harder, the longer you leave it.'

'Do you ever do anything? Draw maybe? Something else creative?'

She shook her head. 'A bit of craftwork sometimes. But it took me years before I'd even look at paintings or illustrations. Sad, aren't I? That's what Neil said anyway.'

'Seems a bit harsh.' Adam didn't want to get involved in this: matrimonial rows and disputes weren't his thing. He'd never thought of marriage as the answer, thought it created too many pressures on a relationship. But just now his thoughts on relationships weren't worth a bean anyway.

'You could take it up again now though. Have you got any of your work here?' He flicked an expectant glance round the room.

'No. And it's not that easy to pick it up again. I never had any formal training, you see. No qualifications. But I was always drawing and painting. When I was seventeen I won a competition to illustrate a scene from a children's book. Everything snow-balled after that. But I haven't got an agent any more.' She shrugged. 'And I'm out-of-date anyway now. Too much new technology I know nothing about.'

Adam nodded but didn't respond. It sounded like an excuse but this didn't feel like a good moment to argue the point. Maybe she didn't want to do it any more.

Slowly he managed to work his way through a whole slice of toast. His stomach felt a little easier. He picked up the mug of tea and sat cradling it. His brain had begun to function more clearly and he glanced round again. There were few decorations up but a scattering of Christmas cards stood on the mantelpiece.

'Are you spending Christmas here or going away?'

'I'm staying here. Laura, my eldest daughter's coming to stay.' She pointed to a framed photograph on the sideboard.

'She's eighteen and has just finished her first term at university. And you? Are you staying in the village for Christmas?'

'Yes. My mother died and my father remarried. He lives in Scotland now. His wife doesn't like me much.' He grinned. 'It's mutual.'

'So you'll be alone? Do you think there's a chance of Zoe coming back?'

The grin faded. He looked at her, wanted to tell her it was none of her damn business and he didn't want to talk about it. But he bit it back. She didn't look so much curious as concerned - and she had bothered to take care of him.

'I don't know.' He shrugged, finished his tea, put the mug down and got to his feet. 'You were very kind to rescue me - from myself.' He forced a smile then found himself drawn to look at the sideboard again. He took a step closer, examining the photograph of Laura and automatically switching to study the second photograph: a younger girl with blonde curls. So this was the child who'd disappeared.

He reached out a hand, wanted to pick it up so he could look at it properly, but felt Claire's eyes on him and let his hand fall.

'And this is your other daughter, I assume,' he said carefully. 'I heard what happened. I'm sorry about that.'

'Yes…Thanks.'

Claire moved closer, picked up the photograph and gave it to him.

'This is Gilly,' she said. 'That was taken on her ninth birthday.'

He studied it. 'She looks full of fun and life.'

'She was.'

He noted the past tense.

'And you've never had any kind of clue as to what

87

happened to her?'

Claire shook her head, face set. 'It was May. The village was crawling with visitors. There was no trace of her. Nothing. It was assumed that she'd been taken by one of them.'

He heard a 'but' in her voice and waited but she didn't elaborate.

'But you don't think so?' he prompted.

She stared at him dully. 'I don't know what to think. See, this is what happens when you have children: you're responsible for them…forever. There's a lot of anguish. Maybe you're wise not to go that way.'

Adam replaced the photograph on the sideboard. 'Are you telling me you wish you'd never had your daughters?'

'God, no, of course not. I'd never say that. There's a lot of joy too.' She hesitated. 'I was never particularly broody but Neil wanted children and I was OK with that. Then when they came I loved them in a way I wouldn't have thought possible, completely, whole-heartedly. I don't regret them for one moment - whatever's happened since, but they are a commitment.' She frowned, looking directly into his face. 'You sound like you're putting Zoe off with excuses. Perhaps you should be more honest with her and make a decision, one-way or the other. And if she means that much to you, perhaps moving from here and having children is what you'll have to do to keep her. It's a balancing act, isn't it - you know, a compromise.'

He laughed contemptuously. 'Do you really think it's that simple?' He felt all his frustration and confusion bubble up inside him. He was nearly shouting. 'You think I should leave now? I've never worked as well anywhere as I have since we've been here. Never. Everything's just come together. I can't go now. Before, living in suburbia, I was… Christ, woman. You have no idea.'

'Calm down, Adam. There's no need to take it out on me. I'm just saying. It's up to you. If you want Zoe back, you might have to change. She obviously wants something different to what you want. At the end of the day it's your choice, isn't it?'

His lip curled. 'And did you decide it wasn't worth making an effort to stay with Nigel?'

Her expression froze.

Adam frowned. 'Sorry. I'm sorry.' He reached out a hand towards her. 'That was out of line. I just...I don't feel ready to talk about it. Look, it's late. I'd better go.'

She saw him to the door.

'Thanks for taking care of me,' he said.

Claire looked out stonily into the night. 'His name's Neil,' she said. 'Not Nigel. And you're right.' She hesitated. 'I'm sorry. I'm in no position to give relationship advice.'

She turned back to look at him and their eyes met.

'Well, thanks again,' he said. 'See you.'

She had closed the door almost before he'd started down the path. He set off up the lane back to the village, his thoughts returning inevitably to Zoe. *If you want Zoe back you might have to change*. The thought settled on him like a cloud all the way home.

Chapter 7

On Christmas Eve Laura came to stay and, seeing her for the first time in weeks, Claire registered her daughter with fresh eyes. Or perhaps that term away from home, being independent, had already changed her. She looked so grown up - and so pretty. As a child she had taken after Claire's side of the family: she'd had fair wavy hair and her mother's slightly ungainly limbs. But with the passing years she had become more like her father. Her hair had gradually darkened and hung more sleekly and her eyes had an expression Claire had often seen in Neil's: self-contained, guarded even. And she had filled out a little too, become curvier. She was no longer a girl.

Claire had put the hair slide safely away and was trying to put the issue out of her mind for the holiday. In the previous days, she had thoroughly cleaned and tidied, had bought cheap paper festoons and draped them along the walls. She had searched the old familiar places where holly grew wild and cut sprigs for the house. Having brought a few old Christmas decorations up from Kent, she carefully unwrapped the Santa Claus candle holder - Laura's childhood favourite - and put it in prime position on the mantelpiece. And she bought a small fir tree and covered it in baubles, tinsel and chocolate decorations.

It was Neil who had picked Laura up from Surrey and

driven her down. He had arranged it with his daughter directly - had given Claire no say in it - and had delivered her to the door where Claire felt obliged to ask him in and offer him a drink. She found herself feeling jealous of the time he had already spent with Laura, hearing her news, and perhaps seeming the more caring parent. She was ashamed of herself and wondered if this was how it was going to be from now on: them both constantly vying for their daughter's attention, competing to be her preferred company, her confidant. It was childish and she knew it demeaned her, though it didn't make the feeling any less intense.

Neil refused the offered drink, dumping Laura's bags inside the door then standing on the doorstep, neither going nor staying. Claire eyed him suspiciously, waiting to close the door.

'Mum says you're coming up to the house tomorrow,' he said.

'Yes. Probably. Laura won't want to go alone.' She hesitated. 'What about Samantha?'

'She hasn't come.' Still he stood. 'It wasn't a serious relationship, Claire. Not like... Well, you know.' He shrugged. 'It was just reaction, I think.' He watched her face. When she didn't reply he abruptly turned away. 'See you tomorrow,' he called, over his shoulder.

Claire went back into the room in time to see Laura standing, staring at the photograph of Gilly on the sideboard. Hearing the door close, she spun round as if caught in something illicit, and quickly came across to give her mother a brief, fierce hug. It was a rare physical show of affection.

*

To Claire, Christmas dinner at The White House felt like a scene from a film she had slipped into by mistake, an old and familiar, much watched film, trotted out every year because it was traditional. It was smooth, so seemingly well-rehearsed, but then it always had been. Claire had not attended one for five years but she had been to countless such dinners before and little had changed. The people were older, of course, and the children had grown. And, though a cousin of Eve's was there and a nephew of Eve's late husband Gerald too, there were now people missing: Gerald himself, of course, and Claire's father who had been a regular guest after Claire and Neil were married. Those first few Christmases had been exciting. Claire had been young and unused to large family gatherings and it had felt warm and embracing. Then, as the years rolled by, she began to find it suffocating, started to experience the first choking constraints of belonging to the Pennymans and their apparently endless expectations.

But sitting at the dinner table now, exchanging polite conversation, hearing Timothy - with alcohol-fuelled expansiveness - recount amusing stories of his vineyard tours from the summer, listening to Julia gently prompt Laura to talk about Oxford, she was reminded just how charming they could all be. Cynically, she thought they put on an effort for Christmas Day, pretending to be one big happy family and carefully papering over the cracks. Or perhaps, she thought with greater honesty, the problem was with herself because she had never fitted in. She didn't want to 'belong'. She couldn't get obsessed with wine production and had always wanted to plough her own furrow, keep her own job and not be subsumed by the vineyard. Had that been wrong? It was hard to be so certain these days.

'Do you think it's changed much then, the village?'

It was Phil asking the question and it brought Claire quickly back to the present. He was sitting next to her but had spoken little until then. His fair hair was rapidly thinning

92

leaving only a few wispy tufts to defend the crown of his head but he seemed uncaring: there had been no attempt to comb them down or mask the fact. Over the years, Neil and Timothy had often teased him about both the way he looked and the way he dressed but, if it had bothered him, it had certainly never changed him.

'No,' she replied. 'Not much. There's that new estate of houses out on the Penmarna road. I gather Tom Merriton sold up the farm?'

'It's a struggle to make a living out of farming these days,' Phil grunted, then paused, his dark eyes examining her, probing. 'Didn't expect you to come back. Any particular reason?'

'No, not especially.'

'Really?' He sounded doubtful. 'Couldn't stay away?' He didn't quite smile.

'Something like that.'

He let it go and now Eve was making a point of asking about the Craft Yard and how it was going, including Claire reluctantly in the sweep of her piercing gaze.

'There always seems to be activity over there,' she added. 'And it certainly brings people to the restaurant, doesn't it Timothy?'

So the conversation turned back to the vineyard, as it generally did.

After dinner they played parlour games. Laura looked embarrassed; Danny escaped to his room. Afternoon stretched into evening and Claire made their excuses and left. Neil walked them to the door and gave Laura the pile of Christmas presents he had left in the hall. While Laura took them out to the car, he gave Claire one too and she was dismayed.

'You shouldn't have,' she exclaimed. Wanting to avoid awkwardness, she had brought gifts for the household:

chocolates and a bottle of port, and a bouquet of flowers for Eve. 'I don't have one for you. I didn't think we'd do this any more.'

'I didn't expect one. But I wanted to.'

Why? she thought. She frowned down at the gift. 'You shouldn't have,' she repeated. 'It's weird.'

'Weird?' He laughed, embarrassed perhaps. 'I don't see why.' He fingered a curl of her hair. 'You're looking so pretty tonight,' he said softly. 'How could I have forgotten just how lovely you are?' He flicked a glance up at the mistletoe, leant forward, and gave her a brief, sweet, warm kiss on the lips, then pulled away. 'Happy Christmas, Claire.'

She frowned at him, resisting the temptation to touch her lips like some lovesick teenager, then hurried away to join Laura at the car. Still she was aware of him standing in the lighted doorway, watching, as they drove back down the hill.

*

'It's been a real struggle these last years, Neil. You must know that.' Eve's voice was soft and low. 'We've managed, of course. We've even done quite well. But it hasn't been easy. And I wonder how long we can keep it up without more help. And your help would be the best help of all. You know there's a future for you here? You do realise that?'

Julia had been fighting sleep but these last sentences brought her round. She'd drunk quite a lot of wine - far more than usual - and the world around her had a soft-edged glow; she was struggling to focus. But this was important.

It was well after seven in the evening and the last of the guests had gone leaving a slipping lethargy to settle on the household. Phil was fast asleep in an armchair some distance away; Danny was in his room, watching some film or other; and Timothy had taken a tray of dishes out to the kitchen, muttering something about putting the dish-washer on. Eve and Neil were sitting conspiratorially side by side on the sofa on the other side of the huge square coffee table.

Through half-closed eyelids, Julia noticed Neil occasionally glance her way. She feigned sleep.

'Do the others agree?' said Neil.

'I wanted to know what you thought. You've had a lot of change in your life recently. I was waiting till it settled down for you. Then when I saw you here today, I thought how content you looked. You looked at home. And even having Claire here didn't seem to bother you.'

'Well, I don't know. It does feel strange to be back here.'

'Of course, it will. But you'll soon pick up where you left off. And I don't think Claire will want to stay so that awkwardness won't be for long.'

'What makes you say that?' said Neil sharply.

'Oh, just a feeling. She doesn't look happy and, now her father's gone… Well, we'll see. But that doesn't matter either way, does it?'

There was a pause. Julia twitched her eyelids open a crack wider. Eve was giving Neil one of her coy, entreating looks. Neil barely seemed to notice. He was frowning, looking up reflectively into some imaginary future.

'Of course it's tempting, mum,' he said slowly. 'I love Bohenna, despite what happened here. But I've got a good job, you know? And I've got friends in Kent; that's where my life is these days.'

'Are you sure it's not Claire who's putting you off? Because I could arrange for her to go.'

'No. No.' Neil twisted in his seat. 'What on earth do you mean?'

'I know the woman who owns that house she's renting. I know I could persuade her to terminate the contract, find some excuse. You know, say that Claire's damaging the place or annoying the neighbours, that sort of thing.' Eve sounded triumphant. She sounded like she was willing Neil to give her an excuse to do this.

'No,' said Neil firmly. 'I don't want Claire hounded out of Bohenna. If she wants to live here, she's entitled.' He shook his head. 'Anyway, that's not the problem and really, mum, I'm surprised at you.'

Eve put one gnarled hand on his knee.

'I just want what's best for you,' she said. 'And for all of us. But if you don't mind her being here, then…fine. She can stay. But you will think about it, won't you? We need you. We need your particular talents here. We've missed them.'

'I'll think about it.'

Timothy walked back into the room and poured himself another coffee from the pot on the table. He stood with his back to the fire and looked enquiringly between Neil and his mother in turn. Julia wondered what he would make of it. But he and Neil had always been close and it was Tim who had been obliged to take on most of the marketing that Neil had done before he left. Tim didn't like it. He was naturally a quieter person, more reflective. Speaking informally to the small groups touring the vineyards was fine - he even seemed to enjoy it - but he didn't like travelling to conferences or speaking at seminars; he didn't like 'selling' the vineyard. He was a home bird.

Julia slipped her gaze sideways towards Phil. He was still asleep. He wasn't going to like this.

She let her eyelids droop again. Maybe it wouldn't happen - though an extra worker, especially one skilled in the ways of the business, would certainly be a help. But they had adapted and there was an equilibrium to the way the vineyard worked now and she wasn't sure she wanted it changed. There would be another salary to pay for a start. And Neil could be domineering; he always thought he knew better.

Either way, Eve wouldn't ask her opinion. She was old-fashioned and thought a man should be the driving force in a business. And she thought the sun shone out of Neil, always had.

*

Laura stayed for a week and returned to Oxford on New Year's Eve. Claire drove her to the station at Liskeard and waved her off, feeling bereft. One of Laura's friends was throwing a New Year's Eve party. It had been arranged on a social media site that they were all on, something Claire neither used nor understood.

'Somebody you actually know?' Claire had queried.

'Yes, of course.'

'You will be careful?'

'Yes mum. It's just a party.'

Driving home again, Claire wondered what she had learned about Laura's life in Oxford. Not much, she decided. She knew the names of a few friends and a couple of the tutors. Laura had been her usual pleasant company, easy to have around, polite, willing, but she was still as reserved as she had always been and shared few confidences. She'd never been the kind of kid to put music on at silly volumes or to lie in bed till midday. Claire sometimes wished she would. Maybe a little rebellion in her soul and more fire in her belly would make her better able to cope with what life threw at her. Laura might have inherited Neil's doggedness but not, it seemed, his thrusting personality. Still, as far as Claire could tell, she seemed happy.

Claire pulled the car to a halt in the muddy space opposite the house and got out. Eddie was watching her from his front window, bundled up in a thick sweater, an old scarf wrapped tightly round his neck. She raised a hand as she walked to her front gate. She did it regularly, obstinately, because he never responded, just watched her suspiciously with a fixed, slightly sidelong gaze.

Once inside, she turned towards the kitchen. Jane had apparently planned nothing for New Year either so Claire had invited her over for the evening, determined to make an effort to get to know her again. She had to make a fresh life; it was both unfair and foolish to be dependent on Laura for company.

She paused by the sideboard. In amongst the greetings cards was the small, oval stained-glass panel Neil had given her for Christmas. She picked it up for the umpteenth time and held it to the light. A kingfisher glowed blue and orange, cleverly shifting tints as she tilted the panel this way and that. There used to be kingfishers along the river and as a youngster she had been enchanted by the iridescence of their plumage. Had Neil remembered? Or had Ted, the glass artist, noticed how her gaze had lingered on this particular panel and given her away?

'Why are you doing this, Neil?' Claire murmured distractedly to the glass panel. 'Do you want to torture me?'

*

'You did say casual, didn't you?'

Jane arrived at Claire's door wearing ankle boots, purple corduroy trousers and an over-sized sweater. As usual a huge shawl had been thrown over the top.

'I did. No airs and graces here, I'm afraid.'

'Don't be afraid. It's a relief. Oh here.' Jane thrust a bottle of red wine and a couple of scented candles at her. 'Some offerings.' She kicked off her boots inside the door and threw off the shawl, looking round. 'You've got it looking nice here,

Claire. Oh and good, you've got the stove lit; it's freezing out tonight.'

Claire relaxed. This was more like the Jane she remembered. The dramatic eye make-up was still there but the smooth-talking professional persona had been sloughed off and replaced by something more natural.

She left Jane warming herself and went through to the kitchen to get a jug of mulled wine. When she returned with a tray, Jane was standing with the photograph of Gilly in her hand and Claire felt the usual freezing sensation inside. Everyone focussed on that picture, 'the girl who disappeared'. It was the same way people were fascinated by conjuring tricks. Ladies and gentlemen, watch and try to work out just how one nine-year-old girl can disappear before your very eyes… Except that I wasn't watching, Claire thought bitterly.

'This must be your lost little girl,' said Jane. 'It's so sad.' She flicked Claire a sympathetic look, put the picture down and picked up the photo of Laura. 'And this is your eldest?'

'Yes. Laura.'

'I think I saw her up at the vineyard one day. How is she?'

'Fine, thank you. Settling in to university life, I think.'

'Good.'

They sat down. Claire poured the mulled wine into two glasses, gave Jane one and invited her to help herself to the snacks she had put out. They ate mince pies and nuts and made small talk. Claire asked politely about Jane's session; Jane enquired after Claire's Christmas. They talked about the Craft Yard and they joked about the Pennyman empire. They discussed the village and what had changed, what was still the same. It was cosy and began to feel reassuringly like the old days of their friendship - before it all went wrong. Claire went to the kitchen to refill the jug with hot wine and replenished their glasses.

'Do you remember that time Neil insisted he could swing right across the river up by 'the steps'?' Jane grinned.

'Ye-es.' Claire slowly grinned too. 'I'd forgotten about that.'

'The steps' were a series of uneven shallow waterfalls up river, each with a long 'tread' before the next. The river was narrower there so the water ran deeper and faster. But there was a birch tree on each bank and they both had branches which reached out over the water, overlapping, a gap of little more than a foot between them. Neil, long-armed and tall for his age, boasted that he had managed to swing, monkey-like, along the branches, crossing the river to the other side.

'Prove it,' Phil had challenged. Phil was a couple of years older and resented all Neil's boasting.

So Neil pulled his shoulders back in an adolescent show of bravado and started well, but something went wrong in the transfer of his second hand to the farther branch and the next minute he was in the water. Later, he swore that a gust of wind had made the branches move at the wrong moment.

'Curious that no-one else felt that wind,' Jane said now.

'Very curious.'

They laughed and drank more wine.

'And then there was the time with the cider,' said Jane.

'Oh yes. Our first hangovers. I was sick when I got home and Dad was furious. Jon played the know-it-all big brother too as if he'd never do anything so stupid.'

Jane pulled a wry smile. 'My mother was cross too. Fiona was with us and she thought I should have been looking after her better.' The smile quickly faded as if she wished she hadn't said it.

'I'd forgotten Fiona was there.' Claire cast her mind back. 'I suppose she was a bit young. What happened?'

'Nothing happened,' said Jane impatiently. 'She had an

embarrassing kiddie crush on Timothy, that's all, but he was with someone else. Can't remember her name now. Her family moved away soon after. Anyway, Fiona walked home by herself, all upset because he hadn't bothered with her. Mum fussed about it but she was fine.'

'It was quite a long way, I suppose.'

'She was fine,' Jane repeated stiffly. 'Mum always fussed over her. Thought she was delicate. And she was – when it suited her. Used it to get me into trouble mostly.' Her upper lip curled with disdain but she glanced up and saw Claire watching her and turned it into a smile. 'Have you been back to the boathouse? Recently, I mean?'

'No. You?'

'No.'

Jane hesitated, swirling the wine in her glass. 'Have you ever thought, Claire, about what would have happened if you hadn't settled with Neil, who you might have met?'

'No, never.' Claire frowned. 'Why? What are you getting at?'

'Nothing. I just wondered - now that you've finished with him. Only life is full of these decisions, isn't it? Things we do on the spur of the moment.'

'Neil wasn't a spur of the moment thing,' said Claire defensively.

'But you were very young.'

'We all were.'

Jane nodded without further comment.

The church clock struck midnight, then the bells began pealing in the New Year. Claire welcomed the distraction.

'Let's drink to the New Year,' she said, 'and…to what it might hold.'

'The New Year,' said Jane, raising her glass. 'Health, happiness and two new men.' She drank, eyes on Claire's face.

After a moment's hesitation, Claire drank too. 'Are you looking for a new man?' she asked curiously.

'Sure. Why not? Aren't you?'

Claire shook her head. 'Too soon.'

She picked up another mince pie; she was feeling muzzy and needed something to soak up the alcohol. She chewed a mouthful, watching Jane's face.

'You know you talked about having a gift? What did you mean exactly?'

Jane met her gaze. 'You don't believe me.'

'I don't know what I believe because I don't understand what it is.'

Jane drank the last of her wine and put it down. Nothing about her suggested she was as drunk as Claire felt.

'I can sense things,' said Jane. 'I can sense when someone's upset or if they're worrying about something...or if they're happy.'

'But we can all do that, can't we?'

'Up to a point. But I feel it more strongly. And I get very strong insights too.'

'In what way?'

'It's hard to describe.' She frowned. 'They come best when I 'read' an object. If I hold something it can tell me things - about its owner, the way they feel, their ailments perhaps, their desires.' She shrugged. 'It varies. Some objects are clearer than others.'

Claire stared at her, saying nothing, frowning heavily.

'You see,' said Jane, 'I knew you didn't believe me.'

'No, I'm just trying to understand. Give me an example.'

'OK.' Jane glanced round the room then got up and crossed to the sideboard, her eyes drifting along its surface. She picked up the glazed panel, held it for a minute then put it down again. She picked up a silver locket on a chain. Claire's mother had found it at an antique market and had sent it to her daughter for Christmas. It was heart-shaped and had a pretty engraved design on the front and was still empty. Claire hoped to find a tiny photo of Laura to put in it.

Jane held it, motionless, eyes closed, head tilted back.

'I'm getting sunshine,' she said. 'Heat.' She frowned. 'And sadness. Yes, someone who had this was very sad…quite recently.' Jane's eyes flicked open and she looked at Claire. 'This is yours?'

'Yes. I was given it for Christmas. It's old.'

Jane looked down at the locket and turned it over thoughtfully. She nodded. 'Yes. The sadness was someone else's, not yours. It's a different sadness.'

'I'm not sad. I'm…' Claire abandoned it. All she knew was that sad didn't describe it. 'So you can sense the previous owner too?'

'Sometimes. The goods are reflections of the person; they hold the owner's energy, that's all. Personal items are the best for getting a reading.'

Jane replaced the locket on the sideboard and moved along. She picked up a long, narrow silk scarf which had been folded and let it fall open, closing her eyes again as it ran through her fingers.

'I'm getting lights. Artificial lights and yet darkness too. Music. Yes. Lots of energy.' She opened her eyes and turned to look at Claire with an expectant expression. 'You wore this to a party perhaps?'

'No.' Claire hesitated. 'I don't do parties any more.'

'Oh OK.' Jane looked disappointed, put the scarf down and turned. 'Well, I'm not claiming it's infallible.' She smiled. 'I think I should be going. But it's been a lovely evening. Thank you.'

She was already slipping on her boots, now reaching for

her coat and Claire joined her by the door.

They embraced. Something of their awkwardness had returned.

'I could help you, Claire,' Jane said softly. 'I know how much you still hurt. I can feel your pain. I could help you let go of the past. Think about it.'

She produced a small torch from her bag and walked away, pausing briefly to wave from the gate.

Claire went to the sideboard, picked up the scarf and carefully refolded it. It was a bit of nothing really, light, insubstantial, pretty. She had found it on the floor in Laura's bedroom, slipped down beside the chest of drawers and forgotten. Had Laura worn it to a party with music and bright lights? Could Jane really do that? Could she tell or was she just making a stab in the dark?

She put the scarf down, opened one of the top drawers of the sideboard and withdrew a small velvet pouch, tipping Gilly's hair slide out onto her open palm. Did it mean Jane could read this? Had Gilly touched it recently enough to leave her mark? What might it say about her, about how she was or where she was? Could an object really do that?

Claire shook her head; it was a crazy idea. This was the wine teasing her thoughts, luring her into quicksand. But just suppose it was true... For a moment there, Jane had seemed very plausible.

She slipped the slide back in its pouch, pushing the notion away, snorting derisively. She wasn't that gullible. There must be something else she could do to track Gilly down. She just hadn't thought of it yet.

Chapter 8

For Adam, all the New Year had brought him was a hangover and Christmas had been even worse. He was glad the holidays were over. The house was too quiet. Adam felt Zoe's absence as a material loss, as if someone had cut a huge hole in the middle of one of his paintings, a space which no amount of patching would ever properly restore. Despite the emptiness he felt shocked too that he was taking it so hard. He had shared his life with several women over the years and he had never before felt as bad as this when they'd broken up - though this had been his longest relationship by far.

Throwing himself back into work, he had found it possible to forget the issues while he was busy. In his down-time it was harder. Reluctantly he became introspective, wondering if Claire was right and he would have to change to get Zoe back. But hadn't Zoe fallen in love with him the way he was? She had said she had. Why did women always have to try to bloody change men, try to crush them and then rebuild them in some kind of one-fits-all mould? Could he change? Did he even want to? Maybe he should have been more amenable to having children.

He conjured up an image of a family group, himself, Zoe, two children, a boy and a girl. Part of him cradled the image, cherished it, felt good about it; the other part felt uncomfortable, repelled even. It didn't sit well. All those practicalities which he had enumerated to Zoe about the difficulties of bringing up a family with their lifestyle and their erratic income jumped to his mind again, but maybe Claire was right and they were just excuses. He earned enough these days to make ends meet. They'd manage. They'd adapt. That's what people did.

But he wasn't sure he wanted a cosy family life; he was scared of the tie and of the commitment it involved. He was an artist, a free spirit, and artists didn't do well when they were tied down. History was littered with them, wasn't it? He tried to bring one to mind and gave up. Perhaps he had already blown it with Zoe anyway and it was too late. His head hurt with the turmoil of his thoughts and he felt alternately heartsick then drained of emotion and he yearned for distraction.

Without intending it, Gilly became that distraction. The conversation with Claire about her lost child had piqued his interest. It intrigued him. He started searching online for information about her disappearance, reading reports and interviews with the police and with local people. He followed up each supposed sighting in the days, weeks and months that followed. There was no shortage of conjecture and opinion from those both near and far. Claire and Neil were discussed at length by people who had never met them. There were hints and accusations but no apparently useful evidence and he began to guess at Claire's confusion and frustration. How does a child go missing in a village of this size where so many people knew her? Usually no-one could do anything here without the other end of the village knowing about it within hours.

But then he wondered about Claire too and whether she was indeed as innocent as she appeared. Perhaps she was simply a good actress. There were questions all over the internet asking how much the police had checked on the parents because - it was suggested - they must have known more than they were prepared to say, for how else could the child so easily have 'disappeared'? Adam was less certain. He was convinced that most of these people were just cranks and troublemakers. Still he thought it would be interesting to learn more about both Claire and Neil from the people who had known them of old.

So he made a list of all the current residents of the village who had been living in Bohenna when Gilly Pennyman disappeared, then he added a cross next to the ones he knew had been living there when Claire was growing up. This had taken some research: casually posed questions in the pub or the vineyard restaurant, earwigging conversations, checking again through newspaper and internet reports, noting down witness names. There were a few. Some of them were people he knew, at least by sight, though there were probably more. Despite a number of incomers to the village over the years, the core of the population hadn't changed. The graveyard - where he had memorably gone sketching one day and frightened an elderly woman putting flowers on her husband's grave by suddenly appearing from behind one of the big crumbling gravestones - was full of memorials to people with the same family names as many of the current residents. And the Cornish brogue softened the tongue of every other person to whom he spoke. It was one of the charms of the village as far as he was concerned: it was small, intimate, timeless.

But how would he set about asking questions without starting the village gossip machine? Unusual activity of any kind aroused curiosity and frank speculation. If he was going to find out anything about Claire Pennyman he needed to be discreet, cunning even.

There was a woman called Trish who sat in the pub

sometimes. Widowed, lonely, she had lived in Bohenna forever - had run the shop for twenty odd years, she'd told him once. She was approachable.

*

Claire reached the old wooden bridge over the river and paused at its centre, looking down at the water as it scurried on its way west towards the River Fowey and then out to sea. How long did it take for the water to reach the sea, she remembered asking her father when she was a child. Ooh, several days I should think, he'd replied, pottering between his rows of seedlings. But how could you tell? she'd persisted. Did the water mix with the River Fowey water or did it stay together in its own stream? Her questions never stopped. You'll have to do lots of learning and find out for yourself, her father would say in the end. Then you'll know more than me. She smiled wistfully at the memory.

The January days had begun to stretch out - the snowdrops had already come out in her garden - and these last days had been marked by a clear sky, a cold wind and a weak winter sun. Now it was a Wednesday afternoon in the middle of the month and Claire was taking advantage of her day off to go exploring. Have you been back to the boathouse? Jane had asked and the question had stayed in Claire's head ever since. Why haven't you, she found herself wondering. Because you're scared? But scared of what? Remembering?

She crossed to the further bank. The public footpath ran to her left, back towards the village. To her right the old fence which blocked access to the path eastwards had been replaced with a stronger one, topped with barbed wire. A sign read: *Private Land, No Access.* She glanced round, carefully climbed the fence and started walking, cutting north soon after on an overgrown track through the trees, though occasional broken stems suggested someone had used it recently. She emerged several minutes later into a large grassy clearing and stopped short. The dense, circling woods blocked out the village and the traffic, everything but the birdsong and a still stretch of water which twinkled in the winter sunshine. It was an uncanny feeling, as if she had stepped back in time.

As lakes went, it was small, maybe the area of three tennis courts. It would have been tempting to call it a pond but the water stayed fresh, fed by a stream from a spring higher up the hill and seeping out underground down to the river. And there was the boathouse, over to her left, a small timber structure, sitting back from the water. Gerald had had it built when Julia, Neil and Timothy were small so they could all use it as a family at the weekend. Somewhere farther up, there was a footpath through the trees from The White House which made it accessible carrying bags of food and swimming gear. But it had never worked out that way because Gerald and Eve had always been working - seven days a week in the early years - just to get the vineyard on its feet. Instead, this clearing had become the youngsters' own adventure playground, away from the eyes of the village – and their parents.

Claire walked slowly towards it. The double doors on the right opened onto a rough concrete slipway - now barely visible under grass – which ran down to the water. The single door and a square four-paned window on the left gave onto a family room. The building was a sorry sight though. The roof was intact but was covered in moss and algae, and a window pane had been splintered. A broken hinge on one of the double doors had allowed it to twist open and it balanced precariously. There was no sign of a boat and she couldn't remember when there had last been one.

Turning the handle on the single door, she cautiously pushed it open. It creaked. A partition separated the boat store from the family room. Once, there had been a huge old upholstered sofa in here, a wooden table and chairs, a clock on the wall and assorted posters. There had been a camping stove, gas lights and a cupboard with odd pots and pans. It had seen swimming parties and picnics, smoking and boozing, secret assignations and their first adolescent sexual fumblings.

The sofa had gone but a couple of chairs and the table remained, all with a fine covering of green slime. The posters had either been ripped down or rotted away. Someone had been in more recently though because the floor had been brushed off and there was a pile of scatter cushions in the corner along with a couple of cheap travelling rugs. And a slight scent hung in the air too which Claire couldn't quite place, a perfume maybe. She stood, slowly looking around, remembering. There were too many memories.

She turned on her heel and walked out, keen for fresh air, wanting to clear her head. She had promised herself that she wouldn't get sentimental and she wandered a few paces away towards the water, watching two mallards rise up from the lake and fly away, leaving eddies in the water.

What makes water wet? she remembered Gilly asking, and her thoughts immediately thrust forward to a different girl, thirty years later. Or maybe not so different. Gilly was always asking questions too.

So where did Gilly go to play? Claire turned round again and looked back at the boathouse. She remembered mentioning it to Mariella and of course the police had searched it and found nothing. But she had only suggested it in desperation. The next generation of Pennymans hadn't bothered with the place much. The boathouse had already become dilapidated by the time Laura, Danny and Gilly were running around and they had shown no real interest. Maybe they associated it too much with their parents.

Gilly loved the riverbanks of course. But where else did she go apart from her grandfather's nursery? Did Claire really know? At one time she thought she did but now she doubted herself. Though Danny might know, she supposed; those two had spent a lot of time together. She dimly remembered talking to him about it when Gilly disappeared but, in the upset of the moment, had no idea what she had asked exactly. She hadn't been thinking clearly, had been turning in circles like a broken compass.

She glanced at her watch. School had not long finished; Danny would still be on the school bus. If she could catch him when he arrived back in the village, she could talk to him away from the vineyard and house, away from the family. She quickly retraced her steps back to the river and, reaching the fence and bridge, pressed on along the river's northern bank, breaking into a jog. She emerged by the stone bridge in the village, panting, at twenty past four, just as the school bus from Fowey came down the hill. A handful of kids disgorged the other side of the bridge and she saw Danny, rucksack on his back, head down, loping heavily back towards her, his long hair flopping over his face.

'Hi Danny,' she said as he drew close.

He looked up, surprised, then immediately wary.

'Hi Aunt Claire. What's going on?' He glanced nervously up the hill towards the vineyard, the first fields of which lay a few yards away to his right.

'Nothing. I just wondered if I could ask you something. Are you in a hurry?'

'Well, the thing is…'

'It'll only take a minute.' She smiled, unsure of the best way to do this. 'Now I'm back in Bohenna, I've been trying to…to reconnect with Gilly, you see. I suppose I want to remember her - but in a good way, you know?'

He was staring at her, looking anguished. She smiled again, trying to sound casual.

'Gilly loved to explore, didn't she, and you spent a lot of time with her round the village? I know she loved the river but I wondered if there were any other places you particularly used to go? Anywhere Gilly liked to play?'

He was shaking his head already. He looked terrified and she hadn't wanted that. And he wasn't saying anything either, though he'd never been a big talker and now he was in that defensive and rebellious phase of adolescence.

'I'm not accusing you of anything Danny,' she added hastily. 'I just wondered where you played...generally. Can you remember?'

'Just the river,' he muttered. He edged a couple of steps up the road. She followed him. 'And the pond in Libby's Wood. We went there sometimes.'

'Of course, yes, the pond.' The police had searched that too. 'Nowhere else?'

His eyes flitted around but wouldn't settle on her face.

'Not really.'

'You're sure? You never went anywhere else, just on the spur of the moment maybe?'

He dropped his head forwards, looking at his feet, and his heavy fringe of hair fell back over his face. He shrugged. 'Well...maybe...sometimes...' He stopped abruptly.

'Yes?' she prompted gently. 'Where?'

'Gilly...well, sometimes she liked to go places she knew we weren't supposed to go.'

'OK. Like...?' He didn't make any suggestions. 'Maybe Piltons' orchards?' she offered, smiling. 'Scrumping?'

'Well, yeah. We did go there a couple of times.'

'Anywhere else?'

'Can't remember. Anyway, I didn't always go with her.'

112

'Did you tell the police that she liked to go places she shouldn't?'

He snorted derisively. 'Yeah, right. Like I was going to tell them that.' He looked at her, curiosity getting the better of him. 'What's the point in asking now anyway?'

'Like I said, I'm just…' She shrugged. '…trying to get a feeling for…'

Daniel's phone rang and he grabbed it out of his pocket, staring at the screen as if it might save his life. 'Look, I've gotta go. I'm going to meet someone.'

'Thanks, Danny,' she called after his retreating back as he strode up the lane to the vineyard.

Then she turned away, unaware that Phil was standing at the edge of the lower field of vines, watching her intently.

*

It was the Friday night when Adam saw Trish in the pub, sitting in her favourite place in the lounge bar, a half pint of stout on the table in front of her. The pub was quiet but for a group of youths playing darts in the public bar.

Adam bought himself a pint, talked to Dave for a few minutes, then turned and made a point of catching her eye. She liked to chat; company was the main reason she came to the pub at all.

'All right Trish?' he said. 'Quiet tonight.'

'Yes,' she said. 'Time of year.'

He glanced at her glass: it was nearly empty. 'Can I get you one?'

'Well, I won't say no. Thank you. I'll have the same again, please.'

He bought a half of stout and took it across to the table.

'Mind if I join you?'

'Be my guest.' She watched him sit. 'You're alone too

113

then.' She picked up her glass and drained the previous half. 'She not coming back then, your girl?'

'Doesn't look like it.'

'I'm sorry. But you're still hoping?'

He shrugged. This wasn't the conversation he'd planned, nor did he want it.

'You know Adam, since I lost Howard, I notice all sorts of things I'd never bothered with before: who's with who; who's fallen out; who's looking out of sorts. It's not that I'm being nosy. I just notice. Not enough to do, see? Anyway, I am sorry.'

'Thanks.'

She picked up the new half. 'Cheers,' she said, raising the glass.

He asked her about Howard and her face lit up and she talked at length. She asked about his work and appeared to listen to his answer. Then out of the corner of his eye he saw Tim Pennyman come to stand in the public bar and wait to be served, saw the man glance across, and Adam postponed his questions about Claire. In any case, Trish suddenly announced that she was leaving.

'Two drinks is my limit or I'll fall over walking home.'

'I'll walk with you if you like. I'm going now too.'

She got up stiffly and a little unsteadily and he put a hand to her elbow. Stepping out of the front door into the fresh air, a cigarette flared with light as someone nearby drew on it.

'Evening both,' said Nick Lawer, and exhaled a cloud of smoke.

Adam nodded. Trish said, 'Evening, Nick,' and slipped her hand through Adam's arm as they began to walk up the dark street. He waited until they were out of earshot.

'Do you remember the day Gilly Pennyman disappeared, Trish?'

'Of course.' She glanced up at him. 'Such a lovely girl. It was a tragedy. Why do you ask?'

'I only heard about it recently. It's hard to believe she could just disappear without a trace in a place this size.'

'Yes, isn't it?' she replied ambiguously.

'Do you know Claire Pennyman?'

'Claire Hitchen - as was. Yes.' She looked at him slyly. 'Why, have you heard stories about her?'

'No, not exactly.'

'When the child went missing, there were plenty going round. Some said she must have done something to the child herself.' Trish shook her head. 'But Claire Hitchen was never like that and most people didn't think it.'

'So what was she like?'

'Claire? A spirited sort of a girl but gentle too. I remember her coming in to the shop one time with a baby bird that had fallen out of its nest. Another time she was crying over a badger that had been run over. Bit of a tomboy maybe but she was never mean or vicious.'

'You knew her growing up then?'

'Of course. Her father ran the nursery for years. Great plantsman he was. Good man too, Charlie Hitchen. Came to church regular. But then his wife upped and left him and he struggled to keep an eye on the two children. Jon was older than Claire and more stay at home. Claire roamed. And she was one of a bunch of kids when they were older, always hanging around together. Lord only knows what they got up to.'

'That's when Claire hooked up with Neil Pennyman then? They were childhood sweethearts.'

'Ye-es.' She hesitated. 'But she was with Phil Borlase to start with.' She glanced up at him as they walked. 'It was Jane as went with Neil back then.'

'Jane Sawdy? You mean, Neil dumped Jane for Claire?'

'Yes. Well. You know teenagers: always in and out of love.' The lightness of her tone sounded forced.

They had reached her gate and she turned away and sidled through. Adam closed it behind her and she came round to face him.

'Jane can't have been too happy about it though,' said Adam. 'How did she react?'

Trish sniffed. 'We-ell, you know... They say there were poison pen letters. And I heard Jane took some things of Claire's and burnt them, made a big bonfire on some rough ground down near the river. But you can't believe everything you hear.' She shrugged. 'They didn't speak much after, mind you, but Jane was going away to university anyway.'

'Interesting. OK, so tell me about Neil...'

She cut across him. 'I'm not going to say any more. And a word of advice, young man: don't get involved in other people's affairs, even if you're trying to help. They usually end up blaming you for it rather than thanking you. And I'm not sure it would be wise to go after Claire Pennyman, if that's what you're thinking.'

He was about to deny it but she was already tottering away up the path to her front door.

''night, Adam,' she called over her shoulder.

He walked slowly home. So it seemed likely that Claire Pennyman was the confused and grieving mother that she appeared to be, after all. But he was more exercised by the other things Trish had told him. He found himself wondering if the shared past of a small group of childhood friends in this insular community could have had any bearing on the disappearance of Gilly Pennyman.

Chapter 9

'Don't you understand?' Julia hissed into the mouthpiece. 'Daniel doesn't want to remember. Do you know just how much he suffered after Gilly disappeared? He was bad for weeks… for months afterwards. He was completely traumatised.' Claire tried to speak but Julia cut across her. 'He blamed himself. He was only nine too, you know. I will not have him being upset again or made into a scapegoat.'

'I had no intention of making him a scapegoat,' Claire said. 'Honestly, Julia. I'm sorry. I didn't want to upset him either. I didn't realise.'

'No, well perhaps you should look around a bit more, Claire. It's not all about you, is it? And do you really think you're going to find out anything now - after all this time? Just dragging it all up, causing a lot of unnecessary grief.'

'No. Of course. Look Julia, I am sorry. Really.'

Claire sounded genuinely penitent, mortified even, but Julia hadn't forgiven her yet.

'Well, don't you go asking our Danny questions again,' she almost spat. 'He's got exams this year too. He needs to be able to concentrate. So no more questions. I'm warning you, Claire, d'you hear?'

Julia disconnected the call but continued to hold the phone in her hand, still bristling with anger and frustration. Phil hadn't told her about Claire's meeting with Danny; she had found out about it quite by chance. She had been due at a meeting in the village on the Friday evening but had forgotten her gloves and had popped back upstairs to get them. That's when she'd overheard him cross-questioning the boy in his bedroom. 'What was Claire saying to you?' he was asking. 'What did she want to know?' She'd found herself standing on the landing, eavesdropping to find out more. In her own house. It had made her feel shifty and cheap.

'When was this?' Julia had asked Phil afterwards. 'You mean you waited two days to ask him? And you didn't tell me?'

'I wasn't sure how to bring it up,' he grunted. 'And I didn't want to upset you.'

Maybe it was true. He had clearly been waiting for an opportunity to speak to Danny when he'd be sure Julia wasn't there. Either way, she let it go though it gnawed at her all the same.

Not for the first time, she found herself wondering if Phil ever regretted that his youthful fling with Claire hadn't lasted. Julia had seen the way Phil looked at Claire at Christmas. If Neil hadn't stolen Claire's heart, would she and Phil have remained a couple? He had never talked about Claire but that meant nothing. The man ran deep and even after all these years, she struggled to guess what he was thinking.

As for what Danny knew, she had no idea - and she didn't want to find out.

She put the phone down, glanced at her watch and hurried off towards the winery. They had started racking the wine again and it would be a relief to be busy.

*

Claire took the change from the woman on the till, picked up her tray and looked round for somewhere to sit.

Initially, she had refused to go near the barn restaurant, unwilling to stray too much onto Pennyman territory. But it hadn't taken long for her to realise that her resistance was childish and the restaurant - a large, bright space with a self-service counter at one end and a run of patio doors overlooking the vineyard at the other - was an ideal place to occasionally take her lunch break. If she didn't go there, it was her loss; no-one else cared. And only once had she seen Tim passing through, routinely checking that everything was OK. Eve was never there.

Today, Adam was sitting at one of the window tables. She had seen him there a few times, looking introspective and detached, but this time he looked up as she came to a table nearby and casually invited her to join him, pulling a cellophane-wrapped sandwich across the table to make space for her tray.

'I see you had the soup today too,' she said, sitting down. 'Any good?'

'Not bad. Better than the tinned stuff I usually eat anyway.'

She smiled and they ate for a few minutes in silence.

'Any news?' she asked, conversationally.

He looked up, apparently surprised. 'Yes, actually. I've just been given a commission for a set of paintings for a corporate headquarters.'

'Congratulations.'

'Thanks. It's a bit daunting but the money'll be useful.' He glanced at her speculatively. 'And you?'

'Me? No. Nothing.'

Adam looked up the room and dropped his voice. 'I've got another commission too. It's supposed to be a secret but you won't tell, will you? Or maybe you already know about it?'

Claire frowned, swallowing a mouthful of soup. 'You're being cryptic. I've no idea what you're talking about.'

'I gather it's Eve Pennyman's seventieth this year and the family want me to do a painting for her of the vineyard and house.'

Claire pulled a face and shook her head. 'I knew it was her seventieth but I didn't know about the painting. Whose idea was that then?'

Adam finished the soup and pushed the bowl away. 'I don't know. It was Julia who rang me. I'm going to do some sketches and take them round to show them.'

He pulled the cellophane off the sandwiches and they fell silent again. Claire picked up the last piece of her bread and fingered it, glancing across at Adam.

'You said Jane talks to you when you're working. How well do you think you know her?'

He shrugged. 'Not very. Probably not as well as you do.'

'It's years since I knew her well and she didn't do this natural healing thing back then.' She hesitated. 'I was wondering if you think she's genuine with all these séances and things?'

'Genuine? You mean, does she believe it?' He smiled, grimly. 'Yes, I think she believes it. She's not a fraud in that way.'

'But she is a fraud, you think? You don't think she has any special gifts?'

'No, I don't. I don't believe in all that psychic stuff so I'm afraid I can't take it seriously.' He picked up his second sandwich but didn't start it and looked back up at her. 'Why? Do you?'

'No. Not really. It's just...' She frowned. 'Jane came round to me for New Year's Eve and said she could 'read' people's belongings, that she could see things about them if she held something that was personal to them.' She hesitated again, put the last piece of bread in her mouth and looked round as she ate, checking there was no-one who could hear. She dropped her voice. 'She held a scarf belonging to Laura and she seemed to know all about where Laura had worn it. It was spooky.'

Adam stared at her thoughtfully, chewing mechanically. 'Nah,' he said. 'She must have picked something up from things you'd said. These people use all sorts of information they glean along the way - odd things they've seen or overheard.'

'I thought you said you thought she was genuine?'

'She probably doesn't realise she's doing it - picking up signals, I mean. Maybe things come to mind and she forgets she's read about it somewhere or overheard someone talking.'

Claire wrinkled up her nose. 'I don't know. Jane's bright - always has been. I can't believe she wouldn't remember that she'd heard something before.'

'If you want to believe something enough, you let yourself. Why are you so interested in it, anyway?'

She pushed her bowl away and sat back in the chair. 'I was just a bit surprised. That's all.'

He finished eating and took a mouthful of coffee, studying her face.

'I'm guessing you were thinking of giving her something of Gilly's. What did you think she would be able to tell you?'

'Don't be absurd,' she responded crisply. 'Why would I do that?'

'Oh, come on. Given what happened to Gilly, it wasn't rocket science to work out what you had in mind.'

She picked up her mug of tea and didn't reply.

Adam leaned forward. 'I was reading about Gilly's disappearance. It's hard to understand how it could happen in

121

a place as small as this.'

'I know,' said Claire lugubriously. 'That's what everyone says. And everyone has an opinion too.'

'I've been reading them. There are a lot of sick people out there.'

'Tell me about it. Some people talk as if you didn't care or even wanted it to happen. You try to ignore it all but it hurts just the same.' She frowned, looking at him curiously. 'What made you read about it?'

'I seemed to be the only person in the country who didn't know about it. And it intrigued me.' He smiled. 'Anyway, look, if you ever want to talk it through or test out a theory…' He stabbed at his chest with an emphatic finger, the smile broadening. '…I'm your man. I've become a mini-expert on who said what and when.'

'This is not a game,' she hissed, annoyed at his flippant tone. 'Or…or…or a cheap whodunit for you to solve. And why the hell would I want to talk to you about it?'

'Because you're the one who brought it up,' he hissed back, glancing towards an adjacent table where two women were looking in their direction. He gave Claire a warning look. 'There you were talking about Jane's 'gifts' and reading objects,' he muttered. 'It was pretty obvious you were thinking about Gilly. So clearly it's on your mind. It was only an offer.'

Claire put the back of her fingers to her mouth, staring at the table, calming herself. He was right of course. In many ways she was more cross with herself than with him.

'I'm sorry,' she said. 'I overreacted. It's just…'

She shook her head, unsure what to say. She was so touchy these days and she hated it. She took another mouthful of her now cold tea, then abandoned it, mumbled a few parting words and left.

Tim was standing near the counter as she walked back to

the door, looking her way, and she wondered how long he had been watching her. He smiled genially and sauntered across to join her.

'Hello stranger,' he said. 'How are you?'

'Fine, thanks. And you?'

'Oh yes, I'm good. I was thinking, Claire...?' He hesitated.

'Yes?'

'You should come over to my place sometime - have a coffee or a drink or something. We could catch up.'

He's desperate to know what's going on, she thought.

'Thanks. I will,' she lied. 'Sorry Tim, I have to go. I need to get back to work.'

'Sure.'

She crossed the road back to the Craft Yard. What with the women eavesdropping at the neighbouring table, the restaurant staff and now Tim, in a couple of days she'd probably hear on the village grapevine that she and Adam were having a torrid affair. At the very least, Neil would be sure to hear about it, and the thought made her smile.

*

After several days of indecision, it was the last Friday of the month when Claire finally went back to the Natural Healing unit.

'Claire,' Jane said serenely as she walked in the door. 'How lovely. I was just thinking about you. I had a feeling we would meet today. It's amazing that we work so near and yet hardly ever see each other.'

'Isn't it?' Claire rammed a lock of hair behind her right ear nervously then put her hand down on the counter top, tapping a rhythm with her finger. In the pocket of her jacket she fingered the velvet pouch with her other hand.

'Can I help you with something?' Jane prompted.

'Maybe. When you came round to my house, you said you could 'read' objects, that they could tell you things about their owner.'

'Yes.' Jane looked at her expectantly.

'The thing is, I've got something of Gilly's and I wondered if you could…I mean, I'll pay you of course. It would be a business thing. Only, I'd need you to promise to keep it to yourself.'

'My consultations are always confidential,' said Jane primly.

'Yes, of course.' Claire pulled the velvet pouch out of her pocket, glanced towards the door to check there was no-one around, then tipped the hair slide onto her palm. She held it out for Jane to see.

'It's this. Could you use this to tell me something about her?'

Jane picked it up and examined it, turning it over and back again.

'What exactly do you hope to find out?' she asked, at length.

'I'm not sure. But I don't think she's dead. We can't assume it, can we, just because she hasn't returned?' Claire's voice became more urgent. 'She might be being held somewhere against her will. We hear about that happening all the time. She might be somewhere near here. I want to know what happened to her. I want to find her. And maybe this slide will give you some information about her.' She gestured with a desperate hand. 'A sensation of the place she's being kept, maybe. Anything which might help.'

An expression of pity crossed Jane's face, fleeting and gone, and she was studying the slide again, sucking her lower lip. She looked up into Claire's face.

'I sense there's something else you're not telling me.'

'No.' Claire shook her head. 'What else is there to know?' She met Jane's gaze levelly.

'If I don't have all the information, it will make it harder for me to get a reading.'

Claire's stomach twisted with disappointment. After days of arguing with herself, she had quashed all her misgivings to do this out of desperation to do something - anything - which might move her forward. But this was insane.

'I shouldn't have come,' she said and held out her hand for the slide. 'It was stupid of me. What did I really expect you to do?'

'No,' said Jane. 'Don't give up, Claire. I just said it would be harder, not impossible.' She still fingered the slide and Claire let her arm drop. 'If you're sure there's nothing else you can tell me?'

'No. There's nothing else.'

Jane nodded slowly. 'Then I'll see what I can do. It's not the most personal of items, is it? Even so, I'll try.'

'Gilly did love it though. It was her favourite.'

'Good. Well, I think this will require some time so you'll have to leave it with me for a couple of days so I can meditate on it.'

'No, I can't do that.'

'Then I can't help.'

Their eyes locked.

'All right,' said Claire. 'But please take care of it, Jane, won't you? I know it's not much but it is important to me.'

'I understand, Claire.' Jane offered a sympathetic smile. 'Don't worry, I'll look after it. If you give me that pouch, it'll protect it when I'm not working with it.'

Claire passed it over. 'When will I hear from you?'

'As soon as I've had a chance to work on it. Not long.

125

Two or three days maybe.'

Claire hesitated, then gave a brief, terse nod. 'OK. Thanks.'

*

Claire struggled to settle. Laura rang on the Sunday and she put the slide out of her mind, determined to make the most of these rare and precious moments with her daughter. But as soon as the call was ended it intruded on her again. She wished she could talk to someone else about it but there wasn't anyone. Neil came to mind regularly; she even got as far as picking up the phone to ring him but didn't. He was the first person she always thought of but he'd be the last to understand. He'd tell her to get rid of the slide, tell her she was crazily obsessed, tell her that only a really sad person would take a hair slide to a supposed psychic and expect the woman to tell her something about its owner - even if that owner *had* been Gilly, which it almost certainly wasn't. In a quiet and insidious voice, common sense told her that she agreed with him.

But still she hoped because she couldn't bear not to, because it felt like the last chance she had of doing anything constructive to help Gilly.

Jane rang on the Tuesday evening, apologising for having taken so long. It had needed a lot of meditation, she said.

'Would you like to come to my house?' she suggested. 'It would be more private. Come tomorrow night after work, say six o'clock?'

Jane lived in a Victorian house set back off the road north out of the village about three-quarters of a mile towards Lostwithiel. Claire remembered it from childhood visits. It had seemed enormous then with two generous floors plus a cellar. The other houses in the tiny hamlet had been agricultural cottages, built to serve a large farm long since broken up and sold off. Claire took the car and parked it close up on the road outside. It was pitch dark but a light on the corner of the building lit up both Jane's small Peugeot on the drive and the path to the front door. The faint tinkle of wind chimes like the ones in the shop drifted to her on the breeze as she rang the bell and waited. There was a light misting of rain in the February night air.

Opening the door, Jane smiled broadly. 'Come in,' she said. 'Welcome.' She peered outside. 'Miserable night, isn't it? Come and get warm.'

The long hallway was as bright as the unit, painted in warm, pale colours which almost glowed in the artificial light. On one wall was a large mirror and on the other, a large sign read: *Peace, Joy, Light.* Jane showed Claire into the front room. The curtains had been drawn and the only light came from candles. The room was bare save for a long low table covered with a white cloth and a tall candle at each end, two chairs pushed back against the wall, and several cushions strewn on the wooden floor. Nightlights in small glass bowls were positioned around the perimeter of the floor.

'Would you prefer a chair or are you happy to sit on a cushion?' said Jane. 'Sitting together on the floor is more natural, makes it easier for us to share. But if you'd prefer...?'

'No, cushions are fine.'

Claire quickly dumped her bag on one of the chairs and got down on the floor. Increasingly she just wanted to get this over with; she wanted to leave.

Jane closed the door, walked to the table and picked up the slide. Claire had seen it there, centred between the candles, like an offering to the gods. Now Jane was sitting cross-legged on a cushion next to her, hands held in her lap, palms up, one resting on the other, the slide on top. She sat erect, chin held high, and closed her eyes.

Claire wondered if she was supposed to close her eyes too.

'Perhaps you'd like to close your eyes,' murmured Jane.

Claire did, then opened one a crack and looked sideways at her companion. She seemed to be completely immersed in herself. Claire envied Jane's composure, her apparent self-containment. And she seemed to have an uncanny way of guessing what Claire was thinking.

'We must concentrate on Gilly,' Jane was saying. 'We have to focus on her completely if we are to pick up her energy.'

Claire tried to think about Gilly. Nothing happened. She struggled to believe in this quasi-religious ritual and had to keep telling herself to focus.

'It's always good to have more than one mind willing the energy to us,' Jane was intoning in an even, mellifluous voice. 'I have done the preparatory work but you are so close to Gilly. The strength of your bond and emotions will help to guide and lead her to us.'

'But surely…' began Claire.

'Sssh,' said Jane softly. 'Relax; think of Gilly; imagine her here, with us now, a bright energy.'

Claire took a deep breath and let it out slowly. A succession of images began to run through her mind: Gilly falling over and cutting her left knee in the same place she always did; Gilly as an unlikely curly blond Virgin Mary in the school nativity play, looking angelic; Gilly rapt, watching a Punch and Judy show; Gilly's face on the front of the newspapers in the shop. It was all too busy, too confusing.

'Concentrate, Claire.'

She took another deep breath and tried to imagine her little girl standing in front of them instead. And for a moment she did. Gilly was there, smiling, her head tilted slightly to one side in that quizzical way she had. She was even wearing the hair slide as if she had reached forward and taken it from Jane's hand. Claire felt as if she could stretch out her own hand and touch her, maybe hug her. She felt her chin start to wobble and pressed her lips together hard.

'Ye-es,' said Jane. 'Yes, I'm getting something now. Oh yes.'

Claire squeezed her eyes tighter still, willing it to be true, concentrating even harder on the image of Gilly she had burning into the back of her eyelids.

'I can see trees...' said Jane. 'Yes. Yes, trees tossing in the breeze.'

There was a pause. Claire wished she could see them too. She could hear Jane breathing in little gasps as if she was experiencing something deeply emotional. Then she moved in some way. Claire wanted to open her eyes to find out what she was doing but didn't dare.

'I can sense water...yes, it's somewhere near.' Jane tutted. 'It's coming and going. It's not strong.'

'What's not strong: the sensation of water?'

Jane ignored her. Maybe she hadn't even heard her. She was almost whimpering, her breath still coming in little gasps.

'Is she all right?' Claire asked. No reply. She raised her voice. 'Is she all right?' she demanded. 'Is she in pain?'

'No.' Jane's voice had an absent note as if she were speaking from far away. 'No, she's not in pain.'

'Where is she?' Claire thought of those sheds of Nick Lawer's; she couldn't get them out of her head. 'Is it dark?'

'No. No, I don't think it's dark. Not at all. No. And she's all right. Yes. Yes, she's happy.' Jane's breathing settled, the tone of her voice brightened. 'She's all right. Isn't that wonderful? She's all right.'

Claire felt a touch on her arm and snapped her eyes open.

The image of Gilly instantly disappeared. There was no-one standing in front of the table and the room felt bleak and cold. She shivered. Jane turned to look at her, smiling.

'But how can she be all right?' Claire demanded, frowning. 'She's been taken from her family. She's alone somewhere. Where is she? Can't you see where she is?'

Jane's smile shrank. 'I'm sorry Claire. I can't tell you exactly where she is. It wasn't that clear. But now at least we know she's all right. She's content. That's something isn't it? Doesn't that make you feel better? Wherever she is, she is content.'

Claire stared, her face puckered in disbelief. 'And that's it? But what about the trees…and…and the water? I mean that could describe almost anywhere in the village. You can't get far away from trees and water in Bohenna. Can't you be more specific?'

'Well, it might mean Bohenna, I suppose,' said Jane doubtfully. 'But it could be somewhere else. Maybe it was somewhere by the sea - you know, the way the feeling of water came and went. I don't know. I told you: it's just a feeling, Claire. It's not a vision exactly.'

Claire continued to glare at her as the realisation slowly sank in that this was all she was going to find out. She had been so stupid, so gullible. How had she allowed herself to think this would be meaningful in any way? If Jane really believed it, she was sad. But better that, Claire thought, than the intentionally deceitful fraudster that would be the alternative.

She reached over and grabbed the slide from Jane's hand, then scrambled to her feet. The velvet pouch was on the end of the table and she took that too and slipped the slide inside. Her hands were shaking. Picking up her bag from where she had dumped it on the floor, she produced her purse.

'I owe you,' she said curtly, trying to contain the bitterness of her disappointment.

'Oh, Claire, it's all right. I don't want you to pay me.'

'No, I insist. This is what you do, isn't it?' Take money from people for giving them false hope, she wanted to add. 'Your job,' she said instead.

She found a twenty pound note and two tens and put them on the table. The altar. She walked to the door. Jane was already on her feet. She picked up the money and followed her quickly out into the hall, catching up with her by the front entrance. She put her hand flat against the closed door.

'You don't have to give me this. It's too much anyway.' She tried to give it back but Claire wouldn't take it so she rested her hand on Claire's arm. 'Claire, let Gilly go. There's a herbal remedy I could give you which might help if you'd like, something to help you banish the past and look forward. You've got to accept that Gilly's content and it's time for you to move on. Really, it's time.'

'No,' said Claire, angrily. 'It's not up to you to tell me what I've got to accept. And I don't want herbal remedies. I just wanted your help. I wanted you to tell me something useful. Where she is. I wanted to know how I can find her.' Claire took a deep breath and let it out in a shuddering sigh. 'I expected too much. It's my fault, I know that. I wanted to believe you could do it.' She stared into Jane's eyes as if she might read exactly what was going on behind them. 'I don't believe it, you see. Maybe you really do believe in all this garbage but I don't. I'm sorry. I'm sorry for you and I'm sorry for me too. We should never have done this. I…'

She pressed her lips together again and put her hand to the door latch.

'Sooner or later, you'll have to move on, Claire,' said Jane peremptorily. 'I'm telling you.' Her hand was still pressed against the door, stopping it being opened. 'You're not helping yourself.'

She fixed Claire with an accusing gaze, then dropped her hand and Claire immediately escaped into the night. When she got into the car she couldn't go anywhere because her eyes were too full of tears to see. So she sat in the dark, rocking her sorrow.

Chapter 10

The large kitchen breakfast room in The White House lay to the front of the building and benefited from a sweeping bay window which looked out proprietorially over the vineyard. Unzipping his portfolio at the kitchen table, Adam extracted a succession of large sheets of paper and glanced round, searching for the best place to display them. He settled on the window seat hugging the bay and carefully propped his drawings up for the Pennymans' consideration. Eve was out, he had been told - gone shopping in Truro with a friend - so they were safe for at least another couple of hours.

He stepped back and glanced round his audience. Julia was there. So too was Phil - looking completely disinterested - and both Timothy and Neil Pennyman. It was the first time Adam had met Neil and he was intrigued to see the two brothers together. They were recognisably related: both had the same long face with a slightly square jaw; both had the same greeny-blue eyes. But Neil was taller by at least a couple of inches, his brown hair a few shades lighter. Tim was slighter, had dark hair, prominent eyebrows and a restless manner. Adam had met Timothy several times because it was he who mostly dealt with the Craft Yard. He was easy to talk to, superficially friendly at least, though didn't always follow up on his promises. On first inspection, Neil appeared a harder character, more likely to unapologetically stand his ground.

But the brothers clearly got on well, exchanging odd remarks, making jokes. Now, however they had fallen silent and had stepped a couple of paces forward to study the pictures.

'These are the sketches I did,' Adam said, 'to show the different views you get from various places in the vineyard.'

'I don't know,' said Tim. 'Mum's never shown much interest in paintings or 'art' before. Is she really going to want this?'

'We've been through all this, Tim,' Julia said impatiently, putting a hand on his shoulder. 'Please don't let's argue about it again. It's not just a painting. It's a painting of the vineyard and the house that mum and dad set up and worked so hard to make a success.'

'I wasn't arguing,' Timothy protested. 'I was just saying. We want it to be a special present.'

'I'm sure our artist here understands that,' said Neil smoothly.

Adam managed a smile. 'The beauty of a painting is that I can move things around a little to get a better composition or to emphasise a significant feature. And I can edit anything out which you don't want or which might spoil the view.'

'I dare say you can,' said Neil. He flicked Adam a dismissive glance. 'So come on, Tim.' He leaned forward, moving his gaze from one drawing to the next. 'Help us choose the best view.'

'What do you think, Phil?' asked Julia.

Phil gave the pictures a brief inspection. 'Surely, the point is: which view would your mother like best? What would mean the most to her?'

The three siblings looked at him, then at each other, apparently surprised.

'Why didn't you think of that, clever clogs?' Timothy muttered to Neil.

Julia pointed. 'That one. I think mum'd like that angle.'

They argued about it for a few minutes and Adam left them to it. He found himself imagining Neil with Claire, trying to see them as a couple. What had attracted them to each other and what had driven them apart? The answer to the second part was maybe easy - the disappearance of Gilly - but he wasn't sure it was ever that simple. He'd thought about these things a lot lately, ever since Zoe walked out. When did attraction stop being enough? How much do you need to have in common to stay together? When did compromise push you too far away from yourself? He thought he knew all the questions but he had no idea about the answers.

The family finally agreed the view they thought Eve would like the best and Adam talked them through the other options of size and approach. Ideally he would have carte blanche to do a painting the way he saw it but for a commission of this type, he recognised the need to compromise. There it was again, that word. So he was capable of compromise. He wondered why there were times when it seemed more palatable than others.

Neil was asking about the price and trying to barter and Adam forced himself to concentrate and hold firm. Neil was casually but expensively dressed and drove a BMW which was parked outside. The Pennymans, between them, could afford his prices for a commission. They came to an agreement and Adam collected up his drawings and left.

*

Standing in front of his work table three quarters of an hour later, Adam was tapping a brush with monotonous regularity against his thigh, staring at his current work, a view across the estuary from Fowey towards Polruan, a picture which he suspected had already gone astray. It certainly wasn't coming out the way he'd originally had in mind and he sighed heavily.

A movement caught his eye and he used the excuse to look up, just in time to see Neil Pennyman walking purposefully into the Craft Yard and turning left, then out of sight. Adam shifted sideways to get a better view but Neil had disappeared so the only place he could have gone was into V and C. Adam reluctantly returned to his work, keeping one eye on the yard. It was another half hour before he saw Neil Pennyman walk away, his step as brisk as ever. He looked like a man who was always on a mission.

Adam did some desultory work on the piece but putting on more and more layers of paint, he knew from experience, never sorted out a problem painting. He abandoned it; he needed perspective.

He walked to the window and looked across towards V and C. That lunch he had shared with Claire in the restaurant still lingered in his mind. She had thought his interest in Gilly's disappearance ghoulish or a source of cheap entertainment maybe. Perhaps she was right. It didn't touch him emotionally and he hadn't handled it well either. Given what had happened and what she had been through, it was hardly surprising that she didn't appreciate his interference and that bothered him. And now he wondered how she felt about having her ex-husband walk in on her like that, so confident, presumptuous even. He let these thoughts drift through his mind, then, on an impulse, left his studio and walked across to see her.

Claire was standing at the back of the unit facing a large mirror which was propped up against the wall. She wore pink rubber gloves and had a bottle of spray glass cleaner in one hand, a cloth in the other and, as Adam approached, was rubbing ferociously at the surface of the mirror. She glanced up but carried on rubbing.

'Hi,' he said.

'Hi. Can I help?' She squirted another mist of cleaner on the glass.

'I wanted to apologise.'

She straightened up then and turned to look at him, frowning.

'Apologise?'

'For seeming...' He shrugged lightly, uncertain what the word should be. '...uncaring, I suppose - the other day when we were talking about your daughter. I didn't mean it that way. I just wanted you to know.'

'Oh. Forget it.' She turned away to start cleaning again - though the mirror looked spotless to Adam's less exacting eye - then suddenly looked back at him and smiled. She looked so different when she smiled that he thought he could see exactly why Neil Pennyman had fallen for her twenty odd years ago. Against the weary disappointment of her face, the smile looked happy, cheeky even; it transformed her. 'I'm impressed,' she said, eyes almost glinting with amusement. 'A man who apologises. Wonderful.'

'Sarcasm doesn't suit you - but I had thought maybe I could buy you a drink,' he added, though he hadn't previously thought anything of the kind. 'You know, so there's no hard feelings.'

'Oh,' she said again. The smile had gone and again a frown puckered her brow. She appeared to be having a mental argument. 'I'd like that,' she said.

'Great. What about, say, Friday night? We could meet at the pub maybe?'

'That would be great.' She was smiling again. 'But could we possibly make it the Thursday instead? I'm off on the Friday and working the weekend.'

'Yeah, OK. Good. Say...' He shrugged. '...seven

o'clock. Maybe we could eat there too? I'm sick of beans on toast.'

'OK. And Adam?'

He had started to leave but stopped and turned.

'Yes?'

'You don't owe me a drink. I was rude. It was uncalled for. I'm sorry too.'

'Don't be.'

Adam went back to his studio, a little stunned - and a little bit pleased with himself too.

*

Adam was already in the lounge bar of The Swan when Claire arrived at seven, sitting at a table in the corner by the fireplace, a pint of beer on the table in front of him. There was a smattering of people in the public bar but the lounge was otherwise empty. He got up when he saw her and met her by the bar, bought her a drink and they took a couple of menus back to the table.

For several minutes they studied the menus intently, holding them up, using them as protective shields against conversation. Claire glanced surreptitiously at her companion a couple of times. He looked tidier than usual, his stubble neatly shaved, the collar of a polo shirt visible, folded over a tidy woollen sweater. A silver earring fashioned in the shape of an artist's palette dangled from his left ear.

'Have whatever you want,' he said eventually. 'It's on me, remember.'

'No, it's all right. Let's go Dutch.'

He feigned shock. 'A woman who refuses to accept a free meal? Wonderful.'

'Oh OK. *Touché*. I suppose I asked for that.'

'Certainly did. Are you always this independent?'

'No. Yes. It's just…look…' She put the menu down and leaned forward onto the table. '…the truth is I feel kind of awkward. I was married for twenty-one years. I guess I still am, technically, till the Decree Absolute comes through. And Neil and I were together very young, so this is kind of odd for me. I'm finding being single…strange.'

She stopped, wishing she hadn't started this and unwilling to explain how confused she sometimes felt at not being half of a couple any more. She didn't want to seem needy, pathetically desperate for a male companion. In any case, how can it be so hard to just be yourself, she kept wondering. Had she forgotten who she was? Some days she was scared that Claire Hitchen didn't exist any more, that she had been subsumed into a marriage and now she was gone.

'Don't feel awkward.' Adam broke into her thoughts, speaking lightly, amused at her earnestness. 'I suggested the meal so it's only fair that I pay.' He smiled ruefully. 'Anyway, I owe you for rescuing me from a damp river bank at Christmas. So relax. I've had commissions, remember. Just get on and choose a meal, will you?'

She gave in and ordered scampi; Adam chose steak and, before he could get to the bar to order, Dave Spenser's daughter, a twenty-year-old Goth, slouched up to them with a notepad, then slouched away again.

Adam took a pull of beer and sat back. He looked round appreciatively. 'I like this place.'

'It hasn't changed much.'

'That's why I like it.' He regarded her speculatively. 'Can I ask you a question?'

'Ye-es. Probably.'

'It's not personal. I was over at The White House the other day, showing my suggestions for that seventieth birthday commission.'

'I heard. How did it go?'

'Not bad. There seemed to be some disagreement between them, but it was resolved.' He hesitated. 'What I wondered was: are they the sort of people to come through? I mean, are they likely to change their minds when I've already put in the work?'

'Didn't you take a deposit?'

'Yes. But it'll only cover the materials if they don't want the painting. Not the time.'

'Well, I shouldn't worry. They're not like that. They're hard-nosed about their business but they're pretty straightforward.'

He grunted. 'Unless they hate the painting of course...'

'I'm sure they'll love it.' She smiled but the smile quickly faded. 'Neil came to see me after your meeting with them,' She paused, running a finger round and round the rim of her glass. 'He's decided to come back to work at the vineyard. Eve asked him to at Christmas apparently.'

'Really?' Adam took another swig of beer and licked the foam from his lips. 'To judge from your expression, this comes as a surprise?'

'Yes.' Her foot started its regular bounce on the floor beneath the table. 'I thought he was settled in Kent. He had a good job - though he's got to work notice there so he won't be coming immediately.'

'He might change his mind yet.'

She thought of the conversation again, of Neil asking her if his return would bother her. 'I know it'll be kind of odd, Claire,' he'd said, 'for both of us.' He had tried to give the impression that he wouldn't do it without her approval but she doubted that. Something he had said or the manner in which he had said it made her suspect he had already given his notice and planned the move.

'I suppose the surprising thing was that he suggested leaving Bohenna in the first place,' she said.

'*He* suggested it? Why?'

'Why do you think? It was like living in a nightmare here: speculation, press, memories, endless gossip and innuendo. Honestly, it was a relief to go. But then I think we both questioned it afterwards…in different ways.'

He nodded, frowning. 'What's that noise?'

'It's my foot. Sorry.' She quelled it. 'Anyway, I don't want to talk about Neil.'

'Agreed. No Neil. No Zoe.'

She immediately opened her mouth to ask about Zoe, then closed it again.

The food arrived and they ate. They talked idly of art and music and books - she hadn't seen him as a reader for some reason - and they compared opinions and mostly disagreed. When they'd finished eating, the waitress reappeared to remove the plates and give them dessert menus. Adam ordered more drinks.

'I saw you jogging once, a while ago.' He studied the choice of dessert. 'The blueberry cheesecake,' he said promptly. 'No competition.' He folded the menu flat and put it on the table. 'Impressive - jogging, I mean. Do you do it often?'

Claire put her menu down too. 'I'll have the ice-cream sundae.' She picked up her wine glass. 'I jog most days. Sometimes it's a struggle to make myself go but I nearly always feel better for it.'

'I should do more exercise. Maybe when spring comes.'

'Ah, a fine weather exerciser.' She wagged an admonishing finger at him. 'You'll never get fit if you don't do it regularly. Though, I didn't do much till the last couple of years. When I was young I was skinny with sticks for legs.

Then when Gilly disappeared I comfort ate and ended up with a spare tyre. I started jogging in Kent because a friend did and I found it helped somehow, kept me sane. So I kept doing it.' She produced a smile. 'Burns off my angst, I guess.'

'Really? You mean you'd be even more touchy if you didn't jog? Imagine.'

She withered him with a look. 'Be grateful that you probably won't find out.'

They finished dessert and had coffee. Adam pressed her to stay for another drink. Not keen to return to her empty house, she agreed, but insisted on buying the round herself.

Standing, watching Dave pour the drinks, Claire saw Phil walk into the public bar, saw him notice her and nod a greeting, then watched his gaze slide sideways to see who she was with.

She took her change and returned with the drinks to the table, handing Adam his whisky.

'Was that Phil Borlase I just heard in the bar?' he muttered.

'Yes. Do you know him?'

'Not really. What's he like?'

'He's OK.' She looked back up to the bar. There was no sign of him but from that angle she couldn't be sure. She dropped her voice. 'We sometimes used to compare notes on how overpowering the Pennymans can be. We were the outsiders. But he seems to have integrated pretty well these days.'

'A little bird told me that you and Phil were once childhood sweethearts.'

'Sweethearts?' She laughed. 'Hardly. Who told you that?'

'They also said that Neil was with Jane back then. Isn't it true?'

'Yes. Sort of. I did go out with Phil but not for long. We

weren't sweethearts,' she added, indignant. 'We were just kids. Why do you care?'

He swirled the whisky round in his glass, watching the colour flicker and change in the yellow artificial light. 'You and Jane don't see much of each other, do you, considering you were friends as children? I saw you go across to her unit a couple of weeks ago and that's it. The bird suggested that the teenage love-switch had caused a serious rift. I was curious.'

'How *do* you get any work done if you're constantly watching to see who goes where,' she said tartly.

'I just look out of the window now and then, waiting for inspiration to strike. You must know what it's like. But I suppose illustrators are more sophisticated than that?'

'Sophisticated? Are you joking? I used to work in a cheap lean-to conservatory built on the back of the house. And I was always playing catch up to deadlines. It focussed my mind.'

'Interesting, but you're avoiding the point. Was there a big blow-up with Jane?'

Instead of the teenage row, Claire's thoughts skipped to the painful evening spent at Jane's house, trapped in that sterile front room. She felt Adam's expectant gaze on her.

'Jane and I did fall out,' she said. 'She was upset when Neil ditched her for me. And she blamed me for stealing him - but I didn't lure him away or anything. Phil and I had already drifted apart and we all used to hang out together anyway. I thought it was unfair and I was upset too. We argued. Badly. She didn't speak to me. Soon after she went off to university and I stayed here, drawing my pictures and then marrying Neil. That's all there was to it.'

'So she did build a bonfire with your things then?'

'Can we drop this?'

'But these things might be important, Claire.' He glanced round again. There was no-one at the bar. 'Who else did you

143

hang out with back then?'

'Julia…Tim…Fiona. Sometimes other kids from the village but not regularly. There weren't many others.'

'Who's Fiona?'

'Jane's cousin. She was younger and wasn't there all the time.'

'Where did you meet?'

'All over. On the riverbanks, on the green sometimes.'

She stopped. These were personal memories, some tender, some funny, some poignant. She kept them carefully packaged up, preferring to feel in control of how she thought about them - and of how much of them she was prepared to share.

'We often met in the clearing,' she added slowly, 'and round the boathouse. It's on Pennyman land, set back from the river in the woods. You can get to it from the house or the river. Explain why this is important?'

'I've been trying to think through all the connections. They say a child is most likely to be taken by someone they know. Which would probably mean someone *you* know.' He shrugged apologetically. 'I know it's none of my business. I'm not trying to interfere, only help.'

'I can't see how our childish schoolyard infatuations could have any bearing on Gilly. And I don't get your logic: Gilly didn't know Jane. She had moved away.'

'But she'd come back. Before she came to the Yard, Jane worked for a couple of years in Bodmin, before that five years at a place on the edge of Fowey. She told me. You're saying you never saw her?'

'No.' Claire frowned, thinking back to that first catch-up conversation. Jane hadn't told her a lie about where she had been but she had neatly evaded the issue.

'I'm not suggesting that Jane's involved,' he added. 'I

don't see it and it seems unlikely, especially if she didn't know Gilly and she wasn't living in the village, but you see the point I'm making?' Adam drank the last of his whisky. 'Everyone assumed it was a tourist, an outsider. But it's much more likely that it was someone that Gilly would trust. Possibly someone you didn't know; more likely someone you did. Someone close. That's what I've gathered from newspapers anyway - the high profile stories.'

'Someone close?' She stared into his face. 'I don't see that.'

He held her gaze. 'Maybe because you don't want to.'

Her frown deepened. Her thoughts settled on Jane again, niggling at her. 'I did take something of Gilly's to show Jane, you know – just in case she could read it.' She shrugged.

'And?'

'It was a waste of time. Gilly was content, she said. Content. And that was supposed to make me happy.' Claire blew out her lips in disgust. 'She went into a sort of trance, said she saw trees waving in the wind - and water, except that it came and went.'

'What did you give her?'

'A hair slide. She sat and held it while we conjured up Gilly's energy. It was…it was…' She failed to find a suitable word and gave up.

They sat in silence but Jane's behaviour and her economy with the truth lingered in Claire's mind.

She finished her wine and stood up, slipping her coat back on. 'Thanks for the meal, Adam. I enjoyed it.' She smiled. 'Now you have more than repaid my hospitality.'

Adam slung his jacket on and walked with her to the door. Outside it was dark but there was a clear sky and stars twinkled brightly.

'I could walk you home, if you like,' he offered.

'Thank you, but it's not even ten minutes' walk. And I have my torch.'

She pulled the torch out of her pocket and waved it in front of him triumphantly, then set off walking - a little unsteadily - the dark roads back towards her house. Reaching the junction near the bridge, she thought she heard a noise and turned round but saw no-one and carried on walking. Adam's words still rang in her ears: *Someone you know. Someone close.*

And her mind flipped back to an early spring evening twenty-four years previously and the red and flickering glow of a fire on the further bank of the river, its flames caught and attenuated by their watery reflections. And a dark figure standing by the side of it, faceless in the half-light and yet clearly looking her way defiantly across the water.

Chapter 11

Claire slept in the following morning. When she came to she was heavy in head and limb, unused to drinking so much, and it was nine-thirty when she finally pushed the curtains back and stood looking out over her back garden to the trees beyond. From this window she could see most of Eddie's patch too, his neatly tilled vegetable plots and the little hen house and run at the bottom of his garden.

And she saw Eddie himself. He was walking in that stiff-legged, rolling gait of his down the path towards the hen house and then the next minute he was falling forwards to land face downward on the ground. Claire watched him anxiously. He didn't move. She grabbed her dressing-gown, throwing it on over her pyjamas, and forced her legs into activity. Automatically snatching up her phone, she slipped on an old pair of deck shoes by the back door and a couple of minutes later she was in Eddie's garden, running down the stone path to reach him.

'Eddie,' she called softly, getting close, worried what she might find. He was lying half on the path, half over a flowerbed to one side, and he lay slightly twisted with one arm beneath him.

'Eddie, are you all right?' She reached out a hand and touched him on the shoulder.

He lifted his head and began struggling to turn over but he

was caught up in a bushy hydrangea, wedged between its dry, chunky stems and dead, brown flower heads.

'I'm stuck,' he grunted. 'Give me a hand.'

'Here.'

She grabbed his free hand and he pulled, stiffly swinging himself free, enough to allow his trapped arm to move and he eased himself out of the bush onto the path where he sat, legs stretched out awkwardly in front of him. He rubbed at his knees, glancing back at the broken stems of the hydrangea, and produced a strange, plaintive grunt.

'I've ruined it.'

'It'll grow again,' said Claire. 'You gave me a fright. Are you all right? Can you stand?'

'I'll just sit here a minute.'

He looked at her sidelong in that way he had. She saw his eyes running over her dressing-gown which had opened to reveal her pyjamas, saw him examining her hair which was wild and tumbled and hadn't yet seen a brush.

'What happened?' She pulled the gown tighter.

'Caught my toe on the brick edgin'.' He pointed to the sides of the path where raised bricks separated it from the flower bed. 'One of them's loose; the devil'd moved. I'll have to fix it.'

She had heard him talking to the hens in the garden, mumbling and making odd clicking noises but she had never had a proper conversation with him before. His voice when he spoke to her now was harsh and flat, with a broad Cornish burr.

'Do you want me to call a doctor?' She brandished the phone from her pocket.

'God, no. Nothin' wrong with me. Not havin' a doctor fussin'. Here.'

He held out both his hands and she heaved him up, bracing her feet against his. For a small man, he felt surprisingly heavy. She looked at him uncertainly.

'Are you sure you're all right? Did you hit your head?'

'I'll be fine dreckly. Don't want no fussin', y'hear?'

'OK, OK.'

She watched him shrug and ease his joints out and the next minute he was tottering away from her towards the hen house as if she didn't exist. She smiled ruefully and turned away.

*

Later that day, having done all the jobs around the house and grabbed a sandwich for her lunch, Claire sat down with a mug of tea and a notepad. As if it might help her think, she put the hair slide on the arm of the chair: a focal point, a talisman perhaps. After the disillusionment of her meeting with Jane, she had felt helpless, dejected that there was no way forward, nothing left to do. But Adam's comments had started her thinking again and she stared at the pad, a pen poised to write down anything or anyone that came into her mind, any tiny detail which might prove significant.

Someone that Gilly would trust. Someone close. It was easy for Adam to say, but Claire struggled to process the thought. Since finding the slide she had accepted that someone in the village had taken Gilly but she had unconsciously assumed that it was someone on the periphery of their world, a relative stranger. If it was someone close... It was unbearably difficult to imagine. It also seemed unlikely. Even so, she had to think it through.

She started by considering the unlikeliest people of all: her own family. Her father had been devastated when Gilly disappeared; he had been a kind and gentle man and he had adored her. The idea that he had had anything to do with his granddaughter's disappearance was unthinkable. In any case, he had died two years since and the slide had only just surfaced. And her brother, Jon, had been living in Canada for nearly twenty years already. He rarely returned to Britain. She mentally ticked them both off with a feeling of relief.

So what about the Pennymans? She was surprised to find that she thought more highly of them than she would have expected, or at least, not as badly, and she failed to see how any of them could be involved. She'd told Adam that they were 'straightforward' and she was convinced it was true. They were arrogant sometimes, high-handed maybe; they were self-involved perhaps and obsessed with their wine and their business; they were insensitive occasionally and clannish. But did any of that make them likely to kidnap a child? And one of their own at that? No. So where did that leave her?

Jane? She had no real reason to suspect Jane. It was difficult to imagine her childhood friend taking Gilly because of a failed teenage romance twenty-four odd years ago. Did petty grudges last that long? She frowned. Maybe. But, as she had told Adam, Gilly had never met the woman as far as Claire knew so she wouldn't have been someone the girl would have trusted. And while Claire realised now there was no future in their friendship, while she distrusted the woman's supposed gifts and her authenticity as a healer or psychic, she struggled to see Jane as a kidnapper. She paused though, pen in hand, and the image of that fire loomed into her mind again. She wrote Jane's name down.

So who else? A family friend maybe. There hadn't been that many friends once Jane had left. Claire's time had mostly been taken up with work and raising a young family. There had been other friends at school but her contact with them over the years had been scant and, since most had moved away, restricted to hastily scribbled news on Christmas cards each year. Though there had been a young couple who'd lived over the road on the estate. She and Neil had gone out with them for a meal a couple of times. He had been an accountant and the vineyard had employed him for a while. But Neil had seriously fallen out with him because of something to do with the vineyard accounts and the Pennymans had employed a new accountant after that. She'd forgotten about that until now, so maybe here was somebody else with a grudge. She felt a buzz of excitement; she was getting somewhere. Except that she couldn't remember his name – or his wife's. Damn. But she could check if they still lived there.

She drank her now lukewarm coffee and looked at the pad in disgust. One name and a question mark. That wasn't going to get her very far. But she was being stupid, wasn't she, because she had forgotten Beattie, their erstwhile neighbour. Patty Miller who'd run the bric-a-brac stall had said Beattie donated something to the stall on the day of the fête but that she had also left goods in the pub garages beforehand. Beattie herself was a sweet and ingenuous soul who wouldn't hurt a fly but she might have seen someone else leaving something there. She also knew everybody and she'd be able to tell Claire if that couple still lived over the road and what their names were. Claire immediately grabbed her coat and went out.

*

The small estate Claire and Neil had once lived on had changed little in the intervening five and a half years since they had left. For the first years of their marriage they had rented, then bought their first house here when Gilly was a toddler. Built in the seventies, the estate was a broad sweeping loop of semi-detached dwellings, the houses brick and breeze block, rendered and painted, with neatly tiled roofs. One or two, she noted now, had extended either into the garage or above it; someone had Japanese-themed their front garden with stones,

151

bamboo, and a decorative water feature. Beattie and George's, though, was as it had always been: a small, immaculately kept lawn surrounded by weed-free beds of carefully pruned roses. George liked his roses.

But it was a strange feeling to walk up Beattie's front drive and look back across the wire-mesh fence at the house where she and Neil had once been so happy. Claire turned away and briskly rang Beattie's bell. This was a little odd too. Only once had she been inside their neighbour's house. Though helpful and charming in many ways, Beattie had also been distant and George could be bad-tempered. Claire had sometimes heard him shouting at Beattie in the garden, complaining about something she had either done or not done, though they had both been good with the girls, giving them sweets over the fence, or fruit from the garden, even returning the occasional errant ball.

The house was silent but there was a car on the drive. She rang the bell a second time.

This time she heard footsteps, the sound of bolts being pulled back, and Beattie opened the door just wide enough to allow her to stand in the gap. Her face crinkled into a smile.

'Claire. How nice to see you. It's been so long since you were here. What can I do for you?'

'Hello Beattie. I wondered if you might have a minute to talk? I'm sorry, I should have rung first.'

'Not at all. What is it?' Beattie glanced behind her into the hallway and pulled the door even tighter.

'Well, there were a few things really.' Claire waited for an invitation inside but clearly that wasn't going to happen. 'I wanted to catch up with a couple we used to know. I've lost touch with them and I wondered if you could help. They used to live over there.' Claire pointed to a house across and further up the road. 'But I'm afraid I've forgotten their names. He was

152

an accountant. I think she worked for the council. He had a moustache, was a bit gingery. She was dark-haired. Do you know them?'

'Do you mean Richard and Meg Poldreen?'

'Yes. Of course. Silly of me to forget.' Claire smiled. 'Do they still live there?'

'No dear. They moved to Lostwithiel - just after you left. Meg works at the library. They've got three children now.'

'Really? That's great. Thank you. And there was something else too...'

'Beattie? Who is it?' George's voice resounded clearly down the hall to the door.

Beattie twisted round and called back. 'It's Claire, from next door as was, *you* know'. She turned back. 'I'm sorry, I really should be going.' She edged the door a little more towards the frame.

'Please,' pressed Claire urgently, 'can I just ask: didn't you leave some things in the garages for the bric-a-brac stall at last year's fête? Did you see anyone else leaving things there?'

'No, dear, I didn't go to the garages. George took them for me. I only took something on the day of the fête because I'd forgotten to put it in the bag.'

'Then maybe George might have seen someone? Would you mind asking him?'

Beattie froze for a second, then shook her head.

'He'd have said. And he went early 'cause he doesn't sleep very well.'

'Beattie, can you remember the day Gilly disappeared? She went to play with her cousin but maybe she came back to the estate. She often used to play on the drive. Did you see Gilly go anywhere or maybe see someone hanging around? Anything odd at all?'

153

'No, no, nothing. I saw nothing. I told the police at the time. And of course, it's such a long time ago now, isn't it? I don't remember anything. I'm sorry I can't be more help but it's nice to see you, dear.' She closed the door firmly before Claire could respond.

Left on the doorstep, Claire stood and rubbed her fingers over her forehead, cross at her impulsiveness. How stupid of her to fire off all those questions like that – desperate and avid, like a woman possessed. But then maybe she was. This quest consumed her, her thoughts dwelling on it several times a day, every day, like flies buzzing round a festering wound. She quickly turned away and headed for home.

Walking up the path to the house she found a box of eggs on the front doorstep, a couple of feathers still attached to the shells. Eddie must have left them. It brought her back to earth. Surprised and touched by the gesture, she took them inside.

*

The February days were lengthening. Up at the vineyard, Phil had started pruning: working his way up and down the columns of vines, cutting back the previous season's growth and choosing the canes which would form the basis of the new shoots for the coming season. Occasionally Julia would go along and help but mostly she left him to it. It was where he was happiest, come rain or shine, and he did the bulk of it himself. There were few other people he trusted to do it right so he preferred it that way.

'Screw this job up,' she had once heard him remark to Chris, 'and you'll mess up the plant for the whole season and reduce the yield. And that costs.' He'd painstakingly shown the young man how to pick the suitable canes then carefully snip off all the others. 'See, you can't rush in, cutting any old thing.' For someone who mostly preferred his own company and who tolerated fools badly, he could be a surprisingly patient teacher if he thought someone was genuinely interested. And he never cut corners. Julia admired both his doggedness and his work ethic. To prune the whole vineyard took him weeks and, by the time he'd finished, the sap would be rising in the canes, making them easy to handle and bend, and he'd go back to the start, looping them down and tying them up. Phil was nothing if not conscientious.

But, with Neil's imminent return, Julia foresaw friction ahead. Phil had never got on with Neil; they were chalk and cheese. They had managed to rub along when they had both worked at the vineyard before, largely because their paths had rarely crossed but time had moved on, new habits had formed. It wasn't going to be easy to turn back the clock.

It was the end of the third week in February when, having worked his notice and taken the last of his annual leave, Neil arrived back in Bohenna. He brought a couple of cases of clothes with him and moved back into his old room at The White House. On the Monday morning he tagged along with Julia around the winery, reading the wine notes and asking questions. Unsure if the red wine was clear enough, she was toying with racking it one more time but didn't ask his opinion, determined not to give the impression that they needed him. She found herself looking for a turn of the lip, waiting on his criticism. Neither came.

In the afternoon, when he'd gone to look at the accounts and the restaurant side of the business with Timothy, Julia made her way down into the vineyard. She came across Phil on the newer slopes up above the house, engrossed in examining the shoots, pinching out the buds he didn't want to grow. He looked up as she came up to join him.

'Problem, Jules?' he asked.

'No. I just came to find out if you were all right. I didn't hear you come in last night and then you went out early this morning.'

'Did I disturb you?'

'Not really.'

'I had to go for a drink, girl. That ridiculous 'reunion dinner' last night with Eve fussing all over Neil... If I'd stayed much longer I'd have said something I shouldn't.' He looked at her bleakly. 'Sorry Jules. You know I don't get on with him.'

He turned back to his task.

'He won't stay.'

'Are you sure about that?'

'I can't see it. He'll get bored. This place won't be big enough for him any more, not after that huge vineyard in Kent.'

'Maybe you're right.' He moved onto another vine.

'Though we could do with the help really.'

'Help, yes. Interference, no. The problem with Neil is: he always has to know better.'

'He won't interfere with you though. It's the winemaking he's after doing.'

'Yeah, not the hard work. All he wants is the glory bit.'

'I work hard too, Phil.'

'That's not what I meant.' He straightened up and looked at her. 'I know you don't see it as the glory bit but he does. Anyway, you do the winemaking great. Look at all those awards you've won.'

'We've won. All of us. We're a team. But that is what he wants to do. That's what Eve wants too: her favourite son as the chief winemaker, his name in the papers. The Pennyman name. She's the one that encourages him. Neil's OK really.'

He snorted and started work again. 'Oh come on, Julia. Why do you always have to defend him? Just because he's family.'

'Well…you know; that's what families are like.'

'Mine wasn't. My brother would've stabbed me in the back, soon as look at me.'

Julia sighed, edging slowly along the vines with him as he worked.

'It's because of Claire that he's come back,' she said. 'It's her fault.'

Phil looked up, frowning. 'Claire? But I thought that was all over.'

'Have you seen them together?' Julia shook her head. 'It'll never be over between them. Even if they only argue forever. Believe me, it'll never be over.'

Phil stared at her, eyes narrowed. 'Nah. You're just being romantic.'

'Romance has nothing to do with it. They got past romance by the time they were twenty. Did you see them together at Christmas? They just…are. Like they've got a cord stretched between them or something, holding them together.' She shrugged and, seeing a weed growing near the trunk of a nearby vine, she bent over to pull it out, uncertain who she was trying to convince, herself or Phil. 'You notice his new romance with Samantha didn't last long?' she added caustically. 'He dumped her like a shot when he was invited to come back here.'

'That means nothing. She was probably just a rebound or something.'

For a few minutes they were silent again but Julia couldn't leave it alone.

'I don't know if Claire engineered for him to come back here or if it was just inevitable once she decided to move down.'

Phil grunted in a non-committal way, shifting his stocky

frame further along the line of vines.

'She's been seeing that artist bloke,' he said.

Julia frowned. 'Who? Adam?'

'Yep. Him. They've had lunch together in the restaurant. And they were in the pub together the other night. So maybe she has finally had it with Neil.'

'That's surprising. I wonder what Neil'll think about that. Still, I don't suppose it'll last.'

Phil didn't respond.

'There's something else, isn't there? What is it you're not telling me, Phil?'

He snipped at a cane, more savagely than usual. 'I heard a rumour.'

'What?' He was silent. 'What, Phil?'

'Apparently Claire's been poking about again.'

'In what way?'

'I heard it in the pub. She went asking Beattie Foster a load of questions. Odd questions, George said, about the day Gilly disappeared. He was cross, thought she was making accusations. Then Nick Lawer pitched in, said he'd found her in his garden a while back, trying to get into his sheds.'

'Has she been pestering Danny again too?' she asked anxiously.

'Not as far as I know.'

'Good.' She kicked with the toe of her boot at a broken piece of wire on the ground. 'If she comes asking us, we must both stick to the same story we gave at the time.'

He stopped working and looked up at her, frowning.

'You do remember?' she said. 'We said we were both together having tea at the house around the time Gilly disappeared.'

He stared at her another minute, then bent to his task again.

158

'Yes. I remember.'

She watched him but he clearly wasn't going to say anything more.

'Are you coming up to the house for tea today?' she asked.

He shook his head so she left him to it, wondering as she often did what exactly he did recall of that day. And if what he remembered made him as concerned as she was about Claire's questions.

Chapter 12

'I miss you,' Adam said softly into the phone.

There was silence. He waited, breath held tight in his throat.

'I miss you too,' said Zoe.

Adam hesitated. It was the first time that Zoe had responded to one of his calls - or his desperate messages - in weeks. She sounded upset; she sounded like she cared. He ached to reach out and touch her.

'We had some great times,' she said.

He winced. That sounded so final.

'Maybe we could meet,' he suggested cautiously. 'Perhaps somewhere neutral, you know? It would be so good to see you. We could talk.'

Again there was silence. 'What's the point, Adam? What would we talk about? I mean, we've been over it, haven't we – everything - again and again? Have you changed your mind about anything?'

'Is it all about me?' he said, voice rising. 'Am I the only one who has to change?'

'Look Adam…'

'I have been thinking about everything you said,' he added quickly. 'I have, really. But there's a lot to think about.'

'I don't think you want to have children,' she said in a flat, resigned voice. 'You're not just putting it off; you don't want it to happen.'

Adam stopped walking up and down and stood, facing his reflection in the dark window pane, eyes unnaturally large and staring. The man looked a little like him but it wasn't him.

'I don't know, Zoe. I'm being honest. I don't know.' He let out a long breath. 'I guess I'm scared.' He'd never admitted it to her before. He had barely admitted it to himself.

'Then I guess that's the problem. Anyway, I have to tell you I've met someone else.'

He felt like someone had punched him in the head; he was stunned. His thoughts whirled pell-mell.

'Someone else? What someone else? Is it serious?'

'I don't know. I'm going to see. I want to find out.' She paused. 'I think you should stop ringing me, Adam. Please.'

He said nothing because he couldn't think of anything to say. He began walking again.

'Adam? Did you hear me?'

'Yes.' He opened his mouth to speak, but didn't and pressed the close call button.

He stared at the phone as if it was culpable in some way, then threw it onto the sofa, the tatty old sofa which still had one of Zoe's throws over it, masking the worn patches and a large wine stain. She had said she didn't want it back. She had left all sorts of things in the bungalow which she didn't want back, any more than she wanted him back. They were all - him included - cast-offs, goods for which Zoe had decided she had no further use. And it hadn't taken her long to find someone new so maybe he had been right all along when he had accused her of two-timing him; maybe she had met this guy ages ago and the whole thing was just a lie. He would be better off without her in that case. She had clearly just been playing him along, an amusement, a convenience.

He needed a drink. There was a bottle of wine open in the

kitchen but he'd barely got as far as the kitchen door when the phone rang again. He'd installed the theme tune to the Indiana Jones movies - some of his favourite films. Just at this moment it really annoyed him. Everything annoyed him. He grabbed the phone, hoping it was Zoe ringing back to say how sorry she was. He thought maybe he would give her a piece of his mind.

'Yes?' he said, savagely.

'Hi Adam,' said a female voice. 'It's Claire. Is this a bad time?'

He mumbled an indistinct negative.

'The thing is, I've been thinking over what you said when we had that meal together, you know, about people who were close? I realise now it would be useful to talk it through. You were right. Would you mind? I thought perhaps you could come here one evening? I could cook us something if you like.'

Adam frowned. His heart was still racing and his body tingled with suppressed anger, frustration and a host of other emotions he couldn't identify.

'Adam? Are you there?'

'Yes. Yes, I'm here.'

'Are you OK?'

'Yes, I'm fine.'

'So what do you think? Would you mind?'

'No.' He found he was shaking his head. He didn't mind at all. It would be a relief to do something different, to have company, female company at that, and somewhere else. His heartbeat started to settle. 'That'd be fine,' he said. 'When were you thinking?'

'I'm off this weekend so how would tomorrow be?'

*

162

Claire walked into the bathroom and checked her reflection in the mirror. She'd heard that Neil had returned and was now living up at The White House. He'd been back a few days apparently though she hadn't seen him herself yet. Given their conversation, she couldn't claim to be surprised but it did feel a little surreal having him in Bohenna too, in the place where they had started out together. First Jane returns, then she did, now Neil. Was that poetic in some way, part of some bigger plan which had brought them all together again? She pulled a face at her reflection. What nonsense.

She fingered a curl of hair off her forehead, wondering if he'd heard yet that she had been out with Adam. It didn't matter that her relationship with the painter was completely innocent and platonic - the whispering voices would be sure to make it something it wasn't.

She checked her watch. Adam would be here in a few minutes. After the bizarre and unsatisfactory conversation with Beattie, she was keen to talk her thoughts through with someone and there wasn't anyone else. In any case, he was a newcomer and a stranger to the whole situation and, even if he did treat Gilly's disappearance as some kind of light distraction, his objectivity could be useful.

He arrived promptly and brought wine though she could already detect the faint smell of alcohol on his breath. They ate at the little table in the kitchen which she had taken the trouble to dress up with a jaunty cloth and napkins and a tiny vase with a couple of daffodils from the garden. She'd made a beef casserole and roast potatoes and the chocolate cake for dessert came courtesy of the supermarket in Bodmin. She needed his help and this was the only way she could think of repaying it.

While they ate, she tried to break the ice with small talk but Adam was quieter than usual, his expression pinched and taut.

163

'Is there something the matter?' she said, at length.

'No, everything's just fine.'

'Good,' she replied doubtfully.

It wasn't until she cleared the plates and put the cake on the table that it occurred to her.

'You've heard from Zoe,' she said.

Adam let out a brief, bitter laugh. 'Oh yes. I've heard. She finally got round to answering one of my messages. Big of her.'

'What did she say?'

'She's met someone else,' he said, exaggerating every word.

'I am sorry.'

'Well, don't be. I've decided I'm better off alone. There's no-one to tell me what I should do or how I should do it, no-one to complain about the way I draw the curtains or how I put my clothes away or where I put the dishes. Hell, I can go days without washing the dishes with no-one to chew my ear off. It's great.'

'Really?' She put a large piece of cake on a plate and handed it to him. 'You don't look like you think it's so great.'

He turned a jaundiced eye on her. 'Thank you. So how should I look? See, that's the problem with women: you always have an opinion on how a guy should be - or not be, how he should look - or not look. It gets very tiring…and impossible to get right.'

She cut herself a slice of cake and didn't respond. She watched him cut into the cake with his fork brutally, like he was exacting revenge on all womankind by taking it out on the innocent sponge. She looked away.

'I see Neil has come back,' he said suddenly. 'How do you feel about it, now he's actually here?'

She looked up, surprised. 'I'm not sure yet.'

He finished his cake; she offered him more but he refused.

'You were together a long time, weren't you?' he said, playing with his wine glass. 'I guess you had your ups and downs. Has there ever been anyone else for you?'

She paused, the last forkful of cake half way to her mouth. 'No.'

'You were never tempted to stray?'

She finished eating and pushed the plate away. 'Only when he went off with his new girlfriend. For spite.' She shrugged. 'To show him – though I don't suppose he'd have cared.'

He nodded. 'See, that's what I thought about Zoe – maybe she's trying to teach me a lesson.'

'Maybe. Or…' she suggested warily, '…maybe you're just trying to persuade yourself?'

'Do you still love him?' he demanded.

'What is this, Adam? Some sort of bizarre counselling session? I suppose sometimes I do. Sometimes I think I love him as much as I did twenty years ago…maybe more. Sometimes I hate him. What's this got to do with anything?'

'Why? Why do you hate him?'

Claire picked up her wine glass. 'Because…' She raised her free hand in a gesture of frustration. '…because he wouldn't talk about Gilly. He cut off from me when I needed him most, said he needed space. I felt like I was in a…a whirlpool spinning round and round all by myself. Then he blamed me for obsessing and driving us apart.'

Adam nodded slowly. 'Men don't talk though. Surely you know that? Scares us to death.'

She flicked him a look, unsure if he was being flippant though his expression was serious enough, intense even.

'I didn't want him to make speeches Adam; I just wanted him to meet me half way.'

He grunted. 'Half way,' he repeated mechanically. 'But every time I try to talk to Zoe I…' He shook his head and drank some wine.

Claire waited but he'd abandoned the thought and was staring moodily into the distance. She got up and cleared the plates off the table and a minute later he appeared to shake off his gloom and helped. Then they took the remaining wine through to the sitting room and sat by the wood-burning stove. Claire poked at it to make it flame up.

'Right,' said Adam, purposefully, 'you wanted to talk something through. Fire away. I'm all ears.'

'OK.' She took a long breath and let it out slowly. 'First, I need to show you something.' She walked across to the sideboard and took the velvet pouch out of the drawer. Standing by his chair, she turned the slide out onto her hand and held it down for him to see. 'I found this. It was the slide Gilly was wearing on the day she disappeared.'

He looked up at her, incredulous. 'You're joking.'

'I would never joke about this, Adam. Here, have a look. Take it.'

He took it gingerly, studied it, turned it over, then looked back at Claire who had sat down again.

'Where did you find this?'

'In a box of bric-a-brac left over from the village fête. The box was given to Penny to sell.'

'At the fête? That's odd. How do you know it's Gilly's?' He studied it again. 'Is it special in some way?'

'No-o, not exactly. It's a cheap mass-produced thing but they make a couple of different colours and this one's exactly like the one Gilly wore. And how many little girls are there in Bohenna who'd have a slide like this?' She glared at him defensively. 'And I've looked online and they don't seem to make them any more. Plus it's got a scratch on the back. Gilly

166

dropped it once and it fell down between the car and the kerb. I think that's when it got scratched.'

He nodded slowly. 'You don't sound certain.'

'I am. I've thought about it a lot. Anyway I know it's Gilly's.'

'Have you told the police?'

'Yes, but they didn't want to know. They said it wasn't proof. They've packed the case up and moved on.'

'They said that?'

'Not in so many words. But it's what's happened.'

'Maybe they just need some good evidence to justify using their meagre resources.'

'You think I'm making it up?'

'I didn't say that. It's just that finding it at the fête doesn't make any sense.'

'Nothing makes any sense,' Claire said heavily, and drank more wine. 'But it proves that Gilly was never taken out of the village.' She looked up. 'Don't you see, Adam, she might be being held somewhere. In a garage or a shed or a cellar. Maybe somewhere quite close.'

'Ye-es. I suppose she could,' he said doubtfully, examining the slide again. 'But how would it get to the fête then? Is this what you gave Jane to read?'

'Yes, but I didn't tell her where I found it.'

Adam reached for his wine and drank, saying nothing.

'I've been trying to track down who gave it to the fête,' Claire continued. 'But it hasn't been that easy. A lot of the stuff was given anonymously, left in big plastic boxes in the pub garages. Dave mentioned someone he'd seen donating but it didn't get me very far.' She told him about the donation by Nick Lawer's girlfriend, about the confrontation by the black sheds in his garden and the subsequent conversation with the police. 'Of the other donations that anyone remembers, some were from newcomers to the village - and our old neighbours, the Fosters, gave some things too.'

'Is that George Foster? Big chap, neat moustache, bit red in the face?'

'Yes. Do you know him?'

'I've seen him in the pub.'

'He and Beattie used to spoil both the girls with treats. Anyway, I went to see Beattie the other day to ask if she'd seen anyone else at the garages, or if she'd seen Gilly that afternoon and she behaved rather oddly.'

'Ah.' Adam nodded wisely. 'That accounts for the looks I've been getting and the way conversations change when I get near the bar. We've been seen together so no-one's prepared to talk in front of me. Perhaps your questions made George nervous. What did Beattie say?'

'She was edgy. Apparently it was George who put the donations in the garage, not her, but she refused to ask him if he'd seen anyone else there. She looked scared.'

Adam drained the last of his wine and went back to the kitchen, returning with the bottle he'd brought. He refilled both glasses and sat down heavily.

'Where was George when Gilly disappeared?' he asked.

'He's retired now but he used to be a delivery driver for a bakery just outside Penmarna.'

'So he might have been around then.'

'After what you said, I've been trying to think of people we've known who Gilly would have met, adults she might have trusted.' She told him about the Poldreens and the grudge Richard might have harboured. 'They're living in Lostwithiel now. Beattie told me. She knows everyone.'

Adam's face puckered into a frown. 'See, that's what I don't get: there are so many people in this village who know everything that goes on. And yet, no-one saw Gilly being taken; no-one seems to know anything at all.'

'I know.' She hesitated, glancing up at him through coy lashes. 'I've been thinking about Jane too.' She waited but he didn't comment. 'I know you like her but I'm wondering if there might be something in that old row we had after all. She behaves strangely around me.'

'I didn't say I liked her. I just said I didn't see her as the type.'

'What is the type then?'

He shrugged, sniffed, took another swig of wine. 'And did you think about the family too?'

For family, she heard Neil. 'Everyone in the family was questioned, Adam. There were no secrets. It was like living in a goldfish bowl - they were all over everything. In any case,' she added coldly, 'there's no-one in the family who's the type either.'

He met her stony gaze but didn't respond and picked up the bottle from the hearth, offering Claire more and, when she refused, refilling his own glass. Then he was back in his chair, hugging the glass, staring into the fire as if he hoped he would see some answer there.

He jerked his head round suddenly. 'Who have you told about the slide?'

'Only you…and Jane. But she doesn't know Gilly was wearing it when she disappeared. And Neil wouldn't believe me anyway.'

'Don't tell anyone else. People are talking enough already. We need to be very careful.'

'We? So you do believe me then about the slide? Are you going to help?'

'I'll try. But we need to be organised. We need a plan.'

They continued to talk it through for another half hour while the contents of the second bottle of wine slowly dwindled. Claire was increasingly convinced that Jane needed to be investigated and she wanted to check out her house.

'No, I should do it,' Adam insisted. 'Remember what happened with Nick Lawer. And I'll see if I can find out more about George Foster too. We can't risk him knowing you're still asking questions about him.'

'But I've got to do something.'

'You check out Richard Poldreen. Then we'll get together afterwards and compare notes.'

Slowly, reluctantly, he got up to leave.

'Thank you,' Claire said to him at the door. 'It's a relief that someone finally believes me.'

A slow, self-satisfied smile spread across his face and he lurched forward, planting a bruising kiss on her cheek. 'You're welcome,' he slurred, as she pushed him gently away. He leaned back heavily against the door frame.

'It's time to go home, Adam,' she said.

'I know: you want me to leave.' The smile faded and he frowned extravagantly. 'You know you're still very attractive, Claire. You mustn't give up on men because of Neil. The man's a fool.'

''Night Adam.'

'Oh OK.' He eased himself upright again. 'Thanks for the meal. It was a good evening.'

'Adam?'

'What?'

'If you're drinking to try and forget Zoe, it doesn't work. Trust me. I've tried it.'

He raised a hand in mock salute and affected to march down the path, pitching a little side to side. She smiled; he was an engaging man. But he talked of being discreet and there was nothing subtle about Adam when he'd had too much to drink. And he clearly still thought this was some kind of game.

She closed the door and leaned against it. He was right about being careful though. She had been foolish to speak to Beattie like that. She couldn't afford to let her heart rule her head and risk anything happening to Gilly because of her big mouth.

Chapter 13

Julia sat in the office, brow furrowed, a sheaf of papers on the desk in front of her, cross-referencing a form she was filling in with a set of printed notes from the computer on one side and her own scribblings in a notebook on the other. This form-filling was the least favourite part of her job, making sure they fulfilled all their legal requirements, checking no further directives had come from government on how, when and if they produced their wine. There were so many rules, so many hoops to jump through, she always felt they had to run to keep up. Sometimes she wished she could get the faceless bureaucratic officials to actually spend a few weeks working in the vineyard with them so they would understand how it really was, here on the ground, battling the weather and the pests and the lack of enough labour and the market and that indefinable thing: fashion in wine. And then there were the costs and the constant balancing of the investment in the latest technology or equipment against their possible benefits.

What she couldn't complain to the faceless officials about, however, was her family, her siblings whose desire to work together and make the business a success could never quite dampen their rivalry or stop their squabbles - or her mother who still thought she knew best even though it had been her husband who had been the galvanising force behind the business before his death, and even though she had no real input to the vineyard work any longer. Still Eve insisted on checking everything, forcing every issue to be repeatedly discussed and argued. Was that her increasing age and insecurity or because she didn't trust her daughter and son-in-law? If Julia hadn't already known the answer to that question, she thought her mother's invitation to Neil had proved it was the latter.

As if reading her thoughts, there was a knock on the door and Neil stuck his head round.

'Hi,' he said. 'Got a moment?'

'Sure.' She put the pen down and leaned back in the chair, watching him as he pulled another chair over and sat down a pace away.

'The winery looks good,' he said.

'Thanks.'

'The new bottling machine will make a difference.'

'I hope so.'

'Sure to.' He licked his lips thoughtfully, glanced at her face but wouldn't hold her gaze. 'I had a good wander round the vines too.'

'Phil said.'

He nodded. 'Well, I had to reacquaint myself with the place. It's been a while.' He hesitated. 'I see we're still growing a lot of Pinot Noir. It's a fussy grape though, isn't it? Temperamental. I'm not saying get rid of it completely but maybe try…'

'It can also produce the most amazing wines when you get it right. Remember? You were here when we made some of them. And dad swore by it.'

'Yes. But he also used to say: learn and adapt. I was going to say there are new varieties being developed all the time, especially for the northern US states and for Canada and Germany. Have you thought of growing Orion?'

173

'Why change a winning formula?' she said crisply. 'It would be a gamble. Anyway, we'd need more land for the transition.' She leaned forward again and picked up her pen. 'Look I've got to fill this in and send it off.'

'We've got to look forward, Julia, not back.'

The tension in Julia, simmering for days, finally blew.

'So you think we live in the past, do you? Not good enough for your standards, Neil? You may have noticed that the vineyard hasn't come grinding to a halt since you decided to leave. Frankly, I think you've got a nerve to come waltzing in here, telling me how we should be doing things when not so very long ago you couldn't wait to get away and leave us to sink or swim. In fact I'm surprised, if we're so backward, that you deigned to come back at all.'

He said nothing but now made eye contact.

'I did have good reasons for leaving, remember? We needed that fresh start. But it didn't work out. And now it feels like a safe time to come back.'

'Safe?'

He looked wrong-footed. 'Safe from feeling quite as much pain. Safe now from all the journos and sick attention.'

'I see.' She leaned back in the chair, her anger fading as rapidly as it had risen. 'Has Tim talked to you about you taking on the marketing again?'

'Yes, he did mention it.'

'You know he hates all that, even though he's done pretty well with it all in all.'

'You're trying to get me on the road again and out of your hair,' he said easily.

'I think we'll be most successful if we all play to our strengths - and you're very good at selling. You know you are. All that side of it: the conferences and seminars and ceremonies, the pitching to supermarkets and wine merchants.

174

Tim can get on with the day to day stuff here: the wine tours, the restaurant, the Craft Yard. He's thinking about opening a gift shop.'

'Yes, he said.' He hesitated. 'Have you seen much of Claire?'

'No. Not since Christmas. Once or twice in the village maybe. I don't get over to the Craft Yard much.'

'Phil tells me she's seeing someone.'

'Did he? Well, she's bound to make new friends, isn't she?'

'Is she…' He didn't finish the thought, hesitated, and got to his feet. 'I think we all need to sit down sometime and discuss our roles and where we think the vineyard is going.'

'Why? What's changed, Neil, because you've chosen to come back? We were doing fine before.'

'I'm not here to challenge you, Julia. I'm here to get involved, to help. And you know it's hard for me too, coming back like this? I want to contribute. Help ease me in, will you? We all need to work together if we want the vineyard to be as successful as it can be.'

She didn't reply and he walked out. For a moment she stared vaguely towards the window, seeing nothing. It was all starting to happen the way she'd known it would. As soon as Claire came back, it had been inevitable that Neil would return too. What on earth had prompted Phil to tell Neil about her seeing Adam? It was just poking at a wasps' nest.

And Neil back at the vineyard? Julia loved her brother but he was a driven man. It was like putting an over-zealous collie in a field of sheep - he always had to try to herd them all together in the direction he wanted to go.

She sighed and bent over her papers again.

*

175

Jane's house stood at the end of a short run of dwellings built along one side of the road and was separated from its nearest neighbour - a small semi - by a rickety, ivy-covered wooden fence. Adam had already driven past it once. Now he turned the car and returned the other way, pulling in to park beside the neighbouring property. A *To Let* sign languished at an angle against the overgrown hedge and a newspaper stuck out of the letterbox. The house appeared to have been empty for some time. That was lucky.

Jane was working. He had made sure of that before leaving. It was not yet two o'clock and a quick glance in at the window of her unit suggested that she was involved in a consultation; he expected to be safe for some time. He got out of the car and, affecting interest in the rental property, wandered nonchalantly into the garden, glancing towards its attached neighbour. There didn't seem to be anyone around. He abandoned the semi and went next door.

The previous day he had been to Fowey, visiting the herbalist's shop where Jane had worked before taking on the unit. The young woman who was now the assistant there - a pretty if somewhat vacuous girl - had been only too happy to talk to him in the absence of the shop owner. Admittedly, he had shamelessly flirted with her, but he had at least found out as much as he could have hoped for: the shop was open every day except Sunday and the girl was allowed one day off during the week, though it was an ad hoc arrangement and the day varied. He had to assume that it had been the same for Jane. She might have been working the day Gilly disappeared or she might not. Short of asking her, there was no way of knowing.

Now walking up the path to Jane's front door, he wondered what exactly he hoped to achieve here. Jane hadn't been living in this house when she worked in Fowey. If she had taken Gilly, where had she been keeping the girl until now and how had she brought her here without being seen? He stopped and looked round. No, it could be done in a place as remote as this, especially at night. He didn't think it likely but it was possible.

He walked round to the back of the house. The central section of the garden had been developed in a circular design with narrow gravel paths separating wedges of cultivation. At a glance he guessed the plants were mostly herbs of some kind. To one side was an old timber shed with a window on one side and a rusty bolt on the door. He pulled it back and glanced inside. It was full of garden tools and bags of compost and he shut it up again and returned to the house, peering in through the rear windows. He saw nothing of any significance and wasn't sure he expected to.

'Gilly?' he called out diffidently, then a second time.

There was no answering sound. A crow in a nearby tree cawed into the silence, making him look round sharply, nerves on edge. According to Claire though, the house had a cellar which might be more promising. When she'd visited the house as a kid, she had been down to its gloomy depths once or twice. Jane's mother had mostly used it to store coal for the fire. So maybe there was a coal chute somewhere?

He found it. At the side of the house, half hidden beneath dead leaves and grit, was an embossed metal cover. He picked up a long, flat stone to work into the notch and managed to lift it. The chute cover was attached by a chain to an inner wall but it allowed access to a narrow channel, maybe ten inches across, which dropped down into the bowels of the house. Again, Adam spoke Gilly's name but there was no answering sound from the cellar, nothing that suggested any life force.

He replaced the metal cover, glanced back up at the house and decided to leave. This was getting him nowhere. He had only come to put Claire's mind at rest. The more he thought about it, the more he was convinced that Jane was just a sad character who channelled her loneliness and frustrations into her oddball work. She was harmless.

*

Claire remembered Meg Poldreen as being petite, softly spoken and a little fragile. She wondered if she would still recognise her; it had been a while. There was no one at the counter when she walked into the library in Lostwithiel, and she glanced round. There were a couple of people working their way along the shelves of books and someone else on a computer. Then a woman came towards the counter pushing an empty book trolley and Claire knew her straight away as Meg. She had a weary, anxious air and had filled out but she still had the same open, easy features and her hair, though shorter, was still dark and wavy. She smiled and came forward.

'Hello,' said Claire. 'I wanted to join the library. How do I do it?'

'It's easy. Have you got some proof of identity with your address on? A driving licence maybe?'

'Er no, not on me.'

'Never mind. I'll give you the form and you can do it again and drop it in.'

'Thanks.'

Meg went behind a counter, extracted a form and held it out.

'You're Meg, aren't you,' said Claire. 'I thought I recognised you. We used to live opposite each other in Bohenna. I'm Claire. Claire Pennyman.'

Meg's eyes opened wider. 'I thought you looked familiar but I couldn't place how. Your hair used to be shorter, didn't it? Straighter?'

Claire laughed. 'Yes. It's naturally curly and I've given

up fighting it now. How are you?'

'Fine, thank you. Busy. We've got three little boys now. A real handful they are but gorgeous all the same. And you?' Her face clouded over. 'Oh, I'm sorry. I remember hearing about your little girl. Terrible thing.'

'Thanks. It's nearly seven years ago already.'

'Yes. I remember the shock. We were away on holiday in Spain when it happened and I was stunned when we got back and heard the news. To think that such a thing would happen in Bohenna.'

'I know. Anyway, thanks for the form. Nice to see you again.'

Leaving the library, Claire felt deflated again. It had been much easier to find out what she wanted than she had expected but, still, it was another dead end and Richard Poldreen had seemed such a promising lead. She hoped Adam was faring better.

*

He wasn't. Adam had established that the bakers George Foster used to deliver for no longer traded and he didn't know where else to find out if the man was in the village on the afternoon of Gilly's disappearance. He could ask him, of course. 'Excuse me, George. You didn't happen to abduct a little girl that afternoon, did you?' Maybe not.

Then he thought of Trish. At that time, she had been working in the shop where they stocked pasties and cakes. Someone must have delivered them and it might have been George - how many local bakers were there in a place this size? In any case Trish was observant and paid attention so she might have heard or seen something else that fateful day which might be of use.

Keen to avoid further gossip, this time he went directly to

her house, calling at the shop the following Thursday after work, buying her a small box of chocolates as an offering. Standing on her doorstep a few minutes later, he could see the flicker of the television in her front room and could hear the strident repeated jingle of a quiz show. But there was no answer to the doorbell and he was on the point of ringing a second time when he heard the latch turn and the door opened.

She looked at him balefully. 'Adam. What are you doing here?'

'I've brought you these,' he said gauchely, thrusting the box of chocolates at her. 'I wondered if I could have a word with you?'

'About what?'

'There was something I was hoping to ask you. Something sensitive.'

'Sensitive?' She glanced up and down the lane. 'Then I suppose you'd better come in.'

The front door gave straight into the living room. She hobbled stiffly to the window and closed the curtains.

'Have a seat,' she said.

'Thanks.'

She didn't offer him a drink. Rather, she had a tense, business-like manner and eased herself down into an armchair.

'You've been seeing Claire Hitchen,' she said accusingly.

'We had a meal in the pub one night, yes.'

'I did warn you about that.'

'Yes. But I'm not sure why. She's single now. Anyway, we're only friends.'

She grunted, still looking at him reproachfully.

'You have to live in a village a long time to understand how it ticks,' she said. 'People think cities are more complex because there are more people. It's not true. Villages are insular and passions run deep - everyone is so involved with

180

everyone else. They have to be to survive because everyone needs everyone else - there's no slack.'

'And your point is?'

'If you tread on someone's toe here, someone else will cry out in pain over there. They probably won't even know why. People aren't as logical as they like to think they are.' She sniffed. 'Anyway, what do you want to know?'

'It was about Gilly Pennyman again, the day she disappeared.'

'I don't know why you're getting involved in that.'

'Because I'm intrigued, that's all. I've been reading about it. But the newspaper reports jump around so. There's no substitute for someone like you who's observant.'

'Oh please, Adam. Don't give me the smooth talk. Spit it out.'

'I know the police checked everyone who was close to the family in any way and anyone who was around nearby. But do you remember anything strange that anyone did, perhaps something out of the way or a change of routine maybe?'

'No, I don't think so.'

She looked at him with a flat, blank expression, shutting him out. For the first time he wondered if he could trust her to tell him the truth.

'Do you know George Foster?' hazarded Adam.

'George?' She snorted. 'Of course I know George.'

'He was a delivery driver back then, wasn't he? Did he deliver to the village shop?'

'Yes. Why?'

'Did he deliver that day? I mean, was he around the day Gilly disappeared?'

'It's a long time ago, Adam. But yes, I think so. He used to come every morning with fresh bread and cakes.'

'Maybe he didn't work in the afternoons then.'

181

'Maybe not. I don't know. I can tell you this though: George's weakness is the horses. He can't resist a bet. And he doesn't like it being pointed out to him. Can't even tease him about it; he gets very touchy, probably because he loses a lot more than he wins. Beattie worries about it but she doesn't dare say anything.' She frowned. 'Mind you...' She stopped short.

'What?'

'I did see him once...' She looked across the room as if staring into a great distance. '...standing by the children's playground, watching...' She nodded slowly. 'Yes, he was watching Gilly on the slide.' Her focus returned and she looked across at Adam sharply. 'But that doesn't mean anything. They were neighbours. It's not a crime to watch children play, especially when you know them.'

'Of course not.'

'What do you hope to gain from all these questions?'

'I'm not sure, Trish. But it's a mystery isn't it? And there must be an answer out there somewhere.'

She studied his face. 'Does Claire know you're doing this?'

'No.' It was more or less the truth. She didn't know he was speaking to Trish.

'Well, you're not doing her any favours. There's nothing to be gained but more heartache by going over it all again.'

She struggled to her feet prompting Adam to stand too.

'When I saw you last time,' he said, 'you didn't get round to telling me what Neil Pennyman was like.'

'Perhaps because I don't know him that well.' She hesitated, regarding him warily. 'He was a confident child, I remember. Didn't like things to get in his way. Always got what he wanted, it seemed.'

'Like he got Claire Hitchen?'

'I suppose so.'

'There was something else, Trish. Did you see Jane Sawdy in the village that afternoon? She was working in Fowey around then.'

'I don't remember,' she said firmly, then frowned. 'I did see her at the fête last year, mind, with Neil Pennyman, talking very intense-like, very cosy. I'd forgotten about that.' She gave a dismissive shake of the head. 'Not something you should mention to Claire maybe. She's got enough on her plate, I reckon.'

She hobbled to the door and put her arthritic hand to the catch but didn't turn it.

'You think it was someone in the village,' she said, staring fixedly at the door.

'Yes. Don't you?'

She turned to look at him. 'The thought had crossed my mind.'

'I'd rather you didn't tell anyone I was asking,' said Adam.

'I wouldn't dream of it.'

Trish opened the door and glanced nervously up and down the road before turning back.

'I don't know anything, Adam,' she said earnestly. 'And it's playing with fire to go nosing round like this. You risk upsetting people and upset people do bad things sometimes.'

He left but her agitation was infectious and he glanced up the street cautiously, unsure who he thought might be watching him. There were a couple of children playing outside a house further along and a woman walking her dog on the other side of the road but no-one was watching the house. He shrugged it off and began the walk home, thinking through the little he had learned. Was Jane talking to Neil significant? Not necessarily: they had known each other since childhood. Still, it suggested an ongoing attraction and that bothered him, mostly because of Claire. He was beginning to think that however things fell, she was going to get hurt.

He rang her that evening, heard her news about the Poldreens and gave her a brief summary of what he'd found out - carefully omitting the news about Jane and Neil. He suggested meeting up again to talk it through but she put him off because Laura was coming to stay for Easter.

Adam put the phone down and got himself a can of beer. This investigation was starting to feel uncomfortable. He was alternately fascinated by it and repelled, finding out things he didn't want to know. There were too many interwoven lives in this village. It was like trying to unravel a section of tapestry; he was scared that if he pulled on one thread too hard, the whole thing might come undone.

Chapter 14

Claire's gaze fixed on the tattoo on the side of Travis's neck. It was only small, discreet even, barely showing under his long, wavy hair but even so, illogical and old-fashioned as it might be, she distrusted a man who had tattoos – especially on his neck.

Travis was Laura's boyfriend apparently. This was recent news. Laura had rung just four days before she was due to arrive for the Easter holidays to say she had been invited to stay at the holiday cottage which her boyfriend's parents owned in Brittany. Would Claire mind? His parents would be there too - and his sister and her boyfriend. It was a large cottage in the country but within an easy drive of the sea.

I live within an easy drive of the sea too, Claire felt like pointing out, though of course she didn't live in a large house nor was it in a foreign and therefore inevitably more exotic location.

'We'd come to you first,' Laura had said, sugaring the pill. 'We thought perhaps we could spend three nights with you and then get the ferry from Plymouth.'

'I've only got two bedrooms,' Claire had said, pointedly. What Laura did when she was away from home was something Claire was prepared to ignore - up to a point - but she couldn't imagine her eighteen-year-old daughter sharing the tiny double bedroom next to her own with a boy she had never previously heard of.

'Travis says he's happy to sleep on the sofa.'

'And his parents are happy with this arrangement - the holiday, I mean?'

It turned out that they were. It also turned out that the ferry tickets had already been bought and that Neil had paid for Laura's.

'We had to get them early because of the Easter crush,' Laura said apologetically.

'And your father got them?'

'No, he just paid for them.'

'So he knew about this trip a while ago?'

'No-o,' said Laura carefully. 'When I said early, I just meant in advance. Dad rang me when we were still discussing what we might do and I mentioned it. That's why he offered to buy the ticket.'

Claire's approval, it seemed, was a rubber-stamping exercise. But she could hear the defensiveness in the girl's voice and didn't want Laura feeling like a blunt weapon in a battle between her warring parents. Disappointed at having so little time with her daughter and with having to share her with this unknown man, still Claire gave in gracefully, aware that she had little choice. And now here they were.

In fairness, Travis was a good-looking boy with tidy - and clean - dark hair and lively eyes. He smiled readily, said all the right things and insisted he didn't want to put Claire out. Over the course of the two days the youngsters spent in her house, he washed dishes, cleared up his bedding after himself and brought in wood for the stove. Claire noticed that he treated Laura well and he was charming to them both. By the time they left her on Palm Sunday morning, he had won her over, leaving her to wonder, a little uneasily, if he always got his own way so readily. But Laura looked happy with him so

186

Claire couldn't fault him. Watching them cuddling up together on the sofa or snatching a kiss when they thought she wasn't looking, brought back memories of herself and Neil when they had been young and in love, memories which had lost none of their warmth despite the events of recent years.

Putting bedding and linens to wash after they'd gone, those early years with Neil ran through her mind again. She hugged the images close even though each one seemed to bring its own particular pain. How come we never understand that we're having the best times of our lives when they're happening, she thought despondently. It's only afterwards, when we wish we could go back, that we realise. Maybe I let Eve and the whole vineyard thing bother me too much. It wasn't really that important, after all.

'But Neil should have told me about Travis,' she said aloud, angrily, pushing the machine door in with a snap and wilfully bursting the rose-tinted bubble of her memories. She turned the dial roughly. 'Always doing things behind my back,' she muttered, and turned away, picking up her phone and ringing Neil's number.

There was no reply and it cut through to the answering service.

'Next time, have the courtesy to let me know that you're helping to ruin all my plans,' she barked into the phone. 'Would it cost you to think about me for once? And did you actually meet Travis before you paid for your daughter's ticket to spend her holiday with the man? Did you really consider her safety or just want to be her darling father?' She ran out of steam and stood, shaking her head. Hadn't she been here before? Was there any point? New start, she reminded herself, trying to calm down. Travis is OK…probably. Save it. She closed the call and walked away.

*

Claire worked through the Easter holidays. She hadn't planned it that way - Penny had reluctantly agreed she could have some time off - but, without Laura, time hung heavily on her hands so she helped sort through a van load of goods Penny had bought at a house clearance, relieved to be busy. Having spent most of Maundy Thursday checking through a suitcase of twenties' clothes, she arrived home to find another box of eggs on her doorstep. It seemed she had finally made a connection with Eddie.

It was her birthday and there was a card on the mat, postmarked from Brittany. Laura had rung her earlier and had told her there was a parcel on the way too. She had sounded cheerful, had been unusually chatty, talking about crêpes and sandy beaches and a firework display. Claire was amazed and pleased and a little bit jealous and wished she weren't.

She put the birthday card on the sideboard next to the one her mother had sent from Greece and put a light to the wood in the stove, then went to get changed. Standing in the kitchen half an hour later, wondering if she could be bothered to cook a meal, she considered ringing Adam to arrange another meeting. Or should she try and speak to Beattie again about George first? Was there any point?

Her thoughts were broken by the sound of a knock on the front door and she was still frowning when she opened it.

'Happy birthday, Claire,' said Neil.

He pushed a large bunch of flowers at her, prettily wrapped in floral paper. She didn't take them and his shoulders dropped.

'Please Claire, I'm sorry. I got your message. I'm sorry about the mix up. It was an honest mistake. I didn't realise I was messing up your plans. I thought Laura had told you all about it.' He looked at her pleadingly. He had nice eyes, Neil: deep ocean-blue wells, long-lashed, expressive. 'Please Claire. Happy birthday *and* a peace offering.'

She sighed and took the flowers. They were her favourites: a mix of carnations, lilies, roses and gypsophila. And now he was holding up a brown paper carrier in his other hand.

'There's a new Chinese restaurant opened in Penmarna. I heard it was quite good and they do take-away so…' He raised his eyebrows in an exaggerated way like a shocked clown. '…I thought maybe you'd like a celebratory Chinese?'

It had been one of their favourite treats, a Chinese takeaway, back when the children had been very young and went to bed early. They'd sit at the table with all the foil cartons spread out before them, picnic-style, and drink white wine. Pennyman wine, of course.

'Didn't it occur to you that I might have something else planned for tonight?' she said.

'Yes.' He hesitated, glanced towards the room behind her. 'But I suppose I hoped not. Have you?'

'Why Neil? Why are you doing this?'

He shrugged. 'I'm not sure. But when I remembered that it was your birthday I just thought I'd like to celebrate it with you. Would you mind?'

'It's not long ago you didn't want to spend any time with me.'

'That's not entirely true, Claire. I was just…confused.'

'Oh come on, Neil. Don't give me that.'

'You said you wanted the divorce too,' he said defiantly.

'I did. I'd had enough. You forced me to it.'

'You forced me to it.'

They glared at each other.

'This is ridiculous.' She shook her head despairingly,

almost smiling.

'I know. Truce?' He grinned and held up the brown carrier again.

She pulled the door back.

'Thank you.' He smiled, bent over to pick up the bottle of wine he'd put on the doorstep and walked in.

They sat at her kitchen table and talked while they ate, safe topics like the weather, the upcoming duck race in the village and Dave Spenser's planning application for a huge conservatory on the back of the pub. Neil told her Tim had a new girlfriend but he hadn't met her yet. He mentioned his mother too but only to joke that she'd forgotten that he was forty-four now and didn't need to have his bread cut into soldiers at breakfast. Claire asked about the people they both knew in Kent and if he'd seen them recently; he asked about the Craft Yard and if Claire was enjoying working at V and C. It was very civilised, very safe.

They refilled their glasses with the remaining wine and took it through to the sitting room. He got down on his knees in front of the stove, poking the logs to make them flare up. She sat in the armchair and watched him. He looked very at home in her little cottage but then he had always enjoyed stoking fires.

'Do you remember that chimney fire we had in the first house we rented?' she remarked.

'I'm never likely to forget it, am I?' He got up and installed himself on the sofa. 'We were young and naive. We assumed the chimney would have been swept.'

'Did we even think about it?'

He grinned. 'No. Not really. We just lit the fire.'

They were silent for several minutes, sipping the wine.

'Do you remember that first holiday we had together in St. Mawes?' he asked.

'Of course.'

'It's not far away is it but it felt like another world. So - I don't know - ordinary and yet so much fun. I think the sun shone every day.'

She smiled. 'It did. My shoulders peeled. Then you ate some dodgy prawns on the quayside and spent a day throwing up.'

'Thanks for reminding me. Very romantic.'

Their eyes met; Claire looked away first.

'Why did you come back to Bohenna, Claire?' Neil asked softly.

She looked back at him, surprised. And irritated too. 'Why do you keep going on about it? Bohenna's my home.'

'It was. But your father's passed away and you had friends in Kent and a job. Laura saw it as home. Why come back here?'

'We've been through this. Laura is grown up now and leading her own life. I was always going to come back. I see you've come back. Why did you leave a good job to rejoin the family firm? You always argue, the lot of you, about everything. What was the point?'

'That is the point, isn't it? It's the family firm. It's where I ought to be. But you didn't have a business to come back to. It's not as though you ever took much of an interest in the vineyard.'

'Well, it didn't take long for the old resentments to rear their ugly heads, did it? Bohenna isn't all about the vineyard, Neil. Other lives do go on here.'

His expression set. He took a long draught of wine, fidgeted in the chair, crossed and uncrossed his long legs, looked round the room. Finally, his gaze settled back on her.

'I saw George Foster a couple of days ago,' he said.

Claire's stomach tightened. 'Oh yes?'

'He said you'd been knocking at their door, asking Beattie a load of odd questions about old neighbours and the day Gilly disappeared and the fête, of all things. And everyone in the village seems to be talking about it.'

'What are you getting at Neil?'

'I want to know if that's why you've come back: to start searching for Gilly all over again?' He leaned forward suddenly, elbows on his knees, the wine glass still in his hand. 'Look Claire, I thought you'd got beyond all this. When I saw you at Christmas, I was…I was blown away by how lovely you still are. And you seemed to be so much more your old self. I thought that was why you'd come back: to find yourself again.'

She frowned, mouth open, stunned by his insight.

'I did.'

'So why the questions? Why start it all over again?'

She took her time, playing with the wine glass.

'I have made a fresh start,' she said slowly. 'But I've been touching base with old friends and the fête question was just a silly thing to do with work - I suppose I should have explained that to Beattie. I asked about Gilly on the spur of the moment. You're reading too much into it.'

'Am I? You've been asking Danny questions too. Are you telling me I'm reading too much into that as well?'

'For a family that argues as much as you do, you share a remarkable amount of information.'

'Don't try to change the subject. You always have to blame my family for everything.'

'Of course I don't. And I'd explain about the questions, but I don't see why I have to and you clearly wouldn't believe me whatever I said.'

'OK, OK.' He sat back, raising a hand in mock surrender and letting it fall heavily onto the sofa at his side.

She downed the last of her wine and stood up. 'Look, I'd offer you coffee but I'm working tomorrow and I've got a few things I need to do before bedtime.'

He didn't move. 'You're dismissing me. But I'd like us to talk, Claire.'

'There's nothing to talk about, Neil. Haven't we already said it all…over and over and over? There's nothing new to say.' She hesitated. 'And I'm not sure I can take any more. It wears me down.'

He stood up too and looked at her fondly and, just as he'd done at Christmas, he reached up a hand to finger the curls of her hair.

'I think you really have found yourself again,' he said. 'You're getting your old confidence back; you're…so much more alive again. You know, I've only recently realised just how much I've missed you. I was a fool. I lost my way there for a while. And I'm sorry.'

He bent down and kissed her gently on the lips. Still stooping, looking into her face, he said, 'Happy birthday, Claire,' then bent to kiss her again but she pushed a hand up against his chest, blocking him and stepped back and away.

'What is it?' he said.

'I don't want…' She stopped. What didn't she want? 'I don't want to get hurt again, Neil. It's history now.'

'You mean, we're history?'

'I don't know.'

'I heard that you were seeing someone else. Is it true?'

'I have been out with someone a couple of times.'

'Adam Thomas.'

'Yes.'

'Is it serious?'

'Not yet. But who knows? How can you tell?' Claire moved towards the kitchen. 'Your jacket's on the back of your chair, isn't it?' She returned, clutching it, gave it to him and walked to the front door. She turned the latch and pulled it open. 'Thank you for the flowers, Neil, and the meal. I enjoyed it.'

He joined her by the door.

'I enjoyed it too.'

He didn't move.

'Don't keep looking, Claire. It's time to let the past go. I worry about you.'

'You don't need to.'

'I think I do.'

She frowned, eyes narrowed. 'Do you know something Neil?'

'About what? I don't know what you mean.'

She stared into his face, trying to read him but she had never found that easy.

'It doesn't matter,' she said and, after a few moments, he left.

An hour later, getting undressed in her bedroom, she heard the house phone ringing downstairs. Her first thought was of Laura but when she picked it up to answer it, no-one spoke. Someone was there though, breathing into the mouthpiece in an exaggerated way, wanting to be heard. She repeated the number and when still there was no reply she hung up and rang 1471 to find out who it was, heart thumping. The number had been withheld. It had happened before.

Chapter 15

The crisp spring sunshine over the Easter break brought droves of tourists back to Bohenna and the Craft Yard buzzed with people. In the preceding month, Tim had employed a landscaper to clear an area of ground beyond the Yard, laying it out as a children's playground with swings, a climbing frame and a slide. It was proving very popular. He had also restarted his tours of the vineyard though the vines were still in bud, the possibility of grapes as yet only an exercise of the imagination.

In the corner of Adam's studio stood a rack of prints of his work in assorted sizes, and greetings cards too, items he could sell inexpensively to passing trade. But with no-one else to help, selling them was a distraction, as were the endless questions and remarks about his work and his wary observation of young children's inquisitive fingers on both his paintings and his work table. So much for open studios, he thought. It was hard to concentrate to get anything constructive done and, though the issue often crossed his mind, he had little time or energy to consider his next move in the search for information about Gilly. And there was also the small matter of the commission from the Pennymans, something for which he had as yet done little preparation and which, with time passing all too swiftly, began to concern him. There was a pressing need to do more sketches and to plan the painting.

On the Wednesday after Easter, frustrated and crabby

with the crush of people milling disinterestedly in and out of his studio, he closed it up, grabbed his rucksack, camera and sketch materials, and wandered off towards the vineyard.

A brisk breeze tugged at his jacket but the weather looked set fair, the bright, clear sky broken only by a scatter of scudding white clouds. Adam turned right before the restaurant and trod purposefully down the side of the nearest field of vines. If by some freak chance he ran into Eve, he planned to apologise for trespassing and pass his presence off as a speculative sketching exercise. He crossed down into the next field, branched left at the bottom near the riverside woods and headed east above the treeline, glancing back frequently, trying to keep track of where he was in relation to the vantage point chosen for the commission.

It was nearly eleven o'clock by the time he reached it and sun bathed the front of the house and cast dancing shadows from the wind-blown trees. Perfect. It was a relief, too, to be out in the fresh air and alone. For more than an hour and a half he worked, sketching, scribbling notes to himself and taking photographs as back up. Around half twelve he heard the throaty grumble of a tractor engine and Phil came into view, chugging up and down the rows of vines, spreading something around their woody stems. Seeing Adam he drew the tractor to a halt nearby, killed the engine and climbed down to join him.

'Painting?' he enquired.

'Drawing. Planning the painting. Do you want me to move? I've nearly finished anyway.'

'In a minute maybe.'

Phil pulled a packet of cigarettes out of his pocket and offered one to Adam. Though the packaging was conventional, the cigarettes looked home-made.

'No thanks. I don't.'

'You're sure now? These aren't your regular cigarettes, if

196

you get my meaning. All my own work.' Phil produced a wry grin.

'Nah, thanks all the same. I've never found anything I can smoke yet which agrees with me.'

'And you a painter? I thought all artists were bohemian types, liked this kind of thing.' Phil looked disappointed and lit a cigarette for himself, cupping the flame from his lighter to protect it from the breeze. He took a hard drag, watching Adam through narrowed eyes.

'You mean you thought we all smoked and drank to excess and took our models as mistresses?'

'Somethin' like that.' Phil took another drag and visibly appeared to relax into his skin. 'How's it going?' He nodded towards the sketches.

'Early days really. But I'll be able to start the painting soon with these.'

'May's the birthday bash. Not long for it to dry is it?'

'I use water-based paints and collage, not oils. It won't be a problem.'

Phil grunted again and nodded. 'I don't understand anything about painting.'

'I sometimes wonder if I do,' said Adam laconically. He glanced in the direction of the tractor. 'Spreading weed-killer?'

'Fertiliser. Makes the buggers grow and keeps 'em strong, helps 'em shrug off pests.'

'I don't know anything about vines.' Adam grinned. 'But I appreciate the wine that comes from them. Drinking is maybe one thing I *do* do to excess.' He bent down and pulled a chocolate bar out of his rucksack, peeled back the foil and bit off a chunk.

'Settled in Bohenna?' Phil enquired without apparent interest.

'More or less. My girlfriend didn't though. She couldn't hack the quiet.'

'Oh? But I heard you were dating Claire Pennyman these days.' Phil took another pull on his cigarette and looked at Adam curiously. 'Or is she calling herself Hitchen again now?'

Naively, Adam hadn't expected this line of conversation but, sensing an opportunity, he thought on his feet.

'The subject of her surname hasn't come up,' he said. 'I guess you knew her when you were kids then, before she got married.'

'Ah.' Phil sucked on his cigarette ruminatively. 'Known her pretty much all my life.'

'Has she changed much?'

Phil's lip curled ruefully. 'Suppose we all have.' He tapped the ash from the end of the cigarette. 'I haven't seen much of her lately. She used to be…' He hesitated, apparently struggling to find the right word. 'Claire always had to be doing. A force of nature she was. Used to roam, chasing crickets, paddling in the pond to get close to the tadpoles, beatin' us lads at our own games.' A smile tugged at his mouth and he brushed the back of his fingers across the rapidly growing stubble on his cheek. 'She was a case.'

This chatty side to Phil was a novelty. On the odd occasion Adam had seen him with the Pennymans he'd said barely a couple of words. Though he dimly recalled seeing the man in the pub before Christmas, singing a succession of carols at the top of his voice, being teased about it and then told to give it a break. He'd had quite a voice. He'd also looked like he'd had a serious skinful.

'Suppose Bohenna must have been a good place to grow up in,' Adam remarked blandly. 'I grew up on the outskirts of a city. Didn't have much freedom to run around there. Not that safe to wander either.' He pulled a face as if suddenly remembering. 'Though of course Claire's kid disappeared here too so I guess it's the same everywhere. But more surprising in a place this size that nothing's come to light.' Adam chewed on another piece of chocolate, surreptitiously watching his companion's face. Phil's expression closed down immediately.

'Ah. It was bad, that.'

Adam nodded, still chewing.

'Claire's told you all about it, I suppose?' Phil glanced up slyly at Adam's face.

'Nah, not really. Not the sort of thing you talk about when you first date, is it? Makes it difficult for me though 'cause I don't really know what happened.'

'And yet she's been going round askin' questions about that day it happened.' Again the crafty look. 'So it must be on her mind.'

'Has she?'

The wind was getting stronger. Phil held the stub of his cigarette cupped in his hand as he drew on it, fixing his now dreamy gaze on Adam. His pupils had markedly dilated. Adam recognised the signs: he'd smoked a reefer or two in his time. He knew the high it could make you feel, the relaxation, the expansiveness; he'd also found that, afterwards, he didn't always remember much about it and later he'd felt ill and been really bad-tempered.

'Can you remember what happened exactly?' Adam hazarded.

'There's nothing much to know.' Phil blew smoke up in a column which the wind immediately whipped away. 'Gilly came home from school, went out to play with our Danny. He stayed for a bit then came home and she never came back. She was like Claire for wandering, see. But she was...trickier.'

'Trickier? How do you mean?'

'Oh, I dunno. Dead stubborn sometimes and she answered back. Kid stuff. You know, pushin' it to see what she could get away with. And nosy too. Always wanted to know what people were doin' and why. Neil used to get real cross with her for it - quick to lose it is our Neil. But she liked her own way - it's likely she got that from him though he probably didn't see it.'

Phil took a last drag on his cigarette, then trod it into the ground at his feet.

'Better get on,' he said shortly and swung himself back up into the tractor.

Adam pulled his things out of the way to let the tractor pass and watched Phil drive on down the row. It occurred to him that, working in these sloping fields, Phil had a good view of the vineyard and a lot of the village beyond. Had he seen anything the day Gilly disappeared? If she had wandered along the river or into the vineyard, wouldn't Phil have been likely to know? Did that mean she hadn't come near? And was he making some particular point about Neil, a veiled accusation for some reason? Of course, it was his own son who had been playing with Gilly that day. Perhaps that was significant. Maybe he was covering for his son? Or himself? But all the family had alibis, didn't they?

Adam finished up his last sketches and notes and packed his things away. Phil's tractor had marched its way up and down the remaining rows on that field and had moved on. Adam thought he'd heard it drive up to the top. It was after one now so probably lunch time. He trudged up himself, all the conflicting ideas and questions swirling in his brain. Along with his conviction that Gilly must have known whoever abducted her, it occurred to him that the vineyard - central to the village in so many ways and effectively her back yard - might hold the key to her abduction. The police would have searched it of course, but the words 'needle' and 'haystack' came to mind. The place was extensive and widely spread - so how easy would it be for anyone else to do better?

*

Claire had baked a cake. She had spent all Saturday morning in the kitchen and now had one cherry cake and two types of biscuits to show for her effort, all cooling. This was exceptional: she had never been a big baker. When the girls were small and she was still doing her illustrations, between working, caring for the girls and running round after Neil, there had never been the time. It had never bothered her - she wasn't naturally domesticated in that way - but she had sometimes felt guilty when the girls had been asked to take something to school. She could tell from their shifting eyes and disappointed expressions that she was probably the only mother who sent them off clutching a supermarket sponge, still in its box.

But Eddie kept leaving eggs on her doorstep and it had become embarrassing. She wanted to give him something in return and she had settled on a cake while the biscuits were an afterthought in a sudden and unexpected flurry of enthusiasm. Now she was icing the cake, trying to mask its slightly lop-sided shape, decorating it with glacé cherries, then wrapping it loosely in foil.

Eddie was in the garden when she walked round, wielding a hoe around his neatly regimented strawberry plants. Claire waited by his back door and called his name and he hobbled across to her with a puzzled and suspicious expression. She nodded at the foil-wrapped plate.

'I made a cake using your eggs. For you.' He didn't immediately respond. 'Shall I put it in the kitchen?'

He reached out two soil-rimed hands and took it off her,

201

stared down at the parcel then looked into her face. He nodded, just once, didn't quite smile, and walked inside, clutching his gift.

Returning to her own kitchen, Claire found Timothy there, standing vulture-like over the biscuits.

She jumped and put a hand to her chest. 'Tim. You frightened me.'

'Sorry. The door was open.' He flicked a meaningful look at the biscuits. 'I was wondering if I could try one?'

'Of course...' She closed the door behind her. '...if you want to be a guinea pig. But I don't know what they'll taste like. They certainly don't look like that in the book.'

He picked one up, took a bite and smiled. 'Delicious.' He crammed the rest of it in his mouth and chewed with affected relish. 'Special occasion?' he said, swallowing. 'Baking for someone in particular? I had heard you were going out with Adam, our local Van Gogh.'

'Of course you had. Hasn't everybody?'

'It's Bohenna, Claire.'

'Mm. Coffee?'

'If you're having one.' He looked back at the biscuits. 'Can I try one of the others?'

'Be my guest.'

She picked up one of the burnt ones from the edge of the tray and ate it while she filled the kettle. It was certainly crunchy.

'I should call more often,' said Tim. He dropped onto one of the wooden chairs by the table and grinned. 'Does my brother get treated to these too?'

'We're divorced, Tim. The final decree came through this week.'

'I know. I was only teasing. Neil said he'd had a meal with you on your birthday, that's all. Like old times, eh?'

202

She was aware of him scanning her face, checking her reaction.

'I don't think I'd have described it that way.'

'No…well.' He glanced round. 'OK here are you? It's a bit dark down this end of the village. Don't you find the trees a bit spooky at night?'

'Not really. I know these trees well, remember.' She spooned instant coffee into two mugs and poured hot water on it. 'Neil said you've got a new girlfriend.'

'Yes. Shannon. Nice girl. Shy though. Haven't risked taking her up to the house yet.'

'Why? Think Eve might eat her? Of course, if her face doesn't fit…' Claire added milk to the mugs and carried them across to the table. 'Is she from the village?'

'No. Fowey.'

She nodded and sipped her coffee.

'We don't see much of you at the vineyard,' he said.

'No, I haven't used the restaurant much these last few weeks.'

'Or called to see us.'

'That's not going to happen, is it Tim?'

'You could.'

'I'm sure Eve would love that.'

He shrugged and drank his coffee. 'Y'know, if you'd made an effort with mum early on, you could have won her over. You were too proud.'

'Is that what it was?'

'You don't think so?'

Claire drank too, considering this. 'I don't know. Maybe. There've been a lot of things I should have done over the years that I haven't. But in your mum's case, I just think she didn't like me. We got off on the wrong foot early on.'

He didn't respond and they sat in silence for some

203

minutes. Claire was convinced he had come for a reason. She waited.

'There was something I wanted to run past you,' he said eventually. He glanced up at her with the coy lift of an eyebrow. 'We've applied for planning permission to extend the shop. We're going to sell gifts as well as the wine so we'll need more space.'

Then he produced his undoubtedly winning smile. He could be very charming, Tim, when he chose.

She found herself smiling back. 'And you're telling me this because…?'

'Because I thought you might like to come and run it for us.' Again the smile. 'You're used to retail. I was speaking to Penny the other day and she seems very happy with your input - you know, the creative eye in arranging goods, stuff like that.'

'Should I be flattered or cross that you're going behind my back talking to Penny about me?'

He looked surprised. 'Flattered, I suppose.'

'And did you tell Penny you were thinking of poaching me?'

'Of course not. Give me more credit than that. But I thought you'd be pleased at the thought of running the shop yourself. That's promotion, isn't it? I'm sure we'll pay you more than Penny does.'

She read something condescending in the tone and bridled.

'Neil put you up to this didn't he? He keeps fussing over whether I've got enough money.'

'Everything doesn't revolve around Neil, Claire,' he said coldly, 'though I know he gives that impression. This was my idea. I was trying to be helpful. If you're not interested, say so.'

She was taken aback at his sudden change in tone; he'd never spoken to her like that before.

'You were the one who brought Neil up first,' she retaliated, feeling childish. 'As for the job...well, I don't know. I'd like to think about it. When do you need to know?'

He drank the last of his coffee and stood up. He shrugged benignly, his anger already dissipated, it seemed.

'There's no immediate hurry. The permission isn't through yet but that won't be a problem. We thought Laura might like to work there too in her holidays. We'll need seasonal staff.'

'I'll tell her.' She stood up too, hesitated, swallowed her pride. 'Thank you. I'm sorry Tim. I am grateful for the offer.'

'Forget it.' He hesitated. 'You know Claire, we all walk in Neil's shadow to some extent.' He paused, appearing to choose his words carefully. 'Even if we don't agree with everything he does. Generally, it's easier to go with the flow.'

He smiled and left and she stared after him, frowning.

*

Adam received a text from Claire suggesting a meal and a chat the following Saturday evening, somewhere out of the village. He came up with The Fox, a pub in Penmarna which had developed a bit of a reputation for its food but when they got there, the place was heaving and there was nowhere to sit, let alone eat.

'I thought you said you'd book,' said Claire.

'I forgot. I'm sorry. I didn't think it would be an issue.'

They went back outside.

'There's nowhere else in Penmarna,' he said, feeling guilty. 'We'll have to drive somewhere else.'

'Everywhere'll be busy by this time on a Saturday.'

'Sorry.'

'Never mind, it doesn't matter.'

They stood. Adam swung his car keys back and forth between his fingers.

'There's the chip shop,' she said. 'They used to do a great fish and chips there. We can talk while we sit in the car to eat them.'

They bought cod and chips each and sat in the village car park eating with tiny wooden forks while the car windows slowly steamed up. Adam glanced across at Claire a couple of times. She was quieter than usual, preoccupied perhaps. Maybe there was an issue with Neil.

'So we can rule out Richard Poldreen?' he said, in an attempt to kick-start the discussion.

'Yes.'

'I'm not really sure about George. I went for a walk on that footpath up above the estate and you can see George's back garden from there. Well, you can with binoculars anyway. I watched him pottering about. He's got a shed but the door was wide open and he was wandering in and out of it, really casual. Gilly could be shut up in the house but it doesn't seem likely. The police must have searched all the houses nearby so where would they have put her?'

He looked at her sideways. 'George had been seen watching Gilly at the village playground, you know.'

Claire quickly turned to look at him. 'I didn't know that. Who told you?'

'I have sources,' he replied cautiously. 'It could have been quite innocent. Lots of people like to see children play, especially if they know them. Most of them aren't paedophiles, thank God.' He broke off a piece of fish and flicked Claire a reluctant glance. 'Of course, we keep talking about sheds and things, assuming that she's still alive.' He hesitated. 'We have to consider the possibility that she isn't Claire.'

'I know.' She stared ahead into the darkness, tight-lipped. 'And if she's dead she could be buried anywhere.'

'I'm afraid so.'

The car filled with a choking silence.

'And you're sure there's nothing to suggest Jane might have been involved?' Claire said.

'Yes. I asked around - carefully - and I checked out her house but there was nothing to implicate her. I think she's just a harmless head-case, Claire.'

'It's not so harmless when you play on people's grief and pain,' she said bitterly.

'No. Of course, you're right. It's not.'

They finished eating without speaking, rolling up the paper into tight balls which Adam threw in the litter bin nearby. He offered to take her back to his place so they could figure out what to do next and ten minutes later they were driving up a narrow lane on the fringe of Bohenna and turning sharp right onto a weed-ridden drive. When he turned the car beam off, the world went suddenly black; there wasn't the light of another house in sight.

'Sorry,' he said. 'I keep forgetting to fix the outside light. Stay here while I put one on.'

Inside, he sent her into the sitting room while he went to get their drinks. It was his tidiest room - a square space with a long low fire surround of flat grey stones and an overpowering matching chimney breast. And Zoe's softening touches were still there because he couldn't bear to part with them: pale floral curtains; a colourful rag rug in front of the hearth; a framed board on the wall with diamond elastics holding a disorganised arrangement of photographs.

When Adam walked in to join her, Claire was standing studying the photos. He handed her a glass of wine and stood at her shoulder, surveying the pictures too though he knew them all too well. There were photos of waves crashing on the shore jostling with moody pictures of both the village and the river. And there were snaps too: him standing on the beach pulling silly faces; Zoe pointing two fingers at a seagull on a wall as if preparing to shoot it; Zoe again, giggling at something and holding a hand up to the camera. And a photo of the two of them together, his arm around her shoulder.

'You probably think I'm stupid to still have them up,' he said.

'It's nothing to do with me. But it can't be easy to keep looking at them.' She looked sideways at him. 'She's a pretty girl.'

He dropped into a chair and put a bottle of beer to his mouth, taking a long pull. 'Yes, she is,' he said tersely. 'And it's not easy to take them down either. Have a seat.'

They sat, cradling their drinks, silent.

'I don't know what to do next, Adam,' Claire said eventually.

'I know. We're not getting anywhere at the moment, are we?' He shook his head lugubriously. 'They make it look so easy in those cop shows, don't they?' He purposely avoided meeting her eye. 'I know you don't want to but I think we have to at least consider the family again.'

'Oh come on, Adam. They were all accounted for.'

'But something might have been missed.'

She shrugged. 'OK. If you want. Whatever it takes.'

'Let's start with Neil. The papers said he was late back from a business trip?'

'He was. He got stuck in traffic. There was an accident on the A road - the one which passes Stonehenge - and the queues were backed up for miles. He didn't get back till nearly seven. The police checked and there was a huge hold up.'

'Right. But it's not conclusive is it? He could have been

anywhere. Don't look at me like that. What about Timothy?'

'Tim was with dad. He often visited the nursery at the end of the afternoon. They got on well. Sometimes he'd help out with an odd job and then they'd have tea together. When I rang dad to ask if he'd seen Gilly, they both started looking for her.'

'Hang on. I need a map so I can place everyone.'

He stretched an Ordnance Survey map out on the rug in front of the fireplace and they both got down on the floor, bending over it. Claire stabbed a finger at her father's nursery which had still been there when the map was drawn.

'Tim was here.'

'And Julia was…where, in the winery?'

'No. She was with Phil, having tea up at the house.' She put her finger on The White House. 'Eve was at the hairdresser's. That would have taken her a while because she goes to one in Lostwithiel. She doesn't like the gossip that goes on in the village hairdresser's - thinks they all talk about her as soon as she's gone.'

'She's probably right. So Julia and Phil are each other's alibi? There was no-one else at the house with them?'

'I think Danny was at the house but he'd probably have been in his room.' She pointed to the extension at the back. 'Bit of a loner. Plays sometimes for hours by himself.'

Adam stared at the map. 'And that's Tim's house there, isn't it?' Adam pointed further along the ridge from the main house. 'Did he have a girlfriend or anyone else staying there?'

'Not then, no.'

Adam nodded thoughtfully and took another pull of beer.

'You see?' said Claire. 'There's nowhere to go with this.'

'Laura was at school?'

'In Fowey. She came back on the school bus. It dropped her here, just this side of the bridge. You must have seen it – it's the only place it stops in Bohenna. She didn't see anything though. She asked where Gilly was when she got home.'

'Someone suggested Neil used to get cross with Gilly. Is that true?'

'Nothing out of the way,' she said guardedly. 'Who said that?'

He hesitated. 'Phil.'

'Why would he say that? Neil was just a typical dad. I mean…' She sighed. '…Gilly did annoy him sometimes. She didn't always do what he asked her as quickly as he'd have liked. He can be impatient. He wouldn't have hurt her though, Adam. He loved her.'

He grunted ambiguously. 'The problem is: no-one seems to have a motive.'

'They haven't. Gilly was a livewire but everyone liked her. Julia used to take her round the winery, showing her how things worked. Tim used to play with her up at the nursery in the afternoon. Even Eve spoilt her.'

'And Phil?'

'He never bothered much with either of the girls. Ploughs his own furrow does Phil.'

Adam finished his beer, staring at the map. 'So Danny left Gilly at the playground. She could have gone along the footpath to the bridge. Then where? Up the river to the next bridge or even the waterfall?'

'Or she could have crossed the bridge and headed west.' Claire pointed in among the woods on the northern bank. 'Libby's Wood. There's a pond there that gets damselflies and dragonflies in the summer.' She looked back up at him. 'But there's nothing else there. The truth is, she could have gone anywhere.'

Kneeling, Adam bent over, letting his gaze wander over the map, at the clusters of buildings each side of the river, at the woods which book-ended them and the countless footpaths weaving in and out of it all. 'I don't know. There must be something we're missing.' He sighed, feeling dispirited and tired, and sat back on his heels. 'You don't think Laura knows something she's not telling?'

'No,' she replied hotly. 'If Laura knew what had happened to Gilly, she'd have said. They were really close.' She shook her head with frustration. 'We're just talking ourselves round in circles. It's pointless.'

He felt her eyes on him, waiting for him to contradict her but he couldn't. He had raised her hopes with his self-important sleuthing and it was she who was going to suffer the most now his little game had come to nothing. He should have known better. He felt bad.

'I'll put some music on,' he said, getting up.

He put on *Prélude à l'après-midi d'un faune* by Débussy - music which he always found soothing - and they dropped the subject and talked desultorily of nothing in particular. Then Claire mentioned, casually, that Neil had turned up at her door with a take-away though what she thought about it wasn't clear.

'I thought there was something on your mind,' he said.

'Neil isn't on my mind,' she insisted, a little too vehemently. She hesitated. 'I had a silent phone call before I came out. Not the first either. Someone's trying to spook me.'

He leaned forward. 'Who?'

'I don't know. That's the point. They don't speak. There's just heavy breathing.'

'You should tell the police.'

'Maybe. But it's probably just some moron who thinks it's funny. I'm not going to be intimidated. The police won't believe me anyway.'

She finished her wine and stood up.

'I'd better go. Thanks for the drink.'

'I'll give you a lift.'

'I'd rather walk, thanks. The air'll do me good.'

He walked with her to the door, lifted a hand to open it but waited, fingering the door catch.

'Sometimes,' he said, 'if I'm really upset about something, I get a sheet of paper and paint it out of my system. There's no plan, I just daub paint on and let the emotion drive it. Colours, shapes…' He shrugged. '…whatever comes out. It can help. Maybe you should try it. Put it on the paper so it doesn't mess with your head.'

'Thanks, but I don't think that would work for me. In any case, I don't have any paints any more.'

'I'll drop some off at V and C then, just in case. Don't be disheartened, Claire. I know we've hit a bit of a wall but we'll think of something.'

'Of course we will.'

She smiled and leaned across to give him a brief kiss on the cheek. He wanted to hug her, tell her it would be all right, but didn't. He didn't think it was true.

He stood on the doorstep and watched her walk down the road. The clouds had cleared and half a waxing moon shed a bleak, white light. He thought about the silent phone calls and, on an impulse, grabbed his jacket and torch and followed her, being careful to keep well back. He wanted to be sure she got home safely.

Reaching Long Lane, she turned right and he held back. She was walking more slowly than usual. The energy she had radiated over these last few weeks seemed to have evaporated and she had an idle, empty air. There was no sign of anyone around though, just the usual night-time sounds: a scuffle under a hedge; the creak of a tree branch shifting; the plaintive hoot of an owl. Nothing sinister. Adam began to think he was fussing but he'd follow her to her house anyway.

He watched her walk up the path to her front door, put her key in the lock and go inside. A light came on.

He was about to turn away when a noise attracted his attention and he looked round sharply. It had come from the trees and sounded like wood cracking underfoot. As he stared, just for a moment, picked out in the dim moonlight, he saw a dark figure standing in the fringe of the woods, facing towards the house.

Then a cloud drifted over the moon and he could see nothing. He swore under his breath and directed his torch that way but the beam was too weak. He moved closer, flicking the light side to side, picking out his path, trying to keep a fix on where the figure had been standing.

'Hey,' he called out.

All he could hear was the distant call of a tawny owl. He edged further into the wood, shining the torch beam around wildly but saw nothing. A patch of ground that looked a little flattened maybe. Or had the whole thing been a trick of the moonlight? There were some old tree stumps here. Perhaps his imagination had given one of them form.

He abandoned the woods and went home. He thought he'd been brave enough for one night. But maybe it would be wiser if Claire stopped her searching after all.

Chapter 16

Up at the vineyard, the Pennymans had spent much of April bottling, corking and labelling, first the white wines, then the red. Then the bottles had to be boxed and labelled, stacked and stored or sent out to retailers. Even with the new bottling machine, it needed as many of them as possible, working as a unit, to keep the process as smooth and efficient as possible. Julia both loved it and hated it. It was the culmination of everything they had worked for all year but it was a nerve-wracking time too. She worried that the wines wouldn't be as well received as the previous year's, that perhaps she hadn't got the blend of varieties quite right. She would only relax when the first reviews came in. At least, she hoped she would.

Neil had been surprisingly supportive and she was grateful. She had almost forgotten what a hard-worker he could be, and efficient too, and his extra help these last days had been invaluable, especially since Phil had not been on his best form. Maybe her brother's return was going to work out after all.

On the last day of the month, with the bottling finally done, Eve called one of her regular meetings. She held them at the end of an afternoon in the dining room of the White House, sitting round the big oak table. It sometimes amused and sometimes irritated Julia that her mother behaved as if they were all executives of a huge multinational company rather than a small, family-run vineyard.

As usual, Julia was the last to arrive and she slid into the vacant seat next to Tim who offered her a brief, welcoming smile. Eve sat at the head of the table as she always did and Neil now sat to her right. His positioning wasn't lost on Julia: Eve's 'right hand man.'

'Thank you Julia,' Eve said drily. 'Now we can get down to business.' She worked slowly through a list of items she had prepared on a sheet of paper, asking for occasional comment, passing on feedback. Julia let it wash over her, answering questions when necessary, her mind too full now of the sparkling wine she wanted to start fermenting.

'And lastly,' Eve was saying, 'we have the possibility of buying more land for the business. There are two separate lots, I believe, which Neil has brought to my attention. Neil, you said you had a map of where the land is?'

Julia sat up straighter.

Neil bent down, pulled several sheets of paper out of a document wallet by the side of his chair and passed one to each person at the table.

'We'd have to do some tests on the soil et cetera before committing to buy,' said Eve, 'but first perhaps we should discuss the issues.' She looked to her right. 'Neil, would you like to start the ball rolling?'

'Yes, thank you.' He stood up. 'Well, of course the vineyard is doing well; no-one could deny that. And I know I haven't been here these last years so I'm sure it feels like I have a cheek to come in suggesting change. It's not criticism in any way.' He glanced towards Julia. 'The whole vineyard: the wine, the tours, the restaurant and now the Craft Yard - it's all going well, isn't it? But having been away I've had the opportunity to see how other people work and some of the latest developments and it seems to me that we're going to

215

have to change to keep up. We can't afford to keep doing so much manually. We'll have to mechanise or we won't cope. It's a basic tenet of business that you have to grow or you fail.'

'Do you know, I've never understood that,' remarked Tim lightly, and received a glare from his mother for interrupting.

'Buying more land and growing more grapes is the obvious next step,' Neil continued, 'and will make mechanisation more cost-effective. I believe we should buy these lots and keep an eye out for more when they come along, even if they're at a distance. We'll be able to experiment with new varieties and a bigger vineyard will be more competitive in every way.'

'Thank you, Neil. Julia?'

Julia hesitated and saw everyone turn her way. She stood up as Neil sat down.

'It won't surprise any of you to know that I disagree. You know my approach to the business. There's no way we can ever compete in quantity with the huge vineyards, however many little parcels of land we manage to grub up. The terrain around here just isn't suitable for large-scale production. In any case, our strength is the quality of our wine and that comes from attention to detail and a hands on approach, both of which will rapidly go by the board if we try to extend ourselves too far.' She could feel herself getting hotter as anger and passion took hold. 'Our constantly increasing sales and the awards we've won prove the point. I see no need to suddenly abandon a winning formula. We've developed a niche in the market. If we extend and throw out our current practices, there's a huge risk we'll produce inferior wine and our reputation'll suffer. It would amount to business suicide. In any case, don't we make wine because we love it? Do we really want to go for big at the expense of the very thing we've striven so hard to develop: a really top quality set of wines? I don't.'

Phil nodded; Tim was frowning. She sat down.

'That's absurd, Julia,' said Neil. 'You can't seriously be suggesting that all the big vineyards produce inferior wine? You just have to change your approach, develop different skills and practices.'

They continued to argue about it for another half hour, repeating well-worn arguments, going round in circles. Tim took Neil's side; Phil backed up Julia.

'I don't think there's anything left to say,' Eve said, to wrap it up. 'Personally, I'm still undecided but the land isn't being auctioned for another three weeks so we've got time to think about it and discuss it again.'

Eve gathered her papers together and fixed Julia with a strained smile.

'Julia, if I could just have a word?'

Neil, Timothy and Phil glanced at them curiously but left without a word. Eve watched them go.

'It occurred to me while we were discussing the land issue that we should invite Daniel to join us for these meetings sometimes, get him involved and understanding all the issues. After all it's his future at the vineyard we're discussing here.'

Julia frowned. 'He doesn't know enough about the business yet to understand what we're talking about.'

'Well, it's about time he did. I notice I still never see him in the winery. Times moving on. He's got a lot to learn and you're not making it easy for him.'

'Well, I don't...'

'Speak to him Julia - or get Phil to. They're close, aren't they? Now that Neil's back, I'm going to suggest he involve Laura too. It's too much for one person to take on. Your father and I struggled and the place was a much smaller operation then. Of course, Neil will likely meet someone and might still have another family - he's young enough - but that would be for the future.'

'Neil is seeing Claire again,' Julia blurted out. She stared at her mother defiantly. 'I don't think we can assume he'll have more children, or, at least, not by someone else.'

'Claire? No. Are you sure? He hasn't told me.'

'Do you think he tells you everything?'

Eve frowned at her daughter.

'Stop this Julia. I know you think you're in some sort of competition with Neil but you're wrong. You're a good winemaker. But Neil has gifts too and my concern is this vineyard. I've got no time for petty rivalries. Neil told me he'd tried talking to you about the land for sale.' Eve's gimlet eyes bored into her.

'He did say something about it yesterday while we were bottling. I was busy.'

'Don't brush him off, Julia. He knows what he's talking about.'

Julia opened her mouth to speak but Eve kept talking.

'We need to make use of all the talent we've got and we need to be adaptable - and that includes you. Suppose you're not well for some reason? I want us to have back-up. I want this family to work as a unit. And, whether we extend our acreage or not, we need Daniel to show some interest and step up to the plate. Stop being so woolly with him. You're not giving him the opportunities he deserves unless he at least learns what's involved here. You and Phil are just letting him sleepwalk into...what?' She shook her head impatiently. 'At Christmas I heard him tell Claire he wanted to be a bass guitarist. Really? A few months ago, he wanted to be a rugby player. He's aimless. Give him something to focus on for goodness sake. Give him a chance and make him feel wanted here.'

Eve took her papers and stumped out. Julia ran a hand

through her wiry hair so it stuck up, then swore loudly, something she rarely did. She hoped Eve had heard her - swearing wasn't allowed in the house - though it was a pathetic act of defiance. She went back to the yard and found Phil leaning against the winery wall, smoking. He turned as she joined him.

'What did she want?'

Julia gave him a brief summary of Eve's demands, then leant her head on Phil's shoulder.

'God, I'm weary,' she said.

'If we've got the money, maybe we should consider growing and mechanising,' said Phil. 'You do too much.'

She straightened up and shook her head. 'No. I'm fine. It's these battles I could do without.'

She glanced into the winery; it was empty but still she dropped her voice.

'Have you heard any more about Claire?'

'What d'you mean?'

He had that faraway look in his eyes again. She wished he'd stop smoking whatever rubbish it was he rolled up in those cigarettes because it was frying his brain. But she saw his gaze start to focus. Claire's name had done it.

'I wondered if she'd been asking any more questions?'

Phil took another drag on his cigarette, brows furrowed.

'Not that I've heard.' He looked at her accusingly. 'I thought you said Neil was seeing Claire again?'

'He is. I overheard him telling Tim. I told you they'd get back together.'

'But I was talking to that painter bloke a few days ago and he gave the impression he was still seeing Claire. And he said she doesn't talk about Gilly much. But *he* did. He was asking all about what happened to her.'

'Was he?' Their eyes met. 'So what did you tell him?'

'Nothin'. Just what everyone knows…about how she went out to play and didn't come back.'

'Good.'

'For Christ's sake, Julia, what did you think I'd say?'

'I don't know. I just…' She hesitated. 'Anyway it doesn't matter what either of them asks, does it, as long as they don't bother Danny…and we stick to our story.'

'No,' he said slowly, his dark eyes on her face. 'Exactly. So let it go, will you?'

He dropped the stub of his cigarette to the floor, ground it down and wandered off moodily. He had been cutting the grass between the rows of vines and Julia watched him climb back up in the tractor, start the engine and set off down the hill again.

She had often wondered why he hadn't made it up to the house that day for tea but she had never had the courage to ask. And that was assuming he could remember…

*

The village Duck Race was an annual event which took place, come rain or shine, on May Bank Holiday Monday. It was organised, and raised funds for, Bohenna Primary School and Adam found the idea intriguing; he had never been to a duck race before. According to Jane Sawdy – his principal informant – yellow plastic ducks were put in the river just upstream of the road bridge and 'raced' downriver to the finishing line by the end of the village green, as demarcated by bunting stretched across the river. Rather than a number, the children had given each of the ducks a name which was written on the side in indelible ink, and punters paid money to sponsor as many ducks as they could afford. Each race was allowed a limited number of ducks and several heats were run during the afternoon with the ducks collected in a net beyond the

220

finishing line each time and taken back up to the bridge.

Adam was keen to go but most of the Craft Yard units intended to remain open for the afternoon and he was undecided, reluctant to go alone. He had been tempted to ask Claire but she wasn't in V and C. In any case, he had barely seen her since their last meeting, whether by design or chance, he wasn't sure. Then Jane had turned up in his studio, asking if he'd like to join her at the races, and the decision was made. He'd grabbed his camera, shut the studio up and now they were already half way down the hill together.

'Go on then,' he pressed, as they walked. 'What's the secret to winning? You must know. You must have worked the averages.'

Jane gave a tinkling laugh. 'The secret, Adam, is: there is no secret. It's complete chance. The fastest current on the river used to be on the north side - that's where the winner always comes down - though the currents have probably changed since we were kids. But you have no say in where the duck will get put anyway, so you have no control over it. Unless maybe you bribe one of the officials.'

'What, bribe a teacher? I can't do that. I'd better resign myself to losing then.'

'You never know. You might get lucky.'

She laughed again. He didn't think he'd ever seen her quite so…what? It was hard to place her mood. Usually she had a studied, carefully managed, cool air, but today she exuded energy in some way, as if she had been left on charge just a little too long.

'When we were kids,' she said, 'we used to race along the path by the river, shouting our heads off, calling out the names of our ducks, willing them to win. Claire's probably told you. I bet she still could - she does all that jogging, doesn't she? But I think it'd kill me now.' Jane glanced up at him. 'In fact, I

221

thought you and Claire would be going together or are you meeting her down there?'

'Oh…you know…' he said diffidently. '…I'm not sure what Claire's doing. Or even if she's working today or not.'

'What?' She stopped walking and turned towards him. 'Are you telling me you've broken up with her?' Her mouth hung open, her eyes puckered with concern.

'No, it wasn't really like that, Jane. We never got beyond, you know, being friends.'

'She's dumped you.'

'No. I told you, we were just friends.'

She scowled at him as if he had done her a personal injury then started walking again, a brisk, angry walk.

'I gather you haven't spoken to her lately then?' he asked.

'No. We bumped into each other the other day in Lostwithiel, but…' She shrugged. '…we don't have much in common these days,' she added coldly.

They walked a few more paces in silence.

'Has she gone back to Neil?' Jane demanded suddenly. 'I bet she has.'

Adam flicked her a pinched look. 'I've no idea.'

She stared at him as if she didn't believe him but let the subject drop and they walked the rest of the way in silence.

The early morning rain had cleared and the sunshine had brought out both locals and tourists. There were families and children everywhere. A booth selling tickets for the duck race was positioned near the river and an array of refreshment stalls circled the green. The haunting smell of cooking meat rose from a hog roast on the edge of the car park. Jane saw someone she knew and made her excuses as if she couldn't wait to leave him.

Adam was relieved to see her go and wandered across to the ticket booth to get some tickets. He bought two for each of the first two races and they put his name down against Arnie and Matilda in the first race and Angie and Larry in the second. The first was due to start at one-thirty which gave him ten minutes to kill. He took a couple of photos, then bought a pork bap from the pig roast and idled with the rest of the crowd, working his way close enough to the river to get a view of the race.

He had just got there when a woman's voice boomed through the loudspeaker.

'The first race is about to start. No more tickets will be sold now. Listen for the whistle everyone.'

The crowd fell silent. The sound of a duck call whistle from up by the bridge crackled through the loudspeaker and everyone leaned forward, trying to get the first glimpse of the yellow ducks bobbing towards them. But just as Adam expected to feel the buzz of excitement too, a feeling of dissociation descended on him. He saw people shouting and children jumping up and down but he barely heard them; they could have been the other side of a glass screen for all he registered. He was acutely aware of how alone he was, a single man, an onlooker. He wasn't involved in the event at all. He had no children and no partner. Maybe he was always an onlooker but that was his choice, wasn't it, because he refused to get involved.

He heard a whoop of delight and looked round. A man nearby had a young child sitting on his shoulders while he grasped the boy's ankles. The child's face was a picture of rapt attention and both father and son smiled broadly as the first duck came into view. Adam felt a rare pang of jealousy at their clear rapport. He noticed children everywhere these days in a way he never had before. A toddler burst into tears to his left, the child's mother desperately trying to calm the child down as his wails grew louder; an older sibling chimed in, shouting at the youngster to be quiet.

Adam needed a drink and he started to ease through the crowd to get to The Swan but Claire's words drifted into his head as he reached the door: *It doesn't help. Trust me.* He sighed heavily and paused. He knew she was right. He'd been trying to forget Zoe in a bottle for months with no real success. In fact sometimes he thought it actually massaged his sorrow, as if that sorrow had formed a life of its own, distinct from Zoe, just an abstract mass of pain, and it needed the alcoholic nourishment to keep it alive. Maybe it wasn't about Zoe at all - perhaps he was just using her as an excuse for not getting on with his life.

Huh. What was that life? Was it destined to be simply a long succession of paintings, punctuated by occasional lads' nights in the pub? Was he going to keep repeating the Zoe experience till he was so old that no girl was interested in him any more? When he was younger, he had assumed, like most people, that he would have a family one day. Had that been social pressure or because he genuinely desired one? He still hadn't resolved that one. The question lurked at the back of his mind and resurfaced whenever his guard was down, often in the bottom of a glass.

He trudged back onto the green, bought a paper beaker of ginger beer from one of the stalls, and stood at a slight remove to drink it, trying to calm his thoughts.

Neil Pennyman passed him, hesitated, turned and stopped, offering a magisterial nod of recognition.

'Painting going well?' he enquired briskly. 'Going to have it done in time?'

'Definitely. It's going really well.' Adam hoped he looked convincing.

Neil nodded again and walked away.

A man was chalking the winner of the first race on a

blackboard by the ticket booth and the woman with the microphone was exhorting people to come and buy tickets for the second race while they still could.

Then Adam saw Claire appear at the end of the path from the bridge and he began to ease back through the crowd towards her. For all her frankly expressed opinions about his life, she usually made him feel better somehow and he could do with her down to earth company at this moment. He needed grounding in some way.

But he was still ten yards away from her when he saw Neil Pennyman walk up to her, lean forward to give her a kiss, and speak. Adam stopped moving and watched them, jostled by the crowd but indifferent to them. He saw that Neil had made Claire smile as though she'd found what he'd said genuinely amusing, and now she was talking herself and laughing, gesturing with her hands and pointing to the river, her face as animated as he'd seen it. So Claire had been telling the truth then: she did still love Neil. It was written in the radiance of her face. Adam wasn't sure he'd ever believed it before.

He finished the ginger beer and walked away towards the road, tossed the beaker in a bin, then paused and pulled the duck race tickets out of his pocket, screwing them up and lobbing them in too. It wasn't surprising that Claire had been so reluctant to discuss Neil and the rest of the Pennymans in their investigation. He might as well forget Gilly. In any case, there was nowhere for their investigation to go; they had reached an impasse and they had ruffled too many feathers - perhaps dangerously. Maybe the hair slide had never been Gilly's anyway. Perhaps Claire's fixation on it had been an act of desperation; in all honesty he had had his doubts.

He started walking back towards the bridge. He had a lot of work to do though his head hurt with so much bouncing around in it. Why was it that he never read relationships right?

He was a sap.

He reached the crowd milling over the bridge, waiting to watch the start of the next race but he barely hesitated, pushing his way through the mêlée and striding up the hill, the sounds of children's shouts and laughter carrying after him.

Chapter 17

Claire stood in front of the long mirror which hung on the back of her wardrobe door and turned first one way, then the other, studying the effect of the dress she was wearing, the third she had tried on. It was the sixteenth of May and she was due up at the house for Eve's seventieth birthday party. Seven for seven-thirty the invitation said. Claire should know - she had read it often enough.

She had mixed feelings about going but Neil had insisted she should come. Turning up at the door with the invitation a few days previously, he'd said he would enjoy it so much more if she were there.

'Otherwise,' he'd said, 'who am I going to spend the evening with? A load of relatives and friends of Eve's I barely know, or my dear brother and sister when we're bound to end up arguing about the vineyard as usual? No, I need you to rescue me. Please say you'll come, Claire. And, if not for me, come for Laura. She'll want your moral support.'

'Has Laura said she's coming?' asked Claire.

'Well, she's been sent an invitation and it is her grandmother's seventieth, after all. Mum's expecting and hoping she'll be there.'

Eve can expect all she likes, thought Claire now, still examining herself in the mirror.

'Oh, it'll do,' she said, out loud. 'God knows, it's no

worse than the others.'

She brushed her hair, grabbed a cotton cardigan from the drawer and went downstairs to do her make-up in the bathroom. Afterwards, walking through to the living room to look for her car keys - she always put them down somewhere different - she saw the hair slide sitting on top of the sideboard in its little pouch and the next minute she was tipping it out onto her hand again.

She kept doing this. The world would stop while she stared at this shiny bit of plastic, handled it, willed it to tell her something, anything. She was so confused that she thought she had got to the point where she would even be relieved to be told once and for all that it had no significance, that it wasn't Gilly's. When had she started having doubts? When had she first dared to acknowledge those doubts? Even now, she struggled to let them linger in her mind and be rationally considered. To suggest the slide wasn't Gilly's after all seemed as preposterous as a politician insisting he always told the truth.

Yet she did doubt. For a while she had managed to convince herself that the silent phone calls proved that she had rattled someone's guilty cage. They were a scare tactic, designed to put her off more investigation. But her conviction hadn't lasted. People got silent calls all the time – computer-generated most of the time - and they had no significance. She saw no pattern to them and they hadn't escalated - if anything, they were happening less frequently. They meant nothing.

And, except for an odd word exchanged in passing at the Yard, Adam hadn't spoken to her since that night at his house. He'd dropped off the art materials at V and C one day when she wasn't there, just as he had promised. They had got nowhere and he had drawn a line under the whole affair; she couldn't blame him.

She carefully replaced the slide in the velvet bag and put it down, found her car keys and left. It wasn't until she was driving up the lane to the house, that an idea occurred to her, something so simple and so obvious that she was amazed she hadn't thought of it before. There was still something she could do to find out where the slide came from. It would be a last throw of the dice and more than a little rash perhaps, but still a risk worth taking. Gilly deserved nothing less.

*

'I just thought you'd like to know,' the woman's voice said in his ear, 'because you and Zoe seemed so happy there for a while and, well, the truth is - Zoe might kill me for telling you this - but I think she misses you. And she's too proud to say so. I think she knows she screwed up by walking out on you so… Anyway, I just rang to tell you. In case you guys can find some way to patch it up.'

Adam thanked her and closed the call. He had just come out of the shower when Zoe's sister, Ellie had called, and he was still dripping, still trying to pull the towel round him with his free hand. He was stunned, thrilled…maybe. Was it true? Did Zoe regret her decision or was this a case of Ellie doing some well-intentioned but ill-judged matchmaking?

He put the phone down on the lid of the linen basket and rubbed himself dry, tension making him do it a little more furiously than usual till his skin tingled. He kept looking at the phone suspiciously as if it weren't to be trusted. This was what he wanted, wasn't it? This was a chance to get back to where they were. He took a deep breath and let it out slowly. He'd been thinking about this a lot, ever since the duck race. He'd thought about the wonderful bond he'd seen between that little boy and his dad and about the joy he'd seen on the other kids' faces when they'd been jumping around, watching the ducks bobbing down the water. They had made him ache a little inside. If he agreed to start a family with Zoe, he was sure that would bring her back because that had been the big stumbling block all along. And he thought the 'living in the middle of nowhere' issue would drop out of the equation. Quid pro quo. It might work.

He dressed, calmer now, then picked up the phone, keyed in her number and waited.

'Adam?' she said. 'I didn't expect to hear from you.'

'Do you mind?'

'Mind? No. No, actually it's good to hear your voice.' She sounded like she was smiling.

'Ellie told me you were flying solo again.' He cringed. What a terrible way to put it.

Zoe laughed. 'Typical sister, eh? It's true though.' She paused. 'I've been thinking about you a lot lately.' Her voice was soft and caressed his ear. 'I have, honestly. Adam, I'm sorry if I hurt you.'

'I've been thinking about you too.' He hesitated. Go for it, he told himself. 'Do you think we could give it another go?'

'Oh Adam, I don't know.' She was silent. He wished he could see her face, have a better idea what she was thinking. He hated not being able to touch her. 'I do miss you...' she was saying, '...but nothing's changed, has it? I don't want to come back to start the same old arguments again. We want different things, don't we?'

'Well, maybe, maybe not. I've been thinking too, wondering what I want out of life.'

A pause. 'Sounds deep,' she said, cautiously. 'Come to any conclusion?'

'Sort of. I've been selfish, Zoe, and I'm sorry. I am really.'

Silence. She wasn't making this easy for him.

'I saw an adorable little boy sitting on his father's

shoulders at the duck race a couple of weeks ago. It made me think what I'm missing.'

'Really?'

'Yes, really. I do want children, Zoe, I've decided. We should go for it.'

'You're sure? You're not going to change your mind if I come back?'

'No. Absolutely not.'

She started to talk, all excitement and plans and he had no idea what because he had zoned out and felt numb. Somewhere in the periphery of his brain he sensed a vague feeling of relief that he had made a decision and he had made Zoe happy. He did want her to be happy. A random thought had him wondering what their children would be like; he sincerely hoped they looked like Zoe.

He glanced at his watch and cut across her chatter. 'Zoe? Are you busy this evening? The thing is, I've got to go up to The White House, to be there while they present a commission I did for them. It would be so great if you could come with me. Would you? I could pick you up if you can.'

*

Claire looked round the huge sitting room of The White House, at the crush of maybe fifty bodies, at the long banner draped across the chimney breast reading *Happy 70th Birthday Eve*, at the big wooden easel by the side of the fireplace which had a white sheet thrown over it. There seemed an inevitability about her coming back to this place. However much she thought she would distance herself from it, still she kept coming back, as if it had some magnetic pull on her. She supposed it did: he was called Neil. And here he came, holding two glasses of wine.

'Who are all these people?' she asked. 'There's a lot of

faces here I don't know - or at least that I've forgotten.'

He grinned. 'When we told mum about the party it grew and grew as she kept thinking of people: neighbours from way back; people she went to school with. Like those weddings where you can't invite Auntie Flo without asking Cousin Sarah in case someone gets offended, she thought they should all come. Fortunately, they couldn't all make it.' He offered her an apologetic look. 'Don't worry. You don't have to speak to them all - or any of them. Just talk to me. Mum'll do the circulating; she's good at that.'

'I remember.'

'You look lovely, by the way.'

'Thank you.'

'So Laura didn't come after all.'

'Didn't she tell you?'

'She sent me a text. I wasn't impressed.'

'She's got exams, Neil. We can't expect her to drop everything and come down to Cornwall.'

'Possibly. But I got the impression she didn't want to come. We are talking about her grandmother here.'

Claire drank some wine and didn't answer. She had formed the same impression when she'd spoken to Laura a few nights previously. Claire found it harder to blame her daughter, though it was a special birthday so maybe Laura should have made the effort.

'Adam's here.' Neil was still watching her face. 'He's going to do the big reveal of the painting later on. Shame we can't arrange a drum roll really. I guess you knew about the painting. Have you seen it?'

'Yes. I mean yes, I knew about it and no, I haven't seen it. Have you?'

'Yes, he brought it up in the week.'

'Pleased?'

'Sure, it's fine.' He looked like he didn't care one way or the other. He paused. 'He's brought a girl with him.'

'Oh?' Claire immediately searched the room with her eyes.

'They're over there.' Neil nodded towards the windows.

'Right. Yes, that's Zoe. She's the girlfriend who used to live with him.'

'I see. Someone suggested that you weren't seeing him any more. Is that true?'

'Who?'

He shrugged. 'I can't remember now.' He studied her face. 'Are you OK?'

'Of course.'

'Was it him who finished with you?' Neil flicked a malevolent glance towards the other side of the room.

So her ex-husband didn't like Adam going out with her, yet now he was ready to dislike him for throwing her over. She grinned at the absurdity of it.

'It wasn't like that, Neil. I told you it wasn't serious. We're just friends.'

He still scrutinised her.

'Were you jealous?' she teased.

A wry smile. 'Maybe.'

They moved round the room and chatted to a few people. Eve spoke to them in passing and was at her most gracious. Then the food was served. A caterer had laid out a buffet in the dining room and had put extra seats and tables anywhere they could find a space. Neil and Claire took their plates of food to a table in the corner where Timothy and his new girlfriend, Shannon, were already installed. Shannon was young, dark-haired and petite. She looked terrified and Claire felt sorry for her, trying repeatedly, without much success, to engage her in conversation. When most people had finished eating, they were served sparkling wine and Eve's brother was standing in front of the fireplace, clapping his hands to get their attention and inviting everyone to toast the birthday girl. Then Adam was uncovering the painting, looking as if he wished he were somewhere else while Zoe stood nearby, looking luminous and smiling incessantly. Claire noticed them both slip away as soon as the presentation was over.

It went quickly - more quickly than Claire had expected - and it was over, and there were people already saying their farewells. Eve stood talking to people by the door and Claire took the opportunity to cross to the painting to take a look at it. A couple of minutes later, Neil was at her side.

'Is it any good?'

She turned to look at him and frowned. 'You commissioned it. Why ask me?'

'You know more about these things.'

She shrugged. 'I think he's caught the view well - the light especially. And I like the texture on the vines. Clever. Yes, it's good but it's a personal thing, isn't it?' She turned away. 'I'd better say goodbye to Tim and Shannon before I go.'

'They've already gone.' He was staring into her face again, imploring her with his eyes. 'You could stay over. You can't drive home after all that wine.'

She refused to meet his gaze. 'I'll walk and come back for the car in the morning.'

'In those shoes?'

'I've got a jacket and some flatties in the car.'

'Then I'll walk with you.'

'If you like.'

They fell into step down the hill and walked in silence, listening to the settling, soothing sounds of a spring night. She wondered if, like her, he was remembering all the times they had done this when they were young. She suspected he did because she felt his hand nuzzling against her own, rubbing back against back then taking it to hold the way he always used to. Time plays such tricks on you, she thought. It was surreal, as if the preceding years hadn't happened, as if there had been no abduction, no escape to Kent, no separation and no divorce.

'Tim was right about Shannon being shy,' Claire remarked. 'But he seems quite taken with her.'

'I think he is. And she seems like a nice girl. It's about time he settled with someone.'

Claire grinned. 'I'm sure Eve wishes he would. She probably can't wait for him to produce more little Pennymans.'

Neil didn't reply, then squeezed her hand, like a warning of the blow to come.

'Mum wants me to ask Laura if she'd like to get more involved in the vineyard.'

'No,' Claire immediately stopped, turning to look at him. She would have pulled her hand away but he held it too tightly. 'No, Neil. Laura's got her own career ahead. She's never shown much interest in the vineyard. Why would she want to throw up her own plans for it? No, you can't do it.'

'I'm not going to pressurise her, Claire. I'll just ask. It'll satisfy mum and then it's over with.'

'It's never over with, not with Eve.'

'It will be. I won't push it. I'm not sure Laura would be any good for the place anyway.' He started walking again, gently pulling her along with him. 'There's no point her doing it unless she's genuinely interested. Eve's just panicking about the future of the family business. It's her and dad's legacy and she thinks it's going to end up leaving the family. You're right: I'm sure she would like more grandchildren. Danny's not showing much interest either.'

'Don't you think children should be allowed to create

their own legacies, follow their own stars? Why should they take on the dreams of their parents? Or, worse still, their grandparents?'

'I love it when you get this passionate about things.'

'Don't patronise me Neil.'

'I'm not. I mean it.'

'You're just trying to change the subject. I don't want Laura's life to shrink to Bohenna and whatever plans Eve has for her. The whole world is before her. Let her fly. I mean it, Neil.'

'I know. And I agree. But I'm puzzled. If you think Bohenna is so small, why come back? You've shrunk your world. Do you ever draw or paint any more? You were so good at it. Those illustrations you used to do were brilliant. So why this? You're still young enough to fly too. And you're freer to do it now.'

She looked across at him, frowning, trying to see his face in the weak moonlight.

'But you didn't like me doing the illustrations. You used to get frustrated when I let things go in the house. You said I was impossible to talk to when I was working on a new idea.'

They were close to the bridge now and a car came down the road, dazzling them with its headlights. They pressed into the verge out of its way then started walking again.

'I know,' said Neil. 'But I was younger then and a fool. I didn't appreciate a lot of things.' They walked several more steps in silence. 'I've made mistakes, Claire. I can't deny it. Some of them were huge.'

She flicked him another look, uncertain. It wasn't like him to admit a fault.

'Me too,' she admitted. 'I was impossible to live with. I think I was trying to punish myself for what happened to Gilly - well both of us really - and it all ended up a tortured mess.'

He gave a short laugh and lifted her hand up to kiss the back of it. 'Hey, how many years has it taken us to say that? We'd have saved a lot of money on lawyers if we'd done it ages ago.'

She smiled but said nothing.

'Do you remember the holiday we had in Brittany before the girls came along?' he said suddenly. 'That tiny little *gîte* with the wonky plumbing?'

'Yes, of course I remember. The weather was amazing but, God, that bed was uncomfortable.'

He glanced across at her. 'We hadn't been married long. Who cared how comfortable the bed was?'

She felt self-conscious and flushed. What a nonsense, after all these years.

'We should go to Brittany again some time.' He grinned. 'Maybe somewhere more upmarket this time - with decent plumbing and comfortable beds.'

'Do you mean that?'

'Of course I mean it.' He glanced sideways at her. 'Would you like that?'

She paused. 'Maybe.' She felt a bubble of excitement forming in the pit of her stomach. 'Yes, that would be fun.'

They reached Dark Lane and the end cottages. Eddie's house was in darkness but Claire had left her outside light on. Neil walked with her up the path.

'You seem to have a carton of eggs on your doorstep,' he said.

'Eddie leaves them.' She bent over to pick them up. They had been pushed in beside a pot of geraniums she'd recently put there. 'From next door.'

'An admirer?'

She smiled. 'You must remember Eddie. Not exactly an admirer but he does at least speak to me occasionally now.

Short sentences.'

She put her key in the lock and, as she turned it, she felt Neil's hand slide slowly, seductively, down her back. Again, her mind played tricks, flicking back in time. She could feel the old passion welling up in them both, the insistence of it, the pull that would not be denied. Jane had simply never understood the way it was between them: there had been no plots or tricks or subterfuge.

Claire quickly pulled away and turned to face him. She had to fight this attraction. Her desire was more complicated now and too intermingled with fear. After all the pain and failure of the past, she needed to be sure.

'Neil, look. I'm not going to ask you in. I don't want us to rush anything.'

'Rush anything? Hell, Claire, we were married for twenty-one years. We're not two adolescents looking for a sweaty grope while our parents are out.'

'No. We're divorced, that's what we are. And the last seven years don't disappear overnight.'

'No, no, I know.'

'The thing is Neil, I don't understand what's happening here.'

He pushed some gravel around with his shoe. 'I'm not sure I do either.' He shrugged, glanced around as if someone might be eavesdropping, then looked back at her expectantly. 'I think maybe we made a mistake. But it's not too late to put it right. Or is it?'

She didn't reply.

'When's your day off next week?' he asked.

'Friday.'

'Perfect. I'm going away on the Saturday for a wine conference. No-one will mind if I take the Friday off. Let's go out for the day. What do you think?'

'On the Friday?'

'Yes. Why?'

'Oh nothing.' She nodded slowly, warily. 'Friday would be good. Perhaps we could go to St. Mawes?'

'St. Mawes it is.' He took hold of her hand and lifted it, this time opening her palm and kissing it with a soft, erotic brush of his lips, then closing her fingers around it.

'Neil?'

'What?'

She hesitated, then shook her head and smiled. 'It doesn't matter now. I'll see you on Friday.'

'I'll give you a ring.'

She watched him walk away before letting herself in. Once inside she leaned her head forward against the wall, hands balled up into fists on either side, and enjoyed the coolness of the plaster against her forehead. It was a shock just how much she wanted him back. She had been very close to telling him about the hair slide too but that wasn't the right moment, standing there on the doorstep.

And he had forgotten what Friday was so maybe that would be a good time to tell him everything.

Chapter 18

Gilly disappeared on a Thursday, the twenty-second of May. Claire remembered the day every year - knew she would remember the date for the rest of her life - and, whatever she was doing, always tried to put time aside to look at old photographs of Gilly and remember her properly: her daughter, Laura's sister, a little girl who did normal little girl things.

For a brief spell after she disappeared, Gilly was stolen from them by the media. She became 'the Cornish girl' who evaporated from an 'idyllic coastal village'; the 'golden angel' taken by an 'evil monster'. 'No child is safe,' roared one tabloid, 'when an innocent can be stalked on her own doorstep.' Little of it was true. Bohenna wasn't on the coast; it was five miles inland. Gilly wasn't taken from her doorstep; she had left the house to play. And she was no angel, golden or otherwise. She was a delightful but perfectly normal little girl who could be both good and naughty. She was affectionate and - for a nine-year-old - surprisingly generous of her time if someone needed help; she loved her parents and her sister and was never slow to show affection; she was quick-witted and funny with an unconscious sense of timing. Claire loved her unconditionally.

But she could grizzle and complain like any child, especially when she was tired; she was terrible at putting her things away and hated being stopped from doing something she had already planned; and she was stubborn and sometimes reluctant to apologise even when she knew she was in the wrong. But for the fact that they put a spotlight on the issue and therefore might bring some information to light, Claire wanted the media to lose interest. She wanted to reclaim Gilly. She didn't want her to be just a propaganda tool or a way to increase the circulation of a flagging title.

The newspaper journalists and television crews hadn't brought anything to light however and they'd quickly left and gone on to the next story. It hadn't crossed Claire's mind for years that there would be any point chasing the media afterwards to help. All that had happened after their exposure was that all the worms had come out of the woodwork, all the twisted people who had to criticise or joke about it or offer knowingly false leads.

But the situation had changed and Claire's new idea was a carefully worded advertisement in *Cornwall Now*, the regional newspaper most read around those parts. An advert which was targeted, specific, asking for anyone with information about a hair slide given to the fête in Bohenna the previous year to come forward, something like that might produce a really useful result. This was a traditional area where people still read the local newspaper and pored over the advertisements. On the Friday, when the bulk of the advertisements appeared, it was particularly well read. It could work. Someone, somewhere - probably nearby - had given that slide to the stall. Someone, close to that person, or maybe even an onlooker, might know who it was.

And then the idea had grown. She could risk mentioning Gilly - she might even hear from someone who knew something about that day. She'd buy a box number from the paper for the replies. It wasn't a fashionable story any more; it wasn't the buzz. Most people would have forgotten about it. But not someone who knew something. Maybe they were just waiting for an opportunity to share what they had seen?

Claire contacted the newspaper on the Monday after the party and arranged for the advertisement to go in the paper for the first time on the Friday, the twenty-second, exactly seven years to the day since Gilly had gone out and never come back. Maybe using the anniversary would spur someone's memory, maybe not. Either way, it felt poetic. It felt right. Her informer could be anonymous if they chose so why wouldn't they get in touch? She wasn't sure how she was going to manage to wait until the advert appeared and the responses came in but she felt good about this. This was going to bring an end to it.

And after that last talk with Neil, she felt sure that now she could tell him and he would understand. It would be wonderful to bring him on board.

*

For Adam, the new dawn with Zoe wasn't working out quite the way he had imagined. She had stayed with him the night after the birthday party and had shared his bed. He had made her breakfast and brought it back to the bed and afterwards they had made love again. Lying afterwards with her head on his chest, the scent of her hair in his nostrils, he had felt at peace, certain that he had done the right thing. But she had left that Sunday evening insisting that she was going to continue to live in her flat in Fowey. It was more convenient for her work, she said, and anyway, they needed time to adjust again.

It seemed that he had misjudged things again. The problem was that the issue of where they were going to live had not gone away. Zoe was adamant that she wouldn't live in Bohenna and she wanted them to start looking immediately at other places they might live, somewhere that suited them both.

He was no fool; he could see what she was doing. It was a test. She was making certain that he would stick to his promises. If she moved back in, she expected that he would let things ride again and avoid the issue and, in his heart, he suspected she was right which made it hard to argue the point.

So he was alone again and the week felt interminable. Adam tried not to think about the course he had set with Zoe but the spectre of living somewhere else - a neat semi somewhere on a neat estate with a neatly fenced garden for the children to play in - hung at the back of his mind. He wasn't against moving in principle but he was scared of where they might end up. He found it hard to concentrate on his work.

On the Thursday afternoon, time hanging heavily, his eyes wandered once more from the stretched paper on his painting board and he watched a handful of people idling around the yard. Tim didn't do a vineyard tour on a Tuesday or Thursday and there were always noticeably fewer people about. He dragged his gaze back to the painting and worked desultorily on. A couple strolled in and disturbed his concentration long enough to buy a set of greetings cards; a woman came in alone, looked through the prints, picked one out and took it to the door, then replaced it in the browser the wrong way up and walked out. He continued working for another hour, then glanced at his watch. It was only four o'clock but he'd had enough. He packed up for the day.

He walked back down towards the village, stood on the old stone bridge for a few minutes, idly watching the water tumbling along beneath him, then continued to the other side but found himself glancing back. He walked this way most days, twice a day, and he thought of Gilly virtually every time, posing himself the same questions. Did she explore the river that day? Who else might have been here? Could she have fallen in? No, the police would have found her if she'd done that. He was frustrated with the futility of these thoughts but, try as he might to put her out of his mind, that little girl wouldn't leave him alone.

He eased himself down the rough steps to the river path and moved under the bridge. The path was just wide enough to be passable if you ducked your head but he preferred simply to stand and listen. He liked the echo of the water here as it bounced and reverberated off the stonework; it was haunting and almost melodic.

A movement caught his eye. On the further bank, heading east away from him, a dark-haired woman wearing a lightweight fringed shawl was walking with a purposeful step. It had to be Jane. He sidled further along the path and emerged from under the bridge on the other side. Already he could only catch glimpses of her between the vegetation but, for all her haste, there was something about her movement that was furtive. Without pausing to question why, he climbed back up to the bridge, crossed it and a couple of minutes later was tracking her along the northern path.

She must be moving quickly - he couldn't see her any more. Or maybe she had cut off on another path though he didn't think he'd passed any. To his right was the river; to the left, the other side of some light scrub, lay the vineyard. He walked faster and it was several minutes later before he caught another glimpse of her up ahead. They were in the woods now, the vineyard no longer visible and Jane was climbing over a fence, then she was gone. He speeded up and a minute later reached the place. To his right was the small timber bridge across the river and, straight ahead, a fence blocking the path with a sign saying it was private. He climbed over it too and struck out along the ongoing riverside path, cutting left through the trees soon after in Jane's wake.

In a little under ten minutes he reached a clearing. This

must be the spot Claire had told him about but she hadn't prepared him for the sweetness of the place. It was hard to believe he was still in the village - it was an oasis of calm. To his left was the little boathouse she had mentioned and ahead of him lay the lake, small but glinting prettily in the afternoon sunshine, reflecting the blue of the sky. Birdsong was all he could hear. He paused and stepped back into the fringe of trees. Jane had stopped further up the clearing and was standing looking at the trunk of a tree beyond the boathouse. He watched her put a hand up to it as if tracing something with her finger, then she turned away and moved off again, walking briskly towards the top of the clearing, shawl flapping. Adam followed.

Jane had picked up a path which struck off from the north of the clearing, uphill in and out of bushes and trees. It seemed to be tracking the route of the stream which fed the lake. Several times he lost sight of her but he stuck to the path and, hot and a little breathless, reached another small clearing, this one strewn with rocks. There was the distinct sound of running water and he eased sideways round a couple of huge boulders, in and out of the bushes. Then he saw Jane's shawl, thrown over a rock some ten yards away and edged further forward, peering through the fronds of a shrub. He stopped short.

They had reached the spring. It was a beautiful spot. Water trickled over a ledge and fell vertically into a small rocky pool. And, as he watched, Jane was peeling off the last of her clothes and stepping into the pool naked, now standing shin deep in the water, stretching her arms up towards the sky as if craving a blessing. She bowed her head a moment then moved across to stand beneath the waterfall, tipping her head back, eyes closed, letting it soak her hair and run down her flesh. Her expression looked at the same time anguished and ecstatic, like that of a martyred saint in a Baroque painting.

245

She's purifying herself, he thought. Or maybe she thinks the water has healing properties. Is she ill – or guilty of something?

He thought he should look away but he found himself magnetised, watching her. Then his skin began to crawl with embarrassment: he was a peeping Tom, a voyeur, and he quickly and silently moved away, retracing his steps all the way back to the lower clearing. He had assumed that she had a secret assignation with someone and now he felt foolish.

In the clearing he walked back over the wildflower-strewn grass, passing on his way a couple of winding footpaths through the trees to his right. One of them was the one which led to The White House; he had no idea where the other one went. And here was the tree Jane had fondled. He moved closer and saw that it had some initials carved into it, worked inside the incised shape of a heart. J and N. Jane and Neil presumably. It was obvious that the woman was still pathetically love-sick, even after all these years but, given the way he had seen Neil looking at Claire, Adam felt sorry for her.

Further along he came to the boathouse and glanced inside, still idly wondering if it had any relevance to Gilly. There was nothing of any interest there. It might once have been the site of carefree youthful fun but now it just looked grubby and dank. On top of Jane's behaviour, everything about it was depressing.

He went home.

*

On the Friday morning Claire was making her way into the village when her phone rang. She had got up early, wanting to make sure she was ready for the trip with Neil, wanting even more to buy her copy of the newspaper before they left.

She stopped walking. 'Neil? Is there a problem?'

'Claire darling. I'm so sorry to let you down but I can't do today. Someone I was supposed to meet on Monday can't make it and offered an appointment this afternoon. I'm going to have to leave soon. I only got his email this morning and I didn't want to ring you too early in case I woke you.'

She felt the sharp sting of disappointment.

'Claire?'

'Yes. I'm here. That's a shame. I was looking forward to it.'

'Me too. I am sorry. But we'll do it again, yes?'

'Of course. It's not your fault. These things happen.'

'I'm afraid so. What will you do? You should do something fun with the day anyway.'

Fun. There were so many things she wanted to say to him and tell him. She glanced up the road, at the people walking dogs and going to buy their newspapers. A car drove slowly past, the driver looking at her curiously.

'Did I hear a car? Are you outside?'

'Yes. I just wanted a couple of things from the shop.' She ran an anxious hand through her hair. She couldn't tell him about the advert on the phone. This was not going well. 'You have a safe journey,' she heard herself say.

'I will. And I'll ring you over the weekend - if that's OK?'

'Yes. Please do.'

'See you next week then.'

She closed the call and began to walk again, consoling herself with the thought that Neil wouldn't see a *Cornwall Now* while he was in Kent so she would have a chance to tell him all about it when he got home.

*

Later that day, Julia drove down to the shop. She nearly always

247

went on a Friday, buying in fresh items for the weekend and her copy of *Cornwall Now*. Busy with work, however, it wasn't until the Saturday evening that she finally got around to reading the paper, sitting alone in their little conservatory, a glass of cider on the table beside her. Danny was out at a friend's; Phil had gone to play darts at the pub where he was in some league or other.

As was her usual routine, she read the news then worked her way through the advertisements. It wasn't that she was looking to buy anything in particular – and she certainly wasn't hoping to find a job - but they were a pleasant distraction, a way to unwind. The adverts reminded her of a world outside her own all-consuming one which, though she loved it, sometimes felt enclosed and constrained, like the image you get when you look down a telescope the wrong way. In any case, she sometimes found the personal adverts very funny.

And it was while she was working her way through the personal adverts that she saw it:

Information sought re child's hair slide donated to Bohenna fête 2014. Reward offered for genuine lead to finding Gilly Pennyman who disappeared May 22nd 2008.

Hair slide? What hair slide? And what would the significance of that be? Julia's blood froze and she stared at the box, reading the words repeatedly over and over. There was no doubting to whom the advert referred nor who had posted it. She couldn't believe it.

She glanced at her watch - it was nine twenty - then picked up her phone. Maybe Neil would be out somewhere wining and dining with other conference delegates, having a good time. She didn't care.

'Julia?' Neil's voice sounded strained. Behind him she

could hear the low hum of voices. 'Is something the matter?'

'You told me Claire had changed. That was just two days ago, Neil. You encouraged her to come to the house, to get involved again. You promised me she'd dropped all this stuff about Gilly. You know what trouble she's going to cause. You said you'd…'

'Hold on, Julia. What's happened?' Neil cut across her, stern and business like. She ran her fingers across her forehead, trying to calm down. She wasn't usually like this.

'She didn't tell you about it then?'

'About what?'

'About the advert…in *Cornwall Now*. She didn't tell you she was going to open the whole can of worms again, have the press down here nosing around, taking photos and printing lies about our vineyard and us?'

'Julia? Julia?' he said coldly. 'You're hysterical. What are you talking about? What advert?'

'OK. I'll tell you what advert. It's this.'

She read it out to him and when she finished there was silence at the other end. There was no longer any laughter; Neil had clearly left the room he had been in. Or maybe the line had gone dead.

'Neil?'

'Right,' he said in a flat voice.

'You didn't know about it?'

'Of course I didn't know about it.'

'What are…?'

'Thanks for calling, Julia. I have to go now. I'll see you next week.'

He cut the call and she swore at the phone and threw it down.

Chapter 19

It didn't work out the way she'd planned. At all. Thinking about it afterwards, Claire could see that she had made mistakes; she could see how she could have done things differently. In fact, maybe she had just been stupid.

On the Saturday night after the advert appeared she received two silent phone calls to her land line. On the Monday morning, when she got back from jogging, there was a note pushed through the door, asking how a dead child could give a hair slide to the fête? The note was made up of words cut out of newsprint - probably from *Cornwall Now* - and glued onto a sheet of paper torn from a notebook.

'I bet you thought that was really funny,' she spat, tearing it into confetti and throwing it in the bin. The fact that someone had watched and waited for her to go out before posting it bothered her more than the note itself.

On the Wednesday, she received another phone call and, when she answered, a shrill, electronic laugh cackled at her until she cut it dead.

It was all absurd and childish but it was unnerving all the same. There were no direct contact details on the advert so someone or maybe several people had worked out who she was and where she was and were amusing themselves at her expense. And that could only mean they were local. The thought sickened her.

The first 'proper' responses - if there were any and she began to doubt there would be - wouldn't arrive for days, forwarded on from the newspaper. Neil wasn't due back from his trip until the following Friday night. She hadn't heard from him, not one phone call, and she recognised the oddness of that, given that he'd promised to ring, but tried not to think about it.

It was on the Friday when the first envelope arrived from the newspaper. Claire had been working all day and found it on the mat when she got home that night. Inside were more than ten letters. She opened the first one.

I saw a little girl, just last week, in Padstow. She looked scared, like she didn't want to be with the man she was with. He was big with a rough dark beard. I didn't like the look of him.

Gilly wouldn't be a little girl any more. Claire exhaled slowly, put it to one side and picked up the next.

I looked up the case. Poor little girl. What were you thinking to let a girl that age go off alone? How irresponsible! You're a disgrace to women everywhere. You didn't deserve to have children. There are women who can't...

Claire shook her head and put that one aside too.

There were others - similarly unhelpful sightings or vindictive tirades. Only one referred to the hair slide, saying that her young daughter had lost one when they were out for the day and could it be the same one? The woman left a telephone number but didn't say where the slide was lost or when. Claire stared at the scribbled note for several minutes and then at the slide. Was it likely that this slide had belonged to that woman's daughter? What were the chances of that?

251

She put the note down and opened the last letter.

Gilly is happy and well and doesn't want to come home. She wants you to leave her alone. She's having a good time now without you so stop chasing her.

Claire felt the deadening sickness of disappointment. But she should have guessed that it would be like this because she'd been here before. Why had she thought the lapse of time would have made any difference? And this last letter hurt the most even though it was surely nonsense. The suggestion that Gilly would be happier and better off with someone else was too horrible, or perhaps chimed too closely with Claire's own fear and guilt.

She glanced towards the clock, wondering if Neil had arrived back at The White House yet. She had still heard nothing from him. Of course he would have been busy but she had hoped that he might at least get in touch as soon as he got home. Had he seen the advert? Maybe he was never going to speak to her again. She was dramatising. Surely, after their closeness the other night, he'd try to see her point of view?

'I don't care,' she said loudly to the room, though saying it still didn't make her believe it. In a rash, angry movement, she swept the letters off the table to the floor and stamped on them.

A few minutes later, she let herself out of the back door, and went out for a run.

When she got home the rear door was open. Someone had found the key she left under a plant pot and it was still in the lock. That someone had thrown a pile of crockery on the floor, smashing it into countless jagged pieces. And on the kitchen table was a small doll with blonde curly hair and a piece of string tied tightly round its neck, like a noose. There was no note though the warning was clear enough. Claire picked it up with fingers that trembled and went outside, looking out towards her back gate and the path into the woods in case whoever did this was still out there somewhere, watching for her reaction. She wanted to laugh it off, loudly, so they could hear that it didn't frighten her, but she couldn't do it. She saw no-one.

She went back indoors, ignoring the crunch of the broken pots under her feet, working to undo the knots holding the string against the doll's neck, desperate to take it off, not allowing herself to ask why it mattered so much. With the string off, she took both the doll and the string to the bin then stopped with them poised over the top of it. Was the doll supposed to suggest Gilly…or herself?

*

Zoe came to stay with Adam again that Friday night. Just as on the previous weekend she brought food with her and spent an hour after her arrival, sorting through the kitchen cupboards and the fridge, discarding out-of-date items and stacking things in order. The previous Saturday she had complained about the state of the bin and had donned rubber gloves and washed it out with disinfectant. Then she had gone through his clothes and bed linens and put the soiled items in the washing machine. Now, having been in the bungalow less than two hours, he watched her washing down all the worktops and the cupboard fronts, tutting under her breath, and felt vaguely guilty as though he had been caught out doing something sordid.

She was organising him and he was grateful. He recognised that perhaps he needed it - he wasn't the kind of man who was good at the 'living alone' thing - but still it left him feeling like he'd been brushed by a tornado. He didn't remember such frenzied activity when she had been living

253

with him, but she hadn't had to cram it all into two days then.

Going into the bedroom, he'd been comforted to see that she had brought back her favourite teddy bear and stuffed badger, positioning them carefully on their bed. She was home again and that was good though inevitably they still argued over what they would watch on television. Zoe liked soaps; Adam liked sport and documentaries. They bickered about music too. Zoe liked loud and modern; Adam liked lilting and classical. He didn't care. He had even missed arguing with her.

On the Saturday they slipped into familiar routines: staying in bed late, going shopping in Fowey, having lunch at one of the pubs and then coming home for the evening when Zoe cooked something Italian. After they'd finished eating and cleared up, he poured them some wine and suggested they watch a film.

'I thought we'd search the agents online,' she countered. 'We need to get started.'

So they sat side by side on the sofa, drinking Italian wine and surfing the property websites and Adam forced himself to concentrate. If he was going to be talked into buying somewhere, he wanted to make sure it was somewhere he wanted to live.

There were several that Zoe liked the look of and a couple Adam thought he might consider. She printed out a bunch of details and they agreed to go driving past some of them the following day to take a look. Then they stopped for the night and Zoe lay against him while they watched an American cop movie.

'Did you see that advert?' Zoe said, eyes fixed on the screen.

'What advert?'

'The one about that girl who went missing?'

Adam bent his head down to look at her, frowning. 'I

haven't seen any advert. What girl? Where?'

'In the paper. I didn't see it either but everyone's talking about it. You know that kid who disappeared from Bohenna a few years ago - what was her name…?'

'Gilly Pennyman.'

'That's the one. Her mother's back here isn't she and apparently she's put some advert in the local rag asking for information about a hair slide. Everyone seems to think she's lost it, poor thing.' Zoe snuggled down more deeply against him. 'Not surprising is it? I think I'd lose my marbles if some sick freak stole my kid away. Maybe we should think about having ours tagged.' She laughed, drowsy with alcohol. 'Do you think you're allowed to do that?'

*

It was nearly eleven on the following Wednesday morning when Julia found Neil in the office, sitting at the computer, adding appointments to the calendar. Tim was there too, flicking through a clipboard pinned with lists of people who had registered for his tours that afternoon.

'Good turnout we're getting at the moment,' Tim remarked as Julia walked up to join them. 'Hey, Julia, check this out.' He picked up a small teddy bear wearing a navy blue sweater with Bohenna Wines embroidered on the front in gold and rocked it side to side in front of her. 'What do you think? I thought we'd try some at the fête later this month with a view to stocking them in the gift shop.'

'You're not serious?' said Julia.

'Of course I'm serious.' Tim looked offended but he'd always had an infantile streak. 'These little toys sell. I've been looking into it. And, come on, everywhere you go you see cuddly toys with some marketing name on them. People lap them up. They'll sell to the tourists, especially the ones with children.'

'You can't Tim; you'll cheapen the whole product if you go down that route,' Julia protested. 'We're a serious wine business.'

'But we agreed on the gift shop,' said Tim. He glanced towards Neil for support though his brother looked preoccupied. 'What did you think we were going to fill it with? Manuals on grape varieties? Bags of compost for the home-grown vine? Neil, what do you think?'

'He's right, Julia,' said Neil impatiently, coming out of the calendar and putting the computer to sleep. 'The gift shop has to be just that. It won't affect anyone's perception of the wine. You worry too much.'

'Fine, fine. I can see I'm outnumbered as usual.'

Neil stood up and walked to the door. She followed him and reached him as he opened it.

'Neil? Wait. Have you spoken to her yet?'

'Do you mean Claire? No.'

'Why not? You've been home for days.'

'Because I can't think of anything to say that I haven't said before, that's why not. So what's the point?'

'I thought you'd want to ask her about the hair slide,' said Julia.

'She's throwing straws in the wind, Julia. It has no significance.'

His eyes flashed with suppressed anger and he banged out of the room.

Julia stared at the door which had bounced slightly and now stood ajar.

She turned to Tim. 'I thought he'd want to know what she was talking about. They've been together so much lately, I was surprised he didn't know what she was going to do.'

Tim put the clipboard down and laid his arm across her

bony shoulder. 'Perhaps he does know what she was talking about.'

'What do you mean? Has he told you that?'

'He doesn't tell me everything, you know,' he said, brows raised archly. 'He can be a bit deep sometimes, can't he? But it's a shame about Claire, isn't it? She'll regret it. All those idiots who chased them last time... Seems like she's putting herself out there for it again, doesn't it?' His expression became serious and his eyes rolled over Julia's face. 'And making life harder again for all of us too. I guess Neil doesn't have as much control over her as he thinks he does.'

Tim raised his eyebrows again and left the office.

Control, thought Julia. She was surprised at his choice of word but, yes, that was the only good thing she had foreseen coming out of Neil's renewed relationship with Claire: she had thought he'd control her. And for the first time she wondered if controlling Claire had been what courting her again had been about all along.

*

Another batch of responses to Claire's advertisement arrived in the post at intervals through the week. They were as pointless, illogical and vindictive as ever. Since it was only a regional paper there was nothing like the number of crank letters they'd received when Gilly disappeared, but they were no less distressing for that. And there were no constructive leads about the hair slide. She had received another couple of silent phone calls too, late at night when, even on these summer evenings, it was dark outside and the rustling, shifting woods seemed to move with the stealth of shadowy unknown footsteps.

In the village, Claire felt as if she had moved back in time to those dark days some weeks after Gilly had gone when, once the first sympathetic pulse of helpful words and activity died down, people had quickly started to take sides. So it was again. Despite the many who offered encouraging words of support, it was the others she remembered: the people who looked at her accusingly when she walked into the shop then purposely looked away, or the ones who whispered to their companions when they saw her in the street and shook their heads. A reporter from the newspaper turned up asking questions around Bohenna and Claire was blamed. People felt the intrusion, the barely-concealed insinuation in a question. He tried to speak to Claire too but she refused, guessing that it was only going to make the situation worse but risking, she knew, a fabricated explanation for her silence. It had been stupid to think a box number would give her any anonymity. Of course everyone knew who had placed the advert. Who else could it have been?

Even Eddie was aware of the gunpowder she had thrown into the fire but she should not have been surprised because he regularly bought *Cornwall Now* - she had seen old sheets of it taped against his greenhouse windows to temper the high summer sun. And he mightn't mix much but he was the sort of silent ghost of a person - shuffling round the village, drinking a quiet pint, ignored - who heard all sorts of local gossip. She was outside, a couple of steps from the back door, throwing scraps out for the birds when he came round with a box of eggs, taking the trouble to walk right round the house to find her. He thrust the box into her hands then stood, not moving.

'Find anything out?' he shouted in his strange, cracked-bell voice.

She frowned, shaking her head. 'No. Nothing.'

He nodded and shuffled away. Ironically, it was the closest they had come to a personal conversation since she'd lived there.

Claire's mood swung up and down. She argued with herself, angry and frustrated at having got nowhere and yet blaming herself too. Had she really thought the advert would bring any answer? Neil had exhorted her to let it go but she always had to know better. He had once accused her of being self-indulgent in her grief and desperation, as if she thought she was the only one who was suffering. Was he right? She'd thought it was all about Gilly. Maybe not. Maybe she had allowed herself to become obsessed. And yet no, for who else was bothering about the fate of her little girl? She was her mother, after all.

The silence from Neil was deafening. He must have seen the advert by now, or at least heard about it because everyone else had, and he hadn't been in touch since he went away. She had tried ringing him to no avail; he wouldn't answer. She had left messages, asking if they could talk, but he didn't reply.

On the Thursday evening, she got out the art things Adam had given her. There were three large heavyweight sheets of watercolour paper, a plywood board, some tubes of paint and a variety of brushes. She taped a sheet of paper to the board, filled a glass jar with water and found a couple of white plates to mix colours on, then stood and looked down suspiciously at the pristine white surface. *Let the emotion drive it.* Was that what Adam had said? *Daub paint on. Put it on the paper so it doesn't mess with your head.* Easier to say than to do. She had never worked like that; her illustrations had been small and finely detailed.

The phone rang. As if he knew she was thinking about him, Adam wanted to know if he could come round. Half an hour later he was standing in her kitchen while she made them coffee.

'I've been meaning to call for days.' He glanced at the table. 'I see you're going to do some painting.'

'Maybe.' She handed him a mug. 'So you're back with Zoe. I'm glad.'

'Yes. It's good.'

They stood around awkwardly.

'I had a reporter come to see me,' he said. 'About your advert.'

She sighed. 'I am sorry, Adam. What did you tell him?'

'Nothing. Someone had told him we'd been dating so he was fishing for what I knew. I said I knew nothing about it. I said we weren't together any more.'

'I suppose he'll have gone to see Neil too then. Oh God, what a mess.' She walked away restlessly. 'Come on, let's sit.'

In the living room, she sat down heavily in the armchair while Adam took a seat on the sofa.

'Are you OK?' he said. 'You look...tired.'

'I haven't been sleeping well.'

'Why did you do it, Claire? It was crazy.'

'The advert? It was desperation. A last try. I had to give it one more shot.'

'I don't suppose anything's come of it?'

She shook her head. 'Nothing useful anyway. Lots of cranks. Stupid messages, threats even. I still don't know where the slide came from.'

'Threats? I don't like that. You should definitely tell the police about those.'

'They're just nonsense. Anyway they'd never track them down. This stuff happens all the time.' She tried not to sound as if she cared but all the negativity had left her feeling wrung out. She couldn't face contacting the police again though - all those questions and recriminations.

Adam was frowning. 'It's interesting that no-one has admitted to donating the slide now there's all this publicity out there. So maybe the person who donated it is indeed the guilty one.'

'Or maybe it's because no-one wants to have anything to do with the crazy woman, or risk being accused of something they haven't done.'

'You're not crazy.' He grinned. 'You just do some crazy things sometimes.' He shrugged. 'Everyone does, Claire.'

'Really? What's the craziest thing you've ever done? It's all right, you don't have to answer that.'

They both fell silent and sipped their coffee.

'So...' she said. 'What now for you and Zoe? Are you going to stay here or move on?'

'We're house-hunting. Zoe thinks we should bite the bullet and buy. She's probably right. We figure we can just about manage a mortgage between us.'

'And children?'

'Oh yes, I gave in.' He smiled again. 'But, hey, I think I'll enjoy it.' He stared into his coffee, studying it as if he were doing a scientific experiment. 'And you and Neil? I saw you together at the party. You seemed to be having a good time. How's that going?'

'It was going well. Then I shot the albatross and put the advert in the paper.'

'He didn't know?'

She shook her head.

'Ah.'

Again they drank, carefully not looking at each other.

'Please tell the police if you're being threatened,' he said, glancing up. 'If it's someone local they'd probably find the bastard.'

'I'm not sure it is just one person. Anyway, it'll stop soon. Bringing the police in would only make it worse. It makes it important, makes me more of a target.' She put her mug down. 'Look Adam, would you mind if we changed the subject?

There must be so many more interesting things we could talk about.'

'Sure. I understand.' He hesitated. 'It's just that I can't stop myself thinking about Gilly, and I wondered if maybe she saw something she wasn't supposed to see...' He paused, searching for a way to explain himself, and she cut across him.

'Please don't. I'm so grateful for all your help but I've decided not to pursue it. I can't do it any more. I'm sorry.' She was surprised at herself, unaware that she had actually made that decision. It was a relief to say it out loud. 'I've caused nothing but heartache and trouble with my desperation to find Gilly. And the truth is I'll never know what happened and I've got to accept it and move on. It's time. That's why I know the stalking'll stop. If I do nothing, they'll lose interest. Everyone'll lose interest.'

'Well, if you're sure... But if it doesn't settle, promise me you'll go to the police.'

'I promise.'

He finished his coffee and got up to go. She showed him out, automatically glancing down to check there was nothing on the step waiting for her. Adam leaned forward and gave her a brief hug.

'Good luck, Claire. I hope everything works out for you. You take care.'

She hugged him back, fiercely. 'You too. Have some beautiful children and love them loads.'

Back in the kitchen, she rinsed out the mugs and returned to the table, trying to focus her thoughts on the paper. *Let the emotion drive it.* Impulsively she grabbed a large brush, dipped it in the water and washed it over the paper, letting it slowly sink in. Then she mixed a bright buttery yellow and added it extravagantly over the damp paper in great swirling circles of colour and watched the water in the pulpy surface pull and feather it softly.

'That's you Gilly,' she murmured. 'Sunshine.'

She mixed a little burnt sienna into the yellow on her palette and dropped it on one side of the paper and saw it spread and mingle with the butter.

'That's your creativity.'

She was getting into this now. She mixed a bright red and dropped a little of that in on the border between the two previous colours. Though a tiny area, the red was bold and strong and fought to dominate the softer colours.

'That's your stubbornness and your love of life.'

Tears had started to fall but she was unaware of them and she was smiling as she mixed a bright green and added it on the other side of the paper.

'That's the beautiful natural world out there that you loved so much. It was your real passion, wasn't it, so I'll put some more in.'

She loaded the brush again and touched it in. The paper was a mass of colours now which shifted, melding into each other as the water seeped this way and that. The tears became so profuse that she could hardly see and she roughly rubbed the back of her hand across her eyes to clear them. She picked up the ultramarine and squeezed a thick worm of colour onto the palette, added burnt sienna to it and mixed them together. Pausing, she stared at the cheery bright colours on the paper.

'But you're not coming back, are you darling?' she breathed, so quietly she could hardly hear herself speak. 'You're...' She baulked at saying the word though she had known for a long time - if she'd had the courage to admit it - that she hadn't been looking for a girl any more, only a grave.

She dipped the brush back in the dark paint and scrubbed it into the yellow, then the red, then the green, dropping in more and more of the dirty blackness.

'And that's you, whoever you are, you bastard,' she spat. 'You destroyed her; you've destroyed us all.'

She threw the brush down and leaned forward onto the table, racked with silent sobs.

'What a stupid, stupid idea,' she gulped. 'Paint it out of your system…How can you? Why did I listen to such a bloody stupid idea?'

She turned and walked out of the kitchen into the sitting room, lifted the pouch out of the drawer of the sideboard and tipped the slide onto her hand. If she hadn't found this hiding in the bottom of the box that day, by now she might have managed to put it all behind her. She might even have got back together with Neil - for a moment there they had been so close – but it was never going to happen now.

At last, she could see the slide for what it was: a worthless piece of plastic. Of course it had never been Gilly's. A confused cocktail of emotions washed through her: embarrassment and anger, frustration and utter desolation. They pressed in on her, crushing her, sucking the air out of her lungs, and she ran to the back door, pulled it open wide and flung the slide as far out into the darkness as she could.

She had no idea where it landed. She heard nothing and she didn't care. Maybe now she would be able to breathe again.

Chapter 20

Claire made an effort to throw herself into work and tried to get some energy flowing, jogging with furious zeal, working up a sweat on the dusty paths by the river. She kept herself busy at home: baking, cleaning and gardening, and reading till all hours. Even so, she felt rudderless and numb, oddly removed from the world around her. All round the village people were gearing up for the fête on the twenty-seventh of June, an event always followed by a dance which, over these recent years, was held in the vineyard restaurant with its patio doors thrown open to the summer night. In the small community, it was one of the major events of the summer. It passed Claire by. If it surfaced in her mind at all she quickly pushed it away, for the fête only reminded her of the hair slide and she was determined to put that out of her mind for good.

As she started to find her feet again, she kept thinking of Neil, and increasingly it bore down on her that she owed him an apology. She should have told him about the slide and explained what she had been trying to do. Gilly was his daughter too. She couldn't blame him for being cross when she had intentionally cut him out of the loop. Regularly she got her phone out but didn't call him. In the end she decided to see him in person and she walked across to the vineyard one day during her lunch break and poked her head in at the office. Julia was the only one there, speaking on the phone, and Claire silently withdrew. Tim was standing behind her and made her jump.

She glared at him defensively. 'I was looking for Neil.'

'And hello to you too, Claire,' said Tim, not quite smiling. 'Neil's not here. He's out for the day.'

'Right. What time will he be back?'

'Late. Anything I can do?'

'No thanks, Tim. I need to speak to Neil but I'll see him again.'

'He's been very busy lately.'

'Meaning?'

'Meaning he's been very busy lately. Travelling a lot.'

'I see.'

She left, knowing that Timothy was still standing there, watching her go. He was clearly covering for his brother. Maybe Neil was somewhere nearby, watching her too; maybe those were the instructions he had left to tell her if she came around looking for him.

The following evening she was pulling weeds out of the front garden - while Eddie stood at the fence, watching, occasionally grunting and pointing at one she'd missed - when Neil came to stand at her front gate. She straightened up and stared at him, a trowel in one hand, a tussock of couch grass dangling from the other.

Neil slipped the catch on the gate and came to stand in front of her.

'I went to see you yesterday,' Claire said, glancing sideways as Eddie wordlessly shuffled away from the fence. 'Tim said you weren't around.'

'Yes. He told me.'

They faced each other, gaze locked. She couldn't talk to him here, in the garden. 'Look, why don't you come in?' She dropped the grass and trowel in the trug, peeling off her gardening gloves and throwing them in on top. 'I'll put the kettle on.'

Neil wordlessly followed her inside.

'I didn't sleep last night,' he said, closing the back door behind him.

Claire looked up from filling the kettle.

'Why not?'

'Because I was thinking about you - and that damn advert. And the very persistent reporter who wanted to know what you'd found exactly, and where. I was cross. And hurt too. And I thought about the party when we really seemed to be…' He pursed up his lips and shook his head impatiently. 'I don't understand what's going on Claire. Then Tim said you'd come to see me. He said you wouldn't say why and I fretted over it all night. This afternoon I decided I had to see you and find out.'

She switched the kettle on and turned to face him.

'I came because I wanted to apologise. I wanted to explain.' She hesitated; she had rehearsed this. 'When I came back here I genuinely meant to make a fresh start. I wanted to put it all behind me and sort my head out. I told you that. And it was difficult at first but it seemed to be working. Then something happened which blew my plans away.'

She paused. His expression gave nothing away but his eyes hadn't left her face.

She told him how she'd found the hair slide and how convinced she was that it was Gilly's, that it meant their daughter was still in Bohenna.

'I wanted to believe that she was still alive, perhaps trapped somewhere not far away. It was a chance I couldn't possibly ignore.'

Neil was frowning now, staring at her lips moving as if she were talking in a foreign language.

267

She took a deep breath and started again, telling him how she tried to trace who had donated the slide and how Adam Thomas had become involved.

'He was at a loose end because his girlfriend had walked out, you see. We let people think we were dating because it covered what we were doing.'

Neil snorted sceptically. 'And what was the upshot of all this grand detective work may I ask?'

'Nothing. That's why I ended up putting the advert in the paper. It was desperation. Adam didn't know anything about it either. As you know, he and Zoe are back together again.'

'I can't imagine what you were thinking, Claire. After all the rubbish we got last time. Why on earth would you put yourself up for it again?'

She frowned. 'So what would you have done?'

'What do you mean?'

'If you'd found something which you thought proved Gilly hadn't left the village, what would you have done?'

He hesitated, put on the spot. 'I don't know.'

'Exactly. It's easy to find fault, Neil. Trying to do something positive and knowing what it should be - that's the hard bit.'

He was unusually silent. 'What response did you get to the advert then?'

'Nothing of any use. The usual. Drat, I forgot the tea.'

She turned and quickly poured it into two mugs, slopped some milk in them and put one on the worktop beside him. He didn't appear to even notice.

'So where is this slide?' he was asking. 'Can I see it?'

'I haven't got it any more. I threw it away. Do you want to come through?'

He didn't move.

'After all that, you just threw it in the bin? You'd better

not tell anyone else or there'll be journalists rooting through your rubbish.'

'Don't make a big thing about it. I threw it outside somewhere. I was cross and upset. It was just a cheap kid's plastic hair slide. It could have been anyone's. I should have listened when the policewoman said that in the first place.'

'You went to the police with it?' He sounded incredulous. 'What did they say?'

'There was a new Family Liaison Officer.' Claire shrugged. 'She thought I was mad.'

'There's a surprise. They aren't pursuing it then?'

'Do you always have to be sarcastic? This is why I didn't tell you about it in the first place. You have to be so superior. And no, they aren't pursuing it. They didn't think there was any point.'

He nodded, hesitated. 'I'm sorry, Claire. I know, I can be a bit...pompous sometimes.'

'A bit?'

'OK. A lot.' He smiled apologetically. 'And I'm sorry you didn't think you could come to me with it. It must have been tough for you.'

'Yes. It was. I can't get away from the feeling that I've let Gilly down. I *wanted* the slide to be hers. I wanted it to be true. And it was all nonsense. All of it.'

She closed her eyes, utterly exhausted. But she could feel Neil prising the mug from her hand and her eyes flicked open to find him putting his arms around her, pulling her close.

'You haven't let Gilly down,' he said, putting one hand to gently press her head against his shoulder, murmuring softly into her hair. 'No-one could have tried harder. It's not your fault.'

'Oh Neil, you know it's...'

'Hush. Don't talk. Let me speak. You know how difficult

I find it to talk about stuff like this.' He paused, still holding her head against him as if he couldn't bear her to look at him. 'I know I didn't support you enough when we moved. I thought the new life in Kent would help us forget and I was so involved in my work, it was easier for me. I know you found it harder to leave Bohenna behind, to leave Gilly behind. Ssh, let me finish. It was me who let you down. I don't know what I was doing with Samantha. She never meant anything. I'm sorry, Claire. I've always loved you. I still do.'

He bent down and kissed her, then pulled away to look at her.

'I'd really been hoping we could try again,' he said. 'Then I heard about the advert and I thought nothing had changed after all. It felt like some sort of recurring nightmare and I didn't know what to do.'

'A recurring nightmare? I know all about those.' She tried a laugh, confused, wanting to lighten the tone. She wasn't sure she could trust this new Neil.

She eased away from him, picked up her mug and drank a couple of mouthfuls of tea.

Neil picked up his mug too and leaned against the units.

'Have you heard from Laura recently?' she asked. 'Did you know she's broken up with Travis?'

'Yes, I rang her a couple of weeks ago. She didn't sound too bothered though. She's probably already met someone else.'

'Do you think so? I thought maybe she was putting a brave face on it. So I suppose you know she's going fruit picking when term ends? Her friend Katie lives in the Cotswolds near a fruit farm.'

'No, I didn't know that.'

'She sent me some photos of the village and the farm. It looks lovely. I'll show you.' She put the mug down and looked round. 'My phone must be upstairs. I'll get it. Won't be a minute.'

She slipped out of the kitchen and ran upstairs. Her bag was on the bed and she pulled the phone out and turned to find Neil standing in the doorway.

'Is it OK for me to come in?' he said.

'Of course.'

She began searching through her phone, looking for the photos Laura had sent, and felt his hand on her shoulder as he came to stand beside her. The heat of his skin was burning through the cotton of her shirt.

'See,' she said, finding them and slowly flicking through the pictures with her thumb, 'doesn't it look nice? I'm quite jealous.'

'We'll visit it sometime.' He barely glanced at the screen. 'Do you still remember the first time we made love?' He was whispering now, lifting his hand to stroke the hair back from her face.

She looked at him sideways, smiling. 'Of course I do. In the boathouse. I was scared to death someone would come in and find us at any moment.'

'That's flattering.'

'You know what I mean.'

'I went back to look at it a few days ago. It's a mess now but it brought back so many memories.'

'I went back too. Yes, a lot of memories. Good memories too.'

He turned her to face him and, for a moment, hesitated, looking into her eyes, posing a silent question. He began undoing the buttons of her shirt and she watched his fingers but didn't move.

'I meant it, Claire,' he murmured, 'when I said I loved it that you were passionate about things. It's what I always think

271

about you, that everything you do is wholehearted. It's exciting. And invigorating. You don't compromise.'

'I do now. I've learnt that you have to if you want to survive.'

She put a hand on his to stop him undoing any more buttons.

'You know, I'm not the same person any more,' she said. 'Are you sure about this?'

'Yes. Aren't you?'

'I'm not sure about anything.'

'We've all changed, Claire. But we're still us. We just need to give ourselves time to readjust. Don't you want to give us that chance?'

She hesitated, silently arguing with herself. Pointlessly. She removed her hand.

He undid the last button and pushed the shirt off her shoulders, then kissed her gently first on one eye then the other. It was what he always used to do before they made love.

*

Adam stared at the painting on his table without seeing it. He wasn't happy. The plans he and Zoe had so carefully and painfully discussed for their future together seemed to be changing again.

It had started with a phone call from one of Zoe's friends. Fran, a girl who worked at the same leisure complex in Bristol where Zoe had been the receptionist, had rung a few days previously. Apparently the girl who'd replaced her as receptionist had been incompetent and Fergus – the manager - had now sacked her.

'Fergus told me to persuade you to come back,' Fran said eagerly. 'Said he'd happily give you your old job again. He's got some agency girl in at the moment.'

When Zoe mentioned that she and Adam were looking to move and start a family, Fran had pressed the point again. She and her partner, Tony, already had two small boys.

'That's perfect, then,' she said. 'Adam can work anywhere, can't he? You don't have to stay buried down there. We could do all sorts of things together again if you come back to Bristol. Wouldn't that be great? We could share babysitters. Or we could leave the kids with the guys while we go shopping.'

Watching Zoe's face while she was having this conversation, Adam had seen her light up as if she had just been plugged into the mains. And even afterwards, even while she was telling him about it and saying, jokily, what a silly idea it was and trust Fran to suggest that, he could tell how the idea still buzzed round her head.

'You aren't seriously considering going back to the Leisure Centre, are you?' he demanded.

'Of course not,' Zoe responded briskly. 'But it's nice to be missed.'

And she'd given him one of those looks he could never decipher and the conversation had been dropped.

They still searched property in Cornwall - they had even made appointments to look round three houses - but they couldn't agree on what exactly they wanted to buy. Zoe wanted sleek and modern; she wanted to live on an estate. Zoe liked manicured gardens; she liked regularity; she liked people around her.

'I can't live on an estate,' Adam insisted.

'Why not?' she asked.

He didn't know. But they made him feel claustrophobic. He'd grown up on a suburban housing estate and felt it choked him; he couldn't wait to leave.

'It's like living in a goldfish bowl,' he offered eventually.

'Everyone watches what you're doing. I'd rather live in a flat in town than that.'

'Don't give me that, Adam. Everyone knows what you're doing in Bohenna too and you love it. Anyway, I'm not bringing up children in a flat. What are you thinking? We need a garden and a lawn for them to play on. I don't see what's wrong with a decent semi on an estate. That one we looked at yesterday afternoon was really nice. It didn't need anything doing to it. It was perfect.'

But Adam wasn't bothered about perfect, he wanted homely. And, more than anything, he wanted to be somewhere that didn't make him feel constrained. He thought they'd agreed on a compromise: a house on the edge of a town where Zoe had access to facilities and things going on, but from which he could see fields maybe. Somewhere he didn't feel trapped.

And then she'd dropped in the line which showed that the conversation with Fran had never entirely left her mind.

'Surely you'd rather live somewhere like that than be back in Bristol, wouldn't you?'

He was irritated – it sounded like an ultimatum – but it bothered him too that perhaps he was being unfair. Left to her own devices, she would take that job at the Leisure Centre. She would be back with her old friends; she could share shopping trips in the city and the occasional night at the cinema. That's what would make her really happy. So maybe a neat little semi on an estate wasn't such a lot to ask of him.

Even so, he thought it would slowly kill him, one neat, perfect room, by one.

'I'm sensing domestic issues,' said a voice behind him. He turned and saw Jane Sawdy standing just inside the door of his studio. He'd been leaving the door open again these warmer days but he hadn't heard her step. She did this sometimes - creeping up on him – and it was unnerving. She took a couple of steps closer.

'You've been sitting staring at that picture for ages and not touched it.'

'I'm waiting for the muse to wake up,' he said drily. 'She's been sleeping a lot lately.'

'To judge by your recent activity I'd have thought she'd gone away on holiday.'

'Yeah. Very funny.'

Jane leaned on the counter that separated the studio space from his tiny gallery.

'Going to the fête?' she asked.

'I suppose. I hadn't thought much about it.'

He had toyed with going, in fact. He had enjoyed it the year before, the simple, old-fashioned nature of the event, the stalls and the games. Last year, he'd won a stuffed rabbit and he'd given it to Zoe who'd smiled and said the right things but had never really entered into the spirit of the day. It was very 'rustic', she'd said. Maybe they wouldn't go after all.

He turned his head to look at Jane. 'Are you?'

'I've been asked to run a fortune-telling booth. I don't like the name but they insisted it was just a bit of fun. I thought I should show willing.'

'Very noble.'

Adam returned his baleful gaze to the painting.

'I might be able to help, you know,' she said. 'With Zoe.'

He snapped his head back to look at her.

'What do you mean?'

'You're still not seeing eye to eye with her, are you? Perhaps if you got me something personal of hers to focus on, and something of yours too…' She looked down at his neck where his gold chain was just visible above his tee shirt. '…that chain, for example. Then I could try and feel how

275

compatible you are.' She hesitated, watching him with what looked like an amused curl to her lip. 'I might be able to sense how well your personalities gel together. Whether you work as a couple, in fact.'

'Of course we work as a couple,' he said crossly. 'We've been together years. You're talking nonsense. Everyone has issues in relationships. It's not all sweetness and light.' He turned back to his painting. 'Look Jane, I need to get on.'

'Of course.' She straightened up but didn't leave. 'You know your aura was a much better colour when you were seeing Claire.'

He turned again, eyes narrowed. 'What? Now you're trying to tell me I should have stayed with Claire? But it was never like that.'

'I'm just saying.'

'You want Neil Pennyman back for yourself,' he said brutally. 'That's why you're saying that. It's not for my benefit, it's for yours. You've never got over him dumping you.'

Jane stared at him. If looks could kill, his mother would have said. Jane walked out without another word.

Adam shook his head and tried to put her out of his mind. Jealous women he could do without.

*

No-one can replicate the first sweet stirrings of a love affair; it's never the same the second time around. Claire knew that; she didn't expect it. And it wasn't the same, but as the next days stretched slowly into one week, then into two and three, things seemed to be going well. She and Neil argued - but then they always had - and sometimes she thought they would be wiser to take it more slowly, but no sooner had she thought it than she was agreeing to another dinner with him or a walk along the riverside or lunch in Fowey. Neil came to her house and helped with some of the more mundane tasks - something he had rarely done before - and several times he shared her bed with a passion which seemed to surprise them both in its intensity. They were getting to know each other again.

Rapidly they reached an equilibrium which was not what it had been before - they were both a little too guarded, too careful and measured for that - and it was perhaps a little stormier, but it was good all the same and too enticing to leave alone. For Claire it was like riding her bike down The Cutting, the lane which ran downhill from the church to Bank Lane, north of the river. The Cutting was perfect for freewheeling - it was quiet and straight and too steep to pedal. They had all done it as kids for the thrill of the speed and the wind in their ears as they gathered a crazy momentum down the hill. Intoxicating, it was. But there was no way to stop once you started, not till you swerved left at the bottom and the ground levelled off onto Bank Lane. You could brake then, or throw yourself down on the grassy bank making the ducks parp a complaint and waddle away. Claire's father told her not to do it - 'you could get hurt' - but she did it anyway. She couldn't resist.

The fallout from the advertisement began to subside. She received another couple of silent phone calls but nothing else was left outside her door and the letters offering false sightings or abuse tailed off. Neil looked at them with her and agreed they were all fakes or cranks. It was at least reassuring to be able to share it with him.

And, just in time for the fête, Laura came to stay for the rest of the summer holidays and Claire told her that she and her father were 'seeing each other again'.

'Really? Are you saying it's serious?'

Claire smiled. Her teenage daughter was talking like the

parent. 'I don't know Laura. Well, I do. I mean it's serious. But, you know…we're going to see how it goes.'

Laura gave her mother a hug.

'But are you happy, mum?' she muttered over Claire's shoulder.

'Yes, Laura, I think I am.' Or I will be, she thought. Yes, I will.

Laura squeezed her a little tighter and Claire closed her eyes in relief. For the first time in years, she dared to think that they were getting over it. They could dare to be happy again - as a family. Then she felt a twinge of guilt for thinking it. Because the guilt wouldn't go away.

Chapter 21

'I don't know why you didn't go and see her yesterday afternoon when she invited you over,' Claire said to Laura, washing out the mixing bowl and utensils and putting them to drain.

You should have got it over with, she wanted to say, but as always bit it back, not wanting to prejudice her daughter against her own grandmother. Laura was entitled to make up her own mind about Eve - though Claire suspected she already had.

'You know why,' said Laura bitterly. 'She was going to have a go at me. Dad says grandma wants me to spend time in the vineyard and show some interest in wine-making. Why the hell would I want to do that? I want a life.'

'Claire.'

'Sorry mum, but really. I'm at uni. I'm not interested in making wine.'

'I know. So it's up to you to say that if she brings it up. You should make a point of seeing her today at the fête. She's going to be there so it's a chance to get it out of the way.'

Claire came to stand in front of her daughter and took hold of her by each arm.

'Look, Laura. It's your life. You choose. I'll back you whatever you decide to do. But you're at an age now when you're the one who has to say it to Eve. She never believes me anyway - you know that. She'll take it from you, if you say it firmly, politely, but like you mean it.' Laura looked at her disbelievingly. 'She will, Laura. You know she and I don't see eye to eye, but she is fair. You have to stand up to her, though, or she'll railroad you. It's no good trying to avoid her and thinking she'll forget. It just gets worse. Trust me.' She smiled at her daughter sympathetically. 'Oh drat, the scones.'

Claire let go of Laura, spun round and pulled the oven door open. She peered in anxiously; the scones still looked pale. Not quite ready? She had no idea.

'I'm so rubbish at this,' she muttered and closed the oven door again, glancing at her watch.

'Why are you making something for the cake stall anyway?' said Laura.

'Hettie Blake asked me so I thought I ought to make an effort.'

It was interesting just how much more popular Claire had become with certain people in the village since she'd been seen going round with Neil again. It was amusing and a little bit irritating but it wasn't a bad feeling; Claire rather liked being included again.

She bent down and peered in through the greasy glass of the oven door, waited another minute, glanced at her watch again and opened it, pulling the top baking tray out and putting it on the stove top.

'What do you think, Laura? Done?'

Laura leaned over and poked the top of one of the scones.

'Yeah. Probably.'

Claire pulled the second tray out and began transferring the scones to a wire rack.

'What will dad say?' Laura asked suddenly.

'What about?'

'Me not wanting to work here.'

'He'll be OK about it.'

Claire's gaze met Laura's. As usual she tried to second guess what lay behind her daughter's shuttered eyes, but couldn't tell. And for a moment she thought Laura was going to tell her something but the next the girl was walking out of the kitchen, speaking over her shoulder.

'I'm getting the bus into Fowey, mum. I'll be back for the fête. I'll see you up there.'

*

Claire was running late as usual. It was already five past two and she was only just leaving the house. The fête officially started at two. Hettie Blake wasn't going to be impressed.

And Eddie was in his front garden, cutting sweet peas from his wigwams and, having seen her, he was already heading for the fence, a small bouquet in his hand. She hadn't the heart to ignore him. He thrust the flowers at her as she came across to join him.

'They're beautiful,' she said, smiling. 'What a lovely scent too. Thank you. But would you mind putting them in some water for me till I get back? I'm already late and I'd hate for them to wilt.'

He grunted and nodded and let his hand drop.

'I'm going up to the fête,' she added. 'I promised some scones for the cake stall. Perhaps I could get you something there. Is there anything you'd particularly like?'

He hesitated with a hint of a guilty smile. 'Chocolate cake?'

'OK,' she said, grinning. 'I'll see what they've got.' She started to move away.

'I never go,' he barked. 'But I saw the posters. That psychic woman's telling fortunes isn't she?'

Claire stopped again and turned. 'So I believe.' She

281

wasn't sure if she found the idea of Jane running a fortune-telling booth distasteful or funny.

'Got a history, that woman y'know.'

She frowned. 'Jane Sawdy? What do you mean?'

'My sister told me just the other day. She lives in Bodmin. I was telling her about the fête and the psychic. *She* said rumour was that that woman got prosecuted for stealing a child.'

A chill ran down Claire's spine. 'What?' she breathed.

'Ah,' said Eddie, nodding. 'Depressed she was, that's what they said. Lost a child herself or somethin'' He sniffed dismissively. 'But it didn't happen in Cornwall.'

He added the last remark as if that made it less important somehow or perhaps more doubtful. He turned away and went back to his sweet peas.

Claire carried on up to the fête, her thoughts running wild.

*

In days gone by, the fête had been held on the little green down by the river. There were black and white photographs of the event, saved for posterity, in a number of old books and periodicals from the nineteen-thirties onwards. But the event had slowly outgrown the relatively small square of green and had moved over the years to two other sites before settling, just three years previously, in a small field adjoining the Craft Yard which had once belonged to Charlie Hitchen and which, now grassed over, the Pennymans offered each year for the village's use. It was unfortunate that it was slightly out of the centre but it did have the advantage that it was relatively flat - something few fields in Bohenna could boast - and was conveniently close to the amenities of the vineyard and Craft Yard, notably their car parks and toilets.

Julia stood behind the Pennyman wine stall, flanked on

each side by her brothers, selling plastic beakers of both red and white wine - and even the occasional bottle - to an apparently endless queue of customers. It was a glorious summer's day and the field was thronging with people. Their stall stood up a slight bank half way along the hedge which ran alongside the road and allowed a good view of the event. She disliked selling wine in this way, thinking it didn't offer it the respect it deserved. 'It's a village, Julia,' her mother had said. 'We're part of it. It's important to do this, show willing.' 'It's good for business,' her two brothers insisted. She supposed they were right. Maybe she just didn't like standing here when she thought she could be doing something more useful. And Tim had arranged a pile of those awful teddy bears on one side of the table and they were selling too. He would be insufferable.

Julia's gaze wandered. She saw Phil weaving slowly through the crowds towards the field entrance to her left. It looked as if he was leaving already though he had promised to help relieve them on the stall later. In the gateway to the field she saw him stop to talk to a woman and a moment later it became clear that it had been Claire. Here she was now, slipping through the crowds, carrying something.

Julia made a point of following her progress. She was heading for the cake stall and proceeded to give them whatever it was she'd been carrying. Julia relaxed a little but still she couldn't stop watching the woman. Claire looked distracted, and Julia, constantly suspicious, wondered what she would do next.

Neil had assured his family that the whole advert issue was a thing of the past, that Claire had abandoned any more efforts to trace where that hair slide had come from, that she wasn't asking questions any more or actively searching for Gilly. He and Claire were 'having another go' he'd said; they were 'getting on really well'; they were 'very happy together again'. But he hadn't explained where Claire had found the slide or why it was so significant to her - he hadn't wanted to talk about it at all - and Julia still felt uneasy, not helped by the fact that, despite his fine words, Neil didn't look happy. He was edgy. In fact, they all were. Something had yet to be resolved, she knew; it hadn't gone away.

The queue was growing and Neil nudged her impatiently. Julia picked up a plastic beaker and put on a smile.

'Red or white?' she shouted above the noise.

*

Claire walked round the field in a daze. She bought a strip of raffle tickets and a jar of jam. She played the tombola and tried to guess how many Liquorice Allsorts were contained in a very large glass bottle. She bought a couple of potted leggy cosmos from the plant stall and struggled to stop them from falling out of the plastic carrier bag they'd been put in.

Her eyes were continually drawn to the small tent at the side of the field with the bold sign *FORTUNE-TELLER* outside. There was a queue of people waiting to go in. Claire toyed with joining it and confronting Jane directly. Caution warned her against it and she kept away. Neil was busy on the wine stall, of course, and she could see no sign of Adam. There was no-one she could share this new information with. In any case, she had made too many mistakes by rushing headlong into things; she wanted to take some time to think.

And Laura hadn't materialised which was starting to concern her. Claire checked her phone again. She had told Laura to ring when she got to the field but there was still no message and no missed call. She pocketed the phone, walked across to the Pennyman stall and joined the queue. Tim smiled and Julia nodded distractedly; Neil served her.

'Where's Laura?' he immediately asked, tipping white wine into a plastic tumbler. 'I haven't seen her.'

'She went to Fowey this morning on the bus. Said she'd meet me up here.'

Neil glanced at his watch, lips compressed.

'Well,' he said grudgingly, 'time yet, I suppose. I told her, you know, that she had to make the effort. After missing mum's birthday bash like that...' He flicked a look along the queue. 'I'll try and get away in a bit, darling.' He was already looking at the next customer. 'A bottle, sir? Yes, what would you like? We've got...'

Claire walked away, clutching her beaker of wine. Yes, Neil was busy. He might plan to leave the stall to join her but, from past experience, that was unlikely to happen. Work still dominated his mind; some things never changed.

She continued her slow tour of the field, exchanging the odd word here and there, looking in on stalls she had so far missed, playing out a part as if, by conforming to the rules of the occasion, all her thoughts would fall into place and line up. She saw Nick Lawer ahead of her at one point, talking to someone, and quickly changed direction rather than bump into him. There was Eve again, standing near the staging, talking to one of the organisers. And at one point Tim passed nearby, taking his break from the stall, walking with an earnest, purposeful step.

She stopped at the book stall, dumped her bags on the ground and worked her way round the square of tables, browsing the paperbacks. She bought a couple, retrieved her bags, and, with still no message from Laura, decided to leave. It was after three now and she was going home to figure out what to do. She paused to send Laura a text and made her way back down the hill.

The house was eerily quiet after the hubbub of the fête.

As she walked through the door, a message arrived melodically on her phone. It was from Laura: *Missed the bus. See you at home later. Will explain.*

Relieved, Claire put the kettle on and unpacked the first bag: runner beans and potatoes, gingerbread and chocolate brownies - the best she could find for Eddie - and the paperbacks. She carefully rolled the other plastic carrier down off the two plants, trying not to snap their shoots and wondering where she could plant them. A piece of paper had settled in among the fronds of one of them and she pulled it out curiously. It looked like a sheet torn from a small notebook and it had writing on it.

If you want to find out more about the hair slide, come ALONE to the church at four thirty. Make sure you're not seen.

Claire felt her heart thump harder and read it twice. She glanced furtively towards the window as if someone might be watching her, then turned the paper over - there was nothing on the back - and read it again. There was no signature, nothing that indicated who had written it. Did this have something to do with Jane? Could she have slipped through the crowds somehow and left it herself? Or maybe it was just a trick, another twisted joke. But it was the fête day after all, which made sense. Someone might be there who had been there a year ago. The same person who had put the slide to the stall? Perhaps that was just what the writer wanted her to think. There again, could she possibly ignore it? No, of course not - just in case.

She glanced at her watch; twenty-five past three. Plenty of time then. It probably wasn't wise to go alone. But the writer mightn't show if he thought she had a companion and she couldn't risk losing the chance of information.

286

She reboiled the kettle and poured the steaming water over a teabag, still staring at the note. She didn't recognise the handwriting. She wasn't sure she knew what Jane's writing was like these days. Mechanically she pressed the teabag into the water a couple of times then extracted it and slopped some milk into the mug, weighing up her options. It would have been good to talk to Neil about it but that was out of the question. He would insist she ignore it and he'd lose his temper. If it was the hoax she suspected, she would have jeopardised their relationship for nothing.

Still she reached for her phone and, on an impulse, rang Adam's number but he didn't answer and it cut to the answering service. She waited for the beep.

'Hi Adam…' She hesitated. 'Never mind. It's nothing important. I'll speak to you soon.'

She cut the call. Maybe that wouldn't have been smart either. She would go alone.

*

The church clock was striking four when Claire closed the front door behind her, its chimes echoing down the valley. Eddie was in his back garden, bending over his rows of strawberry plants, out of sight; she had checked before she left.

The sun was still shining. Wearing a tee shirt, cotton trousers and trainers and holding her phone in her hand, she cut quickly across to the footpath through the woods and followed the zig-zagging track until she reached the river. Glancing up and down the riverside path, she saw no-one and she struck west towards the main bridge. Once there she stood on its arch, nonchalantly looking down into the water while a family she didn't know came the other way carrying bags and a cuddly squirrel and eating ice-cream, clearly coming away from the fête. When they'd gone by she crossed to the other side and walked quickly, keeping to the narrow lanes and cutting up on another footpath until she reached the churchyard gate.

She paused and surveyed all around. She was early. The sound of the fête loudspeaker drifted across to her from further along the hillside, announcing the winners of the various raffles as the event drew to a close. There was no-one visible anywhere nearby; the fête had drawn most of the village. She pushed the gate open, walked up the path and lifted the heavy iron latch to ease the huge oak door of the church open, then slipped into its chill, dark interior.

It was empty. She wasn't sure if she was relieved or sorry. It was a long time since she had been in the church and she hesitated, looking round, feeling the building's calm, dank embrace. Slowly she walked down the main aisle and through into the Lady Chapel. On the far wall was a small polished brass plaque.

Gilly Pennyman
Always remembered

Claire reluctantly raised her eyes to look at it. She and her father had nearly fallen out over this. He'd been a keen church-goer and he had paid to have that plaque put there, was desperate that Gilly should have some sort of memorial so she would never be forgotten. But Claire had hated it because it was too final; it had felt like an admission of loss, a defeat. Now she was confused and didn't know what to think. Her boundaries had shifted; time and repeated despair had brought a measure of acceptance.

She sat down in a pew and waited. Her sight line to the main door was obscured by a pillar. It was four-thirty exactly when she heard it open.

A woman wearing a broad-brimmed floppy sun hat over

straight dark hair came into view, walking slowly up the main aisle. Unconsciously, Claire must have made a noise because the woman's head turned.

'Claire? You came then.'

'Yes.'

The woman took off the hat and smiled. The hair colour was wrong and, with the passage of so many years, it took Claire a full minute to register that the woman was Jane's cousin, Fiona.

Chapter 22

'I met Sam in Fowey.' Laura looked at her mother imploringly. 'You do remember Sam? We were good friends at school.'

'Yes, I remember him, but I thought he'd gone abroad.'

'He did. His dad had a two-year contract in the States but they've been back a year now. Steve's at Exeter uni. Anyway, it was good to see him.' Laura flushed. 'He's really tall now.'

Claire managed to smile. 'And that's good is it?'

'Well, he's kind of hot in other ways too.' Laura flushed and laughed, embarrassed. 'He's asked me out tonight, mum. I told him about the dance. I said I was supposed to go and he said he could come. But it'd be kind of awkward having him at a village do when, like, I haven't seen him in ages and we need to catch up.'

Normally, Claire might have argued the toss. A village dance was surely a good way to have some fun and get to know a boy again without pressure. But she didn't want Laura at the dance. In fact, after what she had heard in the church, it suited her perfectly if Laura was well away from Bohenna that night.

'Go out with him then,' she said. 'Where does he want to take you?'

'A friend of his is having a birthday party at the yacht club.'

'OK.' Claire stretched another smile, trying to appear

relaxed. She hadn't queried Laura's delay in coming back for the fête, hadn't brought the subject up at all in fact. 'How will you get there?'

'He said he could pick me up. He's got a car. And...' Laura stopped, looking awkward.

'What?'

'He said his parents won't mind if I sleep over at his house 'cause...well...' She shrugged. '...it'll be kind of late. There's a spare room.'

'Is there?' Good, and will you use it? Claire wanted to add, but this wasn't the moment for that kind of parental conversation. 'OK, but you take care, won't you?' she said instead, reaching out a concerned hand to touch her daughter's arm.

*

Sam picked Laura up just after seven.

Claire waited until they were out of sight, then went back to the sideboard and opened the top drawer. She pulled out a polythene bag and held it up to look at the hair slide it contained. It had taken her twenty minutes on her hands and knees when she got home from the church to find this at the bottom of the garden. Now she studied it, desperately hoping for inspiration about what she should do. The dance started at seven thirty and Neil would be waiting for her. She didn't have long.

She perched on the edge of a chair, stood up again, sat down, the conversation with Fiona running through her mind for the umpteenth time.

Fiona had been a pretty girl, not striking like Jane and rather flat-featured, but she'd been delicate and fine-boned with pale copper-coloured hair and a soft, breathy voice. She had been remote, Claire remembered, but had only spent occasional holidays with the gang and probably hadn't found it easy to fit in. Adolescents, too preoccupied with fitting in themselves, aren't always that understanding of others.

She was still slight - and bundled up now in an oversized cardigan - but her hair was a heavy dark brown, whether from dye or from a wig, Claire couldn't tell. But something about the woman suggested barely disguised fear.

She's had some mental health issues too. Had a breakdown or something. That had been Jane's dismissive assessment but what did it mean exactly? Lots of people had mental health issues; it didn't stop them functioning just like everyone else. In any case, if what Eddie had told her was true, Jane was hardly in a position to comment.

Fiona sat in the pew next to her. 'You put an advert in the paper, didn't you? About a hair slide that was given to last year's fête?'

'Yes, I did. What do you know about it?'

Fiona fidgeted on the wooden seat, wringing her hands as if they were cold. Maybe they were: the sunshine of the day might have touched the interior of the church in rainbow patterns but it hadn't warmed it.

'I've been arguing with myself for days,' she said. 'I knew I should tell you but I wasn't sure if…' She broke off and looked away, glancing in the direction of the door.

'There's no-one else here, Fiona. Tell me what you know. Please.'

'I think he saw me this afternoon.'

'Who?'

'Tim. I put that slide to the fête, you see. I found it.'

'Tim? I don't understand. You found it where?'

'In a box of Tim's things. We lived together for a while. Didn't you know? We broke up last year.'

'You were Tim's last girlfriend? No, I didn't know.'

Claire frowned, trying to take this in. 'OK, so you found the slide in Tim's things. How? Where?'

'You have to understand, Tim can be really difficult. He doesn't give that impression, does he? But he's got some weird ideas.'

'Weird in what way?'

'He likes to take photos.' Fiona stopped, her eyes flicking around nervously. 'You know, pictures of his women in the nude. I mean, I thought it was a bit of fun at first, a laugh, but he takes it very seriously. He calls it 'art'. Anyway, after a while I decided I didn't want to do it any more and he completely lost it, told me we were through.' Her speech was getting faster and faster, her hands now pressed hard together. 'Most of the time he's so calm, so easy, isn't he? But then suddenly he was like a different person: really angry. He was about to go away for a couple of days with work and he said he wanted me to take my things and be out of his house by the time he came back. Just like that. Spoke to me like I was a bit of dirt under his feet. He got hold of me...and...' She swallowed hard. 'He hurt me.'

Again she looked round, the whites of her eyes showing. She ran a dry tongue over her lips but didn't speak.

'So you left?' prompted Claire.

'Yes. But I wanted to find the photos he'd taken of me. I didn't want to leave them there.' Again she started to babble. 'He's got one of the bedrooms kitted out as a darkroom, and another with a chaise longue and fancy lighting. He keeps his photos there too, with a load of other stuff in a big old cupboard. But the wardrobe was locked and the key wasn't where he usually kept it. I suppose he'd guessed I might look for them. Anyway I looked all around, just nosing, and I found this shoe box, pushed up on top of the wardrobe in the bedroom. He obviously hadn't touched it in a while because it was really dusty and it was full of all sorts of childhood stuff. You know, a little teddy bear and a fluffy duck and Scout badges and games, a compass, a magnifying glass. Silly kid's treasures. And then this hair-slide too. It struck me as odd but I thought maybe it had been his sister's or something - or a previous girlfriend's even. Anyway, I decided I'd take the box for revenge and, later on, I chucked the useless stuff and gave the rest to the fête. I wanted him to see them there, for sale. But it was a silly prank and I don't think he even noticed. He doesn't bother with the stalls. And maybe it's just as well 'cause he'd have guessed it was me. It was a stupid thing to do.'

'But he must have missed the box?'

'Probably not unless he went looking. You couldn't see it unless you stood on something.'

But he'll have gone looking now, thought Claire, because I mentioned it in the advert.

'So where have you been?' she asked.

'I stayed with a friend in Lostwithiel for a couple of months. Then I got a job in Plymouth and moved away. I tried to forget about the whole thing. But I was staying with my friend again and saw the advert in her paper.' She paused, looking at Claire sidelong. 'I didn't like what I was thinking. I guessed it was you put the advert in. My friend had heard you were back in the village and asking questions. That's when I decided to try to see you.' Again she flicked a dry tongue over her lips. 'Do you think that slide was your little girl's? I mean...' She shrugged. '...could there be an innocent explanation for how he came to have it?'

'I don't know, Fiona. I'm...' Claire shook her head, frowning. 'I don't know.' She searched the other woman's face. 'Will you tell the police what you've told me?'

Fiona's eyes widened. 'But there's no proof of anything,

is there? It's just one slide. He'll deny it. And we don't know he had anything to do with Gilly's disappearance. I can't go accusing him of anything. No.'

'We're not accusing him,' Claire said desperately. 'We'll just tell the police what you found and leave it up to them to look into it.'

Fiona shook her head and got to her feet. 'No. It might be absolutely nothing. Maybe he found it lying around somewhere. If I go saying stuff like that to the police, he'll know it was me. He'll find me…If it was him who…you know…Anyway, he has a temper. I've seen it. No, Claire. We'd need some sort of proof.' She glanced round again, pulling the cardigan tight across her skinny body, already edging away. 'Look, I've got to go.'

Claire stood up now and paced restlessly round her little sitting room. She glanced at the clock: time was going on. Fiona was right: there was no proof. And Claire struggled to believe that Tim was involved anyway: Tim had been a friend of Gilly's; he was with her father when the girl disappeared. Perhaps Fiona wasn't a reliable witness after all. But there might be a way Claire could get some proof - *if* Fiona's story was true. It was a long shot and she didn't like the plan but it was better than nothing.

She went upstairs to get changed. If she was going to carry this off, she had to go to the dance, otherwise they would all get suspicious.

*

Claire dressed in a slinky jumpsuit she had bought on a whim and hardly worn. It was more practical than a dress for what she wanted to do and she walked up to the vineyard in trainers carrying a cute pair of soft-soled slippers in a bag.

Neil met her outside and gave her a slow, warm kiss. Her

nerves were so taut, she struggled to respond.

'Great outfit,' he said doubtfully. 'Unusual.'

Then he asked about Laura and wasn't happy with what he heard but, since there was nothing he could do about it, he let the matter drop.

The room was already busy, the volume of chatter and laughter an assault on her ears as she walked inside. Business at the bar was brisk and there were many familiar faces but few people dancing. Adam was there with Zoe, she noticed, sitting at a table in a corner. She smiled briefly in his direction then quickly turned away, dreading him coming across to speak to her. If he mentioned the missed phone call, she wasn't sure how she would pass it off.

She and Neil circulated - Neil was as bad as Eve about playing Lord of the Manor - then settled, inevitably, with Tim and Shannon at a table which fortunately was on the opposite side of the room from Adam. Claire chatted and smiled. She found herself wondering what normal behaviour was. Was it normal for her to smile like this? Was she talking as much as usual or too little? Or maybe too much? Was the dark shadow of suspicion which now haunted her obvious in her face? Could Tim see it in her eyes when she spoke to him? Could he read her confusion and distrust? He didn't appear to; she was clearly a better actor than she thought.

The music got louder. Gradually the large space in the middle of the room filled with jigging, twisting bodies; the room throbbed with sound and movement. Claire danced with Neil with a vigour she was amazed she could muster. Conversation was difficult and involved leaning forwards, speaking slowly and clearly, keeping each sentence brief. Tim asked her if she enjoyed the fête, commented on how popular the teddy bears had been. She liked them, didn't she? he pressed.

296

'Julia's in a snit about them,' he said, 'but she doesn't get that they're just advertising.'

Did she stay on the field to see the Morris Dancing? he asked. He seemed to study her face. Maybe that was just her imagination, her concern that her meeting with Fiona was obvious to him. He looked happy and at ease; he was drinking and laughing. But then he generally did. She found herself seriously doubting Fiona's story but couldn't see any reason why the girl would make it up. Unless she were genuinely unbalanced. She might be. Or maybe Tim had been given the slide by someone else? Maybe he was covering for somebody? Immediately she found herself glancing sidelong at Neil and the thought made her sick to her stomach.

It was around nine when she first rubbed at her temples, brows furrowed.

Neil leaned closer solicitously. 'Are you all right?'

'Just a bit of a headache. I'll be fine. I'll get some water.'

Half an hour later, she said it had got worse and she opted out of dancing. A short time after, she said she would leave because the music wasn't helping.

'I'll go with you,' Neil offered.

'No, you're having a good time. Stay. I'll have to have an early night.' She embraced the table with what she hoped was a brave smile, put a hand to Neil's shoulder and bent down to kiss him. 'I'll see you tomorrow,' she said by his ear.

She walked slowly to the doors, changed into her trainers in the foyer and slipped outside. But for a bashful half-moon, it was dark. Perfect.

She began walking casually along the track towards The White House, then broke into a jog. An earring which had been knocked loose when she was dancing, fell to the ground just past the house entrance, but she didn't notice and kept running. She was desperate to get in and out of Tim's place before he

297

left the dance and went home.

*

Zoe wasn't enjoying the dance - which meant that Adam was struggling to do so too. She had looked miserable from the moment they'd arrived. Or maybe bored would be a better description, he thought. Her sister had originally said that she and her partner would join them but Ellie had called on the last minute to say they couldn't make it. So now they were sharing a table with Ted, the stained glass artist and his wife. They had had a couple of drinks, had even danced once but mostly they sat. It was difficult to talk over the music and Adam had decided he couldn't be bothered anyway. Zoe was cross because he had refused to drive - he wanted to have a drink or two - and she didn't want to walk. But she didn't want to drive either, so she had tottered up the road in inappropriate shoes which had got muddy and had blamed him for it.

Occasionally he looked across at Claire on the other side of the room, sitting with Neil and his brother, and wondered why she had tried to ring him that afternoon. She had left no message either which seemed odd. Though at least she and Neil appeared to be getting on well. He had seen them dancing together and talking, heads pressed close. It had occurred to him recently that he and Zoe didn't really talk. Or rather they both talked but they didn't have conversations any more; they expressed opinions or said what they had done that day but they didn't communicate. Did they ever really listen to each other? He had begun to doubt it.

'More drinks anyone?' he asked, grabbing his glass and standing up.

'I thought we weren't going to stay late,' Zoe said peevishly.

'It's still early.'

298

Adam looked expectantly round the others at the table and Ted asked for another pint. There were no other takers so Adam strolled to the bar but when he got back Ted was on his feet. He'd had a call from the babysitter saying their youngest son wasn't well. They had to go.

'They're going to give me a lift home, Adam,' Zoe said, already standing. 'I'm tired and I can't face the walk back.'

'You want a lift too, Adam?' Ted offered.

Adam didn't. He wanted to stay and drink. Even if he'd wanted to leave, he wouldn't now. He wished Zoe a good night and offered a facetious smile. He was being small-minded, he knew, but he could see a pattern emerging in their relationship these days and he didn't like it. He watched them go and took a long pull of his pint, savouring it.

He sat, idly watching the swirl of dancers, hearing but not listening to the music and the undertow of laughter and conversation. He was only half way down his pint when he noticed Claire put a hand to her head, stand up and say something to Neil, then head for the door. Maybe she wasn't well. He took another swig of beer. There was something about her behaviour that struck him as odd. The DJ started the next track, playing *I Can't Dance*, by Genesis, and the floor rapidly filled up again.

Without being sure why, Adam got up, eased his way round the periphery of the dance floor, weaving between tables and the crush of onlookers, and made the door. There was no-one in the foyer. He stepped outside and peered towards the road back down to the village. There was no sign of Claire but she couldn't have gone far - unless she was running. And why would she do that?

He stepped further away from the building, out of range of the security light, let his eyes accustom to the darkness and looked slowly round, finally staring long and hard down the lane and her route home. No-one. He walked back inside, worked his way back to his seat and picked up his pint. No doubt Claire was right and the drinking didn't help but tonight he didn't care; he was going to get plastered.

It was three-quarters of an hour later and he had started drinking wine instead of beer - he must be getting old because he couldn't drink beer the way he used to - when he saw Tim take Shannon by the hand and walk purposefully with her to the door.

*

'Does Tim have any sort of burglar alarm?' Claire had asked Fiona.

'No. He never used to anyway.'

'And where does he keep the key to the wardrobe normally?'

'In the drawer of his bedside cabinet.' Fiona had looked at her warily. 'Why? What are you going to do? I'm not going back there.'

'I don't expect you to.'

Clouds in the night sky kept obscuring the fitful moon. Claire jogged carefully but quickly along the track, flicking the beam of her torch sparingly to check her tread where necessary. With the patio doors of the restaurant open to the night, the throb of dance music still came to her on the air. She reached Tim's house and paused, barely daring to breathe, looking all around. The house was in darkness; the place looked deserted. Why wouldn't it be?

It had always been Tim's habit to leave spare keys to the front door underneath a stone at the back of the house. The clouds had scudded over again but she used the torch to pick it out and she found the keys, both on the same ring: one for the mortice lock, the other for the latch. She grabbed them and straightened up, taking a long breath, letting it out slowly. She could do this. She would just let herself in, look round, check out the place for any sign that Gilly had been there and she would be long gone before Tim even considered leaving the dance.

The door moved easily and she pushed it closed behind her. The house was silent.

'Hello,' she ventured hesitantly.

Her voice echoed into emptiness. She repeated it a second time, more firmly, unable to stop herself from hoping. There was nothing. No young voice, trapped in the darkness.

Reluctant to put the lights on, she shone the torch round, refamiliarising herself with the layout: the sitting room to her right at the front; the dining room behind with an arch through to the kitchen. Apart from some new units in the kitchen it looked much the same as it had on her last visit, years before. She glanced round, opened a few drawers and cupboards but didn't see anything of interest and went upstairs.

The room at the front was the bedroom. The clothes draped over a chair and the perfume on one of the bedside tables suggested Shannon regularly stayed there. Claire walked to the other bedside table, opened the drawer and grunted in relief: the key was there. She carefully looked through the drawer and elsewhere round the room, just in case she could find Gilly's necklace. She was clutching at straws. If Tim had been in possession of the necklace as well as the slide, it would have been in the shoe box. Even so, she checked everywhere, just in case, trying to leave each drawer and cupboard as she'd found it. There was no sign of it.

She went into the next room, the study cum photo studio, then into the one at the back which was the dark room. She hadn't realised before how seriously Tim still took his photography. But there was no sign of Gilly and she didn't expect it any more.

She returned to the study. It was just as Fiona had described it with its chaise longue and lighting. A desk stood in one corner with a laptop computer and printer on it and behind her was the crucial cupboard which was tall, maybe three foot wide and made of waxed pine. It had one long door and two drawers at the bottom. She pulled on each drawer in turn. The top one contained packets of photographic and printer paper; the second held silk stoles and scarves in neatly folded piles.

Her nervous fingers fumbled the key in the lock of the door and it creaked open. Four shelves were crammed with narrow box files of photographs, the boxes carefully stacked one on top of the other, each dated on the front. Pulling out a few to examine them, she noticed other key words scribbled on the labels too, such as *landscape*, *seascape*, *portrait* or *still life*.

Uncertain what exactly she was hoping to find and with a sick feeling in the pit of her stomach, she pulled file box after file box out, checking the dates. She was looking for 2008, convinced that there was something here which would give a clue to Gilly's disappearance.

She found a file for 2008. It was labelled *Still Life, Mar - Aug*. It contained countless photographs of flowers or fruit, arrangements of shells and pebbles or linens, open books or pottery but nothing significant that she could see. She kept looking.

On the bottom shelf several boxes labelled *Art* had been stacked together right at the back. Claire pulled them out and opened the first one. Here were the pictures of Fiona. In the first she was naked, reclining on the chaise longue, draped solely with one of the stoles Claire had seen in the drawer. The second was the same with a minutely different pose. There was a big pile of them. Fiona looked so young, her body so immature. It occurred to Claire - something she had never realised before - that Timothy's girlfriends were always like Fiona: slight, gamine, sweet and almost childlike. Like a little girl.

Something banged and Claire jumped, her heart hammering in her chest. She stayed absolutely still and listened, not even breathing. Nothing. She put down the box she was holding and tiptoed to the door, slipping out silently onto the landing and leaning on the balustrade to look down into the hallway. There was no-one there. The bedroom door banged against the frame again and she almost smiled. Her heart settled. The wind had got up outside and there were a couple of windows open creating a cross-draught. She pushed the door further back and returned to the study, conscious that she ought to hurry, but pausing to put the pictures of Fiona on one side. The girl wanted them back.

Claire opened another box. It was labelled *Art, Dec 2007 - May 2008*, and she pulled wedges of photos out in her haste, flicking through them. They were pictures of a different girlfriend this time, standing in the boathouse in the nude, leaning suggestively against one of the walls, looking towards the camera with a sultry expression. Claire worked through them meticulously, photo after photo, then froze when she came to a picture of Laura. And another. And another. She was naked in all of them. And here was another - though badly bent and crumpled, the image was still clear to see.

Claire put a hand to her clammy face, closing her eyes, wishing she could blot out the images but they were still there, imprinted on her retinae. Laura pictured draped over the chaise longue, one knee carefully crooked up; or sat pertly on a stool, looking over her shoulder at the camera; or stood with a long silk scarf draped around her neck, holding one end away from her lithe pubescent body in an affected, hips-thrust-forward pose. A child playing at being a woman. She had been barely twelve when these were taken, a shy, introverted girl, and her mother struggled to take it in. Laura must have been terrified - embarrassed simply couldn't cover it - and yet she had never said anything. But of course she would have been too scared to. So what tactics had the bastard used to persuade her to do this? And how had Claire never guessed? She had completely failed her little girl.

Claire pawed her way desperately through more photos. None of the poses was frankly obscene but they looked it to her. It was painfully obvious now why Laura kept making excuses for not coming back to Bohenna, for not doing things which threw her together with the Pennymans.

Rage bubbled up inside her and Claire wanted to rip the photographs apart, one by one. They were damning evidence of her brother-in-law's perverted obsession. She wasn't a prude. She didn't care that Timothy wanted to take pictures of naked women. He was male; he was human and if the woman didn't mind, fine. But the way he did it was unhealthy: it was secretive and worse than that it was coercive. And he'd proved it by making his twelve year old niece pose too, something Laura would never have done from choice. So what else had he done to her? And what had he done to Gilly?

Thinking of Gilly forced her to calm down. She had to find out what had happened to her; she was certain now that Tim knew. Had Gilly been photographed too? Had she been forced to pose but had something gone wrong? Claire scrabbled through the rest of the files labelled *Art* but could find no pictures of her younger daughter. He had probably destroyed them. She checked randomly through the other boxes, just in case, but there was no sign of her.

Again the door banged. She jumped a mile and her heart

304

went into its headlong drumbeat again - but this sounded like someone rapping on the front door. That was crazy: Tim wouldn't knock on his own front door. Still, maybe she could leave through the back, unseen.

She gathered the pictures of Laura and Fiona together, tried to replace the file boxes the way she'd found them, then panicked and began putting them back any old way. She closed the cupboard door, locked it and dropped the key in the bedside drawer, then tiptoed down the stairs with her stolen photographs, peering towards the front door. It had gone quiet again.

She was standing in the hall, ramming the photos in the bag with her pumps, when someone rapped on the door again.

'Claire?' hissed a man's voice. 'Are you there?'

'Adam?' She grabbed the latch and snatched the door open. 'What are you doing here?'

'Thank God. Keep your voice down, will you? Are you all right?'

'Yes, I'm fine.'

'Good. Then we should go.' He stuck out a hand and pulled her roughly towards him. 'It's past midnight and the music's stopped. Tim might be back any minute. Come on. You can tell me what's going on later.'

'OK, OK, I'm coming.'

She pulled the door to, turned the mortice lock and ran round the back to replace the keys under the stone.

'Go through the woods,' Adam murmured, already putting a hand to her back, urging her forward.

They struck out along the path into the trees.

*

Claire mechanically put one foot in front of the other, her thoughts fragmented and reeling. She tried just to focus on the route ahead as they walked swiftly and silently along the footpath towards the clearing. Adam had a torch but used it little, scared that it might be seen. Claire wondered how he had known where she was but he strode ahead of her now, grim-faced, saying nothing. She knew he would expect an explanation but she wasn't sure yet how much she was prepared to tell him.

'What the hell were you doing?' he whispered eventually, reaching the clearing.

'Someone told me something that made me wonder if Gilly was in Tim's house. But she wasn't.'

They turned right and began to cut across towards the southern bank of trees, walking side by side. The clouds had cleared again and weak moonlight blanched their route over the tufted grass. She could feel Adam watching her but wouldn't look at him.

'Who told you?' he demanded.

'No-one you know, Adam. Anyway, like I said, she wasn't there. There was no sign of her. Nothing.'

'Well it was bloody risky, letting yourself in like that. And alone too.'

'Yes, but I couldn't very well ask him, could I? And I didn't want to waste your time.' She glanced across, offered a pinched smile and looked away.

He frowned. 'You're hiding something.'

'Of course not. What were *you* doing there?'

'I saw you leave the dance and thought something was up so I followed you out. But there was no sign of you and I went back in. Later on I saw Tim and his girlfriend leave.'

She stopped and turned to look at him.

'They left?' She automatically glanced back towards the path to the house. 'How long ago? I didn't see them.'

'A while now. I followed him out too and I saw him lead

her towards the vineyard. To judge from the way the girl was giggling, I got the impression they were planning a bit of passion under the night sky. I wasn't sure how long they'd be or if they'd go back into the dance afterwards. We should keep on walking.' He moved off and she went with him. 'I kept thinking about the odd way you'd left and I figured that if you were trying to escape the Pennymans while they were all busy in the barn, then maybe it was because you were going round the winery or perhaps the house. I thought I should find you before Tim did. Then I saw your earring on the track and that pointed the way.'

He held out his hand, palm up with her earring on it.

'You've worn these before.'

She took it. 'Thank you. That was stupid of me. But you didn't need to bother to follow me.'

'It was no bother. I'd only have got drunk if I'd stayed.' He hesitated. 'And I was worried about you.'

She turned away and walked on, past the boathouse and on to the footpath back towards the river where they had to walk in single file and conversation was impossible. They reached the fence with the *Private* sign, climbed over it and Claire walked to the entrance to the wooden bridge, stopped and turned to face him.

'Thank you for worrying about me Adam.' She half-smiled, affecting insouciance. 'But you didn't need to. I'm OK.'

He didn't reply and clearly wasn't fooled. He was looking at her expectantly, wanting answers.

'Look, it's late,' she said. 'I don't think I should ask you back. Do you mind? I couldn't explain it to Neil.'

'No, I suppose not.' He reached out as if to touch her but didn't. 'You look awful, Claire. What's happened? Surely you can tell me?'

307

'No Adam. There's something I have to work out by myself this time.' She hesitated. 'Don't judge me, will you?'

He stared at her, frowning. 'Judge you? That's a strange thing to say. Why? What are you going to do?'

'I don't know why I said that. I'm very tired. Just forget it.'

His expression hardened. 'OK,' he said coolly. 'Night then.' He walked away without a backward glance.

Her heart ached to part with him like that but she couldn't bring herself to tell him. Not yet. She needed space.

Back in her house, with slow deliberate movements, Claire put the photos face down in a drawer of the sideboard and closed it. She made herself a mug of tea and sat in the armchair, her mind flicking through a succession of images, many of them memories from years before.

She fell asleep in the end, still in the chair with the table lamp on. She had that dream again, only this time Tim was in the woods too and he was chasing her. She was running for her life and screaming at him in her sleep.

Chapter 23

Claire's neck hurt and she rubbed at it and rolled over. She had come to around three in the morning and had crawled into bed but now sleep eluded her. The sun was well up and her bedroom glowed with bright early morning sunshine. Even with her eyes closed, it seemed to burn at her retinae. There was no chance of more sleep.

In any case her brain was too active. Over and over she kept thinking through what she knew, trying to work out its significance, uncertain what to do next. She wondered what time Laura would surface that morning, what time she would return home. Claire would have to ask about those pictures and she dreaded that conversation.

And she wondered again if Laura knew anything about her sister's disappearance. It seemed unlikely but now everything felt up in the air and possible. Claire thought she had been walking around for years wearing a blindfold and her thoughts still whirled with all the implications. This was family. Whatever she thought about the Pennymans, they were her family too. And Timothy, of all people. She was amazed how much it hurt, this betrayal, and amazed too at how scared she was of saying it out loud or sharing it with others, astonished at her reluctance to accept an obvious truth. And how could he have had anything to do with Gilly's disappearance anyway? What could he possibly know, and was she wrong to tie the two issues together?

By six o'clock, she had had enough. She got up and went out for a jog, knowing it was the only thing which might clear her head. It was over forty minutes later when she returned home, sweating and weary, but the run had worked its usual magic. Pounding along the footpaths, something had surfaced in her mind which had made a lot of things fall into place. The way forward now seemed obvious.

But first she had to talk to Neil; this was something they had to do together. She watched the clock and waited. At eight o'clock, she rang him.

He answered promptly. 'Claire? You're up. I didn't want to ring too early, just in case. Are you better? I've been worried. You never used to get headaches.'

'I'm OK. Thanks.'

'Are you sure? You don't sound good.'

'I'm a bit tired.' She cleared her throat. 'Neil?'

'Yes?'

'We need to talk. Would you mind coming down here?'

'Why? What's the matter?'

'It's not something I want to talk about on the phone. But it's important.'

'Oh…OK. Now you're being mysterious. Well, I'm just about to go in the shower. I'll grab some breakfast and come along after.'

'Fine. Only come alone, Neil. OK? Alone.'

*

She handed Neil the photos of Laura.

'Tim took these,' she said simply. 'He's been keeping them hidden.'

She had made coffee, had made herself hold back until they were sitting in the living room. Horrific as this situation

310

was, it was at least a relief to share it with him. She watched his face, waiting for his reaction.

Neil scanned each picture, eyes getting narrower, mouth pinched. He got to the last one and bundled them tightly together again, put them down on the coffee table and pushed them away as if they scorched his fingers.

'Well?' she prompted.

He picked up his mug of coffee and sipped it, eyes staring straight ahead.

'How did you get these?' he said to the air in front of him.

It wasn't the reaction she had been expecting. She frowned.

'Does it matter?' She waited. 'So…' she prompted. 'What are you thinking?'

'I don't know. Lots of things, of course. I'm cross, naturally. He should have told us he wanted to take these. Laura was only a kid really.'

'You don't sound cross.'

'Well, it's difficult, isn't it?'

'No. Well, yes. In a way. But no, he should never have taken them. It wasn't a question of him telling us, like he had some right to do it. It's freaky. I've always liked Tim and I know he's your brother, Neil, but I'm sorry, it's sick. She was twelve. What kind of man takes pictures of his twelve-year-old niece naked like that?'

'He's a photographer, Claire. See…' He gestured impatiently with a hand towards the pictures but didn't actually look at them. '…they're black and white. All arty. That's the way he is. He shouldn't have done it without asking but it doesn't mean anything.'

'You aren't serious?'

'Yes, of course I am.'

'Then why did he do it secretly?'

Neil shrugged, not quite looking at her. 'You know what Tim's like. He seems quite confident but it's all show. Anyway, I'll speak to Laura, check that he asked her, you know…nicely, to do it.'

'No.' Claire was almost shouting now. 'No. You can't do it like that.'

'I'll have a word with Tim too, if you like, explain how upset you are.'

She stared at him, astonished. How upset *you* are. He was dissociating himself from it like he always did and simply refusing to see the implications. And if he spoke to Laura he'd manipulate her to get the answers he wanted. She had heard him do it before.

'Suppose he didn't ask her nicely?' she said. 'Then he pressured her. You think she's going to just come out and admit that now? She's probably still scared of him.'

'Scared of Tim?' He snorted. 'Why would…'

'Of course she'll be scared of him. Anyway, I haven't told you the other thing.'

'What other thing?'

'It's even worse, Neil. Fiona came to see me after the fête. You know Fiona was Tim's last girlfriend - a point you omitted to tell me, by the way. She said that she found that hair slide among Tim's things and gave it to the fête to be sold. Gilly's slide. In a box hidden away with Tim's things.'

She watched him, still hoping for some anger. Something. Anything.

He made eye contact at last and stared at her, incredulous.

'Oh come on, Claire. Not that slide thing again. You admitted it wasn't important. You said you'd thrown it away.'

'That was before Fiona spoke to me. I threw it in the garden but I found it again. Don't you see? Tim had Gilly's hair slide.' She began enunciating slowly and clearly as if to a child. 'He took these photos of Laura. Tim has problems. He had Gilly's slide. He knows what happened to Gilly. We have to make him tell us.'

'Now you're making me cross, Claire. You're being ridiculous. Tim was with your father when Gilly disappeared, everyone knows that. He even went looking for her too.'

Claire stood up, her anger and frustration too great now to contain sitting down.

'*You're* cross? And *I'm* being ridiculous? I'm telling you this because I thought you cared about your daughter; I thought you'd want to know what happened to her. I'm telling you this because you're Gilly's father but, frankly, I'm struggling to remember that. And I've worked out Tim's alibi. In the end it was obvious. Blindingly obvious. My father never wore his watch. He told the time by the sun and in the summer the sun is so high and moves so slowly, it's not as accurate. And most of the time he didn't give a fig what the time was anyway. I imagine Tim turned up later than usual but made a point of mentioning that it was half past four or something. Dad believed it; why wouldn't he? We all believed it. But Tim knows what happened to Gilly. And we need to tell the police.'

Neil quickly got to his feet and put a firm hand on her arm.

'Now come on, Claire. Calm down. You're overreacting. I can't believe what Fiona's saying. She's being vindictive because he dumped her. And she's got a history of it too, hasn't she? I'm sure Jane said she used to make things up when they were kids – stories that used to get Jane into trouble with her mother. She's not reliable. We should ask Tim.'

She felt a moment of doubt. Jane had never said that explicitly to her. So maybe Fiona wasn't reliable. And Claire didn't want to believe it either. Then she remembered the photographs and shook his hand off angrily.

'I believe Fiona,' she said. 'If you ask Tim, he'll just lie.'

313

'You're making something out of nothing. I agree the photos aren't right. He shouldn't have done that. But to suggest he had anything to do with Gilly.' He forced a pained smile. 'That's absurd, Claire. Why should we believe Fiona in preference to Tim? We certainly can't go to the police with any of this. It'd hang over him forever. And I mean…imagine when it got out? The press would be down here again like a shot and the vineyard would be mentioned for all the wrong reasons. This is something we have to keep in the family.'

A heavy, chilling thought settled on her.

'Is that what you've been doing, Neil – keeping it in the family? Did you all know what Tim was up to all along? Did you even know about Gilly and turn a blind eye rather than risk it getting out and muddying the Pennyman name?'

'No, no, of course not.' Neil started protesting before she'd even finished talking. 'What are you accusing us of? Of course we didn't know anything. I didn't anyway. I'm sure the others didn't either.'

'And if you had known… What then?'

He hesitated just a moment too long before replying and Claire felt her anger wash away on a smothering tide of disappointment and resignation. She walked to the front door and opened it.

'You'd better go now, Neil. I need to make a phone call.'

Neil quickly moved to stand in front of her.

'Please don't do this, Claire. We can work it out.' The irritation had gone; his tone was gentle, caressing, conciliatory. 'Don't you care about us?' He came closer still and stroked his hand over her hair. 'Darling, I want us to be together. Can't you see that this'll just drive a wedge between us again? It'll change everything; it'll change us. You're playing with fire. None of us will ever be the same again.' He looked at her wearing an earnest, agonised expression.

She knocked his hand away crossly, squeezing her lips together hard, trying to keep control. All her hopes of getting back together with him were about to be thrown away. And she was the one who was going to do it.

'It's too late,' she said. 'We've already changed, Neil. Nothing can ever be the same again. I've made that mistake before - thinking I could go back.' She held his gaze, unflinching. 'And I'm afraid I simply don't love you enough to abandon my daughters for you.'

He took a step back, looking at her disbelievingly.

'You're not really going to ring the police? Let's talk about this some more.'

'There's nothing left to say.'

His jaw set. 'You're making a big mistake.'

'I hope you're not threatening me. Just go.'

His face puckered in anger and disbelief. He stormed out, kicking wildly at the terracotta pot of geraniums by the door as he went, making it fall over and smash.

Claire closed the door but continued to stand there, staring at it but seeing nothing, shaking. She turned away and picked up the phone.

*

The police took Tim in for questioning and went through his house, checking all his photographs in case there were others of children. They found none. He was asked about the hair slide too but insisted he'd found it on the floor at the nursery some time afterwards. He said he'd taken it home because he wasn't sure what to do with it: he'd been anxious not to upset anyone. He assumed it had fallen there when Gilly was playing and he couldn't bring himself to throw it away because he was so fond of his niece. That was his story and it was extremely plausible; the evidence was circumstantial.

Days had passed and Claire was back at work, trying to keep some routine. Penny was away again in France and Claire was grateful for the space, throwing herself into mundane tasks, trying to stay occupied. Now she was ironing linens - a task she always found soothing, steaming and smoothing out creases, spraying the freshly laundered linen with lavender water.

She had heard about Tim's response to the allegations courtesy of Lyn James, the Family Liaison Officer. At the moment, however, she was more preoccupied with Laura, their stilted conversations going round and round in her head. Her daughter simply wouldn't talk about Timothy.

Sam had dropped her back at the cottage on the Sunday afternoon, had stopped to speak to Claire and left. At that point, Laura had been happy and remarkably chatty; she had had a good time. Sam was 'OK', she'd said. He had been 'no pressure'; he was 'fun'; they'd talked of maybe seeing each other again but hadn't arranged anything definite. So Claire had prattled about other things, had tried to bring the conversation round to the photographs but had quickly realised that there wasn't an easy way to do it. In the end, she had done it perhaps too suddenly and Laura's demeanour had changed almost instantly. She became evasive.

'Did he force you to have the pictures taken?' Claire asked for a second time.

'No. It was just...' Laura appeared to be breathing too hard. 'I...' She hesitated again. 'I don't want to talk about it, mum, OK?'

'Laura, we have to talk about it.'

'Why? I don't want to. It's history. He was just...he was very persuasive.'

'Did he...you know, touch you or anything?'

'God, no. No.' Laura shook her head and looked like she

316

was going to cry. Claire tried to hug her but Laura broke away. 'I'm all right, mum. I'm fine. I just don't want to talk about it.'

'But the police will have to talk to you about it, Laura,' Claire said gently. 'The thing is...there's something else.' Claire had explained about the slide. Laura listened, mouth open, eyes staring, then just backed away and ran up the stairs to her room. Claire watched her go and put her hands to her head in despair. She didn't know what to do.

And when the police interviewed her later, Laura was little more forthcoming. She insisted that 'nothing happened', that her uncle had never touched her. He just told her how to pose. Tim kept insisting his photographs were art - he never meant them to be pornographic - and he had set them up carefully so they weren't.

Claire scoffed at the idea. She put another table runner on the ironing board and put the iron down on it heavily and pounded up the length of it. The police, it seemed, weren't in a hurry to accuse Tim of anything. They were still considering the matter apparently and had released him 'pending further investigations', asking him to keep them informed of his whereabouts. Claire was astonished. What more did they need to see? Cynically she suspected that who he was weighed more heavily with them than what he had done; Eve Pennyman knew a lot of people.

She shifted the runner along the board and hammered down on it again with the iron. She was haunted by how badly she felt she had let her daughter down. Even if Tim hadn't done anything physically to her, Laura had clearly been scarred by his behaviour. And Claire wished now she'd spent longer in Tim's house when she'd had the opportunity, sure that she would have found something else to incriminate him if she'd looked hard enough. She shouldn't have waited to see Neil before ringing the police, either. Tim had probably destroyed a load of photographs as soon as Neil told him what she was going to do. How could she ever have thought that Neil would side with her and the girls against his brother? And now the village grapevine was buzzing with the story of course, each version bigger and more lurid than the last. She had kept away.

The bell rang on the shop door and she looked up. It was Adam. She put the iron down and met him by the counter.

'Adam, I was going to ring you.' She hesitated. 'I wanted to apologise for the way I behaved the other night. I wasn't myself.'

'It's OK. I've heard...' He shrugged. 'I understand.' He ran a finger along the counter top. 'So are the rumours true?'

'I suppose that depends which versions you've heard.'

'That Tim had something of Gilly's which you found? I assume that's the hair slide. They say he was arrested.'

'Yes, it was the slide but, no, he wasn't arrested, just questioned. His ex-girlfriend said she found it in his things. He says he found it on the ground at the nursery.'

'And they believe him?'

'No reason not to, I gather, not at the moment.' She tried not to sound bitter and knew she'd failed.

'There's talk about photographs too.'

'Oh no. How do people find out these things?'

'It doesn't matter. Forget it.'

'No. It's all right. I can tell you.' She explained briefly about Laura and the pictures. 'That's why I'm sure he took her. Gilly either knew about the photos or he tried to photograph her and she wouldn't have it. Honestly it makes me sick to think about.'

He fidgeted.

'How is Laura?' he asked after a pause.

'She's gone to stay with a friend from university. She

couldn't stay here with all this going on.'

'I heard that Tim had gone away too, 'visiting friends'.'

'Yes. So Penny said. In Suffolk. Eve's damage limitation, no doubt. Apparently, if the police permit it, he might be going abroad to 'get work experience at another vineyard'. It's a bad joke.'

They both glanced round as a couple came into the unit.

'Look,' Adam murmured, leaning forward. 'If there's anything I can do to help... Or if you just want to talk, ring me will you?'

'Yes. I will. Thank you.' She tried a smile. 'Please don't say anything about Laura to anyone, will you?'

'Of course not.'

She watched him walk to the door.

'Adam? Are you all right?'

He turned and flashed a smile.

'Of course. I'm fine.'

'And Zoe?'

The blink of a hesitation. 'Yes, she's fine too.'

He left, ambling back towards his studio. She still wasn't convinced – there was something in his manner that bothered her. But as he'd told her himself: men don't talk.

She went back to the ironing and her mind drifted back to Tim, wondering how long it would be before he returned to Bohenna and, more to the point, how long it would be before she found out what he knew about Gilly. As far as she was concerned, she would wait for as long as it took; she wasn't going anywhere until she got all the answers.

*

Julia took the car down into the village, drew it into the car park between The Swan and the green and sat for several minutes without getting out. It was July now and some schools had already broken up for the summer. A woman with two small children sat on the bench, watching her offspring chase each other over the grass, shrieking in their excitement. A couple of retirement age, wearing long shorts and walking boots, walked along the road towards the bridge in single file. They had an air of self-absorbed contentment that Julia envied. Behind her, the doors of the pub were open and she could see Dave Spenser in her rear view mirror, mopping the floor inside. It was still early; there would be many more people swarming over Bohenna later.

She'd been avoiding going down into the village for days, had driven to Lostwithiel for odd items she'd run out of rather than brave all those invasive, curious looks. But she couldn't avoid them forever. She lived and worked here so sooner or later she would have to face them. She took a deep breath, blew it out on a sigh and got out of the car, grabbing her bags and crossing the road to the shop.

Even though he was serving someone else, Julia was immediately aware of Steve Carthy's eyes following her from the moment she walked in. She took a basket and worked her way round the store, pulling things from the shelves with an affected insouciance. She went to the freezer, picked up a packet of burgers and a bag of garden peas and dumped them on top, then grabbed a jumbo pack of crisps on the way to the till. Danny never seemed to stop eating these days.

'Julia, good to see you,' Steve said, as she put the basket down on the counter.

'Morning Steve.'

Holding her purse, she began loading things into her hessian bag as he put them through the till.

He flicked her a probing glance. 'Everything all right?'

'Yes, thank you.'

'We've been hearing all sorts of tales. I'm sure they can't

320

all be true.'

'I'm sure they can't either.'

'But I heard Tim's gone away for a while. Must be difficult at this time of year, without him to do all those vine tours?'

'It's not a problem. Neil's doing them while Tim's away.'

'Oh, that's good then.' He put a loaf of bread through. 'Coming back soon, is he? Tim, I mean.'

'I wouldn't know Steve. Do you tell your sister what you're doing all the time?'

'No, but then she doesn't work with me, Julia.' He smiled obsequiously, said how much she owed him and flung the basket into the pile on the floor by the till. 'Your mum all right? Haven't seen her for a few days.'

'She's fine, thank you.'

She handed him a couple of notes. He rang them through the till and lifted out her change, pausing before he gave it to her.

'Police not finished with Tim yet then?' he asked with an innocent air.

'I'm sure you'll know before I do,' she replied sweetly, holding out her hand.

He counted the money into it.

'Thank you,' she said, and left.

She loaded the bags in the car but locked it again and walked across to the river, cutting down onto the footpath. She needed air and…something else, she wasn't sure what. She stared into the river. After a dry start to the summer with long spells of sunshine it was running lower. It boded well for the vines; they might have a big crop this year and quite early maybe. It was ironic, given that they probably wouldn't have Tim's help when the harvest came. When would Tim return? She truly didn't know. Eve was naively convinced that if he

321

stayed away from the village for a while, it would all die down, that everyone would forget. End of story. But he'd been obliged to give the police his contact details and Julia was equally certain that it wasn't over yet.

Tim had been adamant he wasn't involved. Talking with his family back at the house he had sounded by turns shocked, indignant and upset. She wanted to believe him but the accusations lingered in her mind and both frightened and revolted her. Her brother, messing around with a young girl. And what else might he have done? After all, there was no doubt that Gilly had disappeared. She tried not to let her thoughts go there. But Tim didn't deny the photographs so what on earth had he been thinking?

Could she believe him? After all this was Tim, her kid brother, the young-at-heart and soft-hearted, generous one. But a small part of her would have preferred that he admit it because then it was settled and she would know that Phil had never been involved. Phil would be off the hook and she could start to breathe again. They could make a fresh start.

The conflict inside her was immense, the guilt for feeling that way difficult to bear. She felt strained to breaking point. Even standing here in this sweetly familiar place and watching the water bubbling past, it felt as though something oppressive was hanging in the air. More would come out yet. They might all be in denial - Eve certainly was - but this thing came too close to them. Deep down, she had always known that.

She turned away and returned to her car to drive back up the hill to the vineyard. She had to put it away from her and think about the vines and the wine; it was the only way she was going to get through this.

Chapter 24

Adam stood in his living room and stared at the display of photographs on the wall. The pictures of Zoe were till there: Zoe on the beach; Zoe pretending to shoot a seagull; he and Zoe together, grinning inanely at the camera, eyes half-closed against the sun.

'It can't be easy to keep looking at them,' Claire had said. No. But it didn't seem to hurt as much to look at them now as it had at that time. Perhaps that was a sign that he had finally made the right decision. More than any real pain, he simply felt sad that it had come to this. And perhaps a little feeble-minded too that it had taken him so long to work out what he wanted and what he didn't. But he had at least given the relationship his best shot; he really had tried.

Some couples seemed to grow together over the years, he thought. They knocked the corners off each other, found interests in common, developed shared passions. Stuck in a canoe together, just the two of them, they understood the need to both be paddling in the same direction. Whereas he and Zoe had kept moving apart. Progressively, their common ground appeared to have dwindled until it barely existed. If they were still both paddling the canoe (and he had sometimes felt that he was doing it alone) they were working against each other and just going round in circles.

In the end, Adam had reluctantly accepted that they

323

simply didn't want enough of the same things and all the wishing in the world wouldn't change that. How can you build a future on that kind of foundation? He had become tired of the endless negotiations, the barbed remarks and accusations - and he'd contributed a goodly share of those himself. He didn't want to be that person any more, that half of a dysfunctional couple. They had lost something along the way - if indeed they had ever had it.

So he had ended it, before it could get any worse.

'You'll be happier without me,' he'd said to Zoe's protests. 'You will, you know. You can go back to Bristol, find someone new, someone who'll make a great father and live the life you want. And I can stay down here and live my sad little bohemian existence with no responsibilities.' He'd even tried a joke. 'Imagine, if we'd had kids, I might have had to get a regular job or something.' He'd shivered, theatrically. 'I'd have hated that.' It hadn't gone down well.

There had been tears - he had even shed a few himself - but Zoe hadn't argued much. Maybe she was relieved; he certainly was. A huge weight had been lifted from his shoulders. Perhaps if he had really loved her, heart and soul, he would have been able to make the sacrifice she needed. Though he wasn't sure - and that didn't seem like a good basis for a future together anyway.

Now he raised a hand and pulled the photos of her from behind the elastic stays and studied them a moment before tucking them in a drawer out of sight.

There was a knock at the front door. The bell only worked occasionally; it was one of the jobs on his list of things to do, the list that never seemed to get any shorter. It was unusual for anyone to come to his door in the evening though, and he automatically glanced at his watch - ten past seven - before walking into the hallway. The front door had two frosted glass panels in the upper half which tantalisingly showed a shape but gave no indication who it might be. He opened the door warily.

'Hello Adam. You probably didn't expect to see me here.'

'No-o. No, I can't say I did.'

'I need to tell you something. In fact, I need your help. Can I come in?'

He hesitated a moment, then stepped back, waving a dubious arm of invitation.

*

Claire closed the phone call and put her fingers to her forehead, massaging her brow. For nearly twenty minutes she had been holding a largely one-sided conversation with Laura and felt she had achieved nothing. Her daughter was back in the Cotswolds with Katie and insisting she was all right. 'I'm having a good time here. Cheltenham's not far away and Dad gave me money to do some shopping. You don't need to worry about me.' To be fair, her voice sounded much the same as usual but Claire couldn't stop worrying. But maybe she was taking the photo thing harder than Laura now. The girl had grown up. She kept insisting that nothing had happened and there had been no more photos. Whatever trauma she might have felt had perhaps slowly dissipated and she had come to terms with it. She had refused counselling point blank. Perhaps making her talk about it would only make the situation worse, dragging up memories she would prefer to forget. It was noticeable that neither of them had chosen to mention Gilly.

After speaking to her mother in Greece, Claire had suggested to Laura that she might like to spend a couple of weeks out there with her grandmother. But Laura wanted to stay in the Cotswolds. 'Sam said he might come up to see me,' she'd said, sounding almost offended. 'Good,' Claire had responded in that falsely positive tone that parents always use when they want to encourage and don't know what else to say. 'That'll be nice then.'

That'll be nice then, she thought now and cringed. What a trite thing to say.

The phone rang in her hand, making her jump, and she assumed Laura had rung back, but it was Adam.

'Can I come round?' he said tersely.

She glanced at the clock: five to eight.

'Of course. Do you…'

'I'll be there in a couple of minutes.' He rang off.

Five minutes later he was knocking at her back door. When she opened it he had his back to her, facing the woods, and, turning, his expression was taut with tension and something else she couldn't place.

'What's happened?' she asked, feeling a shiver of unease.

He tried a smile but it was unconvincing. 'Nothing.'

'Well come in. You don't need to stand there.'

He strode in then stood in the kitchen looking like Gilly used to when she'd broken something and didn't know how to tell you.

'Can I get you a drink?' she offered. She glanced round. That had been rash; she didn't have much worth offering.

'No, I'm fine. In any case, I won't stay long.' He hesitated, put a hand to her arm. 'Can we sit for a moment?'

'Of course.'

He walked ahead of her.

'Adam?' Panic was starting to knot her stomach. 'What is it?'

He perched on the edge of his chair, leaning forward, elbows on his knees, clasping and unclasping his hands.

'I need to tell you something and I don't know how you'll take it but let me finish before you react. OK?'

'OK,' she said doubtfully.

'I had a visitor tonight. Jane Sawdy. Don't look at me like that. She had something to tell me which she thought was important. When I heard it...' He paused. '...I thought maybe it was important. No, Claire, I think she genuinely wants to help. Give her, give *me* the benefit of the doubt, will you?'

'OK,' she repeated, frowning.

'Jane goes up to the spring sometimes,' he said, 'the one that feeds the stream down to the lake. She likes to bathe in the water there - she thinks it's healing. Anyway, she went up there at the end of the afternoon and on her way back she cut through the clearing the way she always does. But this time she noticed some flowers growing. I mean there've been wild flowers growing up there all summer but these were different and unusual so she went for a closer look. They're bee orchids. They're rare round here but she says you see them on roadsides sometimes or waste ground, anywhere the ground has been disturbed. The seeds blow in on the wind but they can lie dormant for years until the conditions are right and up they come. They can be used for some remedy or other - that's why she knows about them. Do you see where I'm going with this?' He looked at her anxiously. 'Disturbed ground?'

Claire leaned towards him. The blood drained from her face.

'I think so. You mean...this might be...' Her face crumpled suddenly and she swallowed hard. She put a hand to her mouth. Now Adam was out of his seat and kneeling on the floor in front of her, taking her hands in his. 'No,' she said. 'Oh no, please not.'

'Claire? Claire? Listen. You knew when you started this that it might come to this. Didn't you? We've talked about this before. And if you're right about Tim, you must have known that there was little chance she would still be alive. There, I've said it. Isn't the most important thing that we find out what happened to her, that we find out where she is?'

She nodded, pressing her lips together, her heel starting to bounce nervously on the floor.

'We can't trust Jane,' she said. 'Have you been there? Does it look like anything important?'

'I haven't been because I thought you'd want to go yourself. Of course I'll go with you if you like. The thing is…' He took a breath and hesitated. '…the ground is pretty flat, she said, but the way the flowers are growing, Jane says it suggests a sort of long oval shape.'

'Dear God,' she murmured. 'Can it be true?' She pulled her hands away from him and put them to her face again, covering her mouth.

'Perhaps we should just tell the police,' he said softly. 'I could ring them if you like?'

'No. No, I want to go and see for myself.' She pulled her hands down and straightened up, raising her chin. 'Even if Jane means well, she may be completely wrong. I'm not going to be made a fool of. Anyway…' Her chin quivered. '…if it is what we think it is, I want to see it first before a bunch of strangers walk all over it.' She looked towards the window. The light was beginning to fade. 'Let's go now. I'll bring a torch. Did Jane tell you where it was exactly?'

'She's in my car outside. She said she'd show us if you wanted to go. She didn't want to come to you directly. She wasn't sure you'd believe her.'

'I see.' Claire took a slow, calming breath. 'I'll put some shoes on.'

They cut through the woods and over the river, walking silently, single file, with Jane at the front, a macabre procession. By the time they reached the clearing, the sun had already sunk below the tree canopy and the surrounding woods were a dark cloak of stillness. Claire shivered though the night air was mild and unusually dry.

Jane led them on then stopped on the edge of the tree line maybe half way between the footpath from The White House and the stream from the spring. She turned to look at Claire.

'Here,' she said, and moved her hand to indicate the ground to her right. 'See the flowers? They're very delicate. You don't tend to see them unless you're almost on top of them.'

Claire came closer, unwillingly, and bent over. She got down on her hands and knees and fingered the tiny blooms, ran a hand over the ground, unsure what exactly she expected to feel.

'I had a sensation,' Jane was saying quietly. 'I felt that someone was here. I stayed here a while to be sure. And I've got it again now.'

Claire looked up at her. 'You think it's Gilly?'

'I know you don't believe me and of course I may be wrong. But yes, I think it is.' Jane looked down at the ground. 'Look at the size,' she added gently. 'It has to be a child.'

Claire thought so too. Tears began to run down her face but she hardly noticed as she stared back down at the small plot of ground. She closed her eyes and found herself mouthing a prayer; she hadn't prayed in years.

Eventually she stood up and gathered herself, groping through her pockets for a tissue. She pulled her phone out too.

'I'll tell the police,' she said.

*

Julia walked into the kitchen of The White House and stopped short. The atmosphere was heavy with something intangible and bad. Neil was standing with his back to the worktop where the filter coffee machine stood, a mug in one hand; Eve was

329

sitting at the table, an untouched cup of coffee in front of her. Both had stopped speaking as soon as she walked into the room and turned their heads to look at her.

'I know I'm late but we wanted to finish tucking in the row we were on,' Julia said into the unnatural silence, forcing a positive note. 'The vines are growing like crazy now.' She frowned. 'Has something happened?'

'Is Phil with you?' said Neil.

'He's just putting some things away. Why?'

'There's been a development.' His expression rigid and grim, Neil turned and put his mug down, reaching for the jug on the machine and pouring coffee into a new mug. He handed it to Julia. 'Milk's on the table.'

She took it without thinking, bent over to take the jug and add milk, then straightened up.

'What?' she demanded. 'Come on, tell me. What's going on?'

'The police have gone to arrest Tim,' Eve said, dully. Her eyes were glazed, lifeless. 'They've found Gilly's body in the clearing.'

Julia's mouth fell open and she looked from Eve to Neil, then back to Eve. Her mother was staring into her coffee again.

'Drink your coffee, mum,' said Neil. 'It'll go cold.'

Julia saw her mother mechanically pick up the cup and put it to her lips.

'Please explain,' Julia murmured, moving across to stand in front of her brother. 'How did they find her? Why do they think it was Tim? Has he admitted it?'

'Jane Sawdy noticed something unusual about a small patch of ground there. Claire went to see it and rang the police. They cordoned it off and were there at first light, digging.'

'Jesus,' Julia said on a breath.

'They're pretty sure it's Gilly because she still had her

little bead necklace on. There'll be tests of course.' Neil's face was drawn, haggard even. He hesitated, let out a juddering sigh. 'There was a thin leather wrist band in the grave too. Just like the one Tim always used to wear. He said he lost it, remember?'

Julia stared at him open-mouthed. 'So it's true.'

'Maybe. Who knows? But the police have been in touch with the police in Suffolk. They're going to bring Tim in and send him down here for questioning.' He looked at his watch. 'Maybe he's already on his way.'

They both fell silent and sipped desultorily at their coffee.

'How's Claire?' Julia said eventually, flicking Neil a glance.

'I don't know. She won't answer when I call. Jane said that painter bloke's with her.'

'Adam?' Neil didn't reply but Julia didn't notice. She shook her head. 'Why? Why would Tim do that? I just...' She couldn't find the words and gave up.

'I don't believe it,' Eve said. She looked up at them, eyes hard and cross now. She looked more like the mother Julia knew. 'I don't believe he did anything to her. It's a mistake. Or he's been set up. I bet Claire had something to do with this.'

'What are you suggesting, mum?' said Julia. 'That Claire...'

'Let's not jump to any conclusions,' Neil interposed quickly. 'We'll have to wait and see what happens.'

Julia caught his eye and saw in his expression what she thought herself: it wasn't a mistake; it was a fact they were all going to have to come to terms with. Life on the vineyard was never going to be the same again.

There was a noise in the hallway. The door opened and Phil came in, the smell of cigarette smoke wafting in with him.

Julia put her mug down and hurried across the room,

flinging her arms round his neck, pulling him close and burying her head on his chest. He laughed awkwardly, putting a hand up to rub her back and glancing at Neil and then Eve.

'What's up with you?' he muttered to Julia.

She didn't reply; she couldn't imagine ever being able to explain to him why she felt like this.

'We've had some bad news,' Neil told him.

Chapter 25

Gilly had been a slight girl. It hadn't been difficult to carry her nor to dig the ground made soft by recent rain, just enough to put her well down out of sight and cover her over. Tim was used to working outside; he had been clever at covering his tracks and the grave was not a big one. Positioned on the tree line, far enough away from the neighbouring trunks to avoid the roots, he had cut the top carefully to keep at least some of the grass layer, then firmed it down hard afterwards and strewn the surface with the odd broken twigs, leaves and moss which were so evident elsewhere in the clearing. With time, the grass had grown more firmly, weeds and wildflowers had spread over it and, with twigs and leaves constantly falling and blowing about, it had blended in seamlessly to its environment.

Claire learnt all this a few days later, after Timothy Pennyman had formally admitted killing Gilly and burying her in the clearing. After the police's rapid initial response, those days felt as if they passed in slow motion, the procedures that followed interminable. Tim had asked if he could see Claire because he wanted to explain himself to her but she refused to go. She couldn't imagine listening to his excuses. Tim had always been a good talker and he had a way with him, clever at winning people over; she wasn't going to get drawn in like that. In any case Lyn James took the time to sit with Claire over a cup of tea and tell her his whole story.

Tim said he was walking back to his house that afternoon when he saw Gilly leaving it. And he could tell from her behaviour that she had found his spare key under the stone at the back and had been inside. When she heard him she turned furtively to look at him and then ran off down the footpath through the woods, the one that led to the clearing. Tim hesitated for a minute or two, undecided, but he had noticed that she was holding something in her hand and he was sure that she'd taken it from his house so he ran after her. She was fast, he said, and obviously knew the track well. He wondered if she'd been in his house before and made a mental note to lock everything up more thoroughly in future.

When he caught up with her she had already reached the edge of the clearing. He grabbed her by the arm but she turned suddenly and twisted out of his grip to face him, all the while backing away, holding one hand behind her back.

As she edged back, Tim crept forward. 'You've got something of mine, haven't you, Gilly? You're going to give it back, aren't you?'

'You've been taking naughty pictures of Laura,' she said accusingly. 'I'm going to show mummy what you've been doing.'

'They aren't naughty, Gilly. They're like those paintings you see. You know - those paintings of ladies with no clothes on? They're artistic and beautiful, aren't they? Well, Laura looks like that in her photographs. She's a pretty girl and I wanted to show that. Doesn't she look beautiful in the pictures? So come on, give me that one back please.'

But Gilly wasn't convinced by his argument and she refused to hand the photograph over so he lunged for her and wrenched it from her grasp and she began kicking him crossly, trying to get it back, fighting with him like a wild cat. And he was rougher than he intended in pushing her away. Somehow he managed to twist her awkwardly while her head was wedged under his arm and the next thing he knew she had gone limp. He laid her on the ground but she wasn't breathing. She had no pulse either and the angle of her head was all wrong. He was stunned. Devastated. She was dead, just like that. He must have broken her neck and he didn't know what to do.

He froze, panic-stricken, then forced himself into action and ran back to the house to get a spade, quickly digging a grave and burying her further up the clearing, taking just enough time to thoroughly cover his tracks. The leather wrist strap must have fallen off when he was putting her in the grave and he didn't notice it until later when there was no way he could risk going back to find it. He had to leave it there.

Then he hurried back to the house, cleaned up the spade and - so he wouldn't be seen - took the long route round the back of The White House to get to the nursery. When he got there, he pretended he was only five minutes late and said the time. He knew Charlie never wore his watch and didn't bother much when he was working so he would take it at face value. Tim had already made tea and chatted for a while with Charlie by the time Claire's phone call came through. He made a big point of searching the nursery and beyond for the little girl who had disappeared.

'He insists that he's really sorry,' Lyn added. 'He said he loved Gilly and he wouldn't have hurt her for the world. She was just like you at that age and he said he has great memories of being with you when you were both kids.'

'He told you to say that?'

Lyn shrugged. 'I thought maybe you'd want to hear it.'

Claire was silent.

'That's what he says happened, anyway,' she said, after a pause. 'But we'll never know the truth, will we?'

Lyn regarded Claire kindly. 'We'll know more when we

get the full report from the pathologist.'

Claire nodded. The story sounded plausible and she wanted to believe it. She wanted to think it had happened that quickly, that Gilly's last moments were lived in that feisty way she had and not in fear. She might learn to live with that.

She asked about the practicalities of the legal proceedings, about how soon the body might be released so she could bury Gilly properly and Lyn promised to keep in touch. Getting up to go, the police officer paused by the door.

'About the hair slide,' she said. 'It wasn't that I didn't believe you, it was more that…'

She hesitated and Claire interrupted.

'Forget it. I wouldn't have believed me either. And whatever we'd done, it wouldn't have made any difference to Gilly by then would it?'

'No… but I'm sorry it turned out this way. Tell me, is Laura all right? I suppose she does know?'

'Yes, she knows. She's upset of course, but she's all right, thanks.'

The officer left and Claire was left alone with her conflicted thoughts.

*

'You know I'm not a great cook,' Adam said apologetically, pouring Claire a glass of white wine. 'I bought a couple of pizzas. Is that OK? I've got some bags of salad and stuff too.' He took a sip of wine himself. 'Oh, and some fancy bread. And there's raspberries and ice cream.'

Claire grinned. 'So you bought up the supermarket, basically.'

'Believe me, it's safer than my cooking. Do you mind?'

'Of course I don't mind. I'm grateful for the company - and the meal. Do you want any help?'

336

'Er, maybe with the salads? They're in the fridge. I put some bowls out. And there's a bottle of dressing there on the top. The oven's already hot so I'll sort out the pizzas while you do that.'

They worked companionably in his kitchen, saying little. Adam flicked Claire an occasional glance, wondering how she was but scared to ask. He hadn't seen her for several days, hadn't wanted to fuss and recognised that she needed some space. He wasn't sure, in any case, how keen she would be to see him or to keep their friendship going. It had been born out of a difficult situation which perhaps she would now prefer to forget. But he had seen her going back into work at V and C that morning and had made a point of going in to invite her over. Now their silence felt surprisingly comfortable. There was none of the charged atmosphere there had been of late with Zoe.

'So you've parted with Zoe?' Claire said now, as if she'd read his mind. 'Are you sure?'

'Oh yes. We're still friends. Better to quit while you're ahead.' He hesitated. He'd heard rumours and didn't know which of them to believe - if any. 'How about you and Neil?'

'I'm afraid there is no me and Neil any more. There are lines, aren't there…' She frowned. '…boundaries you can't cross and hope to survive?' She shrugged, tossing the salad in the dressing one last time and putting the spoons down. 'And we haven't.'

'I'm sorry.'

'So am I.'

He slid the two pizzas into the oven.

'Ten minutes,' he said. 'Let's sit down with our drinks till they're ready.'

He saw her look around the living room as she sat, her gaze lingering for a minute on the remaining photographs on

337

the wall but she made no comment.

'Didn't I see you go over to Jane's unit today?' he asked.

'Yes. I wanted to apologise. I gave her a hard time for a while there. I thought…well, you know what I thought. But I am grateful to her for finding Gilly. Do you think she really sensed her there or was it just the flowers that gave it away?'

'Who knows? She probably doesn't know herself.'

Claire hesitated. 'Eddie told me something about her before all this blew up, you know, something which made me wonder, briefly, if she was guilty after all. I wasn't sure if it was true or just more of the usual gossip. So I asked her.' She paused again. 'She lost a baby to cot death, Adam. Did you know?'

He shook his head.

'Apparently she got very depressed. Then one day when she was out shopping, she saw a toddler separated from his mum and she took his hand and just walked off with him. A moment's madness. The little boy was fine but she's been trying to make up for it ever since, she says. I felt awful for her and for all the things I thought about her.'

'You weren't to know.'

'I suppose not - but I think she's more than made up for it now, don't you?'

Adam drank some wine. Claire was staring at her glass. She had drifted off into a world of her own. It was the second time she'd done that since she'd arrived.

'Any news about a funeral?' he asked.

She looked up. 'Yes. Some. They haven't released Gilly yet but they said they will shortly, so I've started looking into it. I'm going to bury her with her grandfather in the graveyard here. They were very close.'

'Are the press driving you crazy? I saw the story's been all over the news.'

338

'A bit. They're pestering for my story but…' She shook her head. '…I don't want to go there. The money would be useful of course, but everything else about it is a nightmare and there's Laura to consider. I won't do it.'

They ate at the table in the kitchen, chatted about Adam's work and the restaurant that was opening up at the end of the village which they both thought a huge gamble, and they talked about Laura. He asked how she was coping.

'She seems to be OK. She's got a good circle of friends and she's away from here, that's the main thing.'

'And you?' Adam pushed away his plate and leaned back in the chair, cradling his second glass of wine. 'How are you?'

She smiled. 'I'm OK too, thank you. Yes. OK.'

He thought maybe she was. Despite her clear sadness, there was an air of peace about her now.

'I suppose it'll be easier once you've got through the funeral.'

'Yes, it will.' She ran a finger around the base of her wine glass. 'Then I'm going away.'

He frowned. Stupidly, he hadn't expected her to say that and he was surprised at the depth of his disappointment. It also felt like she had told him as an afterthought and, considering all they had done together, he thought he deserved better than that. He leaned forward.

'Were you planning to tell me?' he demanded. 'Or just slope off, without a word?'

'Of course I was planning to tell you,' she retorted. 'I'm telling you now, aren't I?'

He grunted and sat back, still frowning. 'So where are you going?'

'To Greece, to stay with my mother for a while, just to sort my head out.'

'And then? You're coming back here?'

'No. Not to live.'

'Oh. So where then? I was hoping we could, you know, stay friends, maybe…' He hesitated. '…maybe see a bit more of each other?'

She smiled, cautiously.

'Were you? I'd like that too. But I'm afraid I can't stay here. Penny's talking about opening another branch of her shop further west and asked if I'd be interested. She's looking at some possible sites. Hopefully that means I'll be able to live somewhere else in Cornwall, not too far away.'

Adam drank some wine and thought about this. He sniffed.

'I've wondered lately,' he said casually, 'if having my studio at the Yard has been such a great move. With people wandering in and out and talking at me - generally about nothing in particular and certainly not buying anything - well, I think I'd get more done going back to a traditional private studio. Then I could work on my commissions in peace, and just supply galleries and arrange exhibitions the way I used to. What do you think?'

She nodded thoughtfully. 'I see what you mean. Maybe you're right. But where would you do it?' She looked round the room. 'Here?'

'No, I don't think so. There's nowhere suitable. But it'd be in Cornwall. I like it down here; it suits me. So long as it was somewhere I could paint. So perhaps we'll end up in the same place.' He paused. 'What do you think? Will you get in touch with me when you get back?'

'Of course. But the thing is, Adam…' She grinned, mischievously. '…I could get in touch with you before then, from Greece. There's this thing called the internet – maybe you've heard of it? If you'd like me to, that is?'

He laughed. 'Yes, I'd like that.'

He leaned forwards and raised his glass and she did the same, clinking his glass with hers.

*

Two days later, Claire went back to the clearing. Originally she had wanted to be there when the police dug to find Gilly's body, but Adam had dissuaded her. He'd said she should remember Gilly the way she was. But the police had finished with the burial site now; they had finally filled it all in and removed their tape.

It was a sunny day. Birds sang in the tree canopy and an occasional butterfly fluttered past. A light breeze set the long grasses shivering and whispered through the trees. The clearing looked idyllic, a still and peaceful haven of solitude, as if it had never seen any trauma, as if such a thing would be unthinkable in a place like this.

Claire crossed to where Gilly had been found, paused a few minutes, then turned and looked slowly around. Odd images of Gilly came into her head: a tousle-haired toddler, giggling at some game Laura was playing with her; six years old and her face a picture of determination as she swam the length of the swimming baths for the first time; profuse tears and then a formal garden burial - at which the whole family had had to be present, wearing something black - when her pet hamster had died. Claire shook her head, cheeks wet with tears, but smiling at the memories.

She walked to the water's edge. There were three mallards on the water today, eyeing her from the other side of the lake, weighing up the benefit in coming closer in search of food. She watched them for several minutes then turned and walked away.

Note

Many tributaries run into the River Fowey in southeast Cornwall, some of which are tidal in their later stages. The river in this story is not tidal but is based on those waterways and, like the village of Bohenna and its occupants, is entirely a creature of my imagination. I have tried to conjure up something of the nature of the area however, its small rural settlements and the beautiful, verdant yet sometimes enigmatic quality of the landscape.

Acknowledgements

Many people contribute to the writing of a book, sometimes with information they generously share or even with a simple word of encouragement. It is all valued. I would especially like to thank two friends in the police who kindly gave me their time and the benefit of their professional experience for the background to this novel. Any mistakes in procedure are entirely my own. I should also like to express my gratitude to the numerous British vineyards I have visited - all in the name of research - for the wonderful job they do, not only in producing some fine wines but also for taking the time and trouble to tell visitors how they do it. I learnt a great deal though, again, any mistakes in the processes described are, of course, my own.

A big thank you also goes to two ladies - both called Jane - who always diligently read my work and keep me on the straight and narrow, and to family and friends, near and far, for their continued and precious support.

My thanks also go to Andrew and Rebecca from Design for Writers who produced the stunning cover design.

Last but not least, a thank you to my husband, Dave, for somehow managing to sound interested and be encouraging even when he is listening to a variation on the plot for the hundredth time. I salute his patience.

Deep Water, Thin Ice

Kathy Shuker

When her husband - a flamboyant conductor - kills himself, Alex is mortified that she failed to see it coming. Confused, guilt-ridden and grieving, she runs away to Hillen Hall, an old house by the sea in Devon, abandoning her classical singing career and distancing herself from everyone but her sister Erica.

Hillen Hall, inherited by Simon from his mother and once a fine manor house, is now creaking and unloved. When Theo Hellyon, Simon's cousin, turns up at her door offering to help with its renovation, Alex is perplexed and intrigued, previously unaware that Simon even had a cousin. And Theo is charming and attentive and reminds her strikingly of Simon so, despite Erica's warnings, it is impossible not to want him in her life.

But the old hall has a tortured history which Alex cannot even begin to suspect and Theo is not remotely what he seems. So how long will it be before Alex realises she's making a fatal mistake?

Some reader reviews:

'I couldn't put it down.'

'...fine attention to detail brings the characters & their surroundings to life'

'...sorry to get to the last page'

'...an intriguing and engaging plot...I loved every minute of it'

Silent Faces, Painted Ghosts

Kathy Shuker

Terri Challoner is a young London art curator - talented, ambitious and defensive. Brought up by her moody and taciturn father, her family's past is a series of faceless blanks. Peter Stedding is an acclaimed and ageing portrait painter - brilliant, reclusive and short-tempered. His past contains too many faces, too many disturbing memories he has chosen to forget.

From the studio at his home in Provence, Peter employs Terri to curate his Retrospective. But Terri finds him domineering and obstructive, his household strained and silent. What is Peter hiding and what stories are his family not allowed to tell? And Terri is not what Peter wanted either: she's wilful and challenging and has too many intrusive plans for his exhibition.

Left alone in the studio one day, Terri stumbles upon the dark ghosts of Peter's past. What is uncovered will bring about a shocking collision of both their worlds, turmoil that threatens to unravel the lives of everyone involved.

Some reader reviews:

'...captivates from beginning to end.'

'...full of intrigue and atmosphere.'

'...another excellent novel...'

'I was hooked.'

Lightning Source UK Ltd.
Milton Keynes UK
UKOW06f1329180816

280904UK00011B/191/P